Iron AND Ether

August Li

DSP PUBLICATIONS

Published by
DREAMSPINNER PRESS

5032 Capital Circle SW, Suite 2, PMB# 279, Tallahassee, FL 32305-7886 USA
http://www.dreamspinnerpress.com/

Iron and Ether
© 2015 August Li.

Cover Art
© 2013 Anne Cain.
annecain.art@gmail.com
Cover content is for illustrative purposes only and any person depicted on the cover is a model.

ISBN: 978-1-63216-951-8
Digital ISBN: 978-1-63216-952-5
Library of Congress Control Number: 2014920705
Second Edition June 2015
First Edition published by Dreamspinner Press, September 2013

Printed in the United States of America
∞
This paper meets the requirements of
ANSI/NISO Z39.48-1992 (Permanence of Paper).

For Jerry, my Sasha.
Thanks for being so pretty
and cosplaying with me.

Also for my editor, Jane,
who is often expected to be
more of a magician than Yarrow.

Glossary

Abode of Shades—The realm of the Cast-Down, the unworthy dead, and all those rejected by the goddesses.

Bairn—The second highest title of nobility in Selindria, after "valen."

Baska—An obscenity in a language dead to all but the Order of the Crimson Scythe.

Cast-Down—A term used to refer to those gods and goddesses disowned by The Thirteen because of their wickedness. Most pious Selindrians will not speak of them. In some rare cases, a person can be referred to as Cast-Down.

Emiri—An ethnic group, or possibly a completely different race of people, who arrived in Selindria about 150 years ago. Their name is derived from "*Emir*," the word for the sea in their language. Emiri have no formal homeland and are expert mariners. Their culture and values are quite different from that of Selindrians, and this leads to many misunderstandings.

Eru—The Emiri word for "wind."

Espero—A large and wealthy island nation to the southeast of Selindria, best known for the high population of mages and the arcane university there.

Estrella Lake—A huge freshwater lake in the northernmost corner of Selindria. Aside from providing most of the nation's water, it has a religious significance, is surrounded by shrines and temples, and is often visited by those on spiritual pilgrimages.

Everdale—A fertile valenny near the center of Selindria, which provides most of the kingdom's food, and sister province to Merryvale.

Eyrle—The third highest title of nobility in Selindria, after "bairn."

Fane—A legendary mage-emperor who ruled over a period of unimaginable peace and prosperity eons ago. Eventually he demanded his people worship him instead of the goddesses, and the ensuing war destroyed the known world. No one knows if Fane ever actually existed, but his story is told as a cautionary tale and given as the reason mages are forbidden to rule.

Gaeltheon—A powerful nation to the east of Selindria, across the Kanda River, almost equal in size and wealth.

Kanda River—An enormous river separating Gaeltheon and Selindria. The Kanda is fed by Estrella Lake and considered holy by association.

Lapir Mountains—A huge, impassable mountain range marking the eastern border of Gaeltheon. No one has crossed them in centuries, and what lies on the other side is a subject of speculation.

Lockhaven—An ancient valenny, ruled by the L'Estrella family for as long as anyone can remember. Because it houses the sacred Estrella Lake, Lockhaven is highly respected throughout Selindria.

Meritage—The oldest and largest city in Selindria. Meritage is a port along the Kanda River, and while it is held by the Selindrian monarch, the territory around it is unstable and ruled by barbarians and warlords.

Merryvale—A fertile plain, sister province to Everdale.

Mir—An Emiri ship's captain.

Mu-bo—A spicy Emiri dish made from shellfish.

Muri-ku—A very potent Emiri beverage made from fermented sea plants.

Narxium—A tree producing a fatally poisonous sap. It grows only in the Forest of Elwyd.

Order of the Crimson Scythe—A legendary and unstoppable cult of assassins. Thalil is their patron. While many people doubt the existence of the Crimson Scythe, their symbol, the red crescent, is still the most feared icon in the land. The Crimson Scythe are considered almost supernatural. When they have marked someone for death, that person has no chance of escape.

Selindria—The most powerful kingdom in the known world.

Shagiri—The Emiri word for "death."

Starmont—The highest peak in Selindria, marking the northern edge of Estrella Lake. In the past, many Selindrians believed the goddesses resided atop Starmont, but that belief has been abandoned by all but the most superstitious.

Syrai—The Emiri word for "friend," used to express a wide variety of relationships from casual acquaintance to intimate partner.

Tam—The lowest title of nobility in Selindria as well as a common expression of respect, similar to "sir."

Thalil—A very powerful Cast-Down god associated with seduction, subterfuge, murder, and deceit. He is the patron god of assassins, particularly the Order of the Crimson Scythe. Thalil, usually portrayed as a beautiful youth, is also associated with male beauty and homoerotic love. The Thirteen Goddesses forbid his name from being spoken, and his worship is punishable by death. Thalil is known by many epithets, some of which are: He Who Stands Just Out of Sight, The One You See at the Last, The Whisper Heard Too Late, The Dark One, and The Invisible Blade.

The Thirteen, or The Thirteen Goddesses—The main and most important deities of Selindria and Gaeltheon. They have many sons and daughters, both benevolent and Cast-Down. They are sometimes referred to as the sisters. Each goddess presides over a month, or moon, of the year.

Valen—The highest title of nobility in Selindria, second only to the royal family. Valens rule large holds of land known as valennies.

The Goddesses and Months

Both Selindria and Gaeltheon observe a thirteen-month lunar calendar. Each month, or moon, is presided over by one of The Thirteen Goddesses:

Fayelle, ruler of the first month—A virgin goddess of purity. While compassionate, she is a very demanding goddess who expects perfection from her devotees.

Sarmine, ruler of the second month—The goddess of romantic love and marriage. Most weddings take place during Sarmine's Moon.

Mother Goddess, ruler of the third month—The only goddess without a name, she is the matron of all living things. Her month is a time of devotion and celebration. The Mother Goddess is said to love all her creations, even the Cast-Down.

Myint, ruler of the fourth month—The goddess of warfare, battle, weaponsmiths, armorers, and martial arts. She is the patron goddess of all knights.

Diarana, ruler of the fifth month—The goddess of travel and transition. She is the patron of children coming of age. Certain worshippers of Diarana maintain that the goddess loves and protects men and women who favor the clothing of the opposite gender. This belief is not widely accepted.

Vestrafori, ruler of the sixth month—The goddess of truth and justice, protector of the blind and mute. Vestrafori's priestesses conduct all legal proceedings in Selindria and Gaeltheon, and their verdicts are absolute.

Laud, ruler of the seventh month—A mysterious goddess associated with fate, the passage of time, and abstract concepts. Her devotees live hermitic lives of deprivation and contemplation.

Jelsyn, ruler of the eighth month—The goddess of artisans and merchants. She adores handmade items, particularly woven cloth. Jelsyn is also said to protect the poor.

Berris, ruler of the ninth month—The goddess of farming, plenty, and the harvest. Her festival is one of the most joyous occasions of the year.

Ix, ruler of the tenth month—The goddess of the wilds and protector of forests and animals. Ix is well known to favor those who follow instinct over reason. Ix is also associated with the moon.

Strella, ruler of the eleventh month—The goddess of the sun, stars, and weather, Strella is also a liaison between humans and the goddesses. She carries prayers to the goddesses and guides the worthy dead to their rest.

Illira, ruler of the twelfth month—The goddess of music, poetry, history, and communication. She is the patron of all storytellers and scholars.

Pherara, ruler of the thirteenth month—The goddess of magic and arcane scholarship, and patron goddess of Espero. Most people feel Pherara values only her mages and turns her back on those without the gift. She is not widely worshipped outside Espero.

Lesser Gods and Goddesses

Helwyn—A goddess of solitude and a patron of lonely and abandoned women.

Ilverus—A deity (usually depicted as male) associated with the knowledge of healing elixirs and potions.

Keltha—A daughter of the Mother Goddess, patroness of pregnancy, childbirth, and nursing.

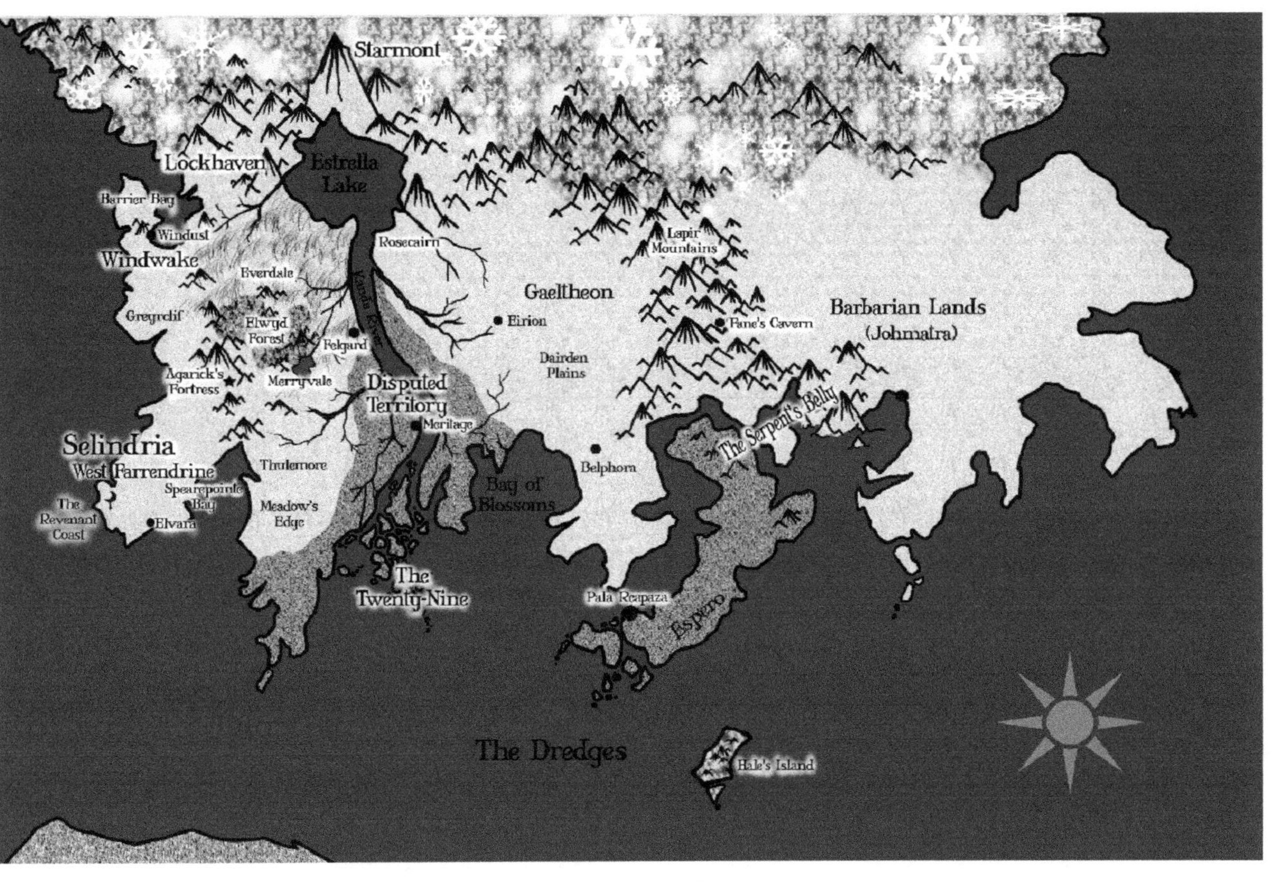

Starmont
Lockhaven
Estrella Lake
Barrier Bay
Windust
Windwake
Everdale
Rosecairn
Lapir Mountains
Gaeltheon
Barbarian Lands
(Johmatra)
Greyclif
Elwyd Forest
Eirion
Pane's Cavern
Felgard
Dairden Plains
Agarick's Fortress
Merryvale
Disputed Territory
The Serpent's Belly
Merilage
Selindria
West Farrendrine
Thulemore
Belphorn
Spearepointe Bay
The Revenant Coast
Elvara
Meadow's Edge
Bay of Blossoms
Pala Reapaza
Espero
The Twenty-Nine
The Dredges
Hale's Island

prologue

THE Dark and Beautiful One rose from his expansive, scarlet, velvet nest, slowly disentangling himself from the languid limbs and strands of silken hair covering his body until he could push himself to his hands and knees and crawl across the field of sumptuous cushions and interlocked flesh. Reverent hands caressed and clung to Thalil as he wove through the maze of arms, legs, adoring faces, and eager mouths, but he brushed them off like cobwebs until he reached the edge of his bed and swung his legs over the side. Moans and laments followed him as he crossed the warm, smooth floor made of eons of bones crushed, compacted, and worn smooth as ivory beneath his bare soles and those of his thousands of lovers and thralls.

Innumerable flames burned within crimson glass lanterns as Thalil made his way slowly across his hall. The lanterns hung from the vaulted ceilings and lined the shining black walls, outnumbering the stars. Images of him in marble, ebony, silver, and gold stared back as he sauntered toward the central fountain, but none, he knew, were as beautiful as the original. He had yet to find an artist with the skill to capture him, and still enjoyed looking at his reflection in his pool best of all.

The Thirteen who called themselves goddesses had prepared a spare and cold realm for those they felt unworthy or wicked—the Cast-Down—an Abode of Shades devoid of pleasure and sensation. Thalil did not reside within it; no, this demesne was of his own making, and his power guaranteed the sisters could neither enter it nor take it from him.

He reached the central chamber of his Crimson Palace and perched delicately on the edge of the great pool at the center, smiling at his image, mirrored back in the thick, rubicund liquid. Because of his mortal children, the blood flowed in an endless supply, always fresh, its ferrous scent robust in the sultry air, and the number of souls wailing outside his fortress walls increased almost by the minute, giving him the power to thumb his nose at the thirteen so-called deities. Thalil rippled the surface of the tarn with his fingertips as he sank down on one elbow to peer into its depths.

Thalil took a moment to watch his children, the brethren of the Crimson Scythe, at work destroying life from the shadows, from the periphery of everything good and wholesome. He smiled as they brought him longer life and greater strength with every throat they slit, and he spent a tiny spark of his might to protect them and increase the fear they inspired as they killed. Then, to entertain himself, he turned his attention to other events occurring in the mortal realm.

On the eastern edge of what the mortals now called Gaeltheon, at the feet of the Lapir Mountains, a small expedition of people chipped into the ancient stone and ice with picks and hand-powered drills. Thalil leaned forward to watch them work, his perfect lips twitching with interest.

The small party had been laboring for nearly a year: their wind-battered tents barely stood beneath the thick layers of rime on the canvas. Their leader, a stooped, elderly fellow called Torkan Mellinger, continued digging and scraping long after his disciples had retired for the night. Though frail of body, passion burned and bloomed around Mellinger like a bonfire, the bright light clear even from afar. Thalil leaned closer, thinking he might like the old explorer's soul to add to his menagerie, but not yet, not before he discovered what made Mellinger laugh aloud and scrub tears from his wrinkled eyes.

Mellinger lifted a slab of rock with his gloved hands, revealing a small alcove preserved through the centuries. Slowly, with appropriate veneration, he began to lift the objects he found inside the cupboard-sized space, exposing them to the wind and stars for the first time in thousands of years. Thalil recognized things from his father's reign, though most of them held little value: a dented golden goblet, a few clouded gems, a dinner fork adorned with jewels, and the brass pegs from a wooden instrument long ago disintegrated. The elderly scholar seemed most intrigued by the few inches of a carved column supporting the forgotten niche, and abandoned his tools to scrape the dust from around it with his hands. As he scooped, Mellinger uncovered a small tablet and brushed it off on his worn sleeve. He blew across it to clear the fine debris from the carved words and brought it near his lantern to read.

Thalil listened with interest to the scholar's whispered words. He doubted many mortals would have been able to decipher the ancient language.

"Long before the arrogance of Fane destroyed the world, the Thirteen Sisters faced an even greater threat on behalf of all humanity…." A deep gouge marred the smooth stone, stealing the words that had been written there. Mellinger skipped over that section and continued. "Fane taught his thirteen disciples the most powerful spell ever wielded by a mortal creature. He taught them the enchantment and sent them forth to purge our world of sin. And the goddesses hunted and destroyed a vile race of demons, older even than the bones of the world. The Thirteen Holy Sisters stripped these creatures of their power, though their essences remain in the shadows, in the most hidden places. Praise to the goddesses. Praise to they who risked themselves to shield mankind from such a vile threat." The old man squinted to examine the illustrations of the vanquished creatures, winged, horned beings larger and more perfect than mortal men, and then continued to read of the so-called goddesses' triumphs against them. Finally, Mellinger whispered, "The power and black evil of these ancient threats remains. Be steadfast in faith to the Thirteen. Without them, the evil will overtake us. Only the goddesses hold these abominations at bay. Be always steadfast in faith."

The old man wrapped his precious find in a few strips of cloth and stumbled to his tent, where he slept with the tablet close to his heart.

Thalil considered.

The mortals had no knowledge of the creatures Fane, his father, had feared so profoundly. They also had no idea Fane had instructed those they knew as goddesses in magic; without his tutelage, the thirteen regarded as divine would have been mediocre mages at best, left out of history, forgotten. Would the knowledge of the old race's existence cast aspersions on his detested mother and her foul sisters, or would it increase the dependence the mortals felt? Should he send one of his children to put an end to Mellinger before his discovery reached the light? It would be an easy task for a Crimson Scythe, barely worthy of one of Thalil's assassins. Or should he let the discovery stir doubt, possibly weaken the foundations of faith the thirteen whores rested upon so comfortably? A new and unknown chapter in the mythology of the Thirteen would certainly be greeted with great interest by the mortals. How would they react to the idea of Fane instructing them? If Thalil knew anything of their nature, and after so many thousand years he felt sure he did, the mortals would fight over the implications of Mellinger's discovery. It could lead to chaos, to rifts, or it could bind the faithful even tighter to their foolish and misguided beliefs. For all his power, Thalil could not divine the future, so he chose to let Mellinger live and bring his revelation to others. He swiped his palm over the roiling pool until another vision emerged.

Thalil saw a sailor, a good-looking, tall, and muscular man called Bartoum Astir. The Dark and Beautiful One easily discerned this man held no exemplary cleverness or skill, but Thalil saw threads of destiny wrapped loosely around the seaman's thick limbs, and he couldn't help but wonder why. He watched as the sailor set foot on the parched shores beyond the mountains. Captain Bartoum Astir had been here before, many times, after discovering the riches these lands held in the form of brightly dyed cloth and gems, as well as powders that enhanced the blandest of foods and kept them from spoiling, but today he'd come for something he felt infinitely more precious. Bartoum made his way from the quayside to the center of the coastal city, to the brothel he'd visited on his first foray to these distant shores. Thalil rolled his eyes as he watched; the dank creases of woman-flesh held so much influence over the men who craved it. He had never understood that, though he understood about lust.

Looking over his shoulder, Thalil surveyed the young men either resting or making love on his large bed and chose one to keep him company: a lithe, bronzed, young creature with wheat-gold waves of hair. He met the gaze of his former assassin, and the young man left the others and crouched behind the Dark and Beautiful One, kissing the soles of Thalil's feet and caressing the backs of his calves. As the young man's warm, damp lips moved up the back of Thalil's thigh, Thalil returned his attention to the pool.

Bartoum, smiling, went to the brothel's madam and offered her a pouch of gold. After trading heavily between Selindria, Gaeltheon, and this newly discovered kingdom, he'd finally managed to save enough. The bent and withered madam took the sea captain's coin and returned with a small, dark-skinned woman. Like all of her countrymen and kin, she kept her head shaved to the skin, and a bright red beaded scarf covered her head. She wore a matching gown, sleeveless, to expose slim arms covered in swirling scars. Similar, deep marking adorned her face and chest, and several gold rings dangled from her ears. A wide line of kohl extended across her eyes like a mask. With a giggle, the whore threw her arms around Captain Bartoum Astir's neck, and he lifted her off her feet and twirled her around. With a few broken words, Bartoum explained that as soon as they returned to Selindria, they would find a priestess and be properly married.

Thalil couldn't tell how much, if any, the girl understood. She seemed happy enough to be leaving the brothel, though. He continued to watch as Bartoum returned to the quayside and put his fiancée aboard his ship. Then he went to trade for the richly dyed thin cloth the noble ladies of Selindria and Gaeltheon so adored and would pay so much to have for their gowns. He bartered common Selindrian things like harrow-wolf furs and twirlhorn bone for sacks of gems and tiny, perfectly made glass beads. Spice, so common to the foreign savages, brought huge sums in Bartoum's home ports, and he and his crew loaded crate after crate of the various roots, dried flowers, and ground minerals onto their ship. Unbeknownst to the sailors, some of the small red lizards common to the area also found their way aboard and curled in the cool shadows below deck. Back home, Captain Bartoum Astir eagerly told a man from his crew, they would make such a profit they'd soon all have fine homes and wives.

"Look there," Bartoum said to his crewman, pointing out over the bay at the many Selindrian ships. "The window to become wealthy by trading with these barbarians is closing quickly. Many sailors know of this place and its riches now. They'll flood the market and drive down the prices of these goods. We must make our gold before that happens, and if we're smart, we'll put away enough to sustain us for the rest of our lives."

"The Emiri raiders have also learned of the riches carried back from this place," a dark-haired sailor with a thick, knotted beard remarked. "Very few ships make it to market with their holds full anymore. Some of the Sea Folk even dare come here, I've heard."

Bartoum nodded. Not far from where they stood, the native people of what the Selindrians referred to as Johmatra worked hard constructing ships of their own, based on Selindrian, Gaeltheonic, and even Emiri design. "These savages have been very keen to acquire maps and charts and have paid well for them. I wonder how long it will be before they build seaworthy vessels and make it to our shores. I wonder what will happen then."

Thalil wondered as well. The people of Johmatra, which was actually a loosely allied collection of nearly a hundred city-states, didn't worship the thirteen goddesses, kept the Emiri as slaves, and slaughtered all common-born mages, who they believed had no right to use up the magic that belonged exclusively to the nobility. All power fell to those who could supposedly trace their lineage to Fane, Thalil's father. Centuries of inbreeding had left these potentates horribly deformed, though many possessed strong sorcery. Thalil didn't think the two cultures would find much in common and longed to see what would occur when they inevitably clashed. Surely his children could help to turn the tide in whichever direction he felt most advantageous. He toyed with the idea of murdering Bartoum Astir and his crew, to possibly slow the coming collision, but he dismissed it. Things had come too far already for him to intervene. He closed his eyes for a moment and enjoyed the light kisses his disciple peppered across his shoulders. Then he let his gaze wander farther up the coast, to one of the Emiri ships Bartoum Astir had mentioned.

A beautiful creature with bloodred hair and brilliant orange eyes captained this particular Emiri crew. As he watched the lithe young man, Thalil realized he had never known an Emiri boy, and he decided he would like to remedy that. They were an appealing people, and this one, who the others called *Sai-Mir*, put the rest to shame. Over the centuries, Thalil had paid the children of Emir little mind, because he possessed nothing he could use to persuade them to spill blood in his name. While comely, the Emiri were indolent and undisciplined. They valued neither power nor permanent wealth, but remained content to lie on their beaches, drink their potent liquor, and steal treasure to squander when the mood struck them. They lost interest in anything as soon as it ceased to amuse them. Thalil doubted they would ever leave much of a mark on history.

But then again....

Thalil leaned a bit closer as the delectable Sai creature and his shipmates skirted the coast with a hold full of jewels, cloth, and spices they'd pilfered from ships who'd traded legitimately for the goods. Sai sat straddling the bowsprit, his graceful legs hanging down and a small smile stretching his lips as he canted his face into the wind. The salty breeze whipped his crimson ropes of hair off starboard, and one of the shells adorning it happened to tap him on his small, round chin. Tugged out of his contented reverie, Sai looked back toward the land, his gaze following a huge flock of seabirds, so many their cries drowned out the rush of the waves. Curious, another common Emiri trait and sometimes a fatal one, Sai pointed, and the woman at the helm steered them back toward the shore, toward a tongue of brown rock jutting out over the foamy surf.

Just as Sai held up his hand to halt his crew, Thalil put his hand on his disciple's slender neck to stop the pleasant movement of his hands and lips. Thalil could not see the future, but he felt the importance of this moment, pregnant with possibility, and knew it would alter the course of the world. After conception, something had to issue forth, for good or ill, Thalil knew. And this moment weighed heavy with… something definitive, as irreversible as the fall of the axman's blade. Thalil almost heard iron strike flesh as Sai pressed a distance glass to his eye.

The Dark and Beautiful One needed no such device to see what went on upon that bony finger of rock; the native people were punishing their slaves. Over a hundred Emiri, their glorious locks shorn to the skin, stood inside a corral. Most of their bodies bore signs of very hard use, but the true horror stood at the center, where half a dozen slaves hung from their wrists. Their captors used dull, serrated blades—clumsy weapons that made Thalil roll his eyes—to make shallow wounds on the prisoners' bellies, inner thighs, backs, and faces. They did not cut enough to do much harm—just enough to lure the seabirds to the scent of blood. Just enough for the birds to wriggle their sharp yellow beaks below the skin and get at the tender muscles and organs—the soft meat of the cheeks or the winding cords of the innards.

Thalil admired the slavers' creativity, but he detested waste. He did not believe in killing a man who still might lift a blade in his name, and if death had to occur, he advocated efficiency; do as you must and move on. The death of these pitiable slaves would take days, and that meant sparing men to guard them. Still, Thalil supposed the display might serve to dissuade the others from rebellion.

Then again, it might not.

Loyalty and obedience based on fear were paltry and fickle compared to devotion based on love. For love, a man would scrape a mountain down with his bare hands until he wore away the last of his bones. For love, genuine love, he would change the place of the stars in the sky, no matter the cost.

Fear could always be overcome, but in Thalil's experience, it was not so with love.

The Emiri captain went white beneath his deep tan, and his small fist curled around the distance glass as he dropped it slowly into his lap. Sai loved his people and the freedom they celebrated.

"Do you love me?" Thalil asked, stroking his disciple's warm red cheek.

"Have I not proven my love for you when I walked in the land of the living, offering you hundreds of lives? I yearned to do more, master, but you called me away. All I have ever desired is to please you."

"Shh. You have and you do. But the world is about to change," Thalil muttered softly, mostly to himself. "I wonder how best to take advantage of what will come to pass."

"Master?" the young man asked, lifting his lips from Thalil's skin and savoring Thalil's sweat by mopping his mouth with his tongue.

Thalil pressed a finger to the center of his disciple's slick, swollen lips and shook his head. "Never mind, beauty. Good times are ahead for me, I think. For all of us. Before long, the mortals will wade through blood to their knees. Doesn't that sound lovely?"

"You are lovely, my master."

Thalil chuckled and raked his fingers through the young man's hair. "Yes, I know. Quiet, now. I have one more thing I wish to see. Would you like to watch with me? Yes? It should be interesting." With his fingertips, Thalil traced circles in the steaming scarlet liquid, and a new image began to form.

"Who is the pretty young man with so much death in his eyes?" the assassin asked.

"He is called Yarroway L'Estrella," Thalil answered as he played with his disciple's nipple. "I have been watching him for quite some time. He has a profound destiny. I think, perhaps, he'll be the one to deliver to me what I most desire. My fondest wish."

"What is that, master?"

Thalil remained silent, reluctant to give voice to his profane aspiration, even safe here within the walls of his Crimson Palace. Instead, he guided his partner's hand beneath his belly to his hardening cock, and the lovely young assassin saw to Thalil's pleasure as Thalil continued to watch Yarroway L'Estrella.

Chapter One

FIERCE wind assailed the mage as he clung to the ice-encrusted rock. It took all Yarrow's strength to hold on and keep from plummeting several hundred feet to the base of Starmont beneath him. His heavy fur-lined cloak whipped out behind him, and ice crystals stung the small strip of exposed flesh around his eyes. Black wool wraps covered the rest of his head and face, as well as his hands and feet inside his heavy leather boots and gloves. When he'd left Windust Castle two weeks ago, the first frost had yet to paint the windows of the ancient fortress, and it only grew chilly enough for a fire at night. Here, at the northernmost border of Selindria and the edge of Yarrow's familial valenny of Lockhaven, the ice never melted. Yarrow squinted against the bright white light and located a narrow ledge a few dozen feet above him. He summoned azure wings made from pure arcane energy, pushed off with his feet, and propelled himself toward it. He beat down with his wings, but they'd never allowed him to truly fly, or at least he hadn't mastered it yet, and he lost momentum just as he grasped the edge of the ridge.

Yarrow caught his breath and waited for his pulse to slow after the shock of nearly falling. Then he pulled himself up on the ledge. Slowly, mindful of the frost beneath his feet, he stood and pressed his back against the rock behind him. Estrella Lake, covered in cloudy ice, stretched for miles below him, as far as the eye could see. At the western shore, near the castle where he'd been born and grown up, the water would be chill but not yet frozen. As children, Yarrow and his brothers had waited until well past midwinter before venturing out onto the ice. Back then, he'd never thought much about Starmont, Selindria's highest peak, though he could see it in the distance from the balcony of his chambers. He'd heard that the Thirteen Goddesses lived at the mountain's pinnacle, but he'd also heard a great wyrm slept in the depths of Estrella Lake. Neither had seemed particularly significant to him; neither really affected his life, and in truth, he had never cared much for unbelievable stories. From a young age, he'd seen them as a means of inspiring fear and securing control. He'd thought himself above them, too smart to be manipulated.

Then. It seemed like a lifetime ago.

Half a year ago, he'd heard the most unbelievable story of all, and the questions and implications it dragged behind it hadn't left him alone since. Unlike the others, the tale he had heard from Hale, a former apprentice of Fane, now living in self-imposed exile, could break the cycle of doubt and manipulation. Hale had seen what really happened when Fane fell, and his version of events had been very different from those Yarrow had heard in the temples as a child. Yarrow felt like the entire world operated beneath a cloak of deception, an illusion no one could see through. It angered him to feel like he'd been duped. He would not be made a fool. Worst of all, he couldn't share his outrage with his partners, because belief in the protection and love of the Thirteen Goddesses brought so much comfort to Duncan, and Sasha's devotion to Thalil was absolute. Yarrow couldn't shatter their faith until he knew for certain he had it all right to the smallest detail. So he'd come here, to the fabled abode of the goddesses, to find out once and for all. What he'd do when he uncovered the answers to his questions, he still hadn't decided.

If Yarrow could believe everything he'd learned from Hale, and he felt he could, the goddesses who he'd been told created and protected the world had once been mortal women. After learning all they could from Fane, they grew jealous of their people's love for the emperor, turned against him, and destroyed him. Well, most of him. If, as Hale suspected, they prolonged their lives and preserved their power by drawing the magic from the world, tapping into the mystic pulse like leeches and leaving little for others with the gift, then what would Yarrow do? He knew what he wanted to do, and he knew his hunger for destruction came from his love of Fane. More accurately, the creature who had once possessed him had loved Fane, eons before the so-called goddesses had been born. Since bonding with the entity, Yarrow had a hard time sorting its memories and emotions from his own, if they could even be sorted anymore. If they were even still distinct. He would get no answers by standing here wondering, though, so he prepared to continue up the mountainside.

Yarrow found a steep, narrow pass between two vertical cliffs. Though he had to crawl on his hands and knees for several hours, it took him closer to the summit. When the path ended abruptly, Yarrow took a moment to sip wine from his flask and choke down a scrap of hard bread. Then he began searching for another way up, eventually locating a cascade of debris he could scale to reach a small plateau. He climbed until well after dark, rested for a few hours, ate more hardtack and dried fruit, and then resumed his ascent. By first light, though his palms and knees were split and bloody and his feet numb within his boots, he hoisted himself over the final ridge and reached the zenith of Starmont.

The thin air made him gasp for breath, and Yarrow pushed his wraps from his nose and mouth as he stepped onto the peak. The frigid air he inhaled stabbed his lungs like iron spikes. At its apex, Starmont was nearly flat. Jagged boulders dozens of feet high wreathed a snow-strewn clearing large enough for several castles, maybe even a small village. Yarrow thought for a moment how impressive it would be to build himself a fortress here, where he could look down on the whole kingdom, and then he turned to take in the view. His breath caught in his throat, and he wished Duncan and Sasha could be with him to witness the grandeur. To the south, even Estrella Lake looked like a small pond, icy blue and glittering in the morning light: just a puddle. To the north, nothing but glaciers and hard-packed snow reached until they curved out of sight with the culmination of the horizon. Part of Yarrow longed to explore land he knew no man had set foot upon in centuries, if ever. He wondered what, if anything, existed beyond their boundaries. He'd learned from his tutors those wastes hadn't thawed since the beginning of recorded time, but if he'd learned anything, he'd come to understand the world was much larger and stranger than anyone imagined. It held many hidden things if one was bold enough to go looking beyond what was written in the books.

Yarrow could contemplate all of that later, though. He'd come here for a purpose: to demand answers, and he didn't plan to leave until he was satisfied.

"You thirteen who call yourself goddesses!" Yarrow yelled, his clear voice echoing across the frozen wastes. "Show yourselves to me! I am Yarroway L'Estrella, and I demand your presence!"

Only the wind, high-pitched, mournful, and sounding almost sentient, answered his call. The unnaturally strong gale kicked up everything in its path and hurled it at Yarrow. Slush, ice, and small rocks battered him until he had to raise his arm to shield his face. Sheets of blowing snow veiled the world, but Yarrow would not be denied. He had suffered much worse.

"Show yourselves, unless you are cowards!" he cried, unfurling his cerulean wings and letting luminescent horns spring from his forehead, reflecting a form that now comprised half of his being. Magic poured from him like a geyser, spilling down the mountainside and shooting into the brightening sky. He knew the power would act as a beacon; no one who sensed enchantment would be able to ignore it. Likely mages as far away as Espero felt the power he unleashed. Not even Yarrow knew what exposure to so much magic might do to the world—or himself. In that moment, he felt like he could haul a castle from the bones of the mountain, and the ground beneath him rumbled at his fleeting desire. He reined it in, had to control it, especially since accessing his full strength made him crave destruction. If he didn't keep a tight hold on his power, he'd level Starmont. The possibility gave him an idea.

"I demand you appear, or I will raze your scared mound to nothing! I will tear its roots from the world and fling it into the sky! What will your faithful make of that? How dare you! I will not be ignored!"

"How dare *you*, little mage?" The answering voice came from the stone beneath Yarrow's feet, from the sky, from the lake waters, from the light on the snow, everywhere. It came out of the ether beyond the bounds of the physical world. Yarrow felt it reverberate through his bones, his guts, that illusive shadow he thought of as his spirit. He fought not to fall to his knees, cover his head, and whimper. No. Never. He knelt before no one. No one would make him kneel. Certainly not this pretender.

A massive form appeared, not only eclipsing the sun but sucking the light from the world. Yarrow tried to look at it, a vaguely female form that shifted and changed as he watched, transforming from a young maiden to a plump mother, then to a wizened crone and back, while sometimes, somehow, displaying all three forms and many others at once. The vision seared Yarrow's eyes until tears streamed down his cheeks and froze to his face, and he still couldn't focus on it directly. It was like a hole burned in reality, a woman-shaped window into the void of eternity. Power like shifting, prismatic flame shot out from its edges until Yarrow felt sure it extended to the ends of the world. It scorched the very sky, turning the clouds to steam.

Still, the mage held his ground. This creature was not superior to him, and he would not let her intimidate him, even though his every instinct told him to throw himself at her feet. Instead, he pulled his magic around him like a net, his wings still extended but ready to fold around him and shield him. "You who call yourself Mother Goddess, I have questions. I have questions, and I will have answers!"

"Who are you to demand anything of me?" The goddess's voice exploded inside Yarrow's skull even as it bombarded his senses from every direction. "You are refuse, and I am the mother and ruler of this entire world."

"That is a lie!" Yarrow shouted. Images he didn't recognize but that felt integral to his being assailed him. "You bitch. You were just a woman, Fane's wife. You learned your power from him and then you—You killed my beloved! My beloved! Do you dare deny it?"

"I owe you nothing. Insect."

"Bitch! Whore! Charlatan! This world was mine! It will be mine again. I will see its people know the truth, and I will bring you down! You and your treacherous sisters are hoarding the world's magic."

"It is our right. We are the Thirteen Goddesses."

"You are no more divine than I am!" Yarrow yelled.

The goddess laughed, and all of reality trembled. Yarrow fell and landed hard on his hip. "Pitiful creature. You have no idea what you are. You do not even know your own heart or your own mind. You are nothing but a frightened little boy. Fane was not so different. Power is much more than something to cower behind, Yarroway L'Estrella."

"I will show you my power! I have wielded it since long before your ancestors existed, since they cringed in the muck and filth like beasts." Yarrow focused his power and compacted it into an arcane spear, which he hoisted and threw into the heart of the nothingness before him. The blackness absorbed the glowing javelin, and the goddess laughed. Yarrow conjured fire, and shot gout after gout at the being, but his flames fizzled and disappeared within her. He shot bolts of lightning at her, but did no damage.

The Mother Goddess chuckled. "I'm growing bored of this, insignificant little worm." She raised her dark hand and swatted Yarrow, lifting him off his feet and sending him flying into the air and over the rocks fencing the mountain clearing. He tumbled down the mountainside, tucking into a ball as he rolled, bouncing off the rocks. He spread his wings to slow his descent and tried to cushion himself with a shell of magic, but he'd used too much power already. He landed hard on a narrow ledge, the breath knocked from his lungs. Ice and stone rained down on him, penetrating the wings he folded over his body and slicing his flesh even through the heavy garments and leather armor he wore.

The goddess stepped down to his level, even her toe towering above Yarrow. "I will crush you into the dirt, grind your bones to powder, Yarroway L'Estrella."

The being's thumb bore down on him, and Yarrow dug deep into his reserves, letting instinct guide his enchantment. He thought of Sasha, of the way the assassin lured his victims close and let them use their own momentum to drive themselves against the tips of his blades. Just as the goddess was about to smash Yarrow into the ground, he conjured a sharp spike from his back. The creature's finger met it, and the goddess pulled back, but only for a moment. It was enough for Yarrow to regain his footing. As soon as he did, he shot an array of fireballs at the Mother Goddess. As before, the behemoth absorbed the energy he directed at her.

You are a taker, beloved, Yarrow's creature had said, back when they could speak in his mind, before they'd fully melded into a single being. With a shrill, triumphant laugh, Yarrow spread his fingers. He located the many magical currents and their tributaries flowing into the dread goddess, and one by one, he dammed and redirected them, letting the energy flow into himself, taking her source of succor. Power sang and crackled through his veins until he felt like he'd burst. The goddess shrieked as she withered in front of Yarrow, and soon a plain, mousy-haired woman, chubby and unremarkable, stood before him. Yarrow raised his fist and smacked her round face, laughing as her lip split and she fell to her knees.

"I knew it," he hissed as he grabbed her hair and wrenched her head back. "Mother Goddess indeed. You are nothing but a hag hoarding the world's magic. I'll put an end to you right now. For my beloved. For Fane, the man you betrayed. To avenge him."

"You ridiculous, broken creature." Blood and foam spattered Yarrow's chest as she spoke. "You cannot even comprehend your own existence. You, the boy living in that small body, never even met the one you call beloved. Let go of me." Stinging heat radiated from the woman, scorching Yarrow's hand, his cheeks, and his eyes. His skin felt like it was melting. He staggered backward, covering his face.

"Fool," the goddess continued. "Insect. You are unnatural, and I cast you down." She regained some of her former stature, and batted Yarrow again, sending him cartwheeling down the hill. All his concentration focused on buffering his body from hitting the sharp rocks and spears of ice, any one of which could destroy his fragile flesh, if not the essence behind it.

As soon as he landed, Yarrow struck. This thing assuming the mantle of Mother Goddess was still weak. He couldn't wait. Ice, for which he'd always felt an affinity, surrounded him, and he used the element he understood so well, breaking off sharp shards and aiming them at his enemy. Soon, the goddess's blood stained the snow, and she hunched nearly buried beneath scraps of the frozen mountain. Still, she laughed at Yarrow.

"You think you're so clever." With a burst of enchantment, she freed herself and sent Yarrow catapulting again. This time, he came to a stop beyond the foothills, almost at the edge of the lake. "You think you understand this world of mine. Let's see if you expected this. Let's see what you'll do now, fragile little flower. Let's see if you can do anything but die."

"You cannot kill me!" Yarrow yelled.

The frozen surface of the lake shattered, thick chunks of ice flying in every direction. The strength of the eruption forced Yarrow's back against the nearest boulder. Frothy water shot from the fissures as something from deep within the lake began to emerge. A talon, old, yellowed, and easily the size of a battering ram breached the surface. Three more claws soon emerged, scarring the stone as the beast dragged itself from the frigid water.

Yarrow spread his wings and drifted onto a boulder as waves of lake water struck the mountainside and froze almost upon impact, leaving jagged, prismatic walls in its wake. Slowly, the head of an enormous creature emerged from the frozen depths. Each of its opalescent scales was as large as a soldier's shield, and its long, narrow head was three times the mage's height. A white eyelid drew back to reveal a yellow iris the size of a temple window, and icicles the size of buttresses hung from the wyrm's bearded jaw. With its huge claws, it heaved itself onto the shore. Yarrow erected a barrier between himself and the mythical beast as the Mother Goddess's laughter echoed around them. He turned to seek her, but she'd already faded away. The wyrm opened its maw and released a great roar reeking of fishy decay, making Yarrow forget the woman as he turned to face it.

The creature's slender, shimmering body extended for probably a half a mile before disappearing beneath the churning waters of the lake. It raised a claw and swiped. Yarrow dove out of the way just in time, but the wyrm's claws cut deep furrows in the rock and sent it showering down, shards battering and slicing the mage's flesh. Its cry of rage made his stomach and organs feel liquefied, and he fought the irrational fear it inspired in him, fought to keep his stomach and bowels from expelling everything they held. He needed fire, and summoned his waning energy to conjure flame from his fingertips. When he waved his burning hand at the creature, it tucked its huge head back against its shoulder. His incantation didn't prevent it from flailing, though, and one of its ice-encrusted whiskers struck his legs and knocked him off his feet. He landed hard, a cloud of snow billowing around him and his fire choking out. The wyrm lifted itself farther from the water, raining cold droplets down on the mage as it regarded him, mouth open to reveal teeth the length of swords. Its rancid breath enveloped Yarrow in huge clouds of mist.

It bit down, and Yarrow's wings closed over him, saving his body from the teeth but not sparing him the impact. He sank deeper into the hoarfrost, and it folded over him like a shroud. For a moment, snow and earth covered his face and stole his vision. He wiped it away and forced himself up on his elbows, digging his way out frantically. Then he gripped the edges of the shallow little tomb and pulled himself up, staggering back onto his feet and facing the beast. He spread his wings and lifted off the frozen ground. The creature swatted at him, and Yarrow dodged to the side, narrowly avoiding its claws. He transformed his wings from sapphire mystic energy to true orange flame. As he extended them, his clothing smoked and his skin blistered, but the wyrm retreated a few feet into the cold water. Yarrow's eyes watered at the pain and stench of his burning skin, but he felt sure he'd driven the beast off at least long enough for him to escape.

He was wrong. The wyrm's head rose from the whitecaps, mouth wide. Before Yarrow knew what had happened, its jaws closed around him, its ancient teeth holding him immobile. It shook its head, rattling Yarrow's brain within his skull, bashing him against the mountain stone. Acting on instinct, he thrashed in an effort to free his pinned arms as the monster's teeth cut his flesh and his blood spilled from its mouth. But it was no use; his body held nothing near the strength of the creature's jaws. Only his magic would save him, and he had precious little left.

Clinging to consciousness, his mind and body begging to pass out and escape the pain, Yarrow fanned the embers burning deep inside his belly. He gave all his energy to feeding that warmth, coaxing it from coals to flame, until he could release the fire. He let it shoot from every inch of his body and smelled scorched fishy flesh as the wyrm dropped him and retreated. Even as it howled, it swiped at him with its claws, and Yarrow had very little strength left to protect himself. He darted behind a wall of fallen rock and snow, isolated a shard of ice, and sent it with all the force he could muster into the creature's amber eye.

The wyrm bellowed in agony as Yarrow's icicle pierced its orb and sent milky fluid steaming onto the snow. In a strangely human gesture, it pressed its webbed foot to its ruined socket and keened, its voice evoking rare compassion in the mage. Yarrow emerged from behind his shelter with his hands held high and his fingers spread open. His scorched clothing hung in ragged strips from his body, offering no protection from the biting wind. The creature, hurt and enraged, lunged for him, catching Yarrow's shoulder with the edge of a tooth and drawing a fresh font of blood that cascaded down the mage's chest. Gripping the wound, Yarrow skirted the edge of the water with the wyrm in pursuit. As it struck again, he dove behind a barrier of jagged stones. One swipe of the creature's claw reduced them to rubble, sending Yarrow fleeing again, his blood leaving a crimson trail in the snow behind him.

Turning, Yarrow concentrated on stealing the heat from the air around the lake water and directed a frigid blast at the wyrm's stomach. He succeeded in trapping it, stopping it from ascending farther from the lake, but as it thrashed, deep fissures cracked the thick ice he'd conjured. The beast's cries felt like they'd split Yarrow's head in two. He ran, doing his best to leap over errant rocks and stay behind what cover he could find. After battling a goddess, even his considerable energy neared its end. Escape was his only option. Besides, a small, silly, romantic part of him didn't want to destroy the magnificent creature, beautiful in its savage power, much like his entity had been before they'd bonded.

Yarrow sprinted toward a cleft in the rocks and what looked like a narrow path beyond. The trail, safely sheltered on both sides by high cliffs of ironstone, lay maybe a half mile away, and Yarrow pushed his body to move faster even as his lungs and muscles protested. He'd almost made it when a huge claw smashed down in front of him, showering him with rime and blocking his way. Seconds later, the creature's head appeared before Yarrow, its huge nostrils steaming and its intact eye regarding him intently. Within that yellow orb, Yarrow saw fierce intelligence, outrage, pain, fear, and confusion. It didn't know why it had been summoned from its slumber and compelled to attack. If he squinted and really opened his senses, Yarrow could see the delicate net the goddess had thrown over the creature's mind: angry, jagged threads filling it with hatred and rage, making it desire nothing but to tear apart any living thing it saw. Yarrow knew that urge, and so instead of attacking the beast again or even preparing a spell to defend himself, he sent a lavender cloud of soothing energy toward it, trying to negate what the goddess had done. At first, it didn't seem to be working, and the wyrm coated Yarrow with freezing spittle as it roared. Fighting his instinct to eliminate the threat, Yarrow spared just enough magic to defend himself and continued using the rest to dissipate the resplendent animal's artificial rage.

He could barely breathe as it thrashed its head and rent the ice with its claws. Dizziness threatened to send Yarrow to his knees, and he clutched a scrap of rock to remain standing. If this didn't work, he didn't know what he'd do. He didn't think he had enough strength left to conjure a wisp of smoke at this point. The wyrm pointed its snout to the snow clouds above and loosed a high-pitched wail that resonated through Yarrow's bones. Yarrow braced himself for whatever would come next, digging deep into his pools of magic for anything he could use to save himself. Bonded with an immortal being or not, he doubted he'd survive being torn to shreds by those massive teeth and claws. He didn't want to survive as nothing but chunks of meat scattered across the mountains.

Slowly, the creature arched its neck toward Yarrow and rested its chin on the frozen ground at his feet. An almost catlike mewling rose from deep within its chest. Yarrow, confused, kept his defenses ready as best he could and waited. Though he expected the wyrm to attack him at any moment, the creature remained docile and complacent. The lid of its remaining eye drooped over its golden iris, and Yarrow reached out with his senses, trying to understand the sudden shift. Grazing the periphery of the beast's mind, Yarrow perceived pride, a singularity of purpose, and, surprisingly, gratitude. It seemed to understand Yarrow had freed it from the so-called goddess's control. Reluctantly, Yarrow took a few steps toward the wyrm and rested his hand against its snout. Much of him still expected it to try to bite his arm off at the first opportunity, but the creature merely huffed out a defeated breath, surrounding Yarrow in a cloud of dank air. Yarrow couldn't help sensing a sort of tenuous bond had formed between himself and the beast.

"Go back to sleep," he said, sending his intent into the creature's mind, letting it know what he wished without language. "Maybe I'll be back for you one day. We'd make quite an impressive sight, riding into battle together."

The white wyrm lifted its head, arched its neck, and looked down at Yarrow. Yarrow detected a mutual respect form between them, and he raised a hand in farewell as the creature sank slowly beneath the frigid waters of Estrella Lake.

Yarrow stood watching until the surface of the water stilled and began to ice over again. Then he collapsed onto a rock and wiped his palm over his face, his hands still trembling. Since bonding fully with the ancient entity he'd encountered as a boy, Yarrow's body had been different. The wound to his shoulder had already closed though the cut had been deep. Before, the presence had healed Yarrow when it grew bored of experiencing pain, but now that they'd become one, Yarrow's flesh mended itself. It wasn't a physical injury that made Yarrow shake and feel like he'd empty his stomach into the snow.

Everything Hale had told him was true; he'd finally confirmed it after the questions had tormented him for months of sleepless nights. Everything his people believed, the very tenets they'd built their world upon, were lies. Those benevolent goddesses everyone believed created the world and looked after its inhabitants were nothing more than opportunistic women who'd stolen power from Fane and then destroyed him. Worse yet, they maintained their strength by hoarding the world's magic. Because of them, mortal casters grew weak, and fewer mages were born with every generation. For centuries, scholars had theorized on the gradual reduction in the world's enchantment. Yarrow now knew the answer those sages sought, but he'd be publicly tortured and executed for even suggesting it.

As if they could execute me.

A few deep breaths of the pure, cold air restored Yarrow's strength, and outrage followed not far behind. He didn't like being duped, and he resented power he could use being stolen. Yes, he knew the truth now, but what would he do with it? He'd be vilified if he spoke it aloud. People liked believing the goddesses watched over them, liked believing the goddesses knew best, so they didn't have to decide their own ideas of right and wrong. Though young, Yarrow had already learned most people would rather be told what to do than have the burden of choosing. They preferred following to forging their own trails.

Yarrow didn't. At that moment, he decided he'd expose the lie if it destroyed him, which it probably would. No altruism or sense of justice led him to his conclusion; he simply didn't like to see the unworthy ordering others around. He never had. After taking a few sips of the wine he'd brought from Windwake, grateful to find his skin canteen had survived the battle, Yarrow lifted his weary body from its perch. He headed in the direction of the small camp he'd made on the western edge of the lake to retrieve the supplies he'd stored there. He'd have to try to repair his shredded clothing. The walk back to Windust Castle would be long and grueling. It would probably take weeks, and Yarrow felt a sudden and severe longing for his lovers. He wanted to lie warm and safe between them for days. Could he reveal to Sasha and Duncan what he'd learned? Would they believe him? Yarrow knew they loved him and that they'd likely give their lives for him, but he also knew they thought him at least half-mad. He wondered what to tell them and just how to phrase it. He supposed he had at least two weeks on the road to sort it out, and he began walking southwest, along the edge of the lake.

After a few minutes, Yarrow stopped and looked back at the apex of Starmont. A watery, lemon-yellow sun hovered just a few feet above the mountain's peak, and the world had grown so quiet it almost hurt his ears. He would build a fortress there. Let the so-called goddesses try to stop him. Let anyone. His icy castle would tower above the kingdom of Selindria and the frozen wastes to the north—a wonder worthy of the lost world of antiquity—and he would sit astride the lake wyrm. First, though, he had more mundane matters to attend to. The time had come to return to Windwake and to Duncan and Sasha. They had much to address.

"Watch for me," Yarrow said, squinting into the bright light reflecting off the icy summit. "Your time is short, you bitch. I am Yarroway L'Estrella. Remember my name and fear me. I will show you no mercy. Expect me soon."

No answer came, and Yarrow wrapped his tattered cloak around himself against the biting wind as he began his long trek home to his lovers and a completely different set of difficulties.

Chapter Two

PLANNING to make his way to the frozen fields beyond the gates of Windust Castle for some practice, Sasha stalked through the torch-lit halls well before dawn. He worried the comfort and lethargy he'd enjoyed since returning from Duncan's wedding in Meritage would dull his senses and let his body become soft and slow. He couldn't allow that—especially if he intended to accompany Yarrow and Duncan in pursuit of his brethren—so he trained for at least three hours before breakfast and again in the afternoon. What he really needed to sharpen his skill was an assignment: an assassination. Unfortunately, at least for a creature like himself, most of High King Garith's enemies had been eliminated, and the united realms of Selindria and Gaeltheon approached something akin to the peace promised at the dawn of this so-called Blessed Epoch.

It wouldn't last, Sasha knew. Those who held power always had to defend against those who stood outside, hungering for control, desperate to claw their way to the top of the heap. To keep the illusion of authority, men like King Garith needed men like Sasha. Human nature never changed. The world had never operated differently, so Sasha knew he would be called eventually. Until then, or until Yarrow returned and the three of them set off on what would likely be an ill-fated quest, Sasha remained restless. He could alleviate it only by exhausting himself on the practice field, training until his body grew so weary his mind could no longer ponder questions he couldn't answer.

Sasha passed a few servants refreshing lamp oil or stoking hearth fires. He didn't expect to see anyone else at this early hour, and so it surprised him when he rounded a corner and found Duncan's new bride sitting on a bench in front of a statue of the goddess of love.

The young woman, Aurauna of Windwake, started at Sasha's approach. She gathered her skirts, stood, and pressed her back against the wall near the statue's alcove. Sasha studied her face in the low light. He'd been taught by the Order of the Crimson Scythe to decipher the most subtle expressions. From her wide eyes, Sasha knew she feared him. That wasn't unexpected. The plumpness and color in her cheeks didn't surprise Sasha either; he'd known for a few weeks now that Aurauna carried Duncan's child, though she hadn't announced it yet. The way the corners of her lips turned down revealed her disgust when she regarded him, and her lined brow showed anger. Still, she held her dress out as she bent her knee and lowered her head to him, saying, "My lord Sasha. The goddesses' favor on you this morning."

Sasha had no time for the false politeness of society—he stood outside such useless rituals—so he didn't return the young woman's greeting. Instead, he crossed his arms over his chest and stared at her pale, frightened face. "It's very early. How is it that you're not still in your husband's bed?"

Aurauna met his gaze. Hatred and resentment made her eyes narrow and a few fine lines creased the skin around them. "We both know Bairn Duncan would prefer you there to me, Tam Sasha."

"I don't suggest you say so to anyone else," Sasha warned.

"Will you kill me if I do?" Aurauna asked, surprising Sasha with her courage.

He shrugged. "Maybe."

"The bairn of Windwake does not love me," the girl said, settling on the bench again and folding her hands in her lap. "You do not have to throw it back in my face. But I suppose the goddesses teach us the Cast-Down delight in cruelty."

Sasha stepped closer to her, making her flinch. "The goddesses are right in that. Remember it, and do not trifle with me. Choose your tapestries and plan your feasts, woman, but don't think you'll steal my lover's affections from me. This is a marriage of political convenience, and as long as you don't try to make it into more, we'll have no problem. We both have our roles to fill, so just don't make any mistakes about what yours is. And if you tell anyone else what we've said to each other, I will make you sorry. That includes Duncan. He doesn't need the added worry of listening to you whine. I will do anything I must to ensure his happiness. Do I make myself plain?"

"You should be ashamed of yourself," Aurauna whispered. "You should renounce your wicked ways and pray to the goddesses for forgiveness. Not that I think they'd ever absolve your many sins. But since I don't wish to die in my bed, I will agree to your terms. I suppose I shall live out my life married to a man who will never want me. I had no choice either, you know. I actually entertained hope—"

"Your hopes do not concern me. Just keep to your place and stay out of my way," Sasha said as he hurried past her toward a small door leading to the fresh winter air. Thalil, the thought of his Duncan touching the simple wench made him want to kill her slowly, using the most nightmarish of the techniques he'd learned. He'd never been such a slave to emotion. He'd only ever regarded sex as a way to pass the time or a way to exert influence until he'd met Duncan and Yarrow. His masters in the order had warned against the sway of passion, warned him to remain cold and let intellect reign. A year or so ago, he'd encouraged Duncan to marry this girl to advance his position and avoid nasty rumors. Had he changed so much? Why had he changed? Sasha turned to watch the girl clutch the hem of her gown and hurry away, forcing himself to assess the situation logically. Her death would not benefit his interests or Duncan's, so he disregarded her. She was of no importance. Continuation of the marriage, at least until it produced an heir, benefitted both of them. Aurauna wasn't significant and therefore was not worth Sasha's energy. He kicked open the door and strode into the dark, chilly air, the frosted grass crunching softly beneath his boots and his breath thick and white against the black sky.

SERVANTS were at work clearing away the breakfast dishes by the time Sasha returned to Windust Castle. A few of Duncan's guests and stewards lingered over their meal in the hall, but in the barracks, the knights and soldiers had finished their food and returned to their training. More and more of them left Windwake each day to join King Garith's efforts to reclaim the land around the Kanda River, between the united realms of Selindria and Gaeltheon, from the mercenary factions and warlords who held them. For the moment, Duncan's lands faced no real threat. The aristocrats conspiring against him had been rousted, exiled, and, when Sasha had been able to manage it without drawing too much suspicion, eliminated. Bandits occasionally attacked merchants on the roads, harrow-wolves proved a nuisance in the winter, and once in a while the Emiri raiders wandered as far north as Barrier Bay, but Duncan could no longer justify keeping dozens of knights and hundreds of soldiers when the king requested them.

Sasha stopped by the kitchens for sausage, breads, boiled eggs, salt fish, cheese, and beer. His strenuous training had left him famished, and his muscles ached and twitched as he ascended the wooden stairs to eat alone in his room, as he always did.

He'd chosen a chamber overlooking the bay, with a single door and two small windows, three stories from the sharp rocks below: a difficult room for another assassin to enter undetected. Sasha set his breakfast on a wooden table by the bed, stabbed at his fire with the poker to coax flame from the coals, and sat down on a bench to pull off his plain black boots. The rest of his sweaty and soiled clothing followed. He couldn't wear his deep red, Crimson Scythe armor at Windust and opted instead for simple, dark garments most wouldn't look twice at as he passed: snug gray trousers, a heavy wool shirt, and a black leather doublet and gloves. They afforded him a measure of anonymity, let him wander the castle corridors undisturbed and ignored, and as such they suited his current purpose. He draped the doublet and gloves over the back of a chair, piled half a dozen knives and daggers on the stand beside his food, and left the rest of his garments for the servants to collect and launder. Running his hand over his chest and belly, Sasha felt the first catch of emerging stubble against his palm. He'd need to shave again the next time he bathed, even though he never knew if Duncan would be able to sneak away from his wife and join Sasha in his bed.

Now it was time to eat. Sasha picked up the clay platter and his knife and prepared to tuck in. A soft sound from the armoire made Sasha hesitate, and he gripped the kitchen knife even as he told himself the old fortress often rattled and creaked, especially in the winter. He turned his attention back to the meats whose aromas made his stomach grumble. Just as Sasha sliced into a juicy link of black pudding, the wooden doors of the armoire burst open. Sasha was on his feet before the splinters of wood struck the stone floor, his plate shattering at his feet and his food scattering across the floor. Naked except for his tiny black satin underpants, Sasha spread his feet into a wide stance and held his knife ready as a man in red leathers Sasha recognized only too well leapt from the wardrobe, a long dagger in each of his hands.

Dark wrappings covered the lower half of the assassin's face, and his hood obscured his hair and forehead, but Sasha met dark eyes narrowed in concentration—cold eyes focused on nothing but their goal. Thalil, he would remember to be more careful what he wished for in the future. If he'd hoped for a chance to test his skills, his desire had been fulfilled and then some.

"Brother," Sasha said, taking a step toward his weapons on the table, trying to avoid the shattered crockery in his bare feet. "You're very bold, coming for me in the light of day, without our master's shadows to protect you."

"You are no brother of mine," the other assassin said, his wrappings muffling his voice. "No one leaves Thalil's service."

Sasha shook his head, unwilling to defend his loyalties again. His heart and soul belonged to the Dark and Beautiful One, and he owed no one else an explanation. Clearly, this man was no green recruit—he waited with his daggers held ready but made no move to attack. Sasha recalled how long it had taken for him to learn the most important aspect of assassination: patience. He also remembered his training and focused on his enemy's gaze. The man's eyes darted downward and to the right, and seconds later he drove the point of his blade toward Sasha's exposed ribs. Expecting the attack, Sasha easily arced his arm to deflect the blow. Steel screeched against steel, and Sasha struggled to push his assailant back. When he succeeded, the other assassin staggered, caught his balance, and raised his blades for another attack.

Their daggers met and bounced off each other, pinging together as they thrust and parried, neither gaining an advantage. Sasha saw his opponent's gaze still focused on the fast, efficient movements of his hands and used the other man's distraction to his benefit. He kicked out, driving his heel into his enemy's kneecap and sending the other assassin sprawling on his back on the bed with a pained howl. Sasha jumped to straddle him, knowing this could only end with one of them victorious and the other dead, but the other assassin rolled and avoided him, throwing his knife as he tucked to protect himself.

The blade nearly embedded in Sasha's cheek, but he caught it just in time and threw it back. His brother in Thalil dove behind the bed, and the weapon ricocheted off the stone wall. Sasha moved toward his table for another blade just as his adversary rose and loosed a trio of tiny, likely poisoned darts. Sasha sliced the sole of his foot on a broken dish but he ignored it, desperate to reach his weapons. He dropped and shielded his head, and the small barbs his enemy launched lodged in the wooden frame of the window. He had to end this, and soon. Sasha leapt onto the bed and crossed it in two large strides, staining his sheets with bloody footprints. He dropped down behind his enemy and prepared to cut his throat, but the other assassin turned and deflected his blow, pushing Sasha off and sending him colliding against the wall. The stone scraped his bare back as the other man got to his feet. Once again, they raised their weapons, faced off, and matched each other blow for blow until both of them sweated and panted at the exertion.

Sasha struck at the other assassin's belly, but this time the other man expected it and caught Sasha's dagger against his own. With his other hand, the man aimed a blow at Sasha's neck, but Sasha lifted his arm in defense. He didn't manage to meet the other brethren's blade with his own, though, and his enemy's dagger dug into the flesh at his wrist, slicing through skin and sinew until his bone stopped it. Blood pouring down his arm, Sasha pulled back and hit the other man in the nose with his fist. The other assassin stumbled back, and his knees hit the edge of the bed, making him sprawl on his back across the red velvet Duncan had hoped would make Sasha feel at home.

Sasha launched himself at his enemy again, and this time the assassin didn't react fast enough to stop him. Sasha's only thought was that if he failed—perished—he'd leave Duncan and Yarrow unprotected. He might not see them again, and Sasha couldn't accept that. He straddled his enemy's groin and drove his dagger down at the man's windpipe. The other assassin blocked. With his other hand, he slashed across Sasha's bare chest, opening a thick gash that bled profusely. Sasha ignored it. He drew back and thrust the point of his knife into the other assassin's eye socket. The man shrieked with an agony that almost split Sasha's ears. When he dropped his weapons to clap his hands over his ruined face, Sasha drew his dagger in a smooth crescent across his throat. The other assassin choked and spit up blood, trembling beneath Sasha for a moment before falling still.

As soon as he knew for sure his enemy was dead, Sasha slid off him and stood at the edge of the bed on feet so torn they barely held him. He picked up his dirty wool shirt and pressed it to the gushing wound bisecting his chest. After tearing off a section of the bedsheet, he wound it around his wrist to staunch the blood flowing from that wound. Then he hobbled to the door, opened it, and glanced up and down the hall. No one else lived in this part of the castle, and the servants avoided it. Sasha called out a few times before he heard footsteps on the stairs. Soon after, a cleaning maid appeared, and Sasha hurried to speak with her before she ran from the sight of him. "Send the bairn to my chambers immediately!"

The young girl went white, nodded, bowed, and sprinted down the hall.

After slamming the door, Sasha went back to the bed and collapsed beside his vanquished brother, heaving to catch his breath and pressing the wad of cloth against his injuries in an attempt to slow the bleeding. *Baska*, he would need stitches, and that meant a visit from the dour healer, Fulgrig. Still, he supposed it beat bleeding to death.

After a few minutes, Duncan pushed the door open so hard it bounced against the wall. Seeing Sasha, Duncan hurried to gather him into his arms, sitting on the bed and drawing Sasha into his lap. "Dear goddesses, what happened here?"

Though everything he'd ever been taught told Sasha to mistrust the comfort and security he felt in Duncan's embrace, Sasha relaxed against his knight's broad chest and trusted his partner to protect him. He let his head droop, resting his temple against Duncan's collarbone. Thalil preserve him, it felt good to trust another to look after him, to know he didn't stand alone. Pain and loss of blood left him chilled and trembling, and he had to admit he needed the help of someone he could trust.

"Duncan, the Crimson Scythe will never let me go," Sasha said, cupping the thick globe of his knight's shoulder and holding tight. "I'll probably make quite a prize to the assassin who manages to bring me down. Fortunately for me, Thalil didn't intend for this one to succeed. But there will be others. They think I abandoned my calling, and they won't stop until I'm dead. By my dark master, it was so easy to forget they hunted me, to pretend I was secure within these walls. No living thing is safe once marked by Thalil. They will not stop until they kill me."

"I won't let that happen." Duncan stroked the back of Sasha's hair and leaned in to kiss his forehead.

"Oh, my love." Sasha brushed his fingers down Duncan's arm, smearing Duncan's crisp tan shirt with his thickening blood until he could wind their fingers together and squeeze, holding on for all he was worth. "I'm to blame. I should have checked the room—"

"This is your home," Duncan said. "I want you to feel safe here."

"I'm safe nowhere in this world," Sasha said. "It's never been any different. My brethren do not fail our god, no matter how long it takes. Not even if it takes generations. Marked is marked, Duncan. It's not something that can be washed away." Almost without thinking, Sasha touched the red crescent inked into the skin between his inner thigh and groin.

"Fulgrig is on his way," Duncan said. "We can talk about this after he tends to your wounds. When you recover, we'll decide what to do about your former brethren. I have had enough of them, and I intend to put an end to this."

Sasha rankled at that. "To stop them coming after me, you mean."

"To stop them doing this to you or anyone else," Duncan said. "I can imagine no better way to leave this world in a fairer state than when I entered it than freeing it from the fear and tyranny of those vile murderers."

"I am one of those vile murders," Sasha said, letting his eyes close. Thalil, they'd had this argument so many times, and he was so tired of it. He almost wished Duncan would either accept him or admit he never would. Existing in this in-between place between himself and the person Duncan expected stretched him thin enough to tear.

"We'll talk about this when your injuries are mended," Duncan said, "and when Yarrow returns from his family in Lockhaven. Right now, you healing is all that matters to me."

"Well, we have a more pressing concern," Sasha said, lifting his head and jutting his chin toward the body of his brother. "If word of the Crimson Scythe loose in Windust Castle spreads, you'll have a panic to quell. It won't take long for your men to trace the source of danger back to me. We need to get rid of this body and make up a story to explain my injuries. Either that, or find a way to keep my wounds secret. The servants and courtiers here don't trust me, but it would do neither of us any good for them to start gossiping about my true calling. You know the worship of Thalil alone is punishable by death. The presence of my dead brother and the condition he left me in might make others wonder what I've done to warrant such a skilled assassin coming after me."

"I can trust my seneschal, Tam Allwynn, to dispose of the corpse," Duncan said. "Goddesses, it will hardly be the strangest thing the poor man has seen since I became bairn of Windwake. I sent a servant to fetch him before I came to you, and he is already on his way. As for your wounds, you'll stay here until they're on the mend. I'd prefer you rest until Yarrow returns, anyway. I'll have the servants bring whatever you'd like to eat, and I'll post guards outside your door."

Sasha rolled his eyes. "Are you trying to make me angry? Honestly, knights protecting *me*?"

"I'll take you angry and safe over the alternative," Duncan said.

"Oh, and who will sit and sing me lullabies and rub my tummy when I can't get to sleep?"

"I will, if it will comfort you," Duncan said, either oblivious to or ignoring Sasha's sarcasm.

Sasha shook his head and then let it rest against Duncan, his neck feeling too strained to hold it up any longer. "By the Cast-Down, you really would. You sweet, simple man. I love you."

"I remember a time when saying those words cut your throat on the way out," Duncan said, just as someone knocked softly on the door. "That will be Tam Allwynn, here to see to the body." He situated Sasha on the pillows and stood to grasp the vanquished assassin by the ankles.

"Wait." With a great effort and almost more pain than he could endure, Sasha pushed himself up on his elbow and looked down at the paling face of his dead brother. He unwound the black wrappings from the other man's face and found a very pleasing countenance beneath; the order valued beauty in its agents, as beauty made manipulation and deceit go down easier. This man had certainly used his fine features to great effect, just as Sasha had so many times. This man had also died thinking his beauty, body, and skill were nothing more than tools to oblige the Dark and Beautiful One, that happiness could only be found through good service. Sasha felt sorry for him; he almost wanted to cry. This man had never found a Duncan or a Yarrow, and because of Sasha, he never would.

What in Thalil's name was wrong with him? Sasha wished his masters in the order would appear and whip him until pain forced all this idiocy from his head, made him focus on what was real and tangible, even if it hurt. When had he become so sentimental, so sickeningly weak? No wonder he'd almost fallen. This man wouldn't want Sasha's pity—he'd be insulted by it. He'd been a capable assassin, and he'd want only a brief acknowledgement of his service before he took his rightful place at their master's side. He'd led the life everyone in the order aspired to: reaping souls for Thalil and then dying for him. The order made life simple, spared its disciples the confusion Sasha faced. With his fingertips, Sasha pushed the other man's remaining eyelid closed.

"May you walk forever in the shadows, brother. May your steps fall forever silent and your blade never miss. May your daggers be forever sharp. May you stand eternally at the shoulder of the Dark and Beautiful One, the Whisper Heard at the Last, and may the light never reveal you as you pass eternity in the Crimson Palace."

"Sasha, this man tried to kill you," Duncan protested gently.

Sasha shook his head. "He did only what I would have done in his place, what you would have done if ordered into battle by your king. He deserves no shame in his death. Duncan—he almost beat me."

The knocking at the door grew louder. "We should see to this matter, Bairn Duncan," Tam Allwynn said through the thick wood.

Duncan hurried to let his seneschal into the room, and the stout older knight scowled at the body and Sasha bleeding on the bed. Though Sasha knew Allwynn was no fool and would easily figure out what had happened, the brawny knight proved his loyalty to Duncan and said nothing as he stroked the long plaits of his beard. "I'll take it out the servants' door, weight it with some stones, and dump it in the bay," he said, clearly annoyed, as if he'd been asked to empty a chamber pot.

Sasha turned away as Tam Allwynn wrapped the body in a sheet and hoisted it onto his shoulder. He knew that before he'd met Duncan and Yarrow, his corpse could have been hauled away like refuse with no one to mourn his passing. Why did that suddenly bother him? It had never crossed his mind before. Sasha focused on the physical pain tormenting every inch of his body, because he could at least understand and deal with it.

A few minutes after the seneschal departed, Tam Fulgrig the healer appeared with his two apprentices and his satchel of nasty-looking tools.

"What happened here?" the old man with the long white beard asked Duncan.

"He fell," Duncan responded.

"Do you think I'm a fool?" Fulgrig asked as he pulled a stool close to the bed and began arranging his instruments.

"I think you're a brilliant man," Duncan said, "and I'm telling you he fell."

The old healer just shook his head and set to work pulling shards of pottery from Sasha's soles with a pair of tweezers. After he wrapped Sasha's feet, he set to stitching the wound across Sasha's chest, then turned his attention to the most serious injury: Sasha's wrist. Duncan held Sasha's other hand as Fulgrig scrubbed it clean and sewed through several layers of severed muscle and flesh. By the time he finished, Sasha was trembling and felt ready to throw up. Fulgrig's apprentice gave him a tonic that alleviated his pain but left him barely able to keep his eyes open. Sasha fought it; every instinct told him to resist letting himself be left vulnerable. Duncan lifted Sasha into his arms and held him while the servants changed the bloody sheets, and Sasha knew he'd be safe. Despite everything he'd been taught, he knew Duncan would never let him come to harm, never leave him, and he let himself forget his worries and sleep.

Chapter Three

DUNCAN sat beside Sasha's bed as he had for the past two weeks, reading from the goddess Myint's treatises on honorable battle while his lover slept. A shaft of white winter light shone through one of Sasha's narrow windows and fell across his slumbering form. The first fine flurries of snow swirled beyond the glass, melting when they touched the stony ground. Though Sasha still looked pale beneath his deep tan, he had been eating more and spending more time alert the past few days.

Watching Sasha, Duncan grew angry with himself. He should never have let this happen. Though he knew going after the Order of the Crimson Scythe might be his last act in the light of the world, he grew restless to begin it. In truth, the peaceful months in Windwake since his wedding had left him empty. He'd always been a soldier—a man who protected innocents with his blade and shield—and he was too old to learn anything else. He longed for the road, the field, decisive action, and a world he understood. Goddesses, he hated politics, hated the sadness he saw on his wife's face every time she looked at him. He had never wanted to marry and had only done so at the king's insistence, to strengthen the ties between the two realms. Other men might find it foolish, but Duncan had never been happier than when he'd been on the road with Sasha and Yarrow, fighting to survive, to eat, to right the injustices they found. He should have been delighted with how far he'd risen—from a simple knight to the ruler of a large and wealthy bairny—but he wasn't. He just wanted to be a soldier again. It might not be as comfortable as being a bairn with a fortress, but it had been simple, and Duncan missed knowing right from wrong with absolute certainty, missed seeing the difference his actions made in the world.

He turned his attention back to his book, but it no longer held his interest. Beyond Sasha's bedchamber, the residents of the fortress celebrated Illira's Moon. Traveling storytellers and minstrels were treated like royalty, given room and board in exchange for their tales and songs, while the common people flocked to their performances. They'd filled the great hall of

Windust Castle for weeks, and the feasting had gone on almost nonstop. Duncan remembered loving the stories and plays as a boy in Thulemore, when his parents' humble household had granted the bards hospitality. He just couldn't find comfort in such simple things any longer. The stories of the great heroes rang hollow to him now; justice didn't always favor the righteous, and after what he'd lived through, Duncan could no longer pretend the goddesses always rewarded good intentions. He could only try to believe the sisters knew best, that they had a plan for his life and would reward his deeds. He had to believe even when it seemed so unlikely.

Someone knocked softly at the door.

"Yes?" Duncan set his book aside and prepared to play the role as bairn of Windwake if needed.

The door creaked open slowly, and a slight youth wrapped in faded black rags, with tangled ropes of white hair hanging almost to his waist, waited at the threshold. Duncan's heart soared at the sight of him, and he hurried to his feet, crossed the room, and folded the smaller man in his arms. "Goddesses, Yarrow. I have missed you. How does your family fare in Lockhaven?"

Yarrow clawed at the back of Duncan's doublet, clinging desperately as he buried his face between Duncan's neck and shoulder. "I'm sure they're well. What has happened to Sasha?"

"The others—"

Yarrow pulled back and looked up into Duncan's eyes, a controlled blaze burning behind his ice-blue gaze. "It's time we did something about this. Time to make them pay for hurting what's ours."

Duncan nodded, so relieved to hold Yarrow again he couldn't form a coherent sentence. Goddesses forgive him, he wanted to take his mage to bed. No, he didn't even want to wait that long—he wanted to take Yarrow against the wall beside the door, their clothing pulled aside just enough to allow them to join. Both of his young lovers made Duncan feel twenty years old himself, but he had to be the voice of reason. "Sasha is badly injured."

"Let me see what I can do about that." Yarrow pulled slowly away from Duncan and went to Sasha's bedside. He crumpled the sheets down to expose their assassin's wounds. At the sight of the puffy, purpled gash winding across Sasha's chest, bisected with thick black threads, Yarrow made an angry scowl, pulled his gloves off, and tossed them on the floor. Canting his head, he spread his fingers and rested his palms on the laceration. Soft blue light clouded out from his hands and sunk into Sasha's flesh. The deep cut, still red and gaping between the stitches, smoothed over to a satiny, pink strip. Yarrow lifted Sasha's injured arm and pressed Sasha's wrist to his mouth. His white eyelashes fluttered as he shut his eyes. His lips moved but he made no sound.

Duncan couldn't see what happened beneath the bandages, but color returned to Sasha's skin, and his eyelids flickered and opened. He tested his fingers, curling and extending them, before he reached up to touch Yarrow's cold-reddened cheek.

Yarrow dropped to the edge of the bed, looking wan. He chuckled and said, "I'm still a sorry excuse for a healer." He dropped his head on Sasha's chest, and Sasha closed his arms around it in a gesture of both protection and possession. "I'm glad to be here, with the two of you again."

Duncan sat down behind Yarrow and petted the back of his head while he smoothed the sweaty tresses from Sasha's face. It pleased him to see Sasha recovering, and he wanted to just enjoy their good fortune for a few moments, but Yarrow had other ideas.

After turning his head and resting his cheek against Sasha's chest, Yarrow said, "As soon as you are well enough, my beloved, we should have a talk with the members of your former order. I don't appreciate anyone threatening what's mine. Time to show them what happens when they do. I have had enough of this."

"I agree," Duncan said, touching the blade of his mage's shoulder, feeling the bone poking against the flesh like the point of a knife. No matter how he tried, he couldn't encourage Yarrow to eat enough. Yarrow seemed to become more ethereal every day, and sometimes Duncan worried he'd one day burn up in an azure blaze, his magic decimating everything physical. They would need that magic to stop the Crimson Scythe, if such a thing was even possible. "But where do we begin?"

"Corbin is waiting in Felgard," Yarrow said, tracing his fingertips along the rungs of Sasha's ribs, clearly tired. "He swore an oath to help me."

Duncan hardly trusted the mage-assassin who'd offered his brothers up in exchange for Yarrow's tutelage, but he had no alternative to suggest. "Do we go to him?"

Yarrow nodded, his eyes shut languidly as he rested against Sasha. "He's already been in Felgard for a few months now. He won't wait forever. We should prepare to travel as soon as Sasha is ready."

"I'm ready," the assassin said in a weak whisper.

"You're not," Duncan protested. "You need to heal completely before we attempt this."

Surprisingly, Yarrow agreed. "Rest, my sweet beloved. We have time. Soon enough, we'll show the world what happens to anyone or anything that dares to trifle with us. Sleep for now, Sasha. I need rest too. My time in Lockhaven has been quite the ordeal." Yarrow moved his hips and legs onto the bed and curled around Sasha. Sasha lifted his injured hand to touch Yarrow's hair, a smile tugging at his magnificent lips. Both of them closed their eyes, and Duncan was only too happy to move to the other side of the bed and lie down behind his beautiful assassin. He draped his arm across both the men he loved and burrowed his face against Sasha's shoulder as he closed his hand around Yarrow's slender arm. He felt their bones, muscle, sinew, and skin, all their essence exposed and open to him. Yarrow smelled of ice, cold, and ether, while Sasha exuded the smoky scents of iron, leather, spice, and blood.

"Your wife is pregnant," Sasha said without opening his eyes. "Has she told you yet?"

"No," Duncan said, "and it isn't important. I'll see Aurauna is well provided for, but I need to know the people I truly love are safe. If… if I don't come back from this excursion, at least I know Windwake will have an heir."

"That isn't going to happen," Yarrow said. "I swear it, Duncan. I won't let anything happen to you or Sasha. I'm stronger than I was before; I can keep you safe."

Duncan couldn't help thinking his mage didn't appear especially strong as he nestled his face into the pillows and fell asleep with his mouth slightly agape. He looked small and vulnerable in his torn, bloodstained clothing, so thin his cheekbone looked ready to tear through the brown skin of his face. How had visiting his family in Lockhaven left Yarrow in such a state? Duncan pulled the bedclothes over Yarrow and tucked him in tightly. He would question him later, after he'd refreshed himself. Then he just lay listening to his lovers breathe. Within moments, Sasha and Yarrow lay fast asleep in each other's arms, their foreheads pressed together and their open mouths only half an inch apart.

Duncan knew such comfort would elude him, so he rose from the bed and spared a moment to look down at the two young men. Goddesses, he loved them. As much responsibility as he felt to the people of Windwake, his subjects, nothing really mattered to him but their safety and happiness. Still, he had another to whom he owed answers, and he reluctantly left Sasha's chamber and went down the hall and stairs to his wife's.

Duncan knocked softly upon the door, and one of Aurauna's ladies-in-waiting opened it. All four of the young women attending Aurauna rose and curtsied when Duncan entered the room. Their fawning made Duncan feel awkward, and he struggled to sound confident when he spoke. "I would like a few moments with my wife."

The girls, who'd been mending Aurauna's dresses, reading from prayer books, or just tidying up the chamber, filed quickly into the hall. After the door closed, Aurauna rose from the padded bench where she'd been sitting at her embroidery, clutched her skirts, and dipped her head low. "Good day to you, Windwake. The goddesses' favor on you."

"And on you, my lady," Duncan said. "Can we sit together?"

"Of course," she said as she put aside her embroidery and covered it with her heavy wool skirts in a clear attempt to conceal it.

"What is that you're working on?" Duncan asked as he sat down on the bench by the window, leaving half a foot of space between himself and Aurauna.

She laughed. "Surely the bairn of Windwake has more important concerns than a lady's embroidery."

"Perhaps, but I'd like to see."

She lowered her gaze as she retrieved the hoop and the square of linen. "Yes, of course, my lord."

Duncan ran his calloused thumb over the delicate threads, afraid to catch and tear them against his rough skin. His wife had sewn an elaborate crag eagle at the top of the sampler, with pale blue windblossoms on either side. Her meticulous stitches spelled out Duncan's name and her own beneath. "What is this for?"

"I… I'm making it for my child," she said. "For our child. Of course, I won't be able to finish it until he or she is born and given a name."

"Is there something I should know?" Duncan asked as gently as possible. With his wife, he always worried something in his tone or phrasing would harm her fragile feelings. He couldn't simply speak without forethought as he did to Sasha and Yarrow.

"I hesitated to tell you at such an early stage," Aurauna said, wringing the fabric of her gown in her hands and not meeting Duncan's gaze. "There's still so much that can go wrong."

"How long?" Duncan asked.

"Two moons."

"Why keep this from me?" Duncan asked.

"It's still possible I'll lose the baby," she answered, pressing a palm to her stomach.

"Why? You are strong and healthy. Is there another reason you didn't tell me, Aurauna?"

She clamped her eyes shut and curled her shoulders forward. "Goddesses forgive me. I… I knew as soon as I conceived you'd stop visiting my chamber at night. I might be young, but I'm not a fool. I know the only reason you come to me at all is to produce an heir. Even when I was an innocent on our wedding night, I could tell you took no pleasure in it. You just wanted it over with. I… I was naïve enough to believe myself special enough to change that, special enough to make you love me. Forgive me. I suppose I still hold to the childish romantic notions of marriage I learned from storybooks."

"The world is seldom as depicted in tales." Duncan didn't know what else to say. "Clearly, you are unhappy here in Windwake. How would you like a new dress? I can send a servant to the market on the edge of the bay. I'm told the cloth coming in from the barbarian lands, beyond the Lapir Mountains, is truly beautiful, a wonder to behold. Is there a certain color you would prefer?"

She shook her head and dabbed at her reddening eyes. Duncan didn't understand her distress. In truth, he'd spent little of his life around women. Before assuming his title, he'd been a knight and lived among other soldiers, often concerned with little besides keeping himself and his brothers alive. This poor girl suffered. She didn't deserve it, and Duncan desperately wanted to comfort her. He just didn't know how.

"Well, how about a fine, fast horse?" he suggested, thinking of gifts he'd like to receive.

Aurauna forced a laugh. "I will hardly be able to go riding when I'm swollen with child."

Goddesses. What else did women value? "Jewelry, then. Or scented oils? Please believe I want you to be content here. Happy."

"Don't trouble yourself, husband. I am well provided for. This is a beautiful castle, and I want for nothing. I never thought I'd be a noblewoman, the mother of the future bairn of Windwake. I'm just being sentimental. Now, what did you come here to tell me?"

"What makes you think I didn't just come for your company?"

"Oh, husband. You never do."

Duncan braced himself. How well he understood viewing what others would consider a blessing as a burden. Most men would give anything for the lands and title he possessed, but in his heart, Duncan wanted to be a knight again. He wanted to protect the people of Selindria with his sword until he grew too old to lift it, then maybe retire to a quaint house back in Thulemore. All this opulence and excess was lost on him. What did he need with a hundred rooms when he could only occupy one at a time? Wealth and power, he'd found, were more trouble than they were worth. He patted his wife on the hand.

"I came to inform you I'll be leaving for a while," he said. "There's a matter that requires my attention."

"Is it something to do with Sasha?"

"Why do you ask?"

Again, instead of answering, Aurauna just shook her head. "Will you be back by the time our child is born?"

"I don't know," Duncan said. "I hope so but… I may not come back. What I must do will be dangerous."

She clapped a hand over her mouth to stifle a little shriek. Duncan touched her shoulder, and she turned to face him.

"I have disappointed you," he said, "and for that, I'm sorry. Truly sorry, and I hope you know I'm sincere. However, I swore an oath to you before the goddesses, and I intend to honor it. No matter what happens to me, you will live in comfort. You'll have the best nurses to aid you in your labors, and to help you care for the child afterward. One of my stewards has helped me draw up papers assuring you will have plenty of money to sustain yourself should anything happen to me. If you produce a boy, he will inherit the title of bairn, and you'll be free to marry again. If not, King Garith has agreed to give you the choice of marrying any man he sees fit to grant these lands to. Even if you decline, you'll receive a monthly stipend from the treasury that should allow you to live quite well. Aurauna, you don't need to worry about the future. No matter what happens, you'll be taken care of."

"You are a good man," she said in a hoarse whisper. "It seems you've thought of everything."

"Yet you're still unhappy." Duncan truly didn't know what more to do. "I'll talk to my treasurer before I leave and see what we can afford to spend furnishing a nursery. You can decorate it however you like. How does that sound?"

Aurauna nodded and scrubbed at her eyes. "Thank you, husband."

"If you need anything else, go directly to the seneschal, Tam Allwynn"

"Yes, my lord."

Feeling like he'd smoothed things with his wife at least a little, Duncan stood and bowed at the waist. "Very good, then." He turned to leave.

"Goddesses preserve you, husband." Aurauna still sounded sad, but Duncan had another idea. His houndmaster had informed him one of the bitches had recently birthed a litter of the long-legged, shaggy hunting dogs prized in Windwake. Many hunters said a pair of Windwake hounds could bring down a harrow-wolf. As he walked toward the staircase, Duncan remembered one of the pups had been a runt: a silvery ball of fur with big brown eyes, a single white sock, and a black tail. He would go to the stables right away and have that dog delivered to his wife, along with a dainty leather collar and a velvet pillow for it to sleep upon.

Chapter Four

THE stars still burned brightly against the dark sky as Yarrow, Sasha, and Duncan loaded supplies onto their horses. Three nights earlier, the first true snow of winter had dusted the rocky ground with a glimmering white powder. It sparkled in the dying light of the moon as the three men mounted up and set off, their animals huffing out great white clouds. Yarrow had slept well between his partners after a night of enthusiastic lovemaking, and he welcomed the challenges they'd meet and overcome together. For at least a few moons, it would be just the three of them again, and that thought gratified the mage as they made their way down the winding path from Windust Castle to the stone-studded steppe below.

After returning from Lockhaven, Yarrow had mended or replaced his damaged gear. He barely noticed the bite of the wind in his new leather trousers, heavy undershirt, wool tunic, fleece-lined black cloak, knee-high boots, and sturdy gloves. He'd wrapped an old blue scarf his Aunt Den had knitted for him around his face to shield his skin from the frigid air. A series of belts held emergency daggers and purses for his coin, and the rest of his worldly goods—a blanket and a few bottles of wine—waited in a single pack slung over his shoulder.

Two days of hard riding brought them to the eastern edge of Windwake by evening. The fertile plains of Everdale stretched out before them, the remains of the grain stalks shimmering with frost by the time they stopped to make camp on the leeside of a small hillock. Yarrow stretched after he dismounted, his thighs and buttocks unused to the saddle and sore. As soon as he'd relieved himself, he brushed his horse down, watered her, and tethered her to a leafless sapling.

Duncan built a fire and made a stew from root vegetables, beans, and dried meat. As Yarrow ate, he tasted the decay in the jerky, and it made him crave warm blood and fresh, living flesh, the hot essence of life against his tongue. Knowing the desire came from some vestige of his creature, Yarrow ignored it and dipped his bread in his broth. Since he'd bonded fully with the presence, he'd been able to smell and taste the slightest hints of death, and whenever he could, he avoided eating flesh. He reached for his wine to wash it from his palate, hoping the others wouldn't notice his distress over a simple meal.

Sasha erected their tent, and they slipped out of their clothes and into a single bedroll. As they made love, Yarrow almost forgot everything beyond the cozy edges of their blankets, just as he had when they'd first met and traveled together. Later, as he dozed between them, he felt complete in a way he only knew on the road, when he had Duncan and Sasha all to himself. If only the rest of the world and its petty problems would leave them be.

For the next ten days, they rode across Everdale without incident. They encountered no one but the occasional traveling merchant and a few patrols of Royal Guards. Only a year or two ago, three men travelling alone would have been temptation for bandits, especially when they turned south and rode along the outskirts of the notorious Elwyd Forest. Maybe there was more to the Blessed Epoch than a flowery name, Yarrow thought, though he doubted anything as simple as a marriage could bring real peace. Peace could only come if people truly desired it, and Yarrow just couldn't find that much faith in people.

They rode southeast and reached Felgard exactly twenty-six days after leaving Windwake—an impressive journey. Yarrow longed to get out of the saddle and happily handed his mount off to a hand at the first stable they encountered.

"How will we find Corbin?" Duncan asked as the three of them walked toward the sprawling port city of Felgard—a notoriously unlawful haven to criminals of all stripes, or at least it had been when Yarrow had last visited. Garith held it now, and his knights patrolled the streets, making cutpurses and whores shy away as they passed. Even though the sun had barely risen, hordes of people clogged the streets, all of them struggling for a scrap of the limited resources.

"I hadn't thought of that," Yarrow admitted. "His letter to me only said to meet him here. I'm sure he wouldn't dare give away any more, in case his message was intercepted." He tried to make some sense of the hundreds of jostling people, most of them covered in heavy cloaks and hoods. They shouldered past, many of them bumping into Yarrow or one of his companions as they stood at the edge of the wide, muddy street. The stench from the gutters, even in the cold, made Yarrow pull his scarf over his nose. The people looked so similar in their worn, dull-colored garments. In a city like Felgard, no one wanted to draw attention to himself. Only the Royal Guards in their shiny plate mail and heavy cobalt capes stood out, looking to Yarrow like they belonged in another world.

Duncan leaned in and spoke next to Sasha's ear. "Are there order safe houses here?"

Sasha nodded. His expression and tone were as flat and icy as Yarrow had ever witnessed. "Three that I'm aware of. The brethren have always had a strong presence in Felgard. Until just recently, criminals and gangs of thugs controlled the city, but none of them would have dreamt of bothering with us. They bent over backward to earn our favor. Thieves, mercenaries, and whoremasters always provided me with any information they could. Of course, that means now they'll happily inform the order of my presence if they know to look for me."

Yarrow considered. "Well, if you know where the safe houses are, let's eliminate Corbin from the equation and save some time. Take me there, and I'll go to the leader of the house and demand they leave us alone."

"That won't work," Sasha said. "The leaders of the individual houses don't have the authority to spare someone who's been marked."

"Then tell us where we need to go," Duncan said. "I would rather not involve Corbin if we can avoid it."

"The problem is, I don't know," Sasha said. "Though I earned some prestige within the order, I am still young. I don't know much about the higher leaders of the order, those who might be able to call this off. We can only hope Corbin does, but we'll have to be careful. As I said, anyone who can will inform on us to gain favor with the order."

"Goddesses," Duncan said. "Why would Corbin walk right into the middle of so many enemies? He's not only put Sasha in peril, but himself as well."

"We'll have to ask him when we find him," Yarrow said, pushing through the crowd in the direction of the river. He didn't know why he wanted to go that way—something about the water and the way it could just carry everything away had always drawn him. He never felt as safe or as free as he did on a ship, surrounded by nothing but water.

"And we've come back around in a circle," Duncan said over Sasha's shoulder. Yarrow realized the knight's strategy: keep Sasha between them. The fact that Sasha allowed it without protest indicated the fear his face and posture so carefully concealed. "We have to find this mage-assassin to get any answers, but we have no idea where to look for him."

"He must have left some sort of a sign," Yarrow said, watching the morning light dance across the rippling surface of the Kanda River. "I just don't know him well enough to know what to look for. I don't feel the faintest trace of his magic. I guess we should just keep looking and hope something grabs our attention."

"This should be the first of many delights," Duncan grumbled. "I suppose we're left with little choice but to wander the streets for now. Keep alert, both of you. King Garith may have reclaimed this area, but it's still a dangerous city."

As they made their way to the quayside, the smell of the river and the fish men hauled from boats to stalls and warehouses mingled with the stench of refuse and unwashed bodies. Civilization, Yarrow had decided long ago, meant stench. He preferred the purity of wild places and fresh air. The longer Yarrow watched the people, the more suspicious he became. This city held dozens or more of Sasha's former brethren, and if they didn't want to be seen or identified, Yarrow wouldn't see them. Every cluster of men in nondescript wraps began to look like assassins. Even the beggars and diseased people huddled between the buildings roused his sudden paranoia. They all seemed to watch Yarrow and his friends. It took all Yarrow's willpower not to extend his azure wings and shield his lovers. Magic coursed through his veins, fighting to spill from his pores. Whenever he felt threatened, the power rushed to protect him. Fear tugged him quickly toward rage, and he reached for his power like a sword. He understood this about himself now, but if he allowed it, he'd alert anyone who might be looking to their presence. He'd led his friends here, and now he didn't know what to do or whom to trust. If, like Sasha, he chose to trust no one, he might miss the opportunity to find an ally. Throughout his life, he'd managed to find his way to wonderful people who wanted to help him; people like Sai, the Emiri ship's captain who'd sailed him halfway around the world with no mention of compensation.

Duncan trusted almost everyone. While Yarrow admired and almost envied the good his knight saw in others, Yarrow had been hurt and exploited too many times to share it. Trusting the wrong person could prove fatal.

What should he do? It had been his idea to stop the Crimson Scythe from hunting Sasha, and his bargain with Corbin that had brought all of them here. What if he couldn't protect them?

My magic is strong, Yarrow told himself. *I'm a great mage....* But could his magic stop an arrow from one of the rooftops or a knife thrown from one of the hundreds of people surrounding them? Could it heal lethal poison? Yarrow wanted to just let his power surge forth and decimate everyone and everything for miles, tear down every potential threat in a single, devastating sweep. He mopped his lips with his tongue as he envisioned it. *No. I am not a monster. I will master this.... This is* my *power, and it will do as I say.*

He stumbled to a bench—just a rough board resting across two barrels—and sat down in front of a shoddy clapboard tavern with an anchor on the shingle above the door. Duncan and Sasha stood in front of him, Duncan furrowing his brow and Sasha looking placid, though he scanned the area and darted his black gaze in the direction of every sound.

"Yarrow?" Duncan asked. "Are you feeling well? Do you need something to eat? I'm sure it's time for the midday meal—"

Yarrow flicked his hand in front of his face and then rested his elbows on his knees. "Honestly, Duncan. How many times must I tell you I can manage to feed myself when I need it? The contents of my stomach are hardly our most pressing problem."

"Then what—"

"Just be quiet and let me think!"

Duncan flinched, and Yarrow reached out and squeezed his gloved hand. "I'm sorry. I'm not angry with you. I'm just frustrated because I don't know what to do, and I'm afraid."

"A rare admission from you," Duncan said.

"I'm not afraid for myself," Yarrow whispered, staring across the lane at a flock of white birds squawking and flapping their wings as they fought over a pile of waste. Against the filthy gray of everything else, their feathers looked so pristine, and their bills were such a bright orange. After a few minutes, a boy in rags swatted the birds away with a broom, shattering Yarrow's brief daydream. He shook his head. "Sasha, what would you do?"

"You're asking how I'd hide and reveal myself at the same time? I suppose I'd leave a signal only you could see."

"Magic?" Yarrow asked.

Sasha shook his head. "Corbin is not the only mage in the order. We don't have many, but we acquire every mage child we can. As you have seen, they can make powerful agents for us."

"Why do you continue to say 'we'?" Duncan asked. "These people cast you aside and put a price on your life."

"A choice of words," Sasha said coolly. "What does it matter?"

"It does matter," Duncan protested.

Yarrow let his attention wander away from their argument. The seabirds had returned to pick over the refuse pile. Two of them tugged a fish's spine back and forth. After a while, another bird, much smaller and with feathers the color of iron, lighted atop a stack of crates. Yarrow squinted at it, thinking he recognized it by its bloodred tail and spindly black legs. It was a rare breed: a Crypt Warbler. The people of Selindria and Gaeltheon considered the carrion birds bad luck and had hunted them almost to extinction. Those that remained haunted desolate cemeteries. Yarrow remembered a snippet of an old nursery rhyme:

Woe to the house where the Crypt Warbler sits
And blinks its bloodred eye
For the goddesses forsake some poor spirit
And he shall surely die.

The bird's eyes did look like droplets of fresh blood, and Yarrow wondered why it would be here by the water. Crypt Warblers, if he remembered his lessons, lived mostly inland, especially around Elwyd Forest.

From the way the bird kept looking at him, Yarrow almost felt like it wanted his attention. To the Shades' Abode with it. Everyone already thought Yarrow mad. He stood, crossed the rutted lane, and reached a hand out to the little creature as the sea birds protested loudly.

The Crypt Warbler hopped onto Yarrow's finger for a second before spreading its wings and flapping into the air. If he focused hard, he could discern a greenish trail flowing from its tail feathers. He could smell death—it reminded him of overripe fruit—sickly sweet and suffocating. He sprinted after it, calling for Sasha and Duncan to follow. Without sparing the time to look over his shoulder to see if they obeyed, Yarrow ran after the bird, pushing people out of his way so he wouldn't lose sight of it. After probably a quarter of a mile, the bird stopped in front of the unlikeliest of buildings: a temple to Fayelle, the goddess of purity.

Nothing distinguished the temple from the pubs, cheap hotels, and brothels around it except a small statue of a woman holding a burning branch standing in the slimy little patch that served as a garden. Time and weather had worn the goddess's features away; she looked like a vaguely woman-shaped blob of pale, peeling stone. Yarrow shuddered, remembering the ill-defined form of the dread goddess he'd faced atop Starmont. But this wasn't Starmont; it was little more than a filthy hovel caked in sea grime and bird dung. Still, Fayelle's disciples had left offerings—burnt symbols of vices they wanted to eliminate from their lives—on the frosty ground at her feet. The Crypt Warbler landed on her head and emptied its bowels.

"Oh, that's just disrespectful," Duncan said, shielding his eyes and shaking his head.

"It's irreverent," Sasha said, "maybe… maybe intentionally so. We in the order mock the goddess of purity over all the rest. We even share a story of Thalil ruining her innocence in the most depraved ways. It's quite an obscene tale."

"Sasha!" Duncan looked like he might be sick in the street.

"What?" Sasha asked, his eyes glittering with amusement. "How is the truth I've been told less valid than the version you believe?"

"Fayelle is a virgin goddess of unshakable virtue!"

"And my Thalil is a master of manipulation, as well as *very* beautiful," Sasha countered. "He seduced your goddess to prove no one is immune to temptation. Those who claim they are the worst sort of hypocrites. Often, those who preach the loudest against vice indulge in it the most. I've seen it, used it—"

"Enough," Yarrow said. "What if you're both wrong? Besides, neither Fayelle nor Thalil will help us now. If we want to accomplish our goal, we have only ourselves to depend upon."

Both of them looked as though they wanted to argue, but they held their tongues as Yarrow followed the bird down a narrow garbage-strewn alley, past a trio of drunkards snoring beneath a moth-eaten blanket. The Crypt Warbler stopped at the back of the temple and scratched at the ground. Fayelle's adherents had planted Maiden's Tears, the goddess's sacred white flowers, but the frail-looking plants struggled to break through the layers of ale bottles and dog dirt. Beyond them was a windowless wooden wall. At the corner, the Crypt Warbler dug up clods of soil. It flew away and didn't return when Yarrow crouched down.

As soon as Yarrow touched the warped boards of the temple, he felt weak and nauseous, his strength ebbing away. *A ward*, he thought. Anyone who crossed it would experience the same effects. Instead of dispelling it, Yarrow fought through the fatigue and reached out with his senses. The rest of the world faded to a dark smudge, and at the end of a blurred tunnel, Yarrow perceived the outline of a door. He pressed his palms against it and sent out a small burst of magic. Magic, like art, could only be imitated to a degree. A master could always detect an original as opposed to a copy. Corbin was a master. If Yarrow guessed right, Corbin's door would open only for Yarrow's unique enchantment, an enchantment no one could really duplicate, especially since Yarrow had never studied under another.

Slowly, the world in Yarrow's peripheral vision solidified, just as a tiny, arched hatch lined in stone appeared before him. Yarrow pulled the brass handle, and the door opened. A set of stairs waited beyond, disappearing into shadow after a dozen steps or so. Excited, Yarrow hurried to enter the passage, though he had to bend almost in half.

Sasha caught his elbow and stopped him. "This could be a trap. I should go first."

"No," Yarrow said. "You're the one they want. I'll go. They cannot hurt me."

"Ridiculous," Duncan said. "We go together. That's how we're strongest."

Neither of them could dispute it, and they made their way slowly down the stairs and into the gloom beyond, with Yarrow leading and Sasha between him and Duncan. Nothing but a cellar waited at the bottom of the steps. Wine casks lined the walls and some smoked meats hung from the ceiling, their savory scent filling the space. Yarrow felt magic now, just a wisp of it dancing in the ether, a faint echo, soft, like the last note of a tune drifting on the breeze, and he crossed the vaulted room to another door, where he found another set of steps leading down.

"Stop," Sasha hissed after they'd descended a few steps.

Yarrow and Duncan froze. Obeying Sasha had saved their lives too many times for them to protest. Their assassin moved to the front of the group and crouched down. In a few seconds, he'd disarmed a razor-sharp trip wire so thin Yarrow hadn't even noticed it.

"If Corbin is hiding in this place, he'll have trapped it to oblivion," Sasha said. "Stay behind me, step lightly, and don't argue. Yarrow, can you give me some light?"

Yarrow conjured a plum-sized orb of bluish-white luminescence and sent it to hover over Sasha's shoulder. He and Duncan lingered a few feet behind as Sasha inspected each of the chipped stone steps. At the bottom, they found themselves in another small room containing only a few pieces of broken pottery.

"Another dead end?" Duncan asked. "What is the point of this?"

"There could be another door hidden by illusion," Yarrow said. He felt enchantment brushing his skin like cobwebs, tickling the edges of his perception. He went to the wall and began running his hands over the old uneven stones.

"Yarrow, wait—"

Sasha's harsh whisper came too late. Yarrow's fingers grazed a stone, and a low rumble sounded as it scraped against the others and sank a few inches into the wall. Duncan spun around and pulled his sword as a cascade of rocks tumbled down the steps and plugged the passageway, trapping them in the tiny room. Seconds later, a noxious green mist began oozing from between the blocks. One whiff of it bit Yarrow's lungs and made it hard for him to draw his next breath. He tasted blood at the back of his throat as he coughed. Grabbing Duncan and Sasha by their elbows, he pulled them close and shielded all of them in a shimmering blue bubble. On the outside of the glass-like surface, the poison gas twisted and crawled like the tendrils of some foul, forgotten sea creature.

Yarrow looked back at the rubble blocking the doorway and the stairs beyond. He could easily blast it away, but that would mean dropping his barrier. He would live, but would Sasha and Duncan survive long enough to make it past the lethal cloud and back up to the next floor? But what other choice did he have? Before long, they'd use up the air inside his protective sphere.

A slim chance was better than no chance, Yarrow thought. "I'm going to get us out of here," he told his companions. "Wrap up your faces and try to hold your breath. As soon as I make an opening, run for it."

"No," Sasha gasped. "Yarrow, I think this gas is Thalil's Kiss. I have never seen it used, but I've heard stories of my brothers employing it to murder dozens of people at banquets. It's a complex mix of rare ingredients and difficult magic. I've heard it smells of cassiette root, which this does. Few people can make it, because it can be just as toxic to the one mixing the components as the victim. If I'm right, we don't have to breathe it for it to be fatal. It will soak into our skin and kill us within seconds. We won't make it the few steps to the doorway."

"What do you suggest we do?" Duncan asked. "Wait for it to dissipate?"

"There's not much air in here," Yarrow said. Beyond their sanctuary, the fog only grew thicker. He could no longer see the stone wall beyond the undulating sheets of grayish green. He let the light he'd conjured blink out to conserve his magic, and the rancid mist seemed to glow. "What do we do? Sasha?"

"Save speech for essential information, to start," Sasha said, wiping a thin ribbon of blood from beneath his nose. "So we don't use up our air."

Duncan nodded and replaced his greatsword on his back. It would do them no more good than Yarrow's magic or Sasha's blades. Yarrow could do nothing while suspended within the enchanted bubble, but as soon as he pierced it, the vapor would kill them—or at least Sasha and Duncan. Yarrow wouldn't accept that. He'd rather perish than have the death of another person he loved on his conscience. He had been responsible for too much pain in his brief life. He looked up at the ceiling. The mist congealed, shrouding the stone supports. Could he wrap his lovers in his azure wings and break through to the upper floor? He just didn't know. The bones of the temple were old and sturdy even if the outside was dilapidated. Could he muster enough force to break through while sparing enough energy to protect his partners? If he faltered for a second, he would lose them.

Sasha stumbled and bumped into Yarrow, knocking Yarrow off balance. Dizzy and unable to recover, Yarrow sank down and sat on his heels. Swarms of glittering fuzz poured in at the edges of his vision, and he realized they'd almost expended their air. Moments later, Sasha sank down and leaned his back against Yarrow's back. His grip on Yarrow's fingers when he grasped them felt weak and shaky.

"I don't want you dying because of me," Sasha said in a strangled whisper.

Yarrow tried to squeeze his hand and found he couldn't muster the strength. He had to concentrate. If he passed out, his spell would dissolve, and he would lose Sasha and Duncan. He bit down on his lip and focused on the pain, but even the pinch of his teeth against the sensitive flesh felt dull and fleeting. He felt himself going numb….

Duncan finally succumbed and dropped to his knees. "I… I'm a knight. I should be able to save you…. Goddesses, is this really the end?"

"No," Yarrow choked. "I… won't let…." He felt heavy, as if iron chains dragged him further and further into the blackness. It took all his will to keep his face above the surface of what felt like thick ink. He could no longer feel his hands or feet, and Duncan and Sasha looked warped and ethereal beside him. They rippled and blinked out for a second. Yarrow shook his head and gritted his teeth until his jaw ached. "I won't…."

"This… this will be the last thing I say in this world," Duncan wheezed, his voice cracking. "I want you both to know how much I love you…. I never thought…. This last year or so has been the richest and best…." He gurgled and choked, unable to continue.

"No matter where we end up, I… I will find you," Sasha said, his voice little more than a weak sigh. "Nothing… will keep me from you, not Thalil, not…."

Yarrow hauled in a lungful of whatever vapor was left inside the bubble, his pain transmuting to anger and giving him a surge of strength. He'd lost enough for ten lifetimes; nothing and no one would steal these men from him. He would wrap them in his wings and release a pulse of magic. He started to let it build in the pit of his belly. It would likely destroy the temple, maybe a section of the city, but it would take the noxious gas with it. The force of it should push the mist away before it could harm those Yarrow loved, and if the ensuing blast took the priestesses of this shrine or others? Well, life wasn't fair.

Just as Yarrow spread his ethereal wings and folded them tight around Duncan and Sasha, ready to decimate everything for a mile or more to save them, the mist began to thin. An archway appeared in the stone, and the sickly green vapor flowed into it. After a few moments, the room cleared, and Corbin appeared in the opening. The other mage didn't protect himself behind an arcane shield, so Yarrow dropped his barrier. Duncan and Sasha remained slumped against him, their eyes closed and their skin waxen and yellowish. The untainted air Yarrow breathed refreshed him, and he gradually grew alert—and angry. He pointed a trembling finger at Corbin. "If they're dead, I'll make you suffer for a hundred lifetimes!"

Corbin, clad in snug black leather trousers, knee-high boots, and a sleeveless tunic made of rows of leather scales, shook his head, tossed his long black hair, and chuckled. Tattered strips of thin black cloth wrapped the stump of his severed arm. Dark leather straps crossed his chest and held a dagger to his side, just below the remnant of his arm. He wore a gauntlet below his wrist that no doubt held hidden blades like Sasha's. Unlike Sasha, he had skin like an ivory statue—almost unnaturally smooth. It contrasted with his black hair and eyes, making him look to Yarrow like the very personification of Death come to claim them. When he spoke, his cold, mocking voice enhanced the effect. "They are not dead. I'm not a fool, Yarroway L'Estrella. Why would I kill my very few allies?"

After a few minutes of breathing unpolluted air, Duncan and Sasha began to stir and gradually sat up. Sasha had his daggers in his hands almost before his eyes opened, and he pointed both blades at Corbin. "Why in Thalil's name would you put us through this?"

Corbin shrugged. "You'd be no use to me if it took so little to defeat you."

Seemingly satisfied, Sasha sheathed his knives. He grasped Yarrow's shoulder to steady himself as he struggled to get to his feet. Duncan rubbed his face and muttered something about being too old for such nonsense.

"You understand I had to take precautions," Corbin explained without apology. "The Crimson Scythe takes offense to its disciples going rogue. But you are here now. Follow me, and I'll tell you what I've learned in the months since I last saw you."

Without waiting for them to acknowledge his words, Corbin turned and soon disappeared down the tunnel. Yarrow stumbled to his feet and then offered his hand to Duncan. All of them took a few moments to breathe and banish their vertigo before they followed the mage-assassin to who-knew-where.

Chapter Five

KING GARITH worried as he waited outside his wife's bedchamber, leaning against the reddish-brown stone of the hall. Queen Cothryn, after announcing her second pregnancy, had expressed a desire to return to her home country of Gaeltheon. To please her, he'd moved their entire household and all their servants to Gaeltheon's oldest and most respected city: Eirion. They'd taken up residence in the ancient castle of Eirion-Vayl, where Cothryn had been born, but her state hadn't improved.

The healer Garith had employed, an elderly woman called Lyorne, who had attended Cothryn's birth and that of her younger brother and sister, emerged from Queen Cothryn's rooms and closed the door softly behind her. She wrung the white apron she wore over her simple blue dress in her wrinkled hands.

"What news?" Garith asked.

Lyorne shook her head. "The queen is having trouble eating and is very weak."

"But why?" Garith asked. "I don't understand. When Queen Cothryn was pregnant with our daughter, the worst she experienced was a desire for arn-nut biscuits. She was happy and healthy right up until Princess Denna Borea was born. And now she can't even rise from her bed? It makes no sense to me."

Lyorne shook her head. "Every pregnancy is different, Your Majesty. She may be carrying a son, which is more taxing to her body. I have tried everything I know to revive her, but she remains weak. There is an old wives' tale...."

"Go on," Garith said.

"It is just a legend, Your Majesty, but the queen has expressed a desire for rare meat. There's an old story that says nothing is better for a woman expecting a son than the raw heart of an awrythe."

"I don't even know what that means," Garith admitted.

"Awrythe are mythical monsters living on the rocky cliffs on the plains of Dairden," Lyorne explained gently. "They are said to have a body like a horse's, but sharp claws like a cat's. They have snakelike tails full of poison, and keen eyesight. The tales say they can even see in the dark, and their sense of smell is second to none. They're a remnant of Fane's world, according to the legends, but many traveling merchants can attest to their existence. Everyone avoids their hunting grounds."

"Good," Garith said, clasping her wizened old hand. "I will hunt the awrythe and bring a fresh heart back to my wife. I will do it for her and our son."

"Majesty, it will be dangerous," Lyorne said, "and… and I am just a midwife and healer, but no one wants to lose you, Excellency. Perhaps you should send some of your knights. You're all that's holding this Blessed Epoch together."

"I won't be lost," Garith said. "And no son of mine will be lost either. I'll slay this creature, and Cothryn will eat its heart and be healed. I thank you for your service."

Lyorne clutched her skirts and curtsied before hurrying away down the hall. Garith smoothed his doublet before walking to the audience with his nobles in the throne room. He had recently passed a law allowing commoners to attend the assemblies and voice their concerns, and he found the massive hall full when he opened the double doors and entered. People from aristocrats in sumptuous velvet to peasants in rags lined the dozens of wooden benches. Tam Lysander, Garith's personal guard, stood to the right of the throne. Seven other knights also surrounded the dais.

Garith tried not to reveal his exhaustion as he sat lightly upon the ornate wooden chair instead of collapsing into it like he wanted to. "Who will speak first?"

One of his stewards stepped to the front of the throng and unfurled a long scroll. The rotund, elderly servant cleared his throat. "There is a petition here from several nobles and landowners throughout Gaeltheon and Selindria, particularly those in the coastal regions. They claim that since the discovery of the sea route to the barbarian lands beyond the Lapir Mountains, raids on the merchant ships by the Emiri have increased tenfold. They are requesting aid and protection."

"I will hear advice on this matter," Garith said. He couldn't imagine what good his knights would do against pirates. Their horses couldn't ride across the waves.

One of the king's advisors, Tam Vartanan, rose from the front row. "What we need is a force that can contend with these vermin, one capable of meeting them on their own turf. I am speaking, of course, of establishing a royal fleet."

"The cost of such a thing will be astronomical," said another man. "How do you suggest we finance it?"

Vartanan faced the other man. "Without ships of our own, we have no chance of ridding our coasts of the Emiri scum. Do you honestly propose we let them continue to rob and exploit our people unchecked? They are making us, and His Majesty, look like bumbling idiots."

Men got to their feet and voices rose in support of both positions. Before long, men shouted and pointed their fingers in each other's faces.

"Sander," Garith said.

The young guard nodded and banged his sword against his shield. "His Majesty will have all of you behave like civilized men! Sit down."

"Does anyone have anything worthwhile to add to this debate?" Garith asked, trying not to sound as weary and overwhelmed as he felt. A young man stood and stepped forward.

"Your Majesty, I am the bairn of Meadow's Edge, and I have traveled all this way to address you on this matter. The situation with the Emiri is more dire than I can impart to you. If it continues, they will push their way inland from the coast and secure even more territory. We really need your help. We also have many sailors and laborers without gainful work. If you choose to construct this fleet, you will have no shortage of craftsman, and these men will gain honest work when they might otherwise turn to crime to sustain themselves. Thank you for hearing me." The young nobleman sat down.

A knight commander standing near the edge of the room spoke next. "King Garith, I feel I would be remiss if I didn't mention how much our efforts to reclaim the land around the Kanda River have cost. It is all we can do to pay the good soldiers who have been fighting for over a year."

"This fleet is necessary!" Tam Vartanan repeated.

"Very well," Garith said. "Tam Vartanan, I will task you with compiling a detailed report. I want to know exactly how much this fleet will cost, how long the ships will take to build, and how we'll find the gold to pay for it. Secure estimates for labor and materials. Explore what, if any, expenses could be cut to finance it. Draft letters to the concerned nobles and let them know we are seeking a solution to this problem. I would also like you to send a message to my cousin Yarroway. He has been promised the lands the Emiri now occupy as his valenny, and I think he should lend his assistance in reclaiming them."

"That is a fine sentiment, my king," Vartanan said, "but where will I send the message? That mad boy…. Forgive me. Your *esteemed cousin* has no permanent residence. Tracking him down could take months or years."

"Send it to the bairn of Windwake," Garith said. "Yarrow will surely be at Windust Castle before long."

"Yes, Your Majesty."

"Is there any other business?" Garith asked.

For the next three hours, he heard his subjects' concerns: mostly requests for money, requests for knights to protect them from bandits and raiders, and petty disputes about borders and the use of roads. Just when the throbbing in his head approached unbearable, the meeting concluded and the great hall began to empty out. Garith rubbed his temples and muttered, "I need a glass of wine. Or maybe a bottle. Sander, will you have your midday meal in my suite?"

"I would be honored, Your Majesty, but I'm afraid there's one more matter you must address first."

"Goddesses, what now?" Garith asked. He wanted a few moments alone with Sander more than he wanted his next breath.

"Three priestesses arrived this morning with dozens of guards and a prisoner. They refuse to speak a word of their business except to you. We found them a room to wait in, but we didn't know what else to do. I'm afraid they're quite insistent."

"Well, you're coming with me," Garith said. He didn't think he could face anything else today without Sander by his side. He needed Sander's strength, and Sander might be the only man in the kingdom who wouldn't hold his support and friendship over Garith's head later. In front of Sander, Garith could afford to show the weakness and uncertainty he sometimes felt.

"Into the heart of the Shades' Abode, if you would ask me," Sander said, meeting Garith's gaze and smiling. For a few seconds, nothing existed for Garith but Sander's lush pink lips, big, blue-green eyes, rosy skin, and the copper curls tumbling into his beautiful face. He'd never known a person—not even his beloved wife—who could ease his mind and lift his heart with just a smile. Every spark of Garith's being wanted to forget about the priestesses and find a place where he could be alone with Sander for an hour. He was king—he had an obligation to his subjects—but was an hour to remember why life was a gift from the goddesses too much to ask?

For the High King of Selindria and Gaeltheon, maybe it was. Garith had no time to pursue his own pleasures or satisfy his heart's demands. Too many others depended upon him.

"I suppose we should get this over with," Garith said.

Sander led Garith to a small, comfortably furnished sitting room. A large bay window afforded a fine view of the windswept plains to the east and the horses grazing on them. Gaeltheon prided itself on its fine horses. Three aged women—a blue-robed priestess of Vestrafori, the goddess of truth and justice, a priestess of Laud in tattered gray, and a plump priestess of the Mother Goddess in elaborately embroidered burgundy vestments—sat around a wooden table. A tray of fruit, bread, and cheeses sat untouched between them.

"Welcome to Eirion-Vayl," Garith said, his gaze wandering to the armed men leaning against the walls and the elderly fellow in manacles who sat on the floor in the corner. "I trust you have been made comfortable. Now, what can I do for you?"

"We will speak with you alone," the priestess of Vestrafori barked. She had a crushed, upturned nose and drooping jowls, like a spinster's lapdog. "Dismiss your servant."

Garith balked. Since assuming the united thrones of Selindria and Gaeltheon, he had endeavored always to keep peace, never show favoritism, and make all his subjects feel valued and respected. He appreciated the implications of his every action, his every utterance magnified beyond what ordinary men had to consider, but he didn't like being bullied. "I am here with a single guard," he said. "You have come with dozens. I must insist my knight remains to insure my safety."

"Unacceptable," said the priestess of the Mother Goddess, drumming her thick fingers on the tabletop. "We must discuss a very delicate matter with you."

"And my guard's discretion is assured," Garith said.

"That will not do," the priestess in purple persisted.

"It will," Garith said. "Forgive me, but I am king and this is my home. You are guests here."

"You are king only by the grace of the Thirteen Sisters, young man," the plump woman said.

"If we cannot reach an accord, I'm afraid our business is concluded," Garith said.

"No!" shouted the man on the floor. "Don't go. Please, Your Majesty, I implore you."

"What is the nature of this man's crime?" Sander asked, pointing an armored finger at the prisoner.

"He is a heretic," the priestess of Laud said in an icy whisper.

"I am a scholar!" the prisoner said.

"Shut your mouth, you heathen," the priestess of Vestrafori snapped.

"I say we let the man speak." Sander crossed the room and offered the frail-looking man a hand, then helped him to stand. Only Sander had seen fit to extend assistance to a broken man. Garith's heart swelled with pride, and he resolved to follow his friend's example.

Sander helped the poor man to a chair and offered him some water. "What is your name, tam?"

"T-Torkan Mellinger, honorable knight. Thank you for the water."

"Of course," Sander said. "Now, what are you accused of?"

"He is disseminating lies and blasphemy—" the priestess of Vestrafori declared in a rough but squeaky voice.

Sander simply held up his gauntleted hand, and the woman bit off whatever she planned to say next. Garith smiled. Sander's inherent grace and power influenced others without the need for him to say base things or resort to threats. If anything, Garith thought, Sander naturally possessed the regal bearing Garith himself had always tried to cultivate. He remembered when, not so long ago, Sander had been rash and a bit obnoxious. Garith had even found that captivating. But then, Garith knew he was a man in love, and Sander's blemishes looked to him like alluring freckles: kisses placed on his pink cheek by the sun. Garith had to remain objective as king, and he had to focus on the matter at hand and stop letting his very desirable knight distract him.

Sander stood beside Torkan Mellinger with his hand on the frail man's shoulder. No one dared to interrupt Mellinger's account.

"I am a simple man," Mellinger said in a weak voice, staring down at his filthy hands and wrists wreathed in iron bonds. Long, shattered nails protruded from his fingertips. "I have always been curious about the past. My only goal has been to reconcile the stories we're told of Fane's golden paradise with some sort of physical proof. I used up most of my life searching in vain, and then, just a few moons ago, I uncovered what I believe are actual relics left behind from Fane's empire. Your Majesty, honorable knight, I am only the messenger. I am nothing more than the man who had the good fortune to dig in the right place. I certainly intended no slight against the Thirteen Sisters. My goal has only ever been knowledge. Truth. Please, radiant lord of the Blessed Epoch, I swear I mean no disrespect."

"What you intend to spread are the most insidious of lies," the skeletal priestess of Laud breathed. "My goddess herself has told me so. You should be called Cast-Down."

"No." Mellinger shook his head, and it seemed to Garith more a gesture of futility than defiance. "I did not author this truth; I only uncovered it."

"What truth?" Garith asked.

"He is a heretic—" the priestess of the Mother Goddess huffed, her outrage clearly stealing her breath.

Garith cut her off. "I would hear what this man has to say."

Chains clinked as Mellinger lifted his hands to rub them down his ashen, sagging face. "After years of research, I found some artifacts from Fane's kingdom. Among them was a fragment of a stone tablet—"

"How dare you?" the priestess of Vestrafori yipped, her voice cracking. "An insignificant insect of a man, making such allegations!"

"Let the man speak," Garith said, more firmly this time.

Mellinger curled forward, either exhausted or just resigned to defeat; Garith couldn't tell. "I found a stone tablet inscribed in an ancient language. It spoke of a race of powerful magical beings... evil and bloodthirsty beings defeated by the goddesses... with the help of magic learned from Fane."

"As if Fane was greater than the sisters," the priestess of the Mother Goddess said, shaking her head. "Preposterous. The goddesses showed that arrogant mage his place. Fane paid for his conceit. I would not see the same happen to you, High King Garith. But if you become too superior, you will not escape the notice of the goddesses and those who serve them faithfully."

"Is that a threat, old woman?" Sander hissed, putting his hand on the hilt of his sword. "I respect and adore the goddesses, but while I live, no one will threaten Garith."

"Your love for your sovereign seems almost... unnatural," the priestess of Laud wheezed.

"Absurd." Sander's cheeks bloomed as red as the sunset, and Garith wanted to press a finger to that heated flesh, feel the warm blood pulsing beneath Sander's skin. Their relationship wasn't unnatural—not yet—but Garith wanted it to get to that point. He'd never felt such a fierce and all-consuming desire for anyone or anything. He enjoyed his wife's bed well enough, but when he looked at Sander, Garith thought he'd willingly beg for scraps in the street for the rest of his life if he could touch him just once.

"Do not defame my faithful soldier," Garith said. "He is only doing his duty."

"Is that all he's doing to service you, Your Majesty?" the fat priestess taunted.

"I am no more than a loyal knight, and I will not have my king slandered. It is my sworn duty to protect His Majesty. From any threat." Sander lifted his chin defiantly, and by the goddesses, he looked as valiant as a picture in a storybook. "I will not have the king insulted in his own home. Tell him what you want from him, or so help me, I will eject you from this castle, no matter how many guards you have brought!"

Garith shuddered at the way Sander defended him, not like a knight performing his work, but like a lover, full of true outrage and concern over Garith's honor. "I agree. I may be young, but I am still a king, and I expect at least a measure of civility. Tam Torkan discovered some relics. What does that have to do with me or my kingdom?"

"They want to destroy what I've found!" Mellinger shouted, his voice parched and breaking. "To destroy that priceless knowledge!"

"It is a forgery full of lies," the priestess of Vestrafori said, "and it should not pollute the minds of the common people."

"Maybe it is," Mellinger said, calming a little. "If you are so confident, release me and let me take my discovery to Espero as I'd intended. Let the knowledgeable mages there study the tablet and either validate or dismiss it. That is all I ask."

"That seems reasonable," Garith said. "Why has this man been so ill-treated?"

"Because he will not reveal the location of this tablet!" the priestess of the Mother Goddess bellowed. "We are here to demand that you, king of Selindria and Gaeltheon, by the grace of the goddesses, sworn protector of your subjects, force him to produce what he has found. It should pass into the custody of the servants of the holy sisters. We should be the ones to study it, not a pack of mages, barely more than heretics themselves!"

"My mother is Esperon," Garith said, struggling to keep his tone even. "Espero is a nation of righteous people, and it is our ally. They are the favorites of the goddess Pherara. Why call them heretics, and why prevent them from examining this man's findings?"

"The mages in Espero would love nothing more than to demonstrate their superiority, even over the holy sisters," the priestess of Vestrafori said. "They would delight in telling everyone Fane the mage-emperor advised the goddesses. That he was greater than they are."

"What if it's true?" Sander asked. "Don't people have the right to know?"

"How dare you suggest such a thing could be the truth?" shouted the priestess of the Mother Goddess as she got to her feet. "The common people are simple and gullible. It is my job as a messenger of the divine to protect them from this sort of corruption. King Garith, do you honestly intend to impede us in our sacred duty?"

Garith considered. Sisters forgive him, he wished he could have asked his mother's opinion, but his mother was not here, and she wouldn't be with him forever. It was time to stop being a child and be a king. If only he didn't harbor such doubt in himself. If only he could have clasped Sander's hand while he faced the three women. But as king, he'd always stand alone in some ways. The decision and its consequences fell to him. "It seems to me that anything this man discovered is his property, and he should be allowed to do with it as he chooses."

All three women opened their mouths, ready to protest, but Garith held up his hand and continued. "I am king. You have asked for my decision, and I have given it. Further, this poor man has committed no crime as far as I can see. I order you to release him at once and never bother him again." When they hesitated, Garith spoke a little louder. "Now!"

Looking sick, the priestess of the Mother Goddess nodded to one of her guards. The man in the shining bronze mail and purple cape took a key from a chain around his neck and unfastened Mellinger's cuffs.

The old scholar rubbed his bruised and bloody wrists. "Goddesses bless you, Your Majesty."

"You have made a grave mistake, King Garith," said the priestess of the Mother Goddess. "As I have told you, the common people want to be led. It is easier for them to be told what to do than to decide for themselves. And the common people come to the temples of the goddesses to be instructed. We are the heads of our orders, and we will turn the people of this kingdom against you if we do not get that tablet. There is not a single peasant in the most remote village who does not visit a rural shrine. We can reach the ears of thousands of people, tam. How many can you personally speak with? Do not doubt for a moment that your rule rests on our whim. If we spread the word that the goddesses oppose you, how long do you think you'll hold the throne?"

Sander drew his sword, and the priestess's guards reacted in kind. "Garith, this is treason," Sander said, his cheeks flushed with righteous passion. "I'll throw the lot of them in the dungeon and let them rot!"

Garith shook his head. Making these women martyrs would not help him. "Stand down, Sander. The priestesses were just leaving."

"We are stronger than you," the priestess in purple warned. "The people trust us over the monarchs who have exploited them so long. Reconsider."

"No," Garith said. "As king, I have a responsibility to protect my subjects." He pointed to Torkan Mellinger, who stood near the door, ready to run as soon as someone granted him the opportunity. "This man is my subject, and he has done nothing wrong. He deserves my protection. Further, I will not let my reign, the Blessed Epoch, be a period of suppressed knowledge. If this is truly to be a prosperous period, we must embrace learning. Truth. That is my decision."

"You will regret this," the priestess of Vestrafori growled, gathering her layered blue skirts as she stood. "Who do you think you are to wage war against the goddesses?"

"That's hardly what I'm doing," Garith said. "I've merely decided the fate of one man. I am a devout servant of the Thirteen Sisters, and I have always been."

"Your people will not believe that if we tell them differently. Further, we have far more gold than your entire kingdom. We can easily eliminate any who might speak against us. We can easily pay those who walk in the shadows, those who never, ever fail."

"Sweet sisters!" Sander rubbed his armored hand over his face. "Are you truly threatening the High King of Selindria and Gaeltheon with the Cast-Down? You would stoop so low as to employ those whose names you won't even utter?"

Garith didn't give them a chance to answer. "Two can play at that game, my fine ladies. I have played it many times before. Does that surprise you? Your empty threats do not frighten me, but you might think twice before speaking against me. I am associated with… many different classes of my subjects. I have personal friends who—how did you phrase it?—walk in the shadows. So test me if you will. I am a young king, but I will not be threatened. By anyone."

"You cannot silence all who speak against injustice," the priestess of Laud wheezed.

"I can try," Garith countered.

"Enough," Sander interrupted. "The king has asked you to leave. Obey his wishes."

Mellinger curled against the doorframe, shielding his head as the priestesses and their guards filed past. As soon as they'd left the room, Garith collapsed into a chair and Sander came to stand behind him. Amidst all this uncertainty, Sander at his back felt good, reassuring. Garith only wished Sander could rest a hand on his shoulder; he craved the smallest connection between them, the smallest overt evidence of the support he knew Sander offered.

Mellinger limped to the table and fell into a chair. "Goddesses bless you, radiant King Garith of the Blessed Epoch."

Garith laughed bitterly. "I suppose we'll see if they grant their blessing. Do you wish something more from me?"

"I don't know," Mellinger said, staring at the holes in the thighs of his trousers. "I am not an evil man. I adore the goddesses; after all, they let me find my way to the tablet. If they didn't want it found, they would have stopped me. Wouldn't they?"

"I don't know." The priestesses had been right about one thing; Esperons were not especially religious, and Garith's mother had been no exception. She had taught him to question instead of believing blindly. He'd also learned little doctrine from his father, who had seen his sword and army as the way to everything. Besides, concrete threats troubled him more than philosophy. "Tam Torkan, the priestesses will try to have you killed. Where will you go?"

"To Espero to deliver the tablet," Mellinger said, appearing self-assured and excited now. "Then back to the ruins. If we keep digging, I am confident we can find more."

"You'll be easy prey," Sander warned.

Mellinger laughed. "I'm an old man already. I have precious little time left. This discovery came late in my life, and I'll do all I can to find all the knowledge available. If… if I fall to the Cast-Down, I suppose it is quicker than disease and age. They will not scare me away, Your Majesty, and I am so glad they couldn't scare you. You will be a great king, remembered by history. For what it's worth, I'll make sure everyone I speak with knows the risk you took. They'll remember you did the right thing."

Garith didn't care about history or posterity at the moment. He reached across the table and patted Mellinger's wizened hand. Being brave as a king surrounded by castle walls and an army seemed easy compared to being an old man, impoverished and alone. "Stay here as my guest tonight. You look like you can use a good meal and a comfortable bed. Tomorrow, when you depart, I'll send a few knights with you. You won't have to stand unprotected against those who would harm you."

"I'll never be able to repay this kindness, Your Majesty," Mellinger said.

"A few knights won't stop the… the ones the priestesses have threatened to employ," Sander said.

"They might," Garith said, looking over his shoulder to smile at Sander. "It would not be the first time, if you recall. Now, Tam Torkan, get down to the kitchens. I will have my servants provide you with everything you require. Get yourself something to eat."

Bowing and muttering thanks, Mellinger backed out of the room. As soon as the door shut heavily behind him, Sander clasped Garith's shoulders and squeezed his tense muscles. Garith caught Sander's wrist and pulled his hand around so he could nestle his cheek into Sander's palm. He closed his eyes, let the scent of Sander's skin wind around him like a comforting blanket, and let Sander support the weight of his head. In moments like this, it was so easy to pretend nothing existed beyond the two of them, and Garith indulged in the fantasy for many minutes as Sander kneaded the back of his neck and leaned forward to breathe into Garith's hair. It made Garith imagine Sander panting against him in a very different situation.

"Do you think those priestesses can really turn my people against me?" Garith muttered without opening his eyes.

Sander leaned in and rubbed the side of his face against the top of Garith's head. He let it rest lightly against Garith as he spoke, his warm breath ruffling Garith's hair. "I don't know, my friend. Maybe. You have done a great deal for your subjects in the short time you've been king. For the first time in memory, the roads are safe to travel and well maintained. No one is going hungry. But people can be fickle. Sometimes I… I think they like to see the mighty laid low. We should make sure they know our version of the events, but I don't know how. You have advisors for things like that. My job is to protect you with my life."

"You must swear to never give your life protecting me," Garith said. "I… don't want to live without you."

"But you're a king. You can't be replaced as easily as I can."

"No one will ever replace you." Garith let his head rest against the back of his chair, angling his face up toward Sander. "Do you not know what you mean to me?"

Instead of answering, Sander pressed his lips to Garith's forehead. Goddesses, it felt good—so good Garith's blood rushed toward his root at just that small press of flesh against flesh. Sander pecked the bridge of his nose, then the tip, and it made Garith's heart stutter. He'd dreamed of a moment like this, so many times, but the reality of Sander's lips brushing his skin surpassed all his imaginings. He angled his head back farther and wrapped his hand around the back of Sander's neck, bringing their lips together—finally. Their mouths grazed against each other, the contact sending jolts of pleasure through Garith's body. He pulled Sander closer and hooked their lips together, with Sander's lower lip between Garith's. Garith ran his tongue along the plump pink flesh, reveling in the taste and texture. Just as he prepared to venture past Sander's smooth teeth, Sander pulled away.

"What's wrong?" Garith panted, his mind reeling with so much lust it almost erased every other concern. He just wanted to grab Sander and kiss him until their lips bled. "Sander?"

Sander just shook his head and went to the window, looking out over the plains with his back to Garith.

"Sander? If you don't want me as I want you—"

Sander turned, a shaft of sunlight gilding his wild copper curls, his cheeks stained crimson and his blue-green eyes pensive. Garith had never seen such a tantalizing sight. "I want you more than anything. Thinking of it tears me apart. But… after today, after all this talk of the goddesses, I am loath to do something so sinful. We are taught it is an abomination. I… I will do it, if you order me…. You are my king…."

His words cut Garith to the core. "Is that the kind of man you think I am? One who would command you to do something that made you uncomfortable? Do you honestly believe I see you as just another servant? Goddesses, Sander! You are my world! My sun and sea and land… my everything."

"I know." Sander crossed his arms over his chest and rubbed his arms. "I know, and I should not have said that. I have only ever wanted to be a good man." He looked up through his red eyelashes. "I love you, but…. No. I just… I love you. But I've been taught all my life that it's wrong."

"I don't want to cause you distress," Garith said, staring deep into Sander's beautiful sea-colored eyes. He didn't want to be the source of the pain he saw in them. "Do you want another post? Would you rather be away from me?"

"No."

"Then… what?" Garith rubbed his eyes. His head throbbed behind them.

"Sisters help me, I don't know."

"Sander, the last thing I want is you suffering because of me. I have only ever wanted to bring you happiness. I thought…. Never mind. Would it be easier for you to serve somewhere else?"

Sander feigned a smile, laughed, and tossed his burnished ringlet curls. "I'd rather suffer with you than without you. And I *would* suffer without you. Can we leave it for now? I... I think we should worry about any threats to your safety."

"I suppose you're right," Garith admitted, running a fingertip along the edge of the cheese platter, wishing he could trace the contours of Sander's lean muscle instead. He had to think like a king now and not a man in love, lust, or whatever all-consuming passion he felt in regard to his knight. "Have a courier sent to Windust Castle."

"With what message?"

"Tell Bairn Duncan... tell him I would like to meet with Sasha."

Chapter Six

As Corbin led them through a warren of tangled tunnels, Sasha kept a careful mental map of his surroundings in case he needed to find his way out or to find his way to the other assassin's hiding place in the future. Here and there, he marked the walls with a slash of his dagger. As they ventured deeper beneath the ground, Sasha caught the many aromas of death: narxium sap, cassiette root, and clot-blossom. The poisonous vapors made him feel at home, like he'd entered an order safe house after a successful mission, but he didn't let them lull him into a false security. He wasn't an order agent any longer; he had no place he belonged, and he couldn't risk pretending he was safe here.

Corbin finally opened the door on his lair, and Sasha, Yarrow, and Duncan followed him inside. Dozens of candles, some inside crimson glass lanterns and others just melted onto errant piles of rock, sprung alight when Corbin waved his hand, bathing the area in shifting panes of scarlet and orange. Surveying the space carefully, taking in and trying to memorize every detail, Sasha decided the other assassin had chosen a fairly secure and defensible location. Crumbling but intact stone columns supported the octagonal chamber's low vaulted ceiling. Decaying arched doorways led to darkened rooms beyond. Sasha thought it might have been a wine cellar or crypt at one time, probably a few centuries or more ago, based on the architecture, and he estimated it lay at least a few dozen feet below the surface. Corbin had done a fair job of protecting the entrance, though now he'd have to reset all of his traps.

Sasha walked to a stone trough where a variety of mushrooms and fungi grew. He recognized some but not all of the poisonous plants. On a table nearby sat a complex configuration of copper pipes and oil-burning lamps. A glowing green liquid dripped from the end of the curlicued tubes into a glass jar. In the silence, every drop resounded as it splashed into the container. Sasha turned to the other assassin and spoke. "Is there at least one other way out of here?"

"Of course," Corbin said, his gaze locking with Sasha's and his expression as frozen as a statue in a cemetery.

"And you've taken precautions to keep it—or them—from being discovered? Or used if they should be? You've placed traps and alerts at every possible way in or out?"

The ghost of a smile flitted across Corbin's lips before fading like mist in the wind. "Would you expect less of a son of Thalil?"

"You are no longer a son of Thalil," Sasha noted, keeping his tone and expression carefully neutral.

"Ah, but only the four of us know that," Corbin said, running his fingertip along the edge of a bloodfern in a pot and letting his blood run down the edge of the delicate fronds when it cut him. "Unlike you, I was clever enough to conceal my failure and avoid being driven from the order and marked."

Sasha fought not to reveal his surprise. "Interesting, and quite a feat. How did you manage it?"

"I'd also like to know," Duncan said.

Corbin shrugged and sucked on his bleeding finger. He went to the far end of the room and sat in a worn red velvet chair, leaned his stump on the arm and canted his lanky body provocatively as he looked up at them through his eyelashes. "It was not difficult. You three left me badly injured, which worked in my favor. None of the others witnessed the bargain I struck with Yarroway, so I returned to the nearest order safe house and spun a tale of how you'd defeated me and escaped. I vowed to fulfill my mission and begged for another chance."

"I have some difficulty believing that," Sasha said, staring hard at Corbin, trying to catch any unintentional facial twitch or grimace that might reveal a deception. He knew Corbin would be studying him just as intently. "The masters of our order are experts at detecting lies. How is it you managed to convince them of the truth of your story? And you failed to kill me three times. *Three times.* How did you get them to overlook such a grievous failure?"

Corbin simply arched a slender black brow at the insult and selected a bottle of wine from those scattered across the tabletop. He held it in his remaining hand as he worked the cork out with his teeth and spat it on the floor. Then he held the wine up in offering, and the firelight glinted off the green glass. "Drink?"

"Oh, thank the goddesses." Yarrow took the seat opposite Corbin, picked up a dented metal goblet, and held it out for Corbin to fill. When he held the bottle up again, Duncan muttered a polite refusal and Sasha said nothing.

"To answer your question, though, br—Sasha…. What can I say? We learn to lie as soon as we can speak, don't we? Lies come as easy to us as our next breath. I'm good at it, as you once were, I'm sure. I can be very convincing, although it did not hurt my cause that the order regards—regarded—you so highly. They are also aware of the extraordinary skill of your knight and mage." Corbin lifted the wine in a mock salute and took a deep pull from the bottle.

Sasha wanted to question Corbin further—he couldn't quite swallow that only Corbin's skill as a liar had saved him—but Yarrow interrupted.

"Sasha and I have spoken of your masters in the order," Yarrow said, excited. He'd always been intrigued by the nuances of the Crimson Scythe and had never bothered to hide it. Sasha had never spoken to Duncan of these details, since he knew his calling made Duncan uncomfortable. Duncan reluctantly accepted what Sasha did, but unlike Yarrow, had never wanted to hear about it. Yarrow seemed to know the time to spare Duncan's feelings had passed. If they were to have any chance of success, Duncan needed to understand how the order worked and why.

"I understand you must report back to your masters after a mission. Sasha told us the story of his first assignment, when he took an earring from the young woman he killed as evidence of his success. So, as I understand it, you must return to the master who assigned your target."

The mage-assassin tilted his head toward Yarrow, clearly a little thrown. It probably surprised him that Sasha had divulged the clandestine workings of their order to Yarrow. They had all been taught that allowing such secrets to pass beyond their brethren was sacrilege. Corbin quickly recovered, letting his emotionless mask slip back into place. "Well, the novice assassins must always report back to their masters, back to their assigned houses. After completing a series of successful missions, we are released and given more freedom. We can return to any safe house after a mission, and when a new target comes to the order's attention, the master of that house chooses the best agent from those available. Sometimes, we are approached outside of the houses, but not often. Yarroway, you're fascinated by this, aren't you? By us."

The two mages' gazes locked as they stared at each other across the table, the curiosity palpable between them. The blue light burning behind Yarrow's eyes flared a little brighter, and Sasha wondered if Yarrow might pursue Corbin if unattached. The mystery and danger of the order had intrigued Yarrow and helped Sasha coax him into the bedchamber, but that initial allure had deepened into something much more profound, and Sasha trusted Yarrow after all they'd endured together and the oaths they'd sworn to each other.

Duncan cleared his throat and Sasha smiled. He knew Duncan trusted them too, but the knight would take offense at Corbin's subtle attempt. Duncan was a protector if nothing else. "We're only here for information that can help us put an end to these killers. Our only desire is to stop them from hounding us."

"Of course," Corbin said, turning his mischievous grin on Duncan, not to seduce him, but to make him uncomfortable, make him nervous and more likely to say something he shouldn't. Sasha had used all these tricks and knew them well.

"You say you're given missions," Duncan repeated. "Who gives them to you?"

"They're given to the assassin in charge of each house," Corbin repeated. "He or she then chooses an agent and assigns the mission."

"Yes, yes." Yarrow sounded a little annoyed and impatient. "Sasha has already explained this to me. I'm asking who gives the targets to the masters of the houses. If you're not willing to tell me, if you don't have anything beyond what we already know to offer us, we'll be on our way. I know the games you play, and I'm too tired to play with you."

"A tragedy." Corbin took another sip of wine and licked the remnants of the burgundy liquid from his lips as Yarrow turned to Sasha.

Sasha sat down on a tattered ottoman and rested his elbows on his knees. "They are called Whisperers. We were forbidden to speak with them, and they never stayed in the safe houses more than a few minutes. They gave the missions to our masters, though I have heard on rare occasions they would approach one of us outside of the order hideouts, perhaps on the road. They… always seemed to find us, to know where we were…."

"And who issued orders to these Whisperers?" Duncan asked.

When Sasha searched Corbin's face, he realized the other assassin couldn't answer either. "Neither of us had risen high enough to have the privilege of that knowledge," Sasha said. For many minutes the room fell silent except for Corbin's poison dripping steadily into its jar.

"All right," Duncan said, "let's take this from the beginning. How does one hire a… one of you? Surely one of you must know that."

Sasha nodded. "There are various methods. One can paint the red crescent on a door or window and wait to be contacted. Of course, doing so is dangerous, since your religion considers it worship of Thalil and punishes it with death. Many people paint the symbol on the door to an abandoned building or even a mausoleum and wait there. Some shrines to Thalil still stand in secret places, and sleeping at one will surely gain an audience with the order, but again, a person caught lingering at one of these forbidden temples will pay with his life if caught by your authorities. Some people are desperate enough to paint our symbol on their palms and go to a place the right person is likely to notice."

"It seems so complicated," Duncan said, finally sitting down on the edge of Corbin's large bed. "Almost… ineffective."

"Those who seek Thalil will always find him," Corbin said. "Besides, it's not always so cryptic. Those children who are found physically unsuited to serving Thalil with blades or magic are positioned in places where they are likely to hear about people looking to hire assassins—taverns and such. They are called Watchers. Their only job is to listen and remember and to report to the Whisperers. The Whisperers may then choose to approach the person in need of our service and offer an arrangement. We are Crimson Scythe. We kill for the glory of Thalil—"

"You kill for money," Duncan interjected.

Corbin shrugged. "What I'm trying to tell you is we don't stoop to settling disputes between street thugs or ridding merchants of their naggings wives."

"So, would one of these Whisperers have the power to call the others off?" Duncan asked. "They're the ones who assign the missions. Could we… convince one of them to leave Sasha alone?"

"No, I don't think so," Corbin said. "I've spent the past few months observing them carefully—without their knowledge, of course. I'm sure the Whisperers report to someone higher in the order."

"Then that is the person we need to seek," Yarrow said. "Tell me how. I'd like to put a stop to this."

"I don't know yet," Corbin said. "The Whisperers are even more adept than the rest of us. They seem to simply disappear."

"Magic?" Yarrow asked.

"Perhaps," Corbin answered. "Though nothing I can decipher or track."

Duncan huffed. "Why call us here if this is all the information you can offer? Some of us have other responsibilities."

"You're welcome to leave," Corbin said. "Although your precious Sasha won't stay ahead of the brethren forever. He'll be quite a trophy for the assassin who offers him to Thalil, and you can't watch over him every second. A second, a breath, or a fleeting shadow is often all we need. Ask him if you don't trust my word."

He was trying to anger and insult Sasha by implying Sasha needed Duncan and Yarrow's protection. An angry man made mistakes, revealed what he should have kept hidden, but Sasha had been trained too well to let his emotions influence him. Yarrow hadn't.

"I have had enough of this! Tell me how to find these bastards, and I'll make them afraid to even think about my beloved again! I'll show them what happens when they threaten what's mine, and no one will ever forget it!"

"Peace, Yarrow," Duncan said soothingly. "We can hardly just go charging into a den full of murderers."

"I think we can," Yarrow said, low and deadly, with a twisted smile. "I can."

"You can't," Corbin said without judgment, simply stating a fact. "No man can, Yarroway, not even you."

"There are things about me you don't know," Yarrow said, neither boasting nor threatening.

"I'd like to know more about you, everything you're willing to give," Corbin said. "But none of it will make me believe you could stand alone against the Order of the Crimson Scythe. We have been stalking the shadows of this world for almost ten thousand years, and Thalil grants us a portion of his might. Not even your goddesses have been able to stop us. I would not want to see you destroyed, Yarroway. The world is fuller and richer with you in it."

"You didn't feel that way when you wanted to cut off my arm and kill me," Yarrow said, looking into his goblet instead of at the other mage.

Surprise made Corbin widen his eyes and unconsciously touch the stub of his severed arm. Sasha smiled, knowing the other assassin had expected Yarrow to fall for his compliments and flirtation. Corbin underestimated Yarrow and Duncan. Sasha would not forget that crucial detail.

"I have reconsidered," Corbin said. "It's true that at one time I desired nothing more than vengeance and sought to disfigure you as you had done to me. I wanted you to watch your friends die as you forced me to watch as you cut down my brothers and sisters. Yet you defeated me again, and in the months since, I have thought a great deal about how best to benefit from the arrangement we reached in the caverns beneath Windust Castle. In spite of all you have taken from me, Yarroway, I think you might give me even more."

"Do you?" Yarrow asked.

"This is getting us nowhere," Duncan said. "You swore an oath to Yarrow, and then you sent a message summoning us here. Do you have a plan to get to these mysterious rulers of your order or not?"

"I have the seed of a plan," Corbin said.

"I am not getting any younger," Duncan grumbled.

"Well, I am staying at one of the houses here in Felgard. I plan to wait for an assignment and then track, follow, or capture the Whisperer who gives it to me. We'll force him to give us information about his superiors."

Sasha couldn't believe what he heard. "Is this a joke? You've already said the Whisperers are more adept than we are. How do you propose we follow one of them? We'll be detected. We'll likely draw the rest of the order. More than that, you and I both know all the brethren are trained to resist suggestion and even torture. The Whisperer will never talk. He'll take his own life before revealing anything."

"I have been working on something to help us with that," Corbin said, glancing at the alchemical equipment on his table. "I think I've formulated a potion that will prevent him from lying or keeping anything secret. I still need to test it, of course. It might end up ruining his mind, but, well, there are always casualties."

"Magic can also help to loosen his tongue," Yarrow said. "I haven't tried it yet, but I have a basic understanding of a spell that can allow the caster to control another's mind."

"Astounding," Corbin said. "Where did you learn such a thing?"

Yarrow stared into his wine.

"Which leaves us the problem of following or capturing one of the Whisperers," Sasha said, "without alerting the rest of the order and revealing Corbin's traitorous nature. If we're found out, he'll be killed on sight, and we'll be back where we started. How do you propose we accomplish this?"

"I'm open to suggestion," Corbin said. "I had considered using my carrion birds as I did to lead you to me. I'm just not sure how far they can venture from me without the enchantment wearing off."

"Do you control the wills of these creatures?" Yarrow asked.

"No," Corbin said as he set his wine bottle aside. He stood and went to a gilded cage near his bed. He opened the little wire door and reached inside. "Magic like that is beyond my understanding at the moment. My pets are just empty vessels." He showed them the iron-colored ball of feathers on his palm, its talons curled and stiff in death. "I sacrifice a wisp of my spirit and pour it into their shells. It is a taxing spell, but it allows me to control them and see through their eyes. It also leaves my true body practically defenseless, as I have to sacrifice my perception to my little spies. I have very little awareness of what's happening around me, so I can only perform the spell when I'm sure I'm safe."

"Which will make it almost impossible to cast after you've been sent on a mission," Sasha said.

Corbin nodded grudgingly, placed the dead Crypt Warbler back in the cage, and locked the door. "A fair point, I suppose. And as I mentioned, I don't know what distance will break the bond between me and my vessel. So far, I have not managed to send one of my birds across the river without shattering the enchantment."

"I can use a similar spell and still remain mostly aware of my surroundings," Yarrow said. "Do you remember when you captured Sasha and I made an illusory replica of Duncan to determine where you were hiding? I put my consciousness into it in a way much like what you've described."

"Ah yes," Corbin said. "I remember your friend stripped, gagged, and tied to that rock." He winked at Sasha, but Sasha didn't fall for his ploy and simply smiled back. "How did you construct such an exact copy of your knight?"

"I used the mist in the seaside cave and just sort of... shaped it," Yarrow said. "Then I put part of my mind in the vessel just as you explained."

Corbin looked genuinely impressed; Sasha could tell it wasn't feigned. "So you had enough magic to create this doppelgänger, project your senses into it, and remain conscious... in both places at once?"

Yarrow shrugged, but Corbin's acknowledgement of his power pleased him, and he bowed his head to hide his grin behind his tangled ropes of white hair. "I suppose I've existed in two worlds most of my life."

"I can only manage the spell with dead things," Corbin said.

The mattress and supports creaked and groaned as Duncan shifted on the bed. Sasha knew the topic made his knight uncomfortable; Duncan's goddesses strictly forbid any magic relating to death or dead things. Only a year or so ago, Duncan would have been unable to stop himself from insulting such practices, but after the war the three of them had survived and what each of them had sacrificed, Duncan knew to consider anything he might use against his enemies. Sasha didn't know if Duncan's loss of idealism was a good thing or not. He'd rather liked his shining defender of righteousness, but as always, things evolved and adapted. Sasha knew he'd been a strong force in bending Duncan away from his absolute views of right and wrong, one of the flames warping the iron in the knight's heart.

Sasha got up and sat by Duncan on the bed, resting his hand on Duncan's knee. Corbin would see the dependence the three of them had on each other as weakness. Let him. Sasha knew their bond gave them strength, a strength Corbin could never comprehend. Any misconceptions the other assassin harbored could be turned against him when and if Sasha needed a hidden blade.

"I would not be comfortable with even a shard of my spirit inside something I could feel decaying," Yarrow finally said, his soft voice echoing in the crumbling chamber.

"Still, we can work together to devise a spell you can use while I distract the Whisperer," Corbin said. "After all, your side of this bargain included sharing your knowledge of magic with me. I haven't forgotten, and I plan to collect."

"Of course," Yarrow said. "Anything to get the order to leave Sasha alone."

"Good." Corbin rubbed the shoulder above his missing arm. Sasha noticed he touched the severed limb often when he spoke to Yarrow, a sure sign he still harbored resentment over Yarrow destroying his arm. "I should return to the safe house before the others wonder about my absence. Come this way. I'll show you a place where you can rest securely."

He led them beyond a collapsing archway, through a darkened hallway, and to a spacious room with a large bed canopied in red gauze at the center. Candlelight reflected off the bed's elaborate iron headboard and the satiny crimson cushions strewn across the mattress. Wine and fruit waited on a table, and incense burned in a dish, making the room smell of exotic flowers and rare woods. Corbin waved his hand, and a cozy blaze sprung alight in the hearth.

"I should go," the mage-assassin said. As soon as he entered the darkened hallway, the shadows enveloped him, and he was gone.

Chapter
Seven

A PORTRAIT of Thalil hung on the wall of the chamber, opposite the bed. Sasha stood looking at the depiction of his god reclining nude on a bed of scarlet pillows, Thalil's black waves of hair spilling over his perfect, adolescent shoulders and his red-tinged eyes looking out from behind sensually drooping lids. Duncan and Yarrow dropped their packs on the chipped stone floor and began removing their armor while Sasha studied the painting, willing his patron to tell him what he wanted from him.

Guide me, Dark and Beautiful One.

Thalil remained silent.

Tell me what you want me to do.

Oh, Sasha....

Sasha turned and looked all around the small room, sure he'd heard a velvety voice, sure he'd felt the words sliding across his perception like honey, so sweet, so smooth... as enticing as the possibility of fresh blood.

"Sasha? Come to bed," Duncan said, standing in the padded gambeson he wore beneath his armor and reaching out his hand.

Yarrow stood next to him in only his trousers with his white hair falling across his slim tanned chest. "Beloved?"

Sasha rubbed his arms, suddenly chilled despite the healthy fire. "I don't like being called that, Yarrow."

"Why?"

"I don't know. Nothing about this sits well with me. I don't trust Corbin, and I don't know if we're safe here."

Duncan stood behind Sasha, rested his cheek against the top of Sasha's head, and enveloped Sasha in his thickly muscled arms. The heat of his body wrapped around Sasha like a velvet blanket, and Sasha leaned back against him. Though it had taken a great effort to go against everything he'd been taught, to abandon his calling, feeling so unconditionally cherished in moments like this made it all worthwhile. It also steeled Sasha's determination not to let either of his lovers come to harm on his behalf. Thalil,

Duncan shouldn't even be here; he had a bairny to rule and a child on the way. Yet—

"I'm glad to have you beside me, Duncan. And you, Yarrow. I'm sorry. I'm very tired, and my mind is playing tricks on me." The painted Thalil seemed to twist his lips into a knowing grin, but Sasha felt sure it was only the play of the flickering light and shadow across the pigment and canvas.

"Is it very strange for you, being back in a place like this?" Duncan asked.

Sasha nodded. "You will not like hearing this, but I feel more like myself than I have in a long while. I can't help feeling like I've come home."

"Windust Castle is your home now," Duncan said.

"Yes, but I don't belong there," Sasha said. It still felt odd to him to discuss his emotions and concerns without fear of Duncan or Yarrow using them against him. "I am not a part of your world. I belong here, watching from the shadows, on the outside."

"I know what you mean," Yarrow said softly as he sat on the edge of the bed to pull off his boots. "I hate all the pettiness of court. All the tiny things people think are important. I like it here too, but because we can all be together without those frivolous concerns. I… we're meant for more. All of us."

"I don't know," Duncan said. "For a simple knight like myself to rise to such a station is rather remarkable. I should be thanking the goddesses every day for my good fortune. I should be happy and fulfilled, yet… yet I feel a certain freedom here, away from all my obligations, with the two of you, who don't expect me to be something I'm not. I feel like I have a concrete purpose."

"What purpose?" Sasha asked. "The destruction of my ancient order?"

Duncan squeezed him tighter and pressed his palm flat against Sasha's belly. "Fighting for one of the men I love. Making sure you can stay with me and we can live out our lives together. We should rest. We have quite the task ahead of us."

Sasha just nodded and reluctantly stepped out of Duncan's arms to disrobe. He pulled the heavy wool shirt over his head and stepped out of his loose trousers. Beneath them, his bloodred order armor hugged his body like a second skin. Though he had to conceal them, he couldn't imagine not wearing his leathers. He wasn't a member of the Crimson Scythe any longer, but the gear they'd provided him was second to none. The scarlet leather was so buttery soft it didn't bunch, creak, or impede his movements. Panels made of woven metal wire sewn between the leather protected his chest, back, and stomach without adding weight or hampering his speed, and razor-sharp spikes enhanced the heels of his boots and the knuckles of his gloves. The armor incorporated dozens of hidden pockets and sleeves for poisons and weapons, including the long, slim blades concealed beneath Sasha's wrists. He'd be a fool not to utilize such superior equipment; it was nothing sentimental, though he did enjoy the aesthetic of the straps and buckles.

After peeling the leather from his limbs, Sasha folded it neatly and set it on the bedside table. He hid a sheathed dagger beneath his pillow and another under the mattress, then got beneath the covers at the center of the bed. As soon as they finished undressing, Duncan and Yarrow joined him, one of them on either side. Yarrow waved his hand, and most of the candles blew out. Sasha lay on his back, and Yarrow curled around him, nestling his face against Sasha's chest and draping an arm and a leg over Sasha. By the Cast-Down, he was thin. His bones poked against Sasha, but his skin was still as soft as a flower petal. In contrast, the bed groaned and sagged beneath Duncan's stature and solid muscle as the knight settled in and reached a long arm across both Sasha and Yarrow. Duncan's whiskers tickled the side of Sasha's neck as he nuzzled close, his warm breath ruffling Sasha's hair. Being tucked between them, toasty and secure, felt so lovely, so perfect, Sasha let his concerns depart and just enjoyed feeling like he knew where he belonged. Yarrow and Duncan's breathing grew slow and steady with sleep, and Sasha lay listening and feeling their bodies pressed so close to his. He would sacrifice anything to keep this, to feel it every night and wake to it every morning.

He still had concerns, though. He worried Corbin had feigned alliance with them to lead them to the order. The mage-assassin had sworn not to harm Yarrow, but Sasha knew from experience how subjective oaths could be. Would Corbin consider it a breach to lead Yarrow into a den of assassins and let one of the others make the killing blow? He owed no allegiance to Sasha or Duncan. Was he planning a way to eliminate them, complete his mission, and earn glory within the order? Sasha would be, in Corbin's position. As he lay listening to his lovers sleep, Sasha replayed the conversation they'd had with Corbin over and over again in his mind, trying to remember any detail that might hint at deception. Corbin had toyed with them, tried to entice Yarrow and alienate Duncan. Why? Why try to weaken an alliance? And why would Corbin have revealed the spells he'd used, along with their limitations? Remembering the way Corbin had fawned over the dead birds, going so far as to lock the door to their cage, also worried Sasha. All of the mages he'd known had been a bit peculiar, but he had to wonder if Corbin had become completely unhinged when Yarrow had taken his arm and forced him to return to the order in disgrace. What would it mean for them and their mission if his mind had gone soft?

Sasha looked at the portrait of Thalil though he could only see the faintest suggestion of it in the darkness. What did his sweet god expect of him? Part of him worried Thalil wanted to punish him for his failure, to teach him a lesson about allowing attachments to form and depending on others. *Don't take them from me,* Sasha prayed. He'd never actually prayed before. *Dark and Beautiful One, please. Please. I will do anything for you, but don't take them. Please, Thalil. Please.*

Staring at the painting, Sasha repeated his entreaty over and over again in his mind. He held on to Duncan and Yarrow with everything he had. He wouldn't let them go. As much as he feared sleep, feared the surrender of vigilance, he was still mortal, and the warmth and security of his lovers wound tightly around him dragged him toward blessed oblivion. Their presence shouldn't let him feel this safe and content, but—

Please, Thalil. Do not take them as restitution for my failure. Let me serve you. I will bathe this world in blood for you, and all I ask is that you don't take their lives.

My sweet son. Fear not. I have plans for you.

Sasha blinked in the darkness and tried to lift his head to survey the room, but he couldn't find the strength. Besides, Yarrow and Duncan still twined around him, pinning him to the bed. He was just tired, flowing back and forth between consciousness and the ether of the dream realm. He could no longer trust his perceptions, so he heaved a sigh and gave himself over to the contentment of Yarrow and Duncan's warm bodies wrapped around him, showing him their love and devotion even in their sleep. Sasha let his eyes close and the tension flow out of his tightly wound muscles. Tomorrow might present challenges, but tonight he'd enjoy the best of what mortality offered. He fell asleep listening to the sounds Yarrow and Duncan made in slumber and breathing their scents.

THE filthy mortal creatures ran screaming from him, but with a single swipe of his glowing blue talons, Yarrow struck them down a dozen at a time. His claws cut through their frail flesh like a warm knife through butter, and blood fountained around him. The mud-streaked mortals in their bits of hide tried to elude him, and some of the foolish ones even tried to fight. He cut through them, reducing them to scattered bits of meat and bone and puddles of blood. While it made an amusing distraction, he'd grown tired of the slaughter over the centuries. As much as he loved the feeling of hot life's blood spattering his face, he craved a distraction.

The distraction came in the form of a beautiful mortal—tall, lanky, tanned, and with shrewd eyes like faceted jewels and lush, full, tempting lips. The bright, brave boy sat at his feet and asked questions. Yarrow instructed him and thrilled at his progress. He hadn't thought the mortals capable of such understanding or power. The boy's mastery of magic surprised and delighted him, and he wanted more from his pupil. He wanted to claim him, mark him as his own.

Some scrap of Yarrow knew he witnessed a dream, the memories of the ancient creature he'd bonded with, but it felt so visceral and fresh he couldn't help getting caught up in the moment. He touched his beloved's full mouth and flat nose. Beautiful. The boy had a red-brown mouth the color of wet clay but a deep pink at the center. He trailed his curved claws down the boy's graceful neck, and his beloved groaned and tilted his face toward the sky. His full lips fell open as Yarrow raked his sharp nails down his chest and over his pert, red-brown nipples. Beloved's belly fluttered, and Yarrow knew he wanted more. He whisked away the tiny triangle of dirty fur concealing his beloved's hard cock and soft, full testicles. Beloved moaned wantonly as he reclined on his back and spread his legs for Yarrow. Yarrow gripped his thighs just above the knees as he pushed his legs farther apart and dipped in to taste him, circling his beloved's untouched entrance with his tongue. The earthy, animal taste of him incensed Yarrow's lust, and he pushed his tongue into the tight heat of his beloved. The boy's cock twitched and dribbled the prelude to his seed.

Yarrow stretched his wings and let them fill the cavern he called home as he gazed down at the beautiful mortal's lust-slacked features. Beloved's amazing lips gaped to reveal his strong white teeth, and his nostrils flared as he panted with need. Yarrow spit on him before aligning his cock with his beloved's opening. He rubbed against the ring of muscle, but in the end he just had to force past it. Beloved gasped and clamped his eyes shut. His back arched off the ground, and Yarrow swiped his hand down his face to comfort him. "Relax, my beloved. Take me."

"Yes, oh yes." Beloved thrust back against him, clenching his muscles around Yarrow's cock. Yarrow thrust in to the hilt, surprised his beloved could handle him. This body in his memories wasn't quite human. Though it resembled a man, it was much larger in every way—larger and more beautiful, with a sheet of black hair, solid-black eyes, slender horns on its forehead, and wings if it chose to manifest them. His beloved might bleed, but the boy risked the discomfort for the chance at a new experience, for wisdom. The creature, and Yarrow through its memories, adored his beloved for the boy's ravenous need for knowledge, for his courage to push everything to the boundaries of what he could endure. Beloved curled his fingers around Yarrow's hipbones and buried his nails in Yarrow's flesh, urging him, daring him. Yarrow thrust, and his beloved cried out. He fought the instinct to let go and pound into the boy; the heat and pressure of being inside him drove all rational thought from Yarrow's mind. But if he gave himself over, he'd destroy the first mortal he had no desire to tear to pieces.

He rested Beloved's ankles on his shoulders and took a breath to ground himself. Beneath him, a burgundy stain spread across his beloved's cheeks and sweat sparkled over his brown skin. Through his parted lips, the boy gulped air as if he'd been underwater. Yarrow brushed the matted hair out of his face and whispered, "Open your eyes. Look at me."

Beloved's crinkled eyelids peeled back slowly to reveal his dark brown irises. In their depths, Yarrow found such fire: curiosity, need, ambition, and courage. A vein of pure iron ran through this young man, and he feared nothing, but his sharp mind and imagination soared beyond the sky and into the ether. His perfection and daring compelled Yarrow to claim him, and he bit his lower lip and whimpered as he tried to resist his body's compulsion to plow into him, thrust until Beloved felt him for a moon's time.

Beloved raked his nails up Yarrow's spine, opening the skin, until he could wind his fingers in Yarrow's midnight hair and pull their faces together. He chuckled against Yarrow's lips and said, "Go on. I'm not going to break."

"I… could break you…. I don't want to…. Oh, my beloved!" In his thousands of years, Yarrow had never felt such need, like he was burning up inside, consumed by the flames rising from this mortal. He didn't care; he wanted to dissolve into this boy's fire, just let himself be burned to nothing. He smashed his mouth hard against the boy's, knocking their teeth together. Beloved opened his mouth to suck on and nibble at Yarrow's tongue, and they began moving against each other, hesitantly at first, but then with a slow, steady rhythm, pulling almost apart before slamming back together.

Yarrow held his beloved's lower lip between his teeth and panted through them, trying to control himself, trying to make it last. He dragged his fingers from the boy's wiry shoulders to his elbows, fighting the urge to open his flesh with his claws. He grasped him below the armpits and rolled so his beloved sat astride him, and then he ran his hands down his lover's lithe waist before grasping his hips and pulling him down. As his partner adjusted, searching for the angle that pleased him, Yarrow muttered the name he had given him over and over. *Beloved.* He could feel the boy's heartbeat as he pushed into him, could see Beloved's pulse shaking his entire body. It was too much, too good, and Yarrow knew it couldn't last long. But he wasn't mortal, and he'd be ready to take his beloved again in no time—

Yarrow snapped awake so instantly he felt sure someone had doused him in icy water. He gasped and instinctively reached for his beloved. When he didn't feel the boy's essence underneath him and all around him, commanding his every perception, he looked around, expecting to find himself in the bed in Corbin's hideout. He'd known he was dreaming, though it had been easy to pretend. Beloved—Fane, Yarrow realized. That primitive boy he'd made love to in his creature's memories had been destined to become Fane—the great mage-emperor who had ruled over the golden age of the world for more than a thousand years. Thinking back to the boy's eyes, Yarrow could see the determination that would make him the master of the world. Though he, Yarrow, had never even touched Fane, he felt a keen pain in his belly at his loss, the loss of his beloved—

No. These were phantom sensations leftover from his creature. The men Yarrow loved were right beside him. He listened for their languid breathing but heard only his pulse whooshing in his head. No warm limbs wrapped around him, and he didn't detect Sasha or Duncan's unique smell—

Yarrow, slightly panicked, patted around him in the darkness. His anxiety increased when he couldn't find either of his partners or even the thick blankets all of them should lie beneath. A cool, smooth surface like polished glass met his questing palms. Even when he scrambled onto his hands and knees and fumbled in the thick shadows, the slick surface extended as far as he ventured.

"Sasha?" Yarrow whispered. "Duncan?" His voice echoed, and he knew he must be somewhere vast. Confused, afraid, and alone, he summoned his magic to conjure a light. Never in his memory, not since he'd been a helpless child, had his magic failed to come at his beckoning, but now he couldn't even manage to make his fingertips glow. Cold sweat broke from his pores as terror seized him. Without his magic, he was helpless. Useless. Weak. Easy prey for anyone or anything looking to exploit him. Frantic now, barely able to drag a breath into his lungs, Yarrow pawed at his waist for the small dagger he kept on a belt, but of course he'd removed it to sleep.

Yarrow's heart raced, and he felt dizzy and feeble, barely able to ball his frail little hands into fists. His magic had been the only thing that had ever made him special, ever made him worth anything. He didn't even dare to imagine what would have become of him without it. After being exiled at fourteen, he'd have surely died in some obscene way without his sorcery. As the third son of a noble family, he was of little consequence even to his mother, who already had an heir and a replacement. Without his magic to protect him, he was nothing but a small man unskilled with weapons: an easy target practically begging to be abused. He tried again to summon even a flicker of power and failed. There was only one other time when Yarrow could remember feeling so frightened, helpless, and abandoned.

"A dream," he said in a trembling whisper. "It's just a nightmare." Still, he didn't want to endure it again, didn't want to be a child at the mercy of his uncle and his knights, held down on a filthy table in the barracks while they took turns—

Slowly, lights flickered around him, but not the smoky torchlight from his recurring nightmare. Instead, columns of colored light surrounded him in a circle. As his eyes adjusted to the glare, the luminescence took vaguely human shapes—female, but still ethereal and wavering. Yarrow sat back on his heels and took a quick count of the phantoms, each glowing a different hue. Thirteen.

Yarrow hurried to his feet. He would not kneel before them. "What do you deceitful harlots want with me?"

"Brave words, coming from a scared little boy," said the brilliant red spirit as it stepped closer to him. As it drew nearer, Yarrow heard the clash of metal against metal, smelled blood and iron. When he stared at what could only be Myint, goddess of battle, he noticed the suggestion of armor, a helmet, and a sword on the shimmering sheet of scarlet forming the silhouette. The goddess looked like a sheet of thin paper cut into the shape of a woman.

"I'm not afraid of you," Yarrow told her. "I am a great mage, and I will bring truth to the people of this world."

"Poor little thing. Your terror is rising from you in sheets, like a hunted animal." A goddess made of green-and-gold light, like the sun breaking through the thick canopy of an ancient forest, stepped in front of Yarrow. She smelled of trees and loam. "This is our world. The wilds are mine, and the rest belongs to my sisters."

"Stolen," Yarrow spat. "First from my beloved and now from every mortal mage. You bolster your power and falsely call yourself divine by hoarding the magic that should belong to every person with the gift. You are worse than charlatans."

The next goddess to approach Yarrow shone with a white light so bright Yarrow thought looking at it might melt his eyes. She smelled of clean linen and cold—the scent of the wind before it snowed. "You are impure and unnatural, Yarroway L'Estrella. What can you possibly do to benefit the people of this world? What interest have you ever had in truth? You should let us help you, let us purge you of your foul black desires, let us purify you."

Shielding his eyes with his forearm, Yarrow pointed his other hand at the radiant being and shouted, "Fayelle, you hypocritical whore! Did you say the same to Thalil when he fucked every opening of your body and you begged for more? No one can live up to what you ask. Yet you ask it, only to make them feel guilty when they fail! It should not be this way."

"You will be judged for your words and actions, Yarroway L'Estrella," said the brilliant blue form of what could only be Vestrafori, the so-called goddess of truth and justice. "Speaking and acting as you have will not go unpunished. It is not too late for you to turn from this path and become a good servant."

"Punish me, then!" Yarrow shouted. "Here I am. What's stopping you? Destroy me. I'm right here. I don't think you can do it."

"Brazen words." Yarrow recognized the voice: the self-proclaimed Mother Goddess. He recognized her form, like a tear in the fabric of reality, sucking all the light and power into the void. "Bold indeed for a whelp who cannot even use his magic. What are you without it? You should plead for our mercy. We can be merciful and kind."

As she approached him, rage flooded Yarrow, washing away the fear and uncertainty he'd felt. He remembered his beloved, and he wanted nothing more than to tear these bitches to ribbons. He was not impotent, and he wouldn't let them make him believe he was. "I *am* my magic," he said, and when he raised his hand, raw cerulean power sheathed it and sparkled down his arm.

The Mother Goddess actually took a step back. "How—how in this realm of our creation—"

"Sister, hush," said a goddess like a swaying, gray sheet of cobwebs.

"Is that all?" Yarrow asked, feeling confident now that enchantment sang in his veins. "I'm tired of this farce."

"How dare you?" asked a goddess like a patch of night sky dotted with stars. Strella: the patron of Yarrow's family.

"You are all liars and usurpers," Yarrow said. "All you've done is hoodwinked the people of this world and stolen their magic. You disgust me. Fight me, if you can. Otherwise, release me from this ridiculous charade."

"And what will you do if we trap you here?" the Mother Goddess taunted.

"I will tear your enchantment to shreds," Yarrow answered. "I have unraveled better spells than this."

"Have you? We destroyed Fane. Do you think we cannot destroy you too? You think we are cruel, but we are merciful, or you would already be dead."

As he prepared a comeback, realization dawned on Yarrow. They didn't know. These almighty goddesses didn't know he'd found the remote cavern where they'd imprisoned Fane and carried a scrap of Fane's essence out of it in his body. It had been the price the great mage-emperor demanded from Yarrow in exchange for his help subduing the creature that had possessed Yarrow. Somewhere, though he couldn't feel it, a faint flicker of Fane had escaped that dank cave inside Yarrow's body. But the goddesses didn't know that. They apparently didn't know he'd been to see Hale, Fane's most beloved apprentice. The spells Hale had placed on his isle to keep others away made the goddesses' magic look like child's play.

"Destroy me, then," Yarrow said. "I have told you, I'm right here. I will not ask for mercy. Go on. Let me see what you can do."

"You will be Cast-Down." The Mother Goddess swiped an undulating limb at Yarrow, but Yarrow easily dipped down and avoided the blow. On his way up, he shot a gout of magic at the creature, stinging her hand and making her retreat a few steps.

"Is that all you've got? You're pathetic." Yarrow's power pulsed around him until he could unfurl his azure wings. All the goddesses but one shied away from his new form. He wondered if they recognized it, remembered it.

A beautiful, silver-haired maiden in a silver gown walked slowly up to Yarrow. Unlike the others, she looked like a human woman instead of a pane of light or a flimsy cutout. Her gray gaze seemed to look into Yarrow as a small smile graced her pale pink lips. Yarrow could see her every detail, down to the silver velvet slippers she wore and the little beads adorning them.

"Are you Pherara, the… the so-called goddess of magic?" he asked.

She nodded, and Yarrow took in the details of her delicate circlet and diaphanous gown. He'd never in his life been attracted to a woman, but he felt a slight pull to Pherara, because she embodied magic, and he loved magic.

"Of course I am, Yarrow," she said with a warm smile. "That's why you can see my true form. You're one of mine. I have always loved my mages and looked out for them. You have been to Espero, so you know this. I would ask you to stand down, to abandon this misguided quest for vengeance for a man you never knew."

"But… but it is a lie!"

"Illusion has its place sometimes, Yarrow. You know this. The world is better for having us and our rule, no matter how it came about."

"Not like this," he said. "The flow of enchantment is dammed by your so-called sisters. If you love your mages, why allow it?"

"It is complex, and you are very young compared to us," Pherara said gently.

"Not really," Yarrow responded. "Part of me is older than you can comprehend."

"What do you mean?" the silvery goddess asked.

They didn't know. They didn't know Yarrow had bonded with the creature that had instructed their emperor—the ancient entity whose eyes Yarrow had looked through as it made love to the boy who would one day become Fane. These goddesses had no idea of the power Yarrow held inside himself, a power even Fane had feared and tried to eradicate.

"I have had enough of this," Yarrow said. "I'm leaving, unless you can stop me." He let his power flow from his veins and skin and manifest as wings, horns, and claws. Then he swiped with his glowing blue talons and shredded the world the goddesses had created to cage him. It fell away like bits of colored paper thrown at a party, and before he knew it, Yarrow found himself in bed, uncomfortably warm beside Sasha, his sweat making the sheets cling to his skin, but glad to feel his heat and solidity.

Duncan snored softly. Yarrow envied his ability to sleep anywhere and through anything. Sasha, though, looked at Yarrow, his black eyes reflecting the last of the dying firelight.

"Another nightmare, my love?" Sasha asked, petting the side of Yarrow's face.

"I suppose," Yarrow said, glad to feel Sasha beside him. It had been so terrifying to be alone. "I don't remember much of it."

"Don't lie to me," Sasha said. "If you don't want to tell me, just say so."

Yarrow sighed and let his head sink into the pillows. Sasha always knew when he tried to hide something. "I'm not lying, be—Sasha. I just don't know what to make of it. I thought I saw the goddesses, but now I'm sure it must have just been my mind trying to make sense of everything. I have been very confused since speaking with Hale. I don't understand anything anymore. That dream—It felt so real."

"Do you want to talk about it?"

"No." Yarrow turned on his side and wrapped his arms and legs around Sasha. Sasha held him close and wound Yarrow in his limbs, letting Yarrow feel his skin, muscle, and bones pressed close. "Soon. Not yet. After...."

"After we destroy the brethren of Thalil?" Sasha whispered against Yarrow's forehead.

Yarrow let that idea percolate through the layers of his mind as he relaxed beside his lover. The Crimson Scythe could be valuable allies against the pretender goddesses, as could Thalil. "After I know you are safe, Sasha. I love you. I would burn the world to ash for you. There's nothing I wouldn't do—"

"Shh. I know. Please rest, my love. Rest and know I won't let anything happen to you. You aren't alone, Yarrow."

"I know. And thank you, my love. It means a great deal to me."

"To me, also." Sasha kissed each of Yarrow's eyebrows before settling his head into the pillows. Duncan rolled and wound his strong limbs around Sasha. Soon, both of them fell back into slumber, Sasha's forehead against Yarrow's and Duncan's face buried in the nape of Sasha's neck.

Yarrow tried to relax, to dismiss the phantasmagorias from his dream. He tried to tell himself his mind had simply conjured images and words to express the doubts he'd felt since speaking with Hale. He was just trying to make sense of it all. He wanted to tell Sasha and Duncan what he'd learned, but why stir doubt in them when they already had so much to face? After, he decided. After Sasha was safe. In the dying firelight, he saw the small picture of Thalil opposite the bed. The Cast-Down god seemed to smile at him, and it gave Yarrow the seedling of an idea.

Thalil.... You have no love for the Thirteen Sisters. Would you stand with me against their lies?

Yarrow stared at the painting for a long time, but after receiving no answer, he let his eyes close and fell into a thankfully dreamless sleep.

Chapter Eight

DUNCAN had never felt so useless. For the past three days, they had done little but hide in Corbin's lair and wait for him to return with some news. That afternoon, the mage-assassin had finally come back to the underground suite. Corbin delivered meat, bread, cheese, eggs, and wine before whisking Yarrow away to a secluded room near the back of the tunnels. He'd said they had to work on spells that would allow someone to follow one of the elusive Whisperers who issued orders to the agents of the Crimson Scythe. The two mages sequestered themselves all afternoon and most of the night, not emerging until almost morning.

Duncan started awake when he heard the clink of glass. He'd fallen asleep with his head and forearms resting on the table. Growing up in the knighthood had taught him to take his rest when and where he found it. On watch, he could remain vigilant and alert as long as necessary, but when the time came to refresh himself, he had learned to trust his brothers in the knighthood to protect him. Part of him knew he was not sleeping in a war tent with other soldiers around him, and the small sound startled him. The noise had come from Yarrow reaching for a bottle of wine. As the mage drank directly from the bottle, his throat rippling as he took deep gulps, Sasha continued sharpening his daggers, sitting cross-legged on the floor in front of the inglenook. He'd likely been at it all night. Duncan had come to understand the contentment Sasha got from action; when something worried or perplexed Sasha, he responded by acting instead of pondering it. Duncan knew, at the moment, Sasha saw keeping his blades sharp as the most important way to spend his time. As for Duncan, he'd fallen asleep out of sheer boredom.

"Yarroway and I have devised a spell to hide someone else in shadow the way I can hide myself," Corbin said. "You remember, don't you, Sasha?"

"Yes. Do you have a point you wish to make?" Sasha didn't look up from his whetstone.

Yarrow spoke. "It's much more difficult to cast that enchantment on another than on oneself. Corbin and I managed to figure it out, but neither of us could maintain the illusion if we were more than a few dozen feet from each other."

"What does that mean for us and our mission?" Duncan asked, sleep lingering in his head and slowing his thoughts. He poured himself some water and drank.

"It means the caster will have to be with the one who follows the Whisperer," Sasha said. "Which means Yarrow, as Corbin will be in the safe house receiving his instructions. The logical thing to do would be for Yarrow to cast the spell on me, and for the two of us to track the Whisperer."

"Where does that leave me?" Duncan asked. "I can't help feeling a little redundant in all this."

Sasha shook his head. "If it comes to a fight, there is no man I'd rather have at my back. Few warriors can face a brother of the Crimson Scythe and prevail. I know from experience you are one of those few."

"I appreciate that," Duncan said, "but you're saying in the meantime I'll be sitting here."

"It will only make it more difficult for Yarroway to try to shield two people," Corbin said. "You do not know how to walk without making noise or avoid attention. It should be Sasha. Now, I'm leaving. The sun will soon rise. I should get back to the safe house before dawn and await a mission. Most of the other agents in the area are occupied, so it shouldn't be long before I'm called. Be ready to follow the Whisperer who gives the order."

Corbin began collecting his gear. He placed the leather bracer with the hidden blade on his forearm and pulled the buckles tight with his teeth. He even managed to secure his straps and the daggers they held with one hand, and then he fastened his long cloak over all of it and pulled his hood over his head, leaving everything but his mouth and pale chin in shadow.

Yarrow stood and caught Corbin's elbow. The other mage turned on the ball of his foot and faced Yarrow, a slight part in his lips that told Duncan he hadn't expected Yarrow's boldness.

"Do you think the Whisperer will appear during the day?" Yarrow asked.

Corbin smiled, and his shadowed eyes glittered. "Even beneath the brightest midday sun, there are always shadows. Watch for the Whisperer." He grasped Yarrow's hand to remove it from his arm and held it for a moment before he let it go, entered the hallway beyond the firelight, and melted into the darkness.

Sasha was already donning armor and weapons, placing his newly sharpened blades in hidden places. "We should give him an hour's start or so, so if anyone is watching him, they won't discern us following."

Yarrow just nodded and poured himself another glass of wine.

"What can I do to help?" Duncan asked, already knowing the answer.

"Wait here until we know where we're going," Sasha said. "Keep your sword close."

"So, nothing," Duncan mumbled. He didn't want to be a child about it, but he'd left the duty to his people behind, thinking he'd be fighting the Cast-Down and protecting his lover. He knew and acknowledged he was out of his element, but he found it hard to accept he could do nothing to aid them. "At least say you won't move on without me."

Yarrow looked hurt. "Of course not."

"Hopefully this won't take long." Sasha crossed the room to place an extended kiss on the apple of Duncan's cheek, and before long, the two of them departed, leaving Duncan alone.

Duncan fried a few eggs over the fire and ate them with a slice of ham and a couple of pieces of bread. He polished his breastplate and oiled the leather straps of his armor. Then, with nothing to occupy his attention, he went to that ridiculously lavish bed that looked so out of place in the collapsing stone room and went back to sleep.

Sasha and Yarrow returned late that night. They'd hidden all day but hadn't seen a single person entering or leaving the order safe house. Maintaining the illusion for so long had left Yarrow exhausted, and he fell into bed without bothering to eat. Duncan could do nothing more helpful than pull his boots off, remove the black leather pauldrons and bracers he wore, and tuck him beneath the crimson-and-gold blanket.

Two weeks passed with little change. No matter how long Sasha and Yarrow watched, they saw no one. Corbin returned every few days with food, but he had no news to share with them. Duncan spent his days exploring the labyrinthine tunnels. Corbin's sanctuary contained dozens of rooms. Some of them had shelves carved into the walls still holding the skulls and bones of the ancient dead. It hardly surprised Duncan that Corbin would choose to make his home in a crypt. The mage-assassin surrounded himself with death. It made Duncan's skin crawl. He should not be sleeping in such a place; he should tear it down as an abomination, but he needed Corbin's knowledge to save Sasha. Goddesses—Could the goddesses ever forgive him for allowing the Cast-Down mage to play with the dead while he stood idly by? Would they forgive him for turning a blind eye to Corbin's sacrilege if it helped him bring down the Crimson Scythe? He just didn't know, and no matter how much he prayed, he never received an answer. From the time he'd begun training for the knighthood at age ten, Duncan had always had a clear purpose. For most of his life, he'd had a clear set of rules to determine right from wrong. Only since meeting Sasha and Yarrow had he realized nothing was that simple.

He'd constructed a mannequin from some scrap boards, straw, and the burlap sack Corbin had used to carry their provisions, and he faced it with a small crossbow, practicing his marksmanship. He had neglected archery as he'd always been a natural swordsman, his size and strength making him capable of powerful blows. Lately, his body had felt the ennui as acutely as his mind, and his muscles cried out for use. Without an opponent to spar against, he'd opted to practice with his crossbow and found he wasn't half-bad at it. After he'd fired all his bolts into the dummy, he went in search of something to eat.

Sasha and Yarrow returned just as Duncan entered the central chamber. "Anything?" Duncan asked without much optimism.

Sasha shook his head, and Yarrow fell into a chair by the table and reached for the wine.

"We're getting nowhere," Duncan said, frustrated and unable to mask it.

"You're right," Sasha agreed. "What do you suggest we do about it?"

"I don't know. Goddesses, this is infuriating."

"I've tried to use my magic to find them, and I can't locate anything," Yarrow said. "The Crimson Scythe are feared and respected for good reason."

"What if Corbin is stringing us along?" Sasha asked.

"Talking about me?" The mage-assassin materialized from the shadows in the hall and joined Yarrow at the table. What was it about mages that made them adore wine, Duncan wondered.

"Actually, yes," Sasha said. "We are wondering what is taking so long. Are we really to believe no Whisperer has visited the house in all this time?"

"What you believe is irrelevant," Corbin said. "The fact is, I have been waiting these past few weeks to receive a mission, yet I have not been given one. I can't say why."

Sasha's exhaustion and irritation cracked his emotionless veneer, and he snapped at his former brother. "Perhaps they see your ineptitude. They're loath to send you out just to fail again."

"I'm afraid you might be right," Corbin admitted. "That, combined with the peace of the so-called Blessed Epoch. There are just fewer people wishing others dead."

"A paltry excuse," Sasha said. "What would you have us do? Just keep waiting?"

"What do you want me to do?" Corbin snapped back at Sasha. "I'm already risking everything to help you!"

"Because we allowed you to live," Sasha pointed out. "Foolishly, perhaps."

"What choice do we have?" Duncan asked, his voice echoing in the crypt. "We have to find the people who can call off the attempts on Sasha's life."

"I've had it with this," Yarrow said. "I say we go into that hideout and make the person in charge tell us what we want to know."

"You're assuming he even knows," Corbin said. "I'm not sure he does. Besides, all that would accomplish would be to alert the rest of the order to our presence and make them aware of our plans."

"And so what?" Yarrow continued. "If we can't use stealth to get to them—which it seems so far that we can't—then let's draw them out. We'll *make* them face us."

Corbin shook his head and took another deep pull of wine. "They won't send a Whisperer. They'll just send agent after agent until all of us are dead."

Duncan could see Yarrow's growing frustration by the increased glow of his eyes. "Well, then," Yarrow said, "we'll destroy the hideout. We'll destroy all the hideouts in Felgard, and then we'll move on to the next town—"

"Where the order will be waiting to meet us," Sasha said.

"Let them," Yarrow said. "If I'm left with no other recourse, I'll rip down every safe house they have until the people ruling the order agree to hear me." He slapped the table, making the bottles on top clink together.

"And what will you do when they send twenty assassins after us?" Sasha asked, too calmly for Duncan's liking. "What will you do when they send fifty? Or a hundred?"

Yarrow got to his feet, fists balled at his sides. A thread of cerulean light outlined him, bright in the shadows of Corbin's crypt. "I will protect myself and the people I love! Let them send a thousand!"

"Yarrow, my dear friend, none of us doubts you would try." Duncan hurried to stand in front of his mage and stroked Yarrow's cheek with the back of his hand. After a few seconds, Yarrow seemed to calm down. The light around him dimmed and then disappeared, and he let his eyelids fall closed as he rested his head in Duncan's hand. "We have to be realistic about this. Smart, not impetuous. I don't want any of us put at risk unnecessarily."

"I'm sorry," Yarrow said in a shaky whisper. "It just makes me so angry that anyone would try to take advantage of us, threaten us."

Duncan shushed him. "Don't apologize. Your devotion is fierce, and I love you for it. You just have to keep control of your anger, or it will burn you and everything around you."

"I know. I'm trying."

Duncan nodded, folded Yarrow in his arms, and kissed him on the top of the head. When he let go, Yarrow slumped back down in his rickety chair, and Duncan took a seat on the edge of Corbin's bed. Sasha stood in the center of the room, his stance wide, his arms bent, and his hands near the daggers at his hips as if he expected an attack. His gaze never left Corbin.

"So we can do nothing but continue to wait," Duncan said, his statement punctuated with a heavier sigh than he'd intended. Goddesses, he grew weary of this dank and gloomy tomb.

"I'm getting better at the shadow-cloaking spell," Yarrow offered. "I'm sure I can keep all three of us hidden now. At least that means you won't be stuck down here."

"I don't want you exerting yourself," Duncan said. "But if you can manage it, I would enjoy some fresh air."

"Good," Corbin said. "I shouldn't linger here. It's getting more and more difficult for me to make excuses to leave the hideout, and the order has eyes everywhere. Every time we meet, we're increasing our chances of being discovered. It might be quite some time before I can return. Thalil willing, the next time we meet it will be to interrogate a Whisperer."

"Why don't we get a few hours of rest before we return to our work?" Sasha said. Duncan recognized the glint in his black eyes and the mischievous curl of his full lips.

"I can think of nothing I need more," Duncan said, locking his gaze with his assassin's.

The three of them retired to the room Corbin had provided while the mage-assassin left the lair. Sasha perched on the edge of the bed, and Duncan knelt to unbuckle his boots. "You were watching Corbin. You never took your eyes off him."

Sasha picked at the buckles of his gloves and pulled them off a finger at a time. "It's no secret I don't trust him. In the order, we're trained to watch the most subtle facial expressions. Often, a person's face will involuntarily give away their deception."

"I cannot imagine being raised in such an environment," Duncan said.

"Raised?" Sasha shook his head. "You misunderstand. The order is not a family; it's a whetstone. We aren't raised, we're sharpened. Our edges are ground to razors."

"And you don't resent that?" Duncan asked.

"Of course not. It made me strong."

Duncan pulled Sasha's boots off and ran his palms over Sasha's calves, feeling iron-hard cords of muscle beneath the creamy-soft leather. He cupped Sasha's knees and kneaded his svelte thighs on his way to the buckles of his trousers. Yarrow kicked his boots off, unclasped his cloak, and let it pool on the floor, then got onto the bed to kneel behind Sasha and comb his fingers through Sasha's hair while Duncan worked Sasha's trousers open and down. On his knees, he walked between Sasha's open legs and planted kisses on the newly revealed golden skin of his belly.

"They really teach you to decipher a person's blinks and twitches?" Duncan asked as he peeled the leather from Sasha's legs and rubbed Sasha through his scant satin undergarment.

"Mmm," Sasha said, his breath erratic as Yarrow nibbled the shell of his ear and pulled his leather coat from his shoulders. "They taught me much more than how to kill."

"What?" Duncan asked as he rubbed his face against Sasha's erection, feeling its veins and ridges against his lips and chin through the silky fabric of his underpants.

"Well, there were informal lessons." Sasha stretched his arms over his head so Yarrow could pull his hooded tunic off. He drew in a shuddering breath as their mage suckled the side of his neck and grazed his nipples with his thumbs. "We—I was taught how to please. People who are pleased are also trusting, willing to help the person who brought them pleasure. I was— oh, Duncan, yes—I was very adept at those skills. Even my master said so. Would you like a demonstration?"

"I would," Yarrow said, and Sasha turned his head so they could kiss and nip at each other's lips.

Duncan pressed his forehead against Sasha's belly and wound his arms around Sasha's small waist. "I don't want anything false. I only want to see your true desire, whether it's artful and cunning or not."

"I have a strange weakness when it comes to you two," Sasha said as he wriggled out of Duncan's grasp to turn around and guide Yarrow back toward the bed's fancy headboard. "I can't feign anything. All my training abandons me. My masters would whip me raw if they knew." He eased Yarrow's legs apart and freed the mage's cock from the confines of his trousers. As he ran just the tip of his tongue up Yarrow's length, Sasha settled on his elbows and raised his hips into the air. "You steal my reason. Still, I have certain skills I can demonstrate for you. Duncan, if you'd undress, you could see what I can do."

Though Duncan already knew, he tore his clothing off and left it scattered across the stone floor. As soon as he found the phial of oil they'd left beneath the bed, he let Sasha treat him to the full presentation as he watched Sasha pleasure Yarrow with his mouth in ways that would put a whore to shame. Hours passed before the three of them collapsed in a heap, their sweat and seed making their skin stick together. Duncan managed to pull the blankets over their tangled bodies before falling asleep with his lips pressed against Yarrow's neck.

When they woke, they all bathed at Sasha's insistence. He claimed a strong odor could give away their position even if the shadows concealed them, so they heated water and filled a large tub. They all washed with a bar of brown soap that left them smelling musky and spicy, just like Sasha, and then they donned their armor and left the lair through a tunnel that brought them up about a half a mile from the river.

Sasha led them to a rooftop across the street from an unassuming stone cottage with a thatched roof. Now that he knew what to look for, Duncan noticed the vague suggestion of a crescent formed by the blocks of the chimney. They huddled in the shade of a balcony over a shop, and Yarrow cast the spell to wrap them in the shadows. Duncan didn't feel any different after the enchantment had been placed, but when he looked at his arm in the shadows, it appeared invisible. When he stretched it out into the sunlight, it seemed to materialize from nothing.

For the first three days, they waited without seeing anyone enter or leave the order safe house. On the afternoon of the fourth day, just as the sun set and painted everything in lavender and gray, a man in a long cloak emerged from the simple door. A heavy hood concealed his face as he looked around before walking slowly down the garden path to the street. Sasha patted Duncan's shoulder and jutted his chin in the caped man's direction. Duncan's pulse quickened; this was finally it!

They let the man get a few dozen feet ahead of them then, with Sasha in the lead, they dropped from the shop's roof and pursued him. When they stayed to the shadows the buildings and trees cast, Duncan could see nothing of his companions but a wavering outline. Sasha and Yarrow reappeared for fleeting seconds when they had to run across a strip of light, only to dissolve back into the darkness. It was disconcerting, but Duncan kept his attention on their quarry. He had no intention of letting the Whisperer out of his sight and returning to Corbin's crypt for another few weeks.

The Whisperer kept to the shadows the buildings cast as the sun sank behind them. In the dark, he practically disappeared, but he always reappeared when he stepped into the dying sunlight, just as the three of them did. The shadows grew longer and heavier, making it more difficult for Duncan to track the man as he walked quickly through Felgard's twisting back streets and alleyways.

"We should take him," Duncan whispered to his companions. "We'll lose him when night falls and he can disappear into the darkness. We should act now."

"Agreed," Sasha hissed. "Get in front of him. Yarrow and I will get his arms. Be quick!"

With a brief nod, Duncan sprinted toward the Whisperer and stood in his path with his hand on the hilt of his sword. Thank the goddesses, they had the bastard now! Sasha and Yarrow stood only a few feet behind him, the assassin holding his blades and the mage crackling with blue sparks of power. The Whisperer approached. He was only an arm's width away, and Duncan reached out to grab his shoulder. They would drag him back to Corbin's crypt and give him the poison that would make him tell the truth. Just then, the sun descended a few final inches, falling behind the clusters of lopsided buildings.

Duncan could no longer see the man they pursued in the shadows that enveloped them, but he knew the Whisperer stood only an arm's length from him. He had nowhere to go. Duncan moved to clutch him, but his fingers curled around empty air. Where a second ago a man had stood, now there was only a shaft of darkness. Duncan looked over his shoulders, sure the Whisperer must be near, must have somehow moved around him, but he saw nothing. He reached out and groped around him, turning back and forth and pawing at the open space but connecting with nothing. Seconds later, Sasha and Yarrow stood in front of him. They looked as confused as Duncan felt.

"What in the Shades' Abode happened to him?" Yarrow spat.

"He's gone... just gone," Sasha observed.

"How?" Duncan asked. "I could have reached out and touched him."

Sasha cursed, and Yarrow punched the wall of the nearest building. "I suppose we should go back to the shop and watch the hideout."

"Was it magic?" Duncan asked. "How did he do it?"

"What does it matter?" Yarrow snapped as he pulled his hood over his head and turned back toward their lookout point. "We missed our chance, and now we'll have to hope for another. I hate this."

They spent the next four days on the roof of that shop before all of them agreed a hot meal and a bath were in in order. Yarrow cast the spell to conceal them, and they headed back to Corbin's hideout.

When they returned to the underground sanctuary, Duncan hurried to remove his breastplate. The armor felt heavier than it ever had, and his muscles and bones ached from carrying it. He left his trusted armor in their room before returning to the central chamber to see what he could use to make them a meal. He found a few eggs and some sausage links and set to heating an iron pan over the fire while Sasha paced the perimeter of the room, and Yarrow collapsed into a chair, clearly worn thin by shielding the three of them with his spell. A nice hot meal would do all of them good, so Duncan cracked the eggs and watched them sizzle next to the meat. Soon, a warm, savory aroma filled the room. Both Sasha and Yarrow took seats at the table, and Yarrow poured wine into three goblets.

Duncan slid the eggs and sausage onto plates and placed them in front of his friends. He dragged a chair to the head of the table and sat down. "What could have happened? We had him."

Yarrow dipped a piece of bread into his wine and nibbled at the crust. "I sensed no magic. I can honestly say it wasn't a spell. I'd have felt a spell."

"Thalil grants us power," Sasha said, pushing his food around on his plate with his knife but not eating any of it. "Thalil grants power to those still in his good graces."

Yarrow snorted. "Magic is magic. It doesn't matter who casts the spell."

"But Thalil is a god," Sasha said.

"Don't be ridiculous," Yarrow snapped.

"Why would you say that?" Sasha asked.

"Yes, why?" Duncan said.

"What makes you think your so-called gods and goddesses are any better than we are?" Yarrow stabbed his fork down so hard the tines embedded in the wood of the table. "The state of the world, for good or ill, should fall to men. Men! If we cannot accomplish something, it is our own limitations holding us back and nothing divine. But what we can do—we could all be gods."

"Yarrow, what a terrible thing to say," Duncan whispered, his appetite departing as he watched the grease congeal along the edges of his fried eggs.

"Why is it so terrible?" Yarrow asked, his eyes spilling blue light at the corners.

"The goddesses made all of us," Duncan said. "Our lives are a gift from them."

"Horseshit."

"Yarrow! What has gotten into you?" Duncan asked.

"The truth," Yarrow said, pushing his untouched plate away.

"Shouldn't we be worrying about the Whisperer and how he managed to elude us?" Sasha asked.

"If not magic, then what?" Duncan asked. "I almost had him in my grasp."

"Perhaps it was just skill," Sasha said. "That few seconds of shadow was all he needed to slip away. That short time when he was out of our sight allowed him to escape. More importantly, he might have known we were following him. If that's the case, we should expect the others to come looking for us."

"Fantastic," Duncan muttered.

Just then, Corbin appeared at the back of the octagonal room, not far from where they sat at the table. "Get your things," he hissed through the black gauze wrapped around the lower half of his face. "We need to leave. Now!"

Sasha was on his feet and holding his blades before Duncan could blink. Yarrow hurried to secure his cloak over his shoulders and pull his hood over his head.

"What?" Duncan asked, still holding his fork as he got to his feet. "What's going on?"

"The order knows someone is seeking them," Corbin said as he hurried to collect phials of poisons and small sacks of powder and toss them into a black satchel. "They may know of this place."

"How?" Duncan shouted as he jogged to their room to retrieve his armor and their packs. With Yarrow's assistance, he secured his battered old plate and threw his cloak overtop.

"It's possible you three were followed when you returned here early this evening. I'm not sure, but someone activated the wards I placed around the edges of this property, and I saw evidence of tampering at one of the entrances. We should not wait to see if I'm right. Follow me."

He turned and disappeared through the archway from which he'd come, and the three of them followed, sprinting through labyrinthine tunnels with only the light of the phosphorescent lichen coating the walls to guide them. Every few hundred yards, Corbin turned and shot a burst of magic at the crumbling walls, sealing off the passageway behind them. They ran for what felt like hours, until every breath Duncan hauled into his lungs felt like broken glass and his thighs trembled with exhaustion. Finally, Corbin slowed down. As he turned to obstruct the tunnel behind them, Duncan leaned his back against the chill, slimy wall, doubled over, and clasped his knees as he panted.

After giving them a few seconds to recover, Corbin led them to an iron ladder bolted into the stone. He climbed up a few rungs and then turned, hanging from his remaining arm. "Yarroway, can you place some sort of ward to slow down anyone who might manage to follow us? If I do it, the order will recognize my magic. As of now, I don't think they suspect me."

"I'll leave them a nice little treat," Yarrow said, grinning as he knelt to press his palms against the stone floor of the tunnel. "Something to twist their guts into knots when they cross it."

Duncan smelled the river when they emerged from the passageway. They'd come out near the southern edge of the city, near an especially rough-looking dock. Nothing but a few torches affixed to wooden poles burned through the thick, chill mist. They all followed Corbin's example and pulled their hoods over their faces. They walked with their heads down past scarred, hardened sailors, thugs for hire, whores, and a few Emiri. Duncan quickly noticed the absence of the Royal Guards in their polished armor.

They entered a tavern. As soon as the door opened, the men seated at the wooden tables turned and drew serrated knives and curved swords. For a few seconds, nothing broke the silence but the exaggerated moans of the whore conducting business in the corner. Slowly, the men drinking in the small, square room with nothing but mud for a floor turned their attentions back to their card games and conversations. Duncan noticed Corbin took extra care to keep his cloak shut and his distinctive armor hidden.

"A room." Corbin slid a silver coin across the filthy bar to the stout, bald man behind it. "The one in the cellar."

The fat man nodded without looking up from his filthy rag and handed Corbin a key. Corbin thanked him, and the three of them followed him to a door on the other side of the room. It led to a narrow stairway with a storage room at the bottom. Smoked meats hung from the rafters and kegs of ale sat against the wall. Some wooden crates held root vegetables, and sacks of flour were piled in one corner. Beyond the foodstuffs was a sturdy-looking, rusted iron door secured with a heavy padlock. Corbin used his key, and the door groaned as he pushed it open.

The room reeked of damp and mold, and it was almost as cold as the wet night outside. Corbin lit the few lanterns dangling from the ceiling. There was no hearth to build a fire in. Looking around, Duncan saw there wasn't much of anything: a tattered rug spread across the packed dirt floor, a thin straw mattress on a low wooden frame, an iron chest, a table, and a chamber pot. Corbin lifted the corner of the rug to reveal a wooden hatch.

"This establishment is a particular favorite of smugglers and the Emiri," he told them. "This door leads to tunnels that come out farther south, in caves near the river. Take care if you have to use it; it is not the only way to reach those caves, and the men inhabiting them might not make you welcome."

"They'll be more welcoming than your people, I'll wager," Duncan said. "Are we safe here?"

Corbin shrugged. "For a short time, but not for long, especially not if the order knows who they're looking for. If it's safety you're after, my fine knight, you should abandon this task and return to your castle in Windwake."

"That is not an option," Yarrow said. "Not until we have the order's word they'll stop coming after Sasha."

Duncan had understood they planned to eliminate, not bargain with, the Crimson Scythe, but he was too tired to argue. Another question occurred to him that he couldn't resist asking. "You are always saying how your order doesn't fail, how no one marked by them can possibly survive, no matter how long it takes. Well, what about High King Garith? Sasha was hired to murder him, but he chose not to. As far as I know, no further attempts have been made on His Majesty's life. Why is that?"

"There has been gossip about this since it happened. The man who employed our order to commit that act perished before he could pay for it," Corbin said. "The last thing we want is to get the reputation for charity."

"So, in theory, if I knew someone had hired you to murder me, and I killed that person before they paid you, or perhaps hired another member of your order to kill them, the mark against my life would be lifted?"

Corbin offered Duncan the crooked grin one might give a confused child: mocking and sympathetic at the same time. "I suppose. Of course, you would have to know who hired me, and you would have to get to him before I got to you. But before any of that, you would have to know your life had been marked in the first place. It isn't like we send out an announcement. Most of our marks never suspect a thing until they see that final flash of steel in the dark. Which reminds me: the three of you should sleep in shifts. It would be wise to always have someone on watch."

"Agreed," Sasha said. "What will you do now?"

"I must return," Corbin said. "I should try to learn how much the order knows about you and perhaps even plant some false information if I'm given the opportunity."

"You still haven't been given a mission?" Yarrow asked.

Corbin shook his head. "I have seen the order punish its agents for failure like this before. The masters will wait for a nearly impossible job, one likely to kill me. If I die, I don't trouble them anymore, and if by some miracle I succeed, I'll have earned my status back. I cannot linger. Should I lock you in from the outside?"

"No," Duncan said quickly. "We'll bolt the door, but I don't like the idea of being trapped."

"Suit yourself."

"I plan to place a ward across the threshold," Yarrow said.

"I'll watch for it," Corbin said as he opened the door and left the chilly little room.

Duncan flopped down on the bed. The coarse blankets felt waterlogged and stank of mold. When he lay back, he saw the thick net of cobwebs covering the ceiling and shuddered as he imagined spiders dropping down on them while they slept. Goddesses, Corbin's tomb had been a palace compared to this place. "Right back where we started," Duncan mumbled.

"No," Sasha said, "now the entire order is likely seeking us. Our position is much worse. I'll take the first watch."

Duncan just nodded, too worn out to even remove his armor and frankly feeling safer with it on. Yarrow stretched out next to him, fully clothed as well, using his cloak to cover himself instead of the reeking blankets. Sasha took his place by the door. As Duncan closed his eyes, he offered a quick prayer to the goddesses for keeping them safe so far and begged them not to let him wake up with a dagger pressed against his throat.

Chapter Nine

THE servants kept the queen's bedchamber dark and as hot as a summer afternoon. Garith perspired beneath his simple shirt and wool tunic as he sat at his wife's bedside. The few candles burning in the chandelier above them illuminated Queen Cothryn's pale face and parched, colorless lips. She had been sleeping for the past few hours. Garith found it bitterly funny that he, High King of Selindria and Gaeltheon, easily the most powerful man in the world, felt so utterly useless. His wife's condition had been deteriorating by the day, and there wasn't a goddess-damned thing he could do.

With a little whimper, Cothryn opened her eyes and lifted her head a few inches from her satin pillows before letting it fall again, clearly lacking the strength to hold it up. Garith hurried to fill a golden chalice and offer her water. She managed to swallow a few sips before she began gagging and turned away from the cup.

"I'm so sorry, Your Majesty," Queen Cothryn said in a voice like the frozen rain pattering against the castle windows.

Garith smoothed the honey-gold hair out of her eyes. Cothryn's skin felt damp and chill despite the three hearty blazes burning in the fireplaces around the room. "What do you have to apologize for, my queen?"

"I… I did something…. I should have thought it out. Now it seems I'll pay for it."

"You are not well," Garith said, dismissing her nonsensical rambling as an effect of her illness. "I should apologize. I am the one who put you in this state. Perhaps it was too soon after our daughter's birth for you to carry another child. Perhaps we should have waited."

She reached up and clutched his shirt, her gentle brown eyes holding his gaze. "My king, this child must survive, even if I don't. No matter what, he must live. Promise me."

Garith sighed deeply. "I wish I could. I have brought you every healer I can find. There is… one last course of action, though I am loath to place much faith in it."

"What?"

"I'm afraid it's an old wives' tale, but the lady Lyorne suggested the fresh heart of an awrythe might help you."

"I have heard that also," the queen said. "It's a superstition leftover from the barbarian horsemen who once roamed the plains."

"I can think of nothing else to do for you, my queen."

"You—You're not planning to go yourself?"

Garith nodded and squeezed her hand. "I will go this very afternoon, as soon as I can get men and supplies ready."

"But what if something happens to you? You are the king, and you're vital to everything we're trying to build. Send your knights to slay this creature."

"No, it is because I am the king that I should go. A king should not ask another to take risks he is not willing to take himself. I should be the one to kill this beast, and I will." He leaned down and kissed Cothryn's clammy forehead. "Rest, and do not give up hope. I will not fail you in this, I swear it."

"I know. I'm not worthy of the danger you face on my behalf."

"Nonsense. Now, go back to sleep. Take care of yourself, and take care of my son. I'll see to the rest."

The queen nodded even as she swiped away the tears spilling down her face.

DAWN was breaking over the Dairden Plains as Garith emerged from his tent. The rosy light lent a fuzzy quality to the frozen grasses and the steppes rising from them at irregular intervals. A few sheep and horses grazed on the brittle vegetation, though most of them had been moved to summer pastures farther south. They'd camped not far from the road, and Sander had assigned only four of the twenty knights they'd brought to keep watch overnight. Here, only two days' ride from Eirion-Vayl and mere hours from the nearest village, they had little to fear beyond bandits, and Sander had doubted even the boldest bandits would attack a hunting party flying the royal banners. Still, he'd insisted on sleeping in Garith's tent with his sword beside his cot.

Garith shook his head as he glanced over his shoulder at his knight sleeping with his arm draped over his face and one of his bare legs poking out from his blankets and furs. Before leaving the tent, he'd stood for probably a quarter of an hour and just watched Sander sleep, fighting the desire to circle his parted lips with his thumb or rake his fingers through his tangled copper curls. Goddesses forgive him, it had taken all his willpower not to pull the covers aside, drop to his knees, and lavish kisses up and down Sander's naked body. Part of him wondered if Sander might not enjoy it, out here on the plains, away from the prying eyes at court, the constant reminder of the Thirteen Sisters, and Garith cursed himself for a fool and a coward for not even trying. But the other half of him loved Sander too much to take advantage of him while he lay dreaming. Garith didn't want to do anything to cause Sander pain or guilt, and so he'd left the tent, hoping the cold morning air might douse some of the fire in his veins.

Even now, he could hear Sander rise from his bed and pull on the studded leather trousers he wore beneath his armor, and Garith had to fight not to watch. Sander came to stand behind Garith, his breath misting around Garith and the heat from his bare chest sinking all the way into Garith's core. When he turned to face Sander, the sight of his pale pink nipples erect in the cold and the dusting of red hair at the center of his ivory chest almost destroyed Garith. He balled his fists and tried to think of something, anything else, anything but how Sander's hard nipples would feel beneath his fingers, his lips—

"It could snow today," Sander said, shielding his eyes and looking east, into the sun. "That might make it easier to track the awrythe. If we ride hard, we could reach the cliffs where travelers have reported seeing the beasts as early as this evening. Then tomorrow, we can begin the hunt in earnest at first light."

Garith nodded, watching the grasses sway and sparkle in the wind. "A good plan."

Sander rested his hand between Garith's shoulder blades and spoke near his ear. "Are you all right?"

"Just worried for my queen," Garith said, only partially lying.

"Understandable," Sander said. "But please don't worry. We'll slay this creature and haul its carcass back to Eirion-Vayl before the first of Pherara's Moon. I swear to do this for you, my king."

"We'll do it together, my friend. Now, let's get some breakfast. We have a long day of travel ahead of us."

Servants emerged from their tents, some to attend to the horses and others to prepare a hearty meal. Not long after, the knights who had been resting appeared in their padded trousers, gambesons, and cloaks, while those who'd taken the night watch retired gratefully for a few hours. Garith knew most of the men on the expedition well; quite a few of them had taken him hunting as a boy back in Selindria. Only one of the knights was new to him, and Garith took his place beside the unfamiliar young man, while Sander sat across the table from them. Garith turned to address the newcomer as a servant put a plate heaped with ham, sausage, beans, bread and eggs in front of him.

"Good morning, Tam…."

"Wyeth Ashlinn, Your Majesty. An honor to be here, King Garith."

"You're much younger than the other knights Tam Lysander selected," Garith noted.

"Aye, I volunteered, Your Majesty," Tam Wyeth said. "I'm a good hunter. I grew up in the north of Everdale hunting harrow-wolves. I thought I could be of service."

"I appreciate it," Garith said, clasping Wyeth's hand, "and I'm sure Queen Cothryn will be grateful for your skill as well."

Garith and his knights finished their breakfast and donned their armor while the servants tore down their tents and loaded them into carts. Then, as Sander had suggested, they spent the day riding southeast. Sander had also been right about the snow—light flurries swirled around them as they traveled. That night, from their camp, Garith could see the cliffs the awrythe supposedly inhabited. The cold had descended like a bird of prey upon the flat land with the retreat of the sun, and the winds had picked up, so all the knights but those on watch chose to eat their dinner in the shelter of their tents. Garith was pleased for the opportunity to eat with Sander, and he took a last glance at the looming bluffs in the distance before opening the flap and entering his pavilion.

Inside, it was warm with the hazy glow of the lanterns and the small fire Sander had lit in the brazier, though the wind smacked the canvas walls and snow skittered beneath the hem. Sander sat at a small round table in just his trousers, with a fur-lined cloak slung over his bare shoulders. Just looking at him sent a chill tumbling down Garith's spine, for more than one reason. Garith rubbed his arms, cold in spite of his padded doublet and wool shirt. "Maybe it's my Esperon blood, but sometimes the cold just sticks to my bones. It doesn't seem to bother you."

Sander smiled and shrugged. "Well, I'm from Greyrclif. We never wore shoes or a cloak until halfway through Strella's Moon as children. But sit down and eat before our stew gets cold. Wine?"

"Please," Garith said, taking the stool opposite his friend and dipping a crust of bread into his broth. As soon as Sander poured it, Garith took a generous sip of wine from his goblet and sighed as it warmed his insides. After only a few slabs of cold meat and hard bread for the midday meal, both Garith and Sander were hungry enough to eat in silence until they'd emptied their bowls. Sander poured more wine, and they dipped the leftover bread into their cups and nibbled at it as they spoke of the upcoming hunt. By the time they emptied the bottle, Garith felt warm and drowsy. "I suppose we should retire. I'd like to ride for the crags at first light."

Sander stacked their dishes for the servants to collect, added a few more pieces of charcoal to the brazier, and stirred up the coals with an iron poker.

"Will you be warm enough?" he asked Garith, the embers washing his face in pale orange and gilding his curls.

Garith wanted to tell him he'd be much warmer if they pushed their cots together and lay beneath a single set of blankets. He wanted to tell Sander how much it would mean just to lie next to him, to listen to him breathing and let his scent wrap around him like a quilt. He wanted to bury his face in Sander's hair and drape his hand over Sander's belly, even if he could go no farther, but Garith said only, "I will be fine, I'm sure."

Sander came up to the stool where Garith sat and unbuckled his cloak. The heavy garment fell across Garith's thighs. "You might as well use this," Sander said. "I'll be fine without it. Don't really get cold, like I said."

"Thank you. Sander, I…."

Sander cupped Garith's cheek and gently inclined Garith's head until their gazes met. By the light of the brazier, Sander's eyes looked like orbs of fire, like molten gold. "What, Garith? What do you want to say?"

"Are you sure you want to hear it?"

Sander took a step closer, so his bare chest and belly waited only inches from Garith's face, the scent of his skin swaddling Garith's every perception, and whispered, "Yes."

With a trembling hand, Garith touched the side of Sander's waist. He'd spent so many days and nights imagining what his skin would feel like, he just couldn't stop himself with it so close. Sander's breath hitched as Garith grazed his torso, the cords of muscle beneath his satiny white skin better than any fantasy. He felt like silken mist over iron, and just the brush of his skin against Garith's finger made heat creep up Garith's neck and onto his cheeks. Garith dragged in a tremulous breath. "I want to say I love you very much. So much I feel like it's tearing me in half. Goddesses, it hurts like nothing I've ever felt, yet I would not be rid of it. Can you understand?"

"Yes." Sander put his rough palm over the back of Garith's hand and guided it across his chest. His heart beat hard and fast beneath Garith's hand, and his fine hair tickled Garith's skin deliciously. "Every time you leave the room, I feel like someone's stabbed me, right here."

"Goddesses, Sander…." Garith could find no words in the mire of lust, uncertainty, and devotion his mind had melted into. All the emotions he'd pushed down for so long burbled up to the surface in a hot, thick geyser he couldn't dam anymore. He got to his feet, knocking his stool over in the process, knit the fingers of his free hand into Sander's hair, and finally claimed his mouth. The boiling heat inside him decimated all rational thought, morality, and worry over the consequences, washed it all away in a torrent until nothing else existed. There was nothing but Sander's slick, swollen lips, warm, wine-scented breath, taut, smooth body and pounding pulse.

Sander kissed him back. He flicked his tongue against Garith's lips and then wiggled it between them as he wound his unoccupied arm around Garith's waist and pulled Garith against him so hard it nearly knocked the wind from Garith's lungs. In that moment, Garith didn't care about anything, not even breathing. He let his tongue bump against Sander's as he ghosted his fingertips down the knobs of Sander's spine until he felt the band of his heavy leather trousers. When Sander didn't pull away, Garith dared a little further, cupping the firm crescent of his ass. Sander growled, grasped Garith's hair, pulled his head back, and dragged his lips up Garith's neck, panting hard against Garith's skin. He was so much different than the queen, so aggressive and desperate, so male…. When he rolled his hips and his erection brushed against Garith's, it almost finished Garith right in his trousers. Then Sander raked his teeth up the other side of Garith's throat and across the emerging stubble on his jaw, and Garith felt sticky wetness in his pants.

Garith pushed Sander back a few inches and tore his doublet open down the center, snapping the lacings before pulling it off his shoulders and letting it fall on the floor. He yanked his wool undershirt over his head and tossed it away before reaching for Sander again. He needed to feel Sander's skin against his own, press their bones together with nothing in between. Garith brought their mouths together, and they twirled their tongues around each other's. They rubbed their naked chests together and groped every inch of each other's heated skin. The friction of Sander's rough palms against Garith's skin made him tingle, made his body spring alight as if it had been numb until this moment. The intensity of the sensation was almost more than he could bear.

"Sander… Sander, can we move to the bed?"

Sander stiffened, going rigid, but he didn't pull away. When he spoke, his breath crashed against Garith's ear like the tide. "Garith, I… I'm a virgin."

With some effort, Garith forced himself to stop rutting against Sander and move out of his arms enough to look into his face. He had to let Sander's comfort come before his lust. Before anything happened between them, he needed to make sure Sander was certain, completely at ease. He wanted his brazen, self-assured knight in all his glory.

"You mean you've never been with a man," Garith said, petting his wild crop of hair. "Neither have I. I never wanted one, not until you."

Sander shook his head, his cheeks reddening in the most alluring way, making him look so vulnerable Garith wanted to shield him from the world, keep him safe in his arms. He'd never envisioned Sander as the one in need of protection, and it ignited something fierce within him.

"No, Garith. I've never been with anyone."

"What? Not a woman either? But… you're so beautiful and such a respected knight. The maidens must fall at your feet."

Sander grinned shyly; Garith had never seen the bashful side of him. He'd only seen Sander banging his sword against his shield and cowing even wealthy aristocrats if they spoke to Garith in a way he didn't like. Garith caught his hand and led him to the cot. Both of them sat on the edge, and Garith rubbed Sander's thigh. Now that he'd started touching him, he couldn't bring himself to stop. He hoped his caresses might bring his friend some ease.

"That might be a bit of an exaggeration," Sander said, "but of course I've had a few offers."

"Not pretty enough for you?" Garith asked. "None of them?"

Sander shook his head and combed his hair out of his eyes. "It was not that. I…. If I tell you something, do you promise not to mock me?"

"Do you really need to ask me that?" Garith asked. He guided Sander's head to his shoulder and kissed the part of his hair.

"My father was a knight of Greyrclif. We lived in the castle. A lot of knights and soldiers came and went. My older sister Ellina… Goddesses. I have never spoken of this…."

"I swear you can trust me."

Sander nodded against Garith's chest and exhaled a damp puff of breath. "My sister fell in love with a knight from another valenny; I don't even know which one. I used to make excuses so she could meet with him. I loved her very much. My mother was so involved with the politics of court, with being better than the other ladies, prettier and in finer gowns, she had little time for me. Ellina practically raised me, because she didn't want to see me reared by servants who didn't give a fig how I turned out. She was lovely, my sister. Long red curls and bright green eyes. The sweetest smile…. As a boy, I couldn't imagine the goddesses could be more beautiful.

"Anyway, she fell in love with this knight and grew heavy with his child. When she found out he had a wife and family, she threw herself off the cliffs into the sea. We didn't even have a body to bury."

Garith's heart hurt as if he'd lost his own sister. "I wish I had some words to offer you, my friend. I'm sorry."

"For a long time, I trained only so I could kill that man," Sander said. "But the goddesses condemn vengeance, and my anger dimmed after a time. Ellina would not have wanted me to be so bitter, so consumed with hatred, so I chose to use my skills to defend the kingdom and the crown. I think she would be proud of me."

"I know she would," Garith said.

"I also swore I would never put another poor girl in my sister's position. I didn't want to father a child until I could do it within a legitimate marriage, so…. So I relied on my own hands." Sander forced a laugh.

"You're such a good man," Garith said, caressing Sander's goose-pimpled arm. "It just makes me love you more. If you must know, I never laid with a woman until my wedding night. The queen knew much more about it than I did. She basically took care of everything. And Sander, you need not worry about putting a child in my belly."

They grinned at each and kissed again, twisting their hands in each other's hair. Hard again, Garith leaned against Sander and lowered him onto the bed, letting his hand roam up Sander's thigh until he could rub the bulge at his root. He kissed down Sander's neck and chest until he could capture Sander's nipple and circle it with his tongue, the way he had dreamed of doing so many times.

Sander arched his back off the cot and pressed his chest against Garith's face. He thrust up against the thigh Garith had let fall between his legs, and he clawed at Garith's shoulders. "So, how will this go? Do you intend for me to play the part of the lady? Or would you rather be the woman?"

Garith chuckled against Sander's skin as he moved down the gully between his stomach muscles until he reached the sparse patch of hair above Sander's trousers and paused there, enjoying the texture against his face. "I don't think it has to be either. After all, think about Bairn Duncan of Windwake and the assassin, Sasha. Does either of them strike you as womanly? What about my cousin Yarroway?"

Sander gasped, maybe with shock, maybe because Garith had begun to roll his trousers down. "You think they—Goddesses, many things make sense now."

"Mm-hmm." Garith peeled Sander's thick trousers down until he had to sit up to slip Sander's boots from his feet and work them off. Sander's cock was beautiful: a little longer and thinner than Garith's with a defined head showing through his hood. Beneath it, red fuzz covered his full pink balls, and Garith couldn't resist cupping them in his hand. "You're more beautiful than I ever dreamed."

Garith rose to his knees to pull his trousers down and free his erection. Sander licked his lips as he looked up at Garith, his eyes glazed with desire. "Sander, show me how you pleasured yourself. Use your hands on me."

Sander opened his mouth as if to speak, but only a groan escaped him as he reached out to touch Garith's cock gingerly, as if he might break it.

"I'm not made of glass, Sander. I'm the same as you." To demonstrate, Garith took Sander's dick in his fist and gave it a hard squeeze before moving it up his length. Sander tossed his head back and moaned. Garith fell against his chest, wrapped an arm around his ribs, and rolled so they faced each other. He caught Sander's mouth and drew Sander's lower lip between his teeth as he continued stroking him. Sander bucked into Garith's hand and closed his fist around Garith's cock. "Oh, yes. Touch me, Sander. I have wanted it for so long. Touch me like you touched yourself...."

"This is better," Sander huffed against Garith's lips. "So much better. Touching you…." He thrust into the tunnel of Garith's fingers, and soon they established a rhythm, circling their hips against each other as they devoured each other's lips. "Garith… Garith, I love you."

Sander's words, his enthusiastic hands and lips, unwound Garith. His whole body tingled and he knew he couldn't last. As much as he wanted to make this stretch into forever, his body tensed with the prelude to release. Sander's strokes grew short and needy, and Garith matched his tempo. They pressed their mouths together and panted and groaned as they thrust and jerked, both of them desperate for completion. Their teeth scraped together and dented and bruised each other's lips. Garith breathed into Sander's mouth and sucked in quaffs of Sander's air, pulling the scent of Sander's hair, wet skin, and dribbles of seed into his lungs, wanting to store the smells and tastes in the back of his throat. He swirled Sander's increasing dew up and down his shaft, then slid his thumb over his tip. It gratified him in ways he'd never imagined to give Sander pleasure like this; he'd worried Sander would never be able to enjoy it, but he was—his belly trembled and his hand shook as he clutched the back of Garith's neck. Both of them jerked clumsily, lost in their need. Sander came first, painting Garith's belly with his hot, white seed, and Garith followed him over the edge moments later. The orgasm tore from the base of Garith's body, so hard he thought he'd pass out. He'd always enjoyed coupling with his wife, but this—His whole body seized and shook, and he held on to Sander as tremor after tremor of bliss tore through him until he thought he'd fall to pieces. "I… I love you, Lysander. I always have…. Goddesses!"

After trembling with pleasure for what felt like forever, Garith slowly became aware of the hard cot beneath him and the silken, pliant body in front of him, slick with sweat and sticky with their seed. He caught Sander's mouth in a deep, slow kiss, gentle and celebratory now that they'd burned through their passion. "I have never been so happy," Garith told his knight, his lover and dearest friend.

"I'm glad," Sander whispered, a shadow over his sea-blue eyes.

Garith propped himself up on his elbow to look down at Sander. "Did you do this just for my benefit? To please me alone?"

"No," Sander said, playing in the sparse hair on Garith's chest, remnants of their spilling drying on his fingers. "I wanted it. I wanted you so badly all the goddesses at once could not have dissuaded me, but now…."

"Now you feel guilty." Garith felt miserable for inflicting such pain on the man he loved. He should have controlled himself. But when Sander had touched him, discipline and decorum had been washed away in a single, devastating wave, and now he cursed himself. He'd been no better than an animal.

"It is wrong," Sander said, bravely not shying from Garith's gaze, "but I would do it again. My dear friend, my love, I want to do it again. I felt so close to you, so connected with you. I already yearn to feel... almost like a single soul in two bodies, sharing breath, a heartbeat. Still, we have sinned against the goddesses."

"A small sin, perhaps," Garith allowed. "Like wearing red during Fayelle's moon, wrong according to the priestesses, but not really harming anyone. It is not like thievery or murder."

"No, I suppose you're right." Sander cuddled against Garith's chest and rubbed the small of Garith's sweaty back. "If it hurts no one, then why do the goddesses say it's wrong?"

"Maybe it is not the goddesses, but those who claim to serve them," Garith said, thinking back to Tam Torkan Mellinger and the priestesses. "Maybe it is just a way to inspire fear in others. I am not the most devout, but how can love, trusting in another person, feeling so happy just to have them near, be unnatural? If what we did was wrong, why was it so wonderful?"

"I don't regret it," Sander said. "I have thought about you... being with you like this, for so long. I already want to do it again. I want to do it every night and wake up to your face next to mine on the pillow. But I don't suppose that's possible."

"It should be," Garith mused. "It just takes a man with the courage to stand up and say so."

"Oh, my king! You must never say something like that. You would lose your crown! Of course, I will fight for you no matter what—"

Garith stopped his tirade with a kiss and then said, "Later, my love. I'm too tired to puzzle over all of this tonight, and we have a beast to hunt in the morning. Right now, I need a piss."

"Should I get you the pot?"

Garith kissed him again. He knew he'd never grow tired of tasting Sander's lips or feeling his emerging whiskers scraping against his chin. "No. You are not my servant. If anything, I'm yours. Besides, it will stink up the tent. I'll go outside." He pulled up the trousers Sander had pushed past his knees but never entirely removed and walked through the tent flap.

A rustling in the brush halted Garith before he could relieve himself. "Is someone there?"

Tam Wyeth Ashlinn emerged from the bracken. "Forgive me, Your Majesty."

"You are not on watch," Garith observed. "What are you doing out here?"

The poor young soldier blushed and stammered. "Ha-having a piss, Your Majesty. The tents are so small that if we use the pot it reeks all night."

Garith laughed and patted the young man's shoulder. "I agree. So let's piss and get in out of the cold, shall we?"

Tam Wyeth seemed to relax, and the two of them took care of their needs before returning to their tents. Garith stretched out next to Sander and pulled the blankets and furs over them. They'd never gotten around to pushing the beds together, and Garith was glad as it forced him to rest his cheek against Sander's chest and wriggle as close to him as possible. He almost wanted to stay awake and relish the sensation of marble-smooth hardness beneath him and thick, warm fur against his back, but they had a dangerous hunt in the morning, and he needed to be alert, so he let himself drift off, sheltered in Sander's strong arms, never more content. For the first time since ascending to the throne, he felt like a man first and a king second.

Chapter
Ten

DAWN broke across the plains, turning the cloudy sky to a splotched, watery gray like diluted ink. The new light on the snow blinded Garith as he sat astride his charger, shielding his eyes against the glare. A few errant flakes skittered across his cold-chapped cheeks, but he didn't think it would snow again. Following his huntsmaster, he nudged his mount with his heels and took off at a trot. The horses huffed out thick, white clouds as their hooves kicked up snow and frozen soil. Sander had spotted a set of tracks, catlike prints as big around as an infantryman's round shield, and the party had been following them since daybreak.

When they rode between the cliffs, a brutal wind whipped Garith's cloak around him. His long hair blew into his face from beneath his helmet, and he had to brush it out of his eyes every few minutes. His guard, his Sander, his precious Sander, riding next to the huntsmaster, held up a hand to halt the others, and Garith reined his animal along with the twenty other knights. They stood in a diamond formation with Sander at the apex and Garith near the center. The world grew white and silent as Sander and the huntsmaster tried to pick up the trail. Nothing but swirling snow and pale ironstone surrounded them until Garith could barely discern the line between the horizon and the speckled sky. The horses pawed the ground impatiently and the hounds snuffled, seeking a faint scent among the ice and powder. Garith rubbed his gloved hands together as he waited for Sander to pick up the trail. When he looked over his shoulder, he saw Tam Wyeth Ashlinn holding his crossbow, nervously darting his gaze between the cliffs boxing them in.

Finally, they picked up a set of faint tracks, mostly obscured by the drifting snow. They followed them around in overlapping circles, trying to outrun the snow the wind sent to hide them. Eventually the huntsmaster decided to split the group and send scouts ahead. The weak, watery sun had slid almost to the center of the smudged sky before they returned.

Horns sounded. "We have spotted the awrythe, Your Majesty!" one of the knights shouted as he pointed to a black silhouette against the snowy gray sky, perched on the edge of a low cliff to the northeast. The four scouts reined their mounts amidst a cloud of dry powder.

"Archers!" Sander yelled, pointing at the blurry black shape. "Get it on the ground!"

Five of the men kicked their horses' sides. A misty trail of snow followed them as they rode to the bluff's edge and raised their bows. Some of the arrows must have found their marks, as Garith heard a high-pitched mewling in the distance. His pulse sped, whether with excitement or fear he couldn't be sure. Though he'd been schooled in combat since he could lift a sword, he'd never been allowed to actually fight. He'd always hated that he was considered somehow too precious, as if other men's blood counted for less than his own. King's son or no, it wasn't like gold flowed in his veins. Clutching the stiff, cold leather of his horse's reins in his left hand and drawing his sword from its sheath by his hip with the other, Garith dug his heels into his dun mare's ribs. The fuzzy silhouette on the crags reared and tumbled to the ground. Garith ignored the shouted warnings of Sander and his huntsmaster as he urged his animal to a canter. Seconds later, he heard nothing but the horse's hooves striking the frozen ground and his pulse thrumming in his head. Everything looked brighter and clearer than before, the edges of the cliffs like cut metal against the sky as Garith approached them.

Garith wasn't prepared for the sight awaiting him on the leeside of that overhang. He'd been told the awrythe resembled a horse, but the creature bleeding into the snow was five times the size of a charger, even more if he counted the tail beating the ground behind it. Pale golden fur covered the awrythe's massive body, and black, dangerous-looking hackles rose like swords along its spine. Ebony claws longer than Garith's blade dug furrows in the frozen ground as the creature writhed and tried to get to its feet. Its tail whipped around, the bony spikes at the end catching one of the archers at his midsection and hurtling him from his horse. The poor man hollered in agony as his back collided with the ground. Blood bloomed around him. The other archers raised their weapons and sent a fresh volley at the creature. Most of their arrows and bolts lodged in its long neck and the rippling muscles of its shoulder. The beast howled again, and blood streamed from the newly inflicted wounds, but it turned on the bowmen and bared its long yellow teeth. A growl rumbled from it, and it sprang, moving much more like a cat than a horse toward Garith's archers.

The awrythe snapped its jaw and ripped away the top of one of the men, crunching his upper body down while his disembodied legs still hugged his saddle. Bile shot against the back of Garith's throat at the sight of his knight's innards sliding down his legs and coiling on the ground, steaming when they hit the snow. The remains of his corpse slid from the horse in slow motion, and when his body fell, the animal nickered, showing square white teeth between stretched brown lips, and trotted away from the stench of death. The other archers' mounts danced backward no matter what their riders did to still them. The remaining men released a fresh round of arrows, and all of them found a mark, though the awrythe did little more than warble at the minor pain.

Garith was a king. A king defended his subjects, served as an example to his knights. With that thought, Garith raised his sword above his head and kicked his horse forward. The awrythe turned its fury on another of the bowmen. As he drew nearer, Garith saw a feline face with bright green eyes the size of dinner plates. A mane of long, bone-colored quills tipped in black wreathed the creature's massive head. When the awrythe gave another bone-melting cry, blood and foamy spittle dripped from its maw and pelted the man in front of it like gruesome hail. The brave archer flinched but didn't retreat, instead raising his bow and firing into the beast's mouth. It howled, thrashed its head, and spit up more blood before lifting a paw to swipe at its tormentor. The man dove to the side, out of his saddle, and covered his head with his arm as he smacked the ground. Claws raked the stallion's side, filleting away skin and muscle and exposing the white bones of his ribs. The horse screamed and dropped to its knees, slipping and stumbling in the fouled snow as it attempted to stand. With another swat, the awrythe tore its throat and silenced it.

As soon as the archer got to his feet, he ran a few steps back and lifted his weapon for another attack. His companions, having retreated a safe distance from the awrythe's teeth and claws, joined him, and soon bolts and arrows protruded from the creature's face, neck, front legs, and chest. They weren't much thicker than the quills around its face, though, and seemed to cause it little more than annoyance. The beast, like any predator, targeted the weakest among them: the archer who'd been unhorsed. The man turned to run, but Garith knew he'd never escape its jaws. He urged his mount mercilessly and closed the distance between himself and the creature just as it opened its mouth to devour another of his men.

With a dry yell, Garith plunged his blade into the horrible thing's flesh, driving his steel deep into the thick sinew where its neck met its shoulder. It took all his strength to yank it free again, and the awrythe's hot blood poured down his arm and sheeted his horse's mane and neck. He'd certainly succeeded in drawing the monster's ire away from his archers.

"Get to safety!" Garith yelled to them without taking his eyes off the awrythe. "Keep up the attack from a distance!"

He couldn't spare a second to see if they succeeded, because the creature turned to face him, baring teeth like thick yellowed daggers flecked with blood. It lunged, and Garith slashed across its face with his sword as his horse danced backward. A seeping gash opened across its flat, black nose, but it only recoiled from the pain for a second. Garith attacked again, but this time his sword pinged on one of the creature's fangs, the impact nearly knocking it from his hand. His next strike sliced its lip, but it never backed away.

"Your Majesty! Garith, what are you doing?" Sander and the other knights had caught up to Garith, and Garith's personal guard sounded both frantic and irate. Garith knew the easiest way to incense Sander's quick temper was to threaten his king. This time Garith had placed himself in danger, and Sander's anger rose at him as it would anyone else. Garith would bet Sander's cheeks were stained red and his lips were trembling with his rage, but he couldn't glance over his shoulder to enjoy the sight.

Sander's shout drew the awrythe's attention, and it craned its overlong neck to watch them, exposing the ribs of its throat. Grasping a handful of his horse's mane to steady himself and leaning forward in the saddle, Garith drove his blade between two of the rungs. The edge of his steel grated along bone, catching and sticking as he fought to pull it free. Clutching hard to his horse with his thighs, he let go of its hair to tug with both hands. More blood and a gust of fetid air followed his weapon out of the beast's throat, and this time it crouched and edged back a few feet.

At the huntsmaster's instruction, the knights fanned out to surround the awrythe, drawing swords and halberds as they encircled it. While some of the men attacked, stabbing at the creature's chest and shoulders, three others rode around to flank it.

"Watch out for the tail!" Garith yelled, remembering Lyorne's warning about poison, but too late. Swinging the appendage like a flail, the awrythe struck two of the knights and swept them from their horses as easily as a servant with a feather duster swept away a cobweb. Their steel breastplates saved both men from being impaled on the spear-like quills, but as one of the soldiers got to his feet, he pulled a smaller barb from his cheek. The toxin acted quickly, sending the man to his knees, retching, before he could take a step. His companion hoisted him up by the armpits and dragged him a little way around the side of the bluff, where they had some shelter.

The rest of the knights assaulted the creature from every angle, stabbing into it with their weapons. Blood and gore matted the creature's fur, and it started to stagger. They were hurting it, wearing it down, but it was like chipping away at a mountain with a pickax. Pain and injury spurred the awrythe's anger, and it turned its deadly teeth and claws on man after man, its movements becoming erratic. It couldn't seem to decide which of them threatened it most. It whipped its tail behind it, the tines plowing up snow, rock, and clods of frozen soil. It managed to catch one of the horses in the legs and topple the poor mare to her side. Her rider screamed, his leg trapped beneath her, and two of the knights ran to aid him and get him out of the fray.

Dozens of arrows stuck out of the rampaging beast, but as long as the awrythe remained on its feet, the men hacking at it couldn't reach much past its belly, and its hackled back and haunches remained almost unscathed. Even though the awrythe had slowed, it still managed to swat and bite at the men, wounding many of them and killing at least one when it hooked its talons into a man with a spear and tore through his armor, shredding his chest and stomach like paper. Half of the hunting party had been killed or injured enough to take them out of the fight. Even the huntsmaster had to retreat when the tip of the awrythe's fang grazed the side of his arm, ripping through his pauldron and slicing the flesh beneath.

Garith tried to land another blow to the creature's neck, but the way it howled and tossed its head, snapping its dripping jaws at anything within reach, made it almost impossible. He managed little more than a few shallow slashes. Off to his left, Sander barely managed to bury his face in his horse's mane and avoid the awrythe's bite. The brittle sound of its teeth snapping shut hit Garith like a cold knife to the lung. They had to kill this thing, and soon. It would bleed out eventually, but he had never encountered such a tough bastard, and the longer it took, the greater the chance they'd lose more men.... The greater the chance he'd lose Sander.

For a horrible second, Garith wondered if the goddesses were punishing him, if they'd seen what had happened last night on that narrow cot—No. He wouldn't let that happen. These men were here out of loyalty and courage. They were here because Garith had brought them to hunt and kill a monster he knew little about for a cure that might not even work. He wasn't going to let any more of them die.

Tam Wyeth's white gelding screamed as the awrythe bit into its flank. From the way the horse's haunches crumpled to the ground and it tried to drag itself with its front legs, its spine had likely been broken like a twig. Wyeth swung his leg over the gelding's back to dismount. He gave the horse a pat and said something Garith couldn't hear before cutting its throat and ending its pain. The brave young knight continued fighting on foot, a cold and determined look on his face as he hacked the awrythe's leg, as if he could chop it down like a tree if he kept swinging. Once it nearly trampled him, but Sander, fighting by his side, managed to catch him by the back of his gorget and toss him out of the way.

The creature dipped its head in their direction, and Garith exploited the chance to stab between its neck and skull: the place most creatures, including men, kept a pulse point. He thrust his arm into the matted hair, and possibly poisonous barbs, hoping his steel gauntlet and chain mail gloves would protect him but knowing he had to take the risk. He met resistance at first, but then his steel sunk into soft flesh, and he pushed until he'd buried his blade to the hilt. As he drew it out, he twisted the metal, and then he stabbed again, squinting and grimacing at the blood fountaining into his face. The gambit paid off. A thick stream of blood poured from the wound and pooled on the ground. The awrythe reeled and almost went down. Just before it crumpled on its side, the beast loosed a horrifying shriek, regained its balance, and began slapping at the knights even more viciously.

Garith had never really been in combat, but he had hunted, and he knew many creatures drew a fresh surge of violence when they felt the chill fingers of death closing around them. "Let's finish this cursed thing!" he shouted to his men. "It killed our friends! Make it pay!"

Some of them responded with battle cries that echoed across the desolate plains. Sander heeled his horse and guided it to the awrythe's left side. Riding almost beneath it, he thrust up with his blade, puncturing the creature's soft belly and piercing it between the ribs. Awful stuff rained down on him, but he kept driving the blade up until the awrythe's back legs folded and its hips dropped to the ground.

"Sander!" Garith shrieked. All he perceived was the awrythe's huge, heavy body falling in slow motion onto the person most precious to him in the world besides his daughter. Sander's horse sensed the danger and bolted, throwing Sander out of the saddle and farther below the dying monster. Fear like nothing Garith had ever felt tightened around his insides, forcing the air out of his lungs and twisting his stomach like a wet rag. He practically leapt from his horse's back and hit the ground running. He saw nothing but the awrythe collapsing onto his friend. Where in the Shades' Abode was Wyeth? He'd been right behind Sander. It didn't matter. Nothing was taking Sander. Garith had only just won him, and he wouldn't let this thing snatch him away.

"Sander, go!" he shouted as he jumped and threw his weight and the point of his sword against the beast's side. If his physical size had matched his degree of desperation, he might have moved it.

The awrythe faltered, and Garith landed hard on his back next to Sander, the wind torn from his lungs. Even though he couldn't breathe, he staggered to his feet, his only concern saving Sander. He grabbed Sander by the blue tabard over his plate and tossed him as hard as he could, tossed him away even though he wanted to curl against him and take shelter in his arms and behind his sword. Mostly, he wanted Sander out of danger. Nothing else really mattered, and Garith felt satisfied when Sander staggered to his feet and reached for a sword he'd left stuck in the monster's innards. The awrythe fell toward him like a mountain hurled by the goddesses. Bent in half and trying to shield his head, Garith ran toward Sander and the knights gathering around him. He felt a hard slap against his back. His chest struck the ground, dragging his breath out again when he'd barely regained it. There was pressure on his wrist, a sharp tug.... Damn, he'd lost his sword somehow.

A sharp pain struck Garith's right foot like lightning. It felt like it burned up his flesh and disintegrated his bone. He screamed. White light erupted across his vision, followed by fuzzy black. That darkness wanted to draw him in, promising sweet oblivion and respite from pain. Garith resisted that honeyed, inky shadow, though; Sander and his men stood on the other side of it, and he would get to them. He willed it away, and the agony returned, but it was the price he paid for standing on the right side of the Shades, and he handed it over willingly.

The awrythe had finally fallen to its side, and it tore up the ground as it thrashed, fighting its impending death to the end. Sander dragged Garith a few dozen feet from the beast and the pool of bloody, churned-up mud surrounding it and dumped him unceremoniously on the ground. Then he picked up a thick spear someone had dropped during the melee, walked calmly to the beast, and drove the weapon into the side of its head, near its eye. It twitched a few times and fell still. The quiet was eerie after the cacophony of battle, the clang of metal and men shouting still echoing in Garith's head as he bent to examine his injured leg. When the awrythe had fallen on him, it had bent one of his greaves and driven the edge of the metal into the flesh above his ankle. He picked apart the leather straps and yanked up on the twisted steel, biting off a scream as he extracted it from his leg. Blood poured out of the deep gash, but so much blood covered every inch of Garith that it just mixed together with the rest, and soon he couldn't tell his own from the monster's. He tore off a strip of his tabard for a makeshift bandage and tied it tightly over the wound. Then, using the broken shaft of a spear as a cane, he limped over to the head of the creature and looked down into its lifeless emerald eye.

THE ride back to camp passed Garith by in a blur. He barely noticed the wintery landscape or the movements of the horse beneath him. He could hardly even feel Sander riding behind him—they'd doubled up since so many of the horses had been lost—but he knew Sander's presence was the only thing keeping him upright in the saddle. Now that the urgency of the battle had passed, Garith felt numb in both body and spirit. Had those men's lives been worth it? What if the cure didn't work and they'd died for nothing? Garith would feel the weight of that guilt on his heart for life. At times like this, his crown felt too heavy for his neck to support. He wanted to say all of this to Sander, but the guard remained silent, cross about something Garith couldn't begin to fathom, so Garith just stared down at the blood clogging the links of his chain mail. Just this once, he considered behaving like an entitled monarch and discarding the whole armor set and commissioning another. He couldn't imagine ever getting the stench out of it.

A cart near the end of their procession carried not only the awrythe's head and its heart in a sealed steel chest, but the remains of the knights who had fallen bringing it down. For one of them, his family would have no more to bury than a pair of legs. A tear slid down Garith's face. He'd hated to put his men in that cart with the monster—to him it dishonored their sacrifice and memory—but they'd only brought one from camp, and he had no choice.

When they got back to the camp, the servants who'd been resting in their tents or talking around fires hurried to take the horses. A flurry of activity followed: men were helped out of their armor, the wounded were taken to the healer's tent, water was heated for washing, barrels of wine were opened, and the evening meat for their supper was skewered onto spits. Garith stood still at the center of it all, frozen in place while colors whizzed by and sounds collided. All of it seemed to happen impossibly fast, and he couldn't connect what he perceived around him with any sort of meaning. He almost wanted to laugh, but he couldn't find the energy. Slowly, because he could imagine nothing else to do, he turned, trudged to his tent, and opened the flap.

Sander followed him into the candlelit space. The servants had already put wine, bread, and cheese on the table. How long had Garith stood in a daze? He looked down at the dried blood coating his hands and arms, cracking and falling off in rusty flakes when he moved. His own blood had soaked the cloth tied around his ankle, and the wound throbbed beneath it. Hunting with his father had always been a sport, as much an excuse for the men to drink and relax as anything else. It had been a welcome respite from court, a chance to use coarse language and tell questionable jokes while away from the ladies, and it had been fun. This—

Garith turned to say something to Sander. He wasn't sure what; he just wanted the balm of hearing Sander's voice. His knight stood facing the rippling canvas wall of their tent, his back to Garith and his arms crossed over his chest.

Garith took a step closer to him and winced when he put weight on his injured leg without the aid of his walking stick. "Sander, have I done something to offend you? Are you cross with me?"

Sander hissed out air and dropped his arms to his sides, his fists balled so tightly the skin over his knuckles looked ready to tear. When he spun around to face Garith, his eyes were squinted with anger, and he curled his upper lip. "I'm a little cross, yes. What in the Shades' Abode did you think you were doing?"

"What do you mean?"

Sander released a portion of his rage in a growling shout. "You absolute ass! You—are—the king—of Selindria." He poked his finger into Garith's chest between his snarled words.

"I don't understand."

"You got between me and that thing! You dismounted and ran toward danger!"

"To save you," Garith protested.

"Exactly! No matter what you say, your life is worth more than mine! And you put it at risk to save me. You have to promise me you'll never do it again."

"I can't," Garith said. He would do it again a thousand times, and he wouldn't tell Sander otherwise. "Please don't be angry."

"Angry? I'm—There's not even a word for it, Garith! If you want to know the truth, I'd like to throttle you. Every time I think of you pushing me out of the way and coming so close to being killed, I just want to hit you in the face!"

"Go ahead, then!" Garith bumped his chest against Sander's. "Hit me if it will make you feel better! But don't ask me to stand aside and watch you die. You say you get angry when you think of it. Well, when I think of it, all I feel is fear. The thought of facing the world without you in it, without you standing by my side…. It makes my blood turn to ice. Don't ever ask me to do it, Sander."

Sander's lips quivered, and he lifted his fist to Garith's chin. Instead of hitting him, he closed his hand around Garith's cheek, dug his fingers into Garith's hair, and pulled their faces together. They opened their mouths to each other and let their tongues nudge against one another. Sander twined the fingers of his other hand around Garith's neck and held Garith almost immobile as he thrust into Garith's mouth. Garith let Sander pump all of his fear and anger into him, and as he clutched at the unforgiving planes of Sander's armor, the dead numbness he'd felt began to dissipate, replaced by a heat that started in his belly and moved up to his chest and down to his root. With every swipe of Sander's tongue along the edges of his teeth or over the roof of his mouth, Garith felt more alive.

They kissed until their lips swelled and they had to break away to steal a breath. Sander rested his forehead against Garith's temple and panted onto Garith's cheek, rubbing tight little circles on the back of Garith's neck with his fingertips. "I just don't want anything happening to you. The world needs you more than me, whether you want to admit it or not."

Garith turned his head and rubbed the tip of his nose up the bridge of Sander's and back down. He pulled Sander's kiss-tender lips between his and nibbled at them lightly. "No man is worth more than another. No life has more meaning than any other. Every life is a gift from the goddesses. Sacred. Equal."

Sander chuckled against Garith's mouth. "If you can get the rest of the world to agree with you, we might find ourselves with a Blessed Epoch after all."

Mirroring Sander's smile, Garith ran his hand over Sander's breastplate and gorget until he could bury his fingers in Sander's hair and peck along his bottom lip. Just as they let their eyes flutter shut and started to lose themselves within each other, the tent flap cracked and they jumped apart.

Tam Wyeth stood at the entrance, backlit by the bright sunlight reflecting off the snow. He nearly dropped the large wooden bucket of steaming water he held as he stared at them with wide brown eyes. Some of the liquid sloshed out and spattered on the rug covering the ground, and it seemed to bring the young knight back to reality. "I… forgive me, Your Majesty. I should have announced myself."

"Yes, you should have," Sander barked, coming around to stand in front of Garith and tug the pail out of the young man's hands. "Why are you bringing us washing water, anyway? We have servants to do that."

Wyeth flushed and stammered. "I… I'm sorry, Tam Lysander. The servants are all so busy, with everyone hurt and hungry and filthy…. I didn't want to keep you waiting until the water got cold.…"

"I appreciate it," Garith said. When Wyeth continued looking at him like he'd sprouted a second head, he added, "That will be all."

The young knight left the tent, and Garith started helping Sander off with his armor. He couldn't imagine ever getting it clean, the sticky blood and grit an inch thick in some places "Do you think he saw us?" Sander asked in a whisper. "Wyeth?"

"I… I don't know." Garith tried not to let Sander see how much the thought troubled him. "If he says anything, we'll just have to tell him he's mistaken."

"It would be hard to mistake what we were doing for anything else," Sander said as he slid out of his domed pauldron and kneaded the meat of his shoulder. "What if he tells someone?"

"We'll deny it. I have a wife and a daughter, with another child on the way."

"I don't," Sander said, removing his chain-mail tunic and letting it fall to the floor in a pool of blood-caked silver ringlets.

"You're young," Garith assured him. "It isn't unusual for a knight your age to be a bachelor. Come on, let's try to scrub this awful stuff away and get something in our bellies. We'll worry about Tam Wyeth when and if we have to. Right now, I just want to get back to Eirion-Vayl. I'll let the men rest for a few hours, but I intend to ride before sunset. I don't want to spend another night here. We have what we came for, and now we need to get it to the queen."

And goddesses help me if it doesn't return her to health, Garith thought. His enemies would see the hunt as nothing more than an expensive waste of life. They'd probably accuse Garith of vanity, of taking into his own hands what should have been left to the Thirteen Sisters. And if Wyeth revealed what he'd witnessed on the heels of those accusations....

Garith forced the paranoia from his mind. He'd been doubting and second-guessing every decision he'd made since ordering that group of priestesses to release poor Torkan Mellinger. He had done the right thing by seeking the awrythe to save his wife and child; he knew he had. If the creature's heart cured the queen, others would agree. If it didn't....

Garith would just have to face the consequences. As a king, his choices carried heavier repercussions than those of other men, so he considered his every decision carefully. Still, not even mages could look into the future.

Chapter Eleven

YARROW still had voices inside his head, specters howling from the ether and screeching at the back of his thoughts. Sometimes they swallowed up the advice his mind tried to give itself, drowning out practicality with fear and the memory of pain. Like unwanted guests, they banged at the doors of his subconscious, refusing to relent until he granted them entry. Sometimes, especially when he got as tired as he was now, he just couldn't hold that door shut, and those voices from the past broke through and trampled him.

Sitting in the corner of the tenth filthy rented room they'd occupied in as many days, Yarrow's skull throbbed as the voices crashed around inside it: the voices of the knights who'd hurt him as a child. After casting the spell to keep them cloaked in darkness for hours a day and sleeping for only a fraction of each night, he couldn't shove them back into the fetid hole they'd crawled out of or slam the iron door shut to keep them contained.

You like that, don't you, boy? This is what you wanted....

"Shut up."

"Yarrow?" Sasha stood with his back to the door, on alert with his daggers in his hands, while Duncan snored softly on the straw-stuffed burlap sack the innkeepers called a bed, preparing to take the night watch.

"I want some wine," Yarrow said.

"There isn't any more."

"Damn."

"Are you all right?" Sasha asked. To anyone else, his tone might sound chilly and unconcerned, but Yarrow knew it was just Sasha's way. Though Sasha still struggled to show his devotion in his voice or face, Yarrow never doubted he felt it.

"I… am," Yarrow answered, reaching out in a plea for Sasha to come to him. "Do you ever have nightmares?"

Sasha crossed the small room. Even with everything he could accomplish through magic, Yarrow couldn't comprehend how Sasha managed to walk on the shoddy floor without even a board creaking.

Sometimes he seemed ethereal, carved from shadow, almost otherworldly. Corbin seemed that way to Yarrow too: a phantom. Yet Sasha's body felt warm beside Yarrow, his arm comfortingly solid around Yarrow's shoulders when he sat down.

"Nightmares… no," Sasha said, resting the side of his head against the top of Yarrow's. "At least I never used to. When I was with the order, I loved nothing, valued nothing—not even my own life. It let me live completely without fear, completely resistant to pain. Immune to threats of any kind."

"And now?" Yarrow reached across to trace the length of each of Sasha's graceful fingers with the tip of his own. Though Sasha had removed his gloves, he still held a dagger tightly in each hand.

"Now…. I know every ugly way a man can die, Yarrow. I know how his tongue will turn black and his lungs will shrivel from narxium sap. I know if I stab him in the right place in his belly, it will take days for him to die. I know the place on the back of his head to strike him and steal every thought and memory of his life. Before, this knowledge was merely a tool in my arsenal, but now…. Now, I imagine these things happening to you or Duncan, and I am afraid. I'm not used to fear, the heaviness of it on my chest. These images do come to me while I sleep sometimes. What is it that troubles you, my dear love?"

Yarrow tried to weave his fingers into Sasha's, but he couldn't while Sasha held his blades. "You can put them down."

"I can't," Sasha said, and Yarrow understood the security Sasha gained from feeling the steel against his palms, and he couldn't snatch it away from him, even if it was false.

"Just memories," he responded to Sasha's question.

"I wish I had known you back then," Sasha whispered, letting one of his knives rest on his thigh and clasping Yarrow's hand. "I would have spared you that pain."

"That's the thing," Yarrow said, holding tight to his warm fingers. "I should have been able to spare myself that pain. Why did I just… let them?"

Sasha turned Yarrow's hand over, brought it to his mouth, and kissed Yarrow's palm. "You were a child. I had been trained to kill by that age. I… I would have stopped them…."

Yarrow heard an unexpected bitterness in Sasha's voice. It surprised him, like biting into a ripe koria fruit and tasting tartness instead of sweet juice. "You can't honestly feel guilty because we hadn't yet met."

"Guilt?" Sasha said, forcing an artificial laugh. "Is that what I feel chewing inside my belly? I thought it was just the hunger to spill blood."

Yarrow shifted to face him and rested Sasha's hand low on his waist before releasing it to brush the feathery black hair out of Sasha's face. "I don't know if you're joking. You are still such a mystery to me. A beautiful, alluring, desirable mystery."

Sasha's magnificent lips curled up into a genuine grin full of mischief and the promise of pleasure. His onyx gaze furrowed right into Yarrow's heart and saw all the horror and regret it held, but didn't shy away. Yarrow dragged his palm up Sasha's lithe, leather-swathed arm and clasped the back of his neck to pull him close enough to kiss. Sasha kissed him back eagerly, taking the reins and wrestling Yarrow's tongue into submission. Yarrow willingly let him take control as little currents crackled across his skin like miniature thunderstorms.

"I would do anything for you," Sasha panted as he rose to his knees and moved between Yarrow's legs, resting a forearm against the wall as he looked down at Yarrow through heavy-lidded, sin-black eyes.

"I know," Yarrow responded, brushing his lips over Sasha's smooth chin, relishing the unique, spicy flavor leaking from his pores. Tasting him not only stoked the fires of Yarrow's lust, it made him feel safe, like he was where he belonged. He wanted more of it and extended his tongue to lick across Sasha's jaw and behind his ear. Sasha groaned and thrust down against him as Yarrow nipped along the shell of his ear.

"I love you." Those words came so freely from Sasha now. Before, saying them had been like coughing up blood for the assassin. As Yarrow peppered kisses down Sasha's neck, then paused to suck up a faint purple oval from his golden skin, Yarrow realized Sasha was free in these moments. The weight of his obligations to Thalil and the Crimson Scythe lifted, and he got to be just a man for an hour. Perhaps that was why he dropped the icy, emotionless mask he usually wore when they made love. Yarrow loved that he could release Sasha from his bonds, release the true Sasha, separate the complex, passionate man from the single-minded assassin. He could strip Sasha bare, lay him open, and, goddesses, Yarrow wanted to liberate him, make him forget all he'd been taught about hiding his emotions. He wanted Sasha so mad with desire he wouldn't be able to stop himself from screaming. His heart knocked against his ribs as he scraped his teeth over Sasha's throat, biting at his skin and denting it into little red depressions.

"Bite harder," Sasha said as he crossed his arms over the small of Yarrow's back.

"Anything for you. Anything you want." Yarrow sunk his teeth into the plump flesh between Sasha's neck and shoulder, and Sasha cried out. Tasting blood, Yarrow whimpered, "I want you…. Sasha…."

At that moment, something scraped against the window of their third-story room. Sasha was on his feet with his back pressed against the wall by the window and his daggers ready before Yarrow even registered the sound.

Yarrow sat up from the corner, his dick hard and his thoughts still hazy with lust. "What is it?" he asked.

Sasha pressed a finger to his mouth to shush Yarrow as he glanced through the dirty glass. On his hands and knees, Yarrow crawled to the bed and shook Duncan's shoulder. The knight snorted and bolted up, reaching for the sword he usually kept at his back. Yarrow pointed to Duncan's weapon resting against the wall, and then he mimicked the gesture Sasha had made, urging Duncan to be silent.

Yarrow turned to watch Sasha's back. The tension bled out of his assassin as Sasha laid one of his knives on the windowsill and opened the shutter. A small, dust-colored bird fluttered into the room and landed in Sasha's palm. Almost as soon as it touched down, it collapsed into a feathery little ball, not to move again. Sasha unfurled a tiny strip of paper from the warbler's leg and then closed the window against the chill night wind. He offered the scrap of parchment to Yarrow, and Yarrow cast the small enchantment to make the writing appear.

"Midnight. The Exiles' Cove. They are watching." The mark of the Crimson Scythe, the crescent dipping blood, punctuated the miniature scroll. "I wonder how Corbin found us. He must have had this poor creature searching the less reputable inns and taverns for hours. What's worse, if he can find us, so can the others. Based on this, they might be looking. We should leave here as soon as we can."

"What time is it now?" The floorboards protested as Duncan stood and went to pour himself water. Yarrow watched the low light accentuate the dip of his spine above his ass and the adorable dimples on his buttocks. He reached up and ran his hand over the back of Duncan's thigh, through downy hair and over thick muscle. Duncan looked over his broad shoulder to smile down at Yarrow.

"It's not long after sunset," Sasha said in answer to Duncan's question. "Maybe half past six."

"And do you know of the location of this Exiles' Cove, where the sorcerer wishes to meet?" Duncan asked, bending to pick up the padded trousers he wore beneath his armor.

"I do," Yarrow answered, those specters from the past jeering so loudly he almost couldn't hear his own voice, reminding him of how he'd let his Rini die. The voice of the creature that had once possessed him taunted him in his memories, just as it had after it had taken control of Yarrow's body and killed Yarrow's cherished Emiri lover with Yarrow's hands. After everything he had suffered, the guilt of what he had allowed to happen to someone who trusted him completely hurt Yarrow more than the rest put together. "The Emiri use it, along with smugglers, pirates, mercenaries and the like. It's not somewhere you'd want to go if you can't look out for yourself."

"You've been there?" Sasha asked.

"Surprised? When I was with Rini, I was practically Emiri myself. I learned many of their secrets."

"How do we get there?" Duncan asked as he continued dressing.

"It's south of the city," Sasha said. He didn't bother to put the loose shirt and trousers on over his armor, only threw a black cloak over his shoulders and fastened it at the neck. "The brethren know it as well, as a good place to procure weapons and materials for very little coin since most of them are stolen. It's also a source of… rarer items. What I don't understand is why Corbin wants to meet in a place known to and used by the order. When we get down into those tunnels, with no one around to hear us cry out, we might find ourselves converged upon by many assassins."

Duncan shook his head, poured some water into his palm, wet his face, and smoothed his long brown hair back. "Wait, what are you talking about? What tunnels?"

"The tunnels are the easiest way to get to the cove," Yarrow said. "There are hatches leading into them from many taverns and warehouses in Felgard. That way stolen and smuggled goods can be brought to buyers in complete secrecy. The only entrance to the tunnels I remember is the one Corbin showed us in the cellar of that tavern where we first stayed. Sasha, do you know of any others?"

"Yes, but they're far from here, which increases our chances of being seen. We might not even reach Corbin in time. We should use the passageway in the tavern cellar."

"But don't you think the order will look for us there?" Yarrow asked. "Isn't there a good chance they're paying the innkeeper to let them know if anyone asks to rent the cellar room?"

"Oh, almost certainly," Sasha said. "That's why we won't ask to rent the room."

"Then how will we get into it?" Duncan asked.

Sasha shot him a smug smile. "Do you think I have ever gone to sleep in a building without knowing at least three ways in and twice as many out?"

WITH Yarrow's spell keeping them swathed in velvety shadow, Sasha had little trouble leading his companions through the back alleyways to the tavern near the river. After so long on the run, even Duncan had learned to move more quietly in his heavy armor. Yarrow jogged along behind them with only a soft swish of cloth. Sasha ran with one eye on the rooftops and every sense acute, ready to pick up the smallest hint of someone following them. The cold and the thick mist spilling onto the banks from the water kept most people indoors, and they disturbed only a few cats eating from refuse heaps before Sasha heard the subdued rumble of the river and creak of the boats' ropes.

Sasha directed them to a neglected little window around the back of the inn. He used a small knife to unscrew the hinges and remove the shutters, then he kept watch while Yarrow and Duncan climbed inside, Duncan's brawn and armor scraping the frame and splintering the waterlogged wood. As soon as they made it safely inside, Sasha hurried to follow, leaning the shutters on the sill from the inside. In the dark and fog, it would fool anyone who didn't know specifically what they were looking for, and it would buy them more time than leaving the shutters lying in the garbage-strewn lane.

It was dark inside, and the smell of onions was strong. Sasha had led them into a small pantry off the inn's tiny kitchen. It was barely large enough for the three of them to stand shoulder to shoulder, and by the flickering light spilling beneath the door, Sasha shifted a few loose boards to reveal a rope ladder leading into the cellar.

Duncan touched his shoulder. "Did you put this here?"

"No," Sasha whispered. "I suspect at one time it was used to access the food stored in the cellar and then probably forgotten about. As I said, I like knowing more than one way in and out of a building. I don't think the current innkeeper knows it's here. You two go. I'll replace the boards."

The ladder took them to the cellar, and Sasha easily picked the lock on the bedroom door at the far end. He rolled up the threadbare carpet and opened the hatch. Yarrow summoned a faint bluish light as they all crouched to look into the narrow opening. It looked deep; Sasha couldn't see the ground at the bottom. No steps, ladder, or even a rope would help them down the dank stone walls. He saw nothing but a series of uneven steel spikes driven into the rock.

"Let me go first," Sasha said. "I can find my way by feel, and Yarrow can follow so both of you will have his light. Duncan, be sure to pull the hatch shut."

Sasha grasped the ledge of the pit and prepared to swing his legs down, but Duncan caught first his wrist and then his gaze. "Sasha, what if it's like you said? What if you get to the bottom and find yourself surrounded? What if we're walking into a trap? What if everything Corbin has said and done up to this point, all the aid he's offered, has just been a way to throw gauze over his true motive, to lead all of us right into the order's hands?"

"It isn't like you to be so suspicious," Sasha noted without judgment.

"After as many times as I've been betrayed in the last few years, I'd be a fool not to expect it," Duncan said. "Besides, we're not talking about temple girls, are we? These people are trained to lie and kill."

Sasha couldn't take offense at his friend's words; they were true enough. He just didn't like to watch as Duncan's ideals and faith chipped away. When he'd first met the altruistic knight, Sasha had found Duncan's optimism the foolish fantasy of a child, but now that he saw it eroding, he wanted to somehow shelter him from the hostile elements, keep him whole and pure. Sasha could suspect and mistrust everyone enough for the both of them. "What do you want to do?"

"I don't see what choice we have," Yarrow said. "The assassins will keep coming after Sasha until we stop them, and Corbin is our only chance to stop them. Don't forget Corbin swore an oath to do me no harm."

"Just you, though," Duncan reminded him. "Not me or Sasha."

Sasha shook his head. He didn't want them in danger; Thalil, he'd given up his very identity, everything he'd defined himself as, to keep them from harm. "I have thought a lot about this, and it very well could be a trap. Corbin could be delivering me to the others to regain his standing in the order. It's what I would have done in his place. Duncan, you have killed the brethren of Thalil, so they won't mind killing you. As for Yarrow.... Even the strongest oath is fluid to us. Corbin swore not to harm you, but he could just be coaxing you toward someone who owes you no such loyalty. I ask again: What do you want to do?"

"I want to protect you." Light poured from the outer corners of Yarrow's eyes like the streaks left by falling stars as he clutched Sasha's wrist. He had told Sasha many times that he would burn the world for him, and Sasha had no doubt Yarrow not only would but could. It both delighted and unnerved him a bit to be loved that fiercely, loved by someone above everyone and everything else in the world put together.

"If they think they'll lay a trap for us, then we'll make them sorry," Yarrow went on. "All they'll be doing is gathering in one place and making themselves easier to kill. I will show them anywhere and as often as I must not to threaten what's mine."

"I... I'm afraid I agree. This is our chance. If we don't take it, we may not get another. I'm not willing to wait. I won't forgive myself if something happens to you when I could have prevented it." Duncan closed his strong hand around Sasha's upper arm, encircling it and almost covering it to the elbow. "I will be ready."

Sasha nodded once, though that weight on his chest grew even heavier, pressing down until it pushed the wind from his lungs and made his heart feel squashed like a rotten apple beneath a boot. Fear would only make him weak, distract him, cause him to make a mistake. He needed to be at his sharpest and best, so he brushed away the horrible visions of what a dozen brothers of the Crimson Scythe could do to his lovers, unsheathed one of his daggers, and held it between his teeth as he grasped the cusp of the tunnel and dropped down. He cast around with his foot until his toes brushed one of the metal spikes, and then he balanced on the ball of his foot and slowly lowered his weight onto the shard of steel. Pawing around, he found another spike near his chest and curled his hand around it. Slowly, knowing one slip would lead him to a bad fall, he made his way down, and the men he loved followed him into the dark.

When Sasha couldn't find the next peg with his toes, he bent at the waist and grabbed the one he stood on, then swung around and caught the wall with the soles of his boots. If he stretched as far as he could, he could just scrape the ground with the edge of his foot. He dropped lightly down and looked up into the tunnel. The slow descent of the ethereal blue glow showed him his companions' progress as they picked their way down carefully. Sasha moved his dagger from his mouth into his left hand and took the time to check for traps as best he could in the almost absolute blackness.

Yarrow and Duncan eventually made it to the bottom of the tunnel, and the three of them began walking as quietly as possible. The mage and knight had learned a great deal about stealth, but to Sasha they still sounded like an army clomping along behind him.

"Should I do the magic to hide us?" Yarrow asked.

"Save your strength," Duncan said. "We're alone for the moment. Aren't we, Sasha?"

"As far as I can tell," Sasha answered, casting around for any hint of a presence: the tiniest sound, a shift in the still, heavy air, even an odor apart from the wormy stink of the dirty river or the mossy smell of the tunnels. "We should be ready, though. Duncan, keep your sword handy. Yarrow, just remember, anything too destructive could collapse these passageways and trap us here."

"I can use something more subtle," Yarrow whispered.

For a long while, they waded through thick shadows with nothing but the occasional flutter of a bat to break the silence. After walking probably a few miles, the ever-present swish of the river filled the caverns as they widened. Up ahead, an orange glow made the rough-hewn rock sparkle. Before long, voices could be heard as people moved through the firelight. Duncan and Yarrow moved a little closer, but Sasha stretched his arms out to keep them a little bit behind him. From the racket ahead, he doubted his brothers were waiting for them, but the people living and doing business in the tunnels could be very rough. Some of them were also mad and violent.

They rounded the corner and stepped into a permanent-looking settlement complete with small shacks made from what looked like wood from discarded ships. Fires burned in stone rings or iron cauldrons, clogging the tunnel with black smoke. A man sat on an upturned barrel carving arrows, a pile of shafts beside him on a table. He grunted and scowled as Sasha and his friends passed by. Somewhere, a hammer struck an anvil with a rhythmic clang. A pack of dogs on heavy chains snarled at them, frothing at the maws but not running to attack. Though more than a dozen people moved through the camp, most of them making, moving, or crating up weapons, no one bothered them until they'd almost made it to the opposite end of the subterranean village.

"Something we can do for you lads?" A huge man, towering almost a foot above even Duncan and twice as broad, blocked their path. He wore nothing but a pair of leather trousers, a matted fur cloak, and a massive ax strapped to his back.

"Just passing through," Sasha said, meeting the man's gaze. He didn't have to pretend not to be afraid. The giant might have size going for him, but even alone Sasha could have brought him down and escaped into the darkness bleeding from the passage walls. "Stand aside."

"Not here to buy something, then?" the big man asked.

"I'm afraid not."

The man's ugly lip curled at one corner, and he reached over his shoulder for the handle of his weapon. "We really only like paying customers down here, boy. You'll be wanting to reconsider spending some gold on some of our fine weapons. Or, if nothing strikes your eye, you can leave the gold and come back another time."

Sasha's teeth wiggled, and the hair on his neck prickled as Yarrow prepared a spell. He knew without looking that Duncan stood ready to draw his sword, but Sasha didn't think it would be necessary. From the edges of his vision, he watched the other residents of the settlement edging out of their hovels, most of them holding weapons. Instead of drawing his own blades, Sasha pushed his black cloak open a few inches, just enough for the man in front of him to see his red leather armor. "We don't want any trouble with you. And I assure you, friend, you don't want any trouble with *us*."

The big warrior's eyes widened for a second, and very slowly, he lowered his hand from the polished wooden handle of his ax and moved it in front of his round belly with the other, his palms turned up, as if any quick movement might earn him a dagger through the eye. Sasha decided the man wasn't a complete ass after all.

"No, friend, you're right about that. No trouble with the family." The others watching muttered their assent, sheathed their weapons, and quickly made themselves scarce. "In fact, if we can be of any service, any at all…."

"You can stand out of our way," Sasha said.

"Aye, my friend. As you say. We meant no disrespect, I promise you that. If you had just announced yourself…." He hurried away, and the air cleared as Sasha and his friends left the little makeshift town.

"Was it a good idea to let him know an agent of the order is in the tunnels?" Yarrow asked. "If one of your brothers questions him, he can describe us."

"True," Sasha said, impressed with his mage's reasoning. "I considered that. I thought it would attract less attention to us than a brawl with a dozen mercenaries. Hopefully by the time anyone thinks to ask after us here, we'll be long gone."

"Let's make sure of that," Duncan said, pointing ahead.

They encountered more people calling the tunnels home as they got closer to the water: small encampments of mercenaries, diseased beggars huddled in rags, a whore here and there, merchants hawking everything imaginable, and a few Emiri sailors peddling illicit goods of their own. Smaller channels branched off the main passageway, light and sound drifting out of some while others remained oddly dark and silent. The cavern widened again, and the ceiling sloped higher. A dome of rock, natural or carved slowly by human hands—Sasha didn't know—provided shelter for the dozens of ships lined up along the riverbank. In some ways, it almost looked like a proper port, with wooden piers stretching out into the dark, oily water, sheds full of crates, and men working to load and unload goods.

"It's got to be getting on midnight," Yarrow said, his otherworldly gaze on the torchlight reflecting off the river. "Where in the Shades' Abode is Corbin?"

"Let's look around," Duncan suggested, and they began walking downstream, weaving through the throng of dangerous men. The few women they encountered looked even more formidable, but they would have to be to survive in a place like this. All the people they passed looked the three of them over before deciding against bothering them. Sasha wasn't surprised; men such as these learned early and well how to spot other capable people, and they survived by avoiding them. He'd known as a small child how to judge a man's abilities and disposition by his posture, the way he moved, his facial expressions, and what he rested his eyes on.

"We won't see him until he wants to be seen," Sasha said. "We might as well let him come to us."

"Let's keep going this way," Yarrow said, jutting his chin down river and to the south. "I feel the faintest hint of… something."

Yarrow had been able to sense the presence of Corbin's magic before, so Sasha and Duncan silently agreed to follow him. As they moved south, the ships on the river thinned out, and fewer and fewer people wandered along the wooden piers or across the wet sand between them. A few Emiri wrapped in heavy furs sat fishing at the end of a wharf. They looked suspiciously at the three men until Yarrow raised his hand and greeted them in their native language. Small holes pitted the wall of rock, undoubtedly leading to more twisting warrens where anyone could be hiding. They passed half a dozen such tunnels before Yarrow stopped in front of one and canted his head.

Without a word, he turned and entered the irregular opening. Sasha looked at Duncan before they both followed Yarrow.

A few feet in, Sasha also detected something: a faint odor of rotting fruit carried by a breeze coming from deeper in the tunnel, the unmistakable stench of decay. Yarrow conjured the faintest luminescence, just a hazy sapphire cloud trailing from his fingers like a ribbon of smoke from a candle someone carried. They picked their way slowly, Sasha in the lead to check for snares. Cracks and irregular openings, some large enough to hide a man, appeared along the walls, and Sasha inspected each one before he let his friends put their backs to them. So far, he'd discovered nothing but shallow, empty indentations. He had always had a sense for danger, and it had kept him alive. Since they'd left their room at the inn, that instinct had been screaming at Sasha that he walked into a trap. Yet he kept walking. He supposed this had to end one way or another.

Water dripped up ahead, echoing in the passageway and scenting the air. They reached a steep decline, and Yarrow lifted his hand so they could see to the bottom. A wide stretch of still water, rippled here and there by droplets sliding down the stalactites, filled the tunnel for as far as Sasha could see. Sasha looked from side to side, the reek of death still tickling his nostrils and the back of his throat.

"It looks like we might as well turn back," Duncan said, rubbing his eyes with his thumb and finger. "I'm tired of this. Tired of him pulling all the strings and leading us on these ridiculous chases. I feel like a child playing hide-and-seek, like I'm stumbling around in the dark."

Sasha saw his lover's frustration in the tight set of Duncan's jaw and the lines etched into his forehead and beside his eyes. He pressed the back of his wrist—the only part of his glove free of blades or barbs—against Duncan's cheek. Duncan looked tired in Yarrow's icy light as he leaned his face against Sasha's hand and closed his eyes for a few seconds. "I'm sorry, my love," Sasha told him, "but I told you this would be nothing like the battles you're used to. Those battles have at least a loose set of rules. For us, the only rules are succeed and survive. Come on. We'll keep looking. Or we can turn back whenever you two say. If you would rather go home, just say the word."

"You're out of your mind if you think I'll just wait around for them to come after you again," Duncan said, pressing a kiss to Sasha's forehead, just below his hairline.

"He's here," Yarrow whispered as he pulled off his glove and ran his fingers over the uneven stone. "I can feel his magic. It's unique… sort of… drawing the life out of everything… making it cold and rotten. Almost like disease floating on the air."

"I don't know if I'm complimented by your assessment of my abilities, Yarroway L'Estrella, even if it is an accurate one." Corbin appeared at the edge of the pool at the bottom of the hill, his face covered in black gauze and his hood concealing his eyes. He wore a full set of order armor similar to Sasha's, if a little simpler, and a heavy cloak over top. "Follow me, and hurry."

Sasha held up his hands to halt his friends and looked down the slope at his former brother. "How do we know you're not leading us to our deaths?"

"You haven't trusted me from the beginning," Corbin observed, neither hurt nor offended. "I expected that. Try to remember your training, br—er, Sasha. The easiest path to the desired result. If I desired you dead, I would have brought a team and ambushed you in the tunnels. There are plenty of places to hide, and I know them better than you. Either come with me or don't. I never asked to help you, if you recall. I certainly won't beg you to accept my assistance."

Corbin turned and skipped carefully along a path of flat stones jutting out of the water. Sasha, Yarrow, and Duncan followed him, and when they reached the tiny cavern beyond, Corbin waved his hand and the smooth rocks sunk back beneath the glossy black surface. They followed the mage-assassin's lead and sat on the smooth floor of the small room, so close their legs nearly touched. All of the faces around Sasha looked like corpses in Yarrow's cold blue light, especially Corbin's when he pulled the wrappings from his mouth and nose.

"There's been an interesting development," Corbin said. "I think I've finally been handed a way to get you into the presence of the order's leaders, provided you—and especially Sasha—can survive it."

Chapter Twelve

THE idea of Sasha possibly perishing brought no end of amusement to his former brother, and Corbin didn't even bother trying to hide the grin on his sallow face.

"I'm sick to death of your games!" Duncan shouted, his deep voice echoing. "This is not a joke. For the love of the goddesses, tell us what you've learned and what you plan."

The smile fell from Corbin's face and his eyelids sagged, making him look mildly annoyed. He turned to Sasha again. "I can see why you like this one, my disgraced brother. So… forceful."

Yarrow surprised Sasha by reaching over and clutching Corbin's hand. His mage felt some camaraderie with Corbin Sasha didn't understand and wasn't sure he liked. Perhaps it was just because they were both sorcerers. Corbin squeezed Yarrow's hand back, lowered his gaze to look at Yarrow through his lashes, and flashed a smile completely different from the one he'd shown Sasha. Duncan shifted uncomfortably.

"Tell us what we must do," Yarrow urged.

To Sasha's complete disbelief, Yarrow seemed to have affected the other mage, and Corbin's tone grew serious. "The master of the house where I've been staying took me aside last night. He told me I've become a liability to the Crimson Scythe, a terrible disappointment after all they've invested in my training. I pleaded for a last chance to redeem myself, and the master told me I would have one, and only one. I had to remedy my failures, and he gave me a mission. As I have told you, agents who the order no longer finds useful are given impossible assignments either as a way for the order to get rid of them or for them to earn back their standing. Well, I have received such an assignment.

"I… I am to find the traitor who failed to kill Garith, then Prince of Selindria, the man I let escape the order's justice on three separate occasions. I am not to return unless I am successful; the master made that quite clear. I am to complete my mission or go to Thalil in the attempt. I—"

"Honestly, how does this help us?" Duncan asked. "Why even bring us here to tell us you're yet another assassin looking for Sasha? We obviously have no intention of letting you kill our friend, so where does that leave us now?"

Corbin wriggled his remaining hand out of Yarrow's grasp and held it up. "You did not let me finish, Tam Knight." He reached for Yarrow again.

"Go on," Duncan said, "though I find it unnecessary for you to hold Yarrow's hand while you do."

Corbin lowered his long fingers to his bent knee. "My master did not let me off so easily. I am required to do much more than just kill Sasha. Sasha is the only agent in known memory to leave the order and survive this long, and they want an example made of him—something far beyond a clean death while he sleeps. I am to capture him and deliver him—alive—to the heads of my order, the Thirteen Shadows, at their temple."

"So you know the location of this temple?" Yarrow's eyes glowed brighter with his excitement. "You can tell us, and we can go there and demand the order leave Sasha alone?"

"I'm afraid it will not be that simple, Yarroway. I was not permitted to know the location of the Temple of Crimson Shadows. I am to bring Sasha to the safe house where I've been staying, and then I will be escorted to the temple to deliver him."

"I ask again, how does this help us?" Duncan's voice was rough, and he sounded physically and spiritually exhausted. "You don't honestly expect us to turn Sasha over to you?"

"There's no other way," Corbin said without passion or pleading. "I cannot return without him. If you will not agree, there is no more I can do for you, and we must part ways, the three of you to return to your home and wait for the order to succeed, and me to go into hiding and await the same inevitable end."

"Let's hear what he has to say," Sasha said, looking at his friends. Duncan's jaw quivered as he clenched his teeth to maintain decorum, and Yarrow stared absently at the rocky fringe lining the cavern's entrance, lost somewhere in his head. "Do you have a plan?"

"I do," Corbin answered. "Let me take Sasha. He will be in no danger until we reach the temple. You two will not be able to follow us directly. The order knows of your friendship and will be expecting that. I have devised a way for you to learn the location of the temple as soon as it becomes known to me, however."

"Go on," Yarrow said.

The two mages looked at each other, and Corbin couldn't quite conceal his trepidation as he spoke. "Yarroway, both of us are capable of putting a sliver of our consciousness and perception into something—or someone—else...."

"Wait," Yarrow said. "I don't think I can agree. I just can't have someone else in my head again... another voice in there trying to yell over the others. It's already so hard for me to cull those voices away to get to my thoughts...."

Sasha wanted to quiet Yarrow before he revealed any more of his weaknesses to Corbin, but expressing concern would only intrigue Corbin more, so he kept his emotion off his face and stayed silent.

"You know, your head is one of the last places in this world I want to go," Corbin said, a shudder in his voice probably no one but Sasha detected. "Besides, I have told you I can only manage the magic when I devote all my concentration to it. That's not something I'll be able to do while guarding Sasha and traveling with my order to the Temple of Crimson Shadows. No, I'm only suggesting *you* put a little of yourself in *my* head. Then you'll be able to see through my eyes and hear my thoughts. I'll be able to speak to you after a fashion and guide you. You just won't be able to answer."

"You could lie to me," Yarrow said.

Corbin chuckled humorlessly. "You'll know. You'll be inside my mind."

"You could sever the connection and leave me blind."

"I could. Yarroway, if you think my magic can best yours, that I can break the spell you put in place, then I understand if you don't want to proceed." Of course Corbin struck at Yarrow's pride and sense of worth. A blind imbecile could see Yarrow held them in great supply, but they were fragile.

Predictably: "You think you're better than me? Absurd. Let's do it. What are we waiting for?"

"Patience," Corbin said. "After we complete the spell, the three of you should leave and go to an inn. The order will be watching me, so we'll have to make it look convincing when I capture Sasha. You'll have to put up a fight but let me triumph in the end. I cannot wait long, but I will give you tonight. After that, expect me."

"It isn't going to be easy to make it look like you beat all three of us." Sasha couldn't resist the barb after enduring Corbin's insults.

The mage-assassin's black gaze met Sasha's. "You'll just have to manage. Be warned, though, I might be a little rough. We can't have the others catching on, can we?"

"I'm sure I can handle anything you can throw at me," Sasha said with a feral growl in his tone. "In fact, I look forward to it."

"First, the magic," Corbin said.

"Wait." Duncan stood and grabbed Corbin by the neck of his cloak, lifting him off his feet in a single, smooth motion. He held Corbin a few inches off the ground as he spoke. "If anything happens to Sasha, I will spend the rest of my life hunting you down, and I swear by the goddesses, I will find you." Duncan gave Corbin a small shove as he sat him down, and the mage-assassin stumbled back a few steps.

"Yes, I can definitely tell what you see in this one, Sasha. Fear not, Tam Knight. After all, how will I hide from you with your very skillful mage watching my every thought?"

"Let's get this done," Yarrow said, getting to his feet. "And just remember, I don't have the same sense of honor as Duncan. I won't be kind enough to just kill you if you let something happen to my be—to Sasha. Imagine what I could do to you from inside your thoughts and know what I'll actually do will be much worse."

"Yarroway, within a few moments you will know beyond a shadow of a doubt if I intend to betray you. You'll know before any of us leave this room. Now, I am ready, but perhaps we should sit down."

"I'll keep watch," Sasha offered as the two mages sat facing each other with their legs folded beneath them, kneecaps touching. He put his back to them and stood near the cleft in the stone. Something about the ritual felt too intimate—almost a penetration of sorts. Sasha wondered if Corbin would somehow understand all the things Yarrow kept hidden from him and Duncan. It made him feel—He wasn't sure he could name the emotion, but if anyone should have access to Yarrow's most intimate fears and aspirations, it should be the men who loved him. Still, this was necessary, and Sasha would stop being foolish. It felt good when Duncan came to stand beside him and curled his hand around Sasha's shoulder.

Behind them, Yarrow hissed, "Just hold still. It isn't going to take me long unless you keep fighting me. Just relax and let me in."

Corbin chuckled and apologized, while Duncan nearly broke Sasha's collarbone when he squeezed it.

For the next several moments, it felt like it had back in Corbin's crypt: dark and damp, with nothing but the rhythmic dripping of the water to break the silence. Sasha rested his weight against Duncan, and Duncan kissed the top of his head and pulled him closer. They stood together while the mages did whatever they needed to do. Sasha saw no flashing lights, nor did he expect any. He'd been around Yarrow long enough to understand sorcery didn't work that way. Like assassination, it involved more patience and subtlety than extravagant display.

Sasha let his mind go slack and clear, concentrating on the overlapping ripples in the dark water, watching the way the bluish-white edges of the circles merged and changed as they bumped up against others, forming intricate and ever-evolving patterns. A shrill scream shattered the momentary peace he'd found, and Sasha whirled around, his daggers in his hands.

Yarrow sat blinking innocently as Corbin screamed his throat raw and waved his arm around his head as if a whole colony of bats had descended on him. He scuttled backward, and even when the wall prevented him from going any farther, he kept pushing with his heels, digging up furrows in the loose gravel on the cavern floor. He buried his face inside his forearm and kept screaming, rhythmic bursts of pure horror Sasha never thought he'd hear from the lips of an order agent. When Yarrow reached out to touch him, Corbin howled and swatted his hand away. Then he pressed his fist between his eyes, curled over his knees, and spent the next quarter of an hour sobbing and retching.

"D-Dark and Beautiful One," Corbin choked when he managed to lift his head and find his voice. His eyes were wide black discs at the center of bloodshot white. "Sweet Thalil! What-What are you?" He rose to his knees, grabbed Yarrow by the cloak, and shook him. "What are you?" Then he seemed to realize he'd touched Yarrow and pulled away as if Yarrow were on fire and wiped his hand rigorously on his thigh. When he looked down at his palm, he started screaming again.

"Stop it," Yarrow said in a quivering whisper. "If I can live with it, so can you."

"I don't know if I can," Corbin responded, staring warily at Yarrow through narrowed eyes. "How do you sleep for even a minute?"

"I… I can't really explain what you're probably seeing," Yarrow said in a voice saturated with shame. "But… not all of it came from my hands. Not these hands. Not Yarrow's hands."

"But it's real?" Corbin gasped. "Thalil—"

"Reality and truth are very open to interpretation," Yarrow replied.

"Not this," Corbin said, his voice a little stronger. "I can… feel the blood on my hands."

"That is nothing new for you," Sasha interjected, moving to stand over Corbin. "Can we count on you, or have you broken your fragile little mind?"

Corbin looked up at Sasha, his skin as white as a corpse. "You have no idea what I have seen, what his presence in my mind has shown me. You would not fall asleep within miles of him, let alone in his bed!"

"Watch your mouth!" Duncan said, biting off each word to keep from shouting.

Corbin staggered to his feet and wiped his sweaty brow on a corner of his cloak. "I-I'm leaving. Wait at least half an hour before following me out. The order is watching my every move. I will stop and buy some supplies so they don't wonder why I came to the tunnels. I will give you tonight, so spend it wisely. Then I'm coming for Sasha. I'll come somewhere public, somewhere plenty of people will see. Sweet Thalil, I can't see the last of you too soon. I want… *this* out of my head."

He shouldered between Sasha and Duncan and hurried across the stones, barely waiting until they rose from the pool. It almost looked like he skipped across the water in his haste to escape them.

DUNCAN closed and locked the door of yet another rented room. At least this one, on a bluff overlooking the river, a mile or so south of the cove and nicer than those they'd stayed in recently, contained a real bed, a chest of drawers, a small fireplace, and a bottle of wine on a small table by the window. Water bubbled in a kettle above the flames, waiting to be poured into a ceramic basin. For the first time in almost two weeks, they had a bar of soap and a cloth for washing.

It surprised Duncan little when Sasha retreated to a stool in a darkened corner and took out his daggers and whetstone. As he scraped his blades rhythmically, he kept his red hood up and his eyes on his task. Duncan could scarcely imagine what plots and plans took shape within his mind. When Sasha hurt or worried, he never expressed it. He responded to pain by plotting and preparing, escaping into himself. Duncan had learned trying to force Sasha into anything, particularly talk when he wasn't in the mood, was as futile as trying make flowers bloom from the frozen ground.

In contrast, Yarrow paced the length of the modest chamber with his fists balled at his sides, swinging his arms and barely containing the veins of magic crackling over his hands. "Those arrogant sons of whores. Even Corbin. I can't believe he expects us to slink around like bilge rats. He might not think I can face the order, but I can tell you he's wrong. I'll tear them to pieces! I'll tear their temples and hideouts apart brick by brick and kill every person who gives Sasha a sideways glance! This is maddening!"

The mage's outburst demonstrated to Duncan just how bad he was hurting; Yarrow responded to pain with anger and defensiveness. He'd been at the mercy of others before, and Duncan knew those childhood wounds still oozed, filling Yarrow with bitter blood until he had to choke it out. He hurried to stand in front of Yarrow and stop his agitated movements. When he closed his hands around Yarrow's wrists, Duncan swore he felt the mage's energy coursing beneath his palms. "It will do no good to upset yourself like this, my friend. Why don't you sit down on the bed, and I'll bring you a goblet of wine?"

Yarrow wrenched his arms free of Duncan's grip. "What in the Shades' Abode will wine do to help? I just want to show them… show them what they'll get for threatening the people I love! Oh, Duncan, I'm sorry. I've done it again, haven't I? You're trying to be kind to me and I shouted at you. Forgive me. I… I'll have that wine, and I thank you. For taking care of me."

Duncan couldn't help smiling as he poured the wine. For his mage to not only admit to needing comfort but apologize for being cross…. He never would have imagined it possible when they'd first met. "You need not say you're sorry." Duncan handed Yarrow the goblet and smoothed his tangled ropes of hair back with his other hand. "I know you're worried."

"I'm not worried! I'm—Ah! I just want to tear something apart!"

"Drink your wine, lad, and before you argue, I am telling you what to do, so just do it." Duncan bent to plant a row of kisses across Yarrow's brow, and Yarrow calmed a bit as he nodded and lifted the cup to his lips.

In the corner, Sasha lifted his dozen or so knives one by one and studied the firelight glinting along the edges, then took a few back to the stone until he was satisfied each one could split a hair. Then he carefully replaced them in the hidden sheaths of his armor or the belts and straps crossing over it. "I wonder if I'll get them back," he said, with no more emotion than if he'd wondered if it would snow on the morrow.

"What do you mean?" Duncan asked, moving to stand in front of Sasha. While Yarrow clung to every scrap of affection, Sasha had to be allowed to ask for it, give his permission, so Duncan waited.

"When I let Corbin take me, the order will disarm me, of course. I wonder what they'll do with my daggers, that's all." He picked up a knife with a ruby red hilt and a long, serpentine blade with a faint crimson gleam to the steel and turned it over and over in his hands. "This was the first blade given to me by my masters in the order. I don't suppose it's likely I'll get it back, even if I live through this. I don't suppose it's important. I know a hundred ways to kill a man with my bare hands, after all. It's… just a very good weapon, well made, and it would be a shame to lose it."

"A very sensible concern," Duncan said, moving his hand a few inches closer to Sasha and reaching out slightly, so if Sasha declined they could both pretend Duncan hadn't attempted to hold him.

Instead, Sasha slid his blade into the sheath on his belt and touched just the tips of Duncan's fingers with his own, tracing tiny circles over the pads. He sighed almost inaudibly as he skimmed his thumb over the heel of Duncan's hand and the inside of his wrist before saying, "I should prepare. I want to wash, in case I don't get a chance again for a while."

"Of course," Duncan said. He went to sit on the edge of the bed with Yarrow, who looked ready to weep as he watched them.

Sasha carefully removed his belts and the straps crossing over his chest, then laid them lightly, silently on top of the dresser. He picked apart the many buckles of his armored leather shirt and shrugged it off, then folded it carefully before placing it with the leather strips. His boots and trousers followed, and then he whisked his tight hooded tunic over his head and discarded his black satin undergarment with the red jewels and charms dangling from the metal ring in the back. He looked over his shoulder and smiled, as if pleased to find Duncan and Yarrow watching him.

As if Duncan could force his gaze anywhere else as Sasha silently crossed the room to the inglenook. He watched the crescents of Sasha's perfect ass round and elongate as he moved, the muscles of his back tugging and playing against each other beneath his dark golden skin. The firelight enhanced the shadows between his lithe, defined muscles and the bright spots where his skin reflected it. Duncan's body reacted to what he saw, and he wanted desperately to taste all that sparkling, bare flesh, to run his hands over that sinew, those dark red nipples—

Next to him, Yarrow drew in a shattered breath. "Oh my Sasha. I always think I know how beautiful you are, but my memory never, ever rivals the real thing."

Sasha looked over his shoulder and smiled, an honest, open smile that reached his eyes and crinkled them to black half-moons. "You're the sweetest men. I have been lucky this past year or so."

"Sasha, this isn't the end! I won't let it be the end!" Yarrow said.

Duncan had to concur. "We return to Windwake together or not at all. As much as I hate to admit it, Corbin's plan isn't half-bad. We'll get through this."

Sasha nodded as he poured hot water into the basin. A shimmering sheet of steam rose and enveloped their assassin like a shroud as he plunged the cake of soap into it and lathered up the cloth. He washed his face, hair, armpits, and groin before sitting down on the stool and taking a small round looking glass and razor from his pack to shave. Yarrow moved his hand up Duncan's thigh, rattling the chain-mail shirt he wore beneath his breastplate when he reached the crease between Duncan's leg and groin. He edged closer to Duncan on the bed, and Duncan stroked the back of Yarrow's hand as he watched the suds and water trace the planes of Sasha's body as they dripped down him and darkened the wooden floor at his feet.

Sasha finished shaving his face and moved on to his neck and chest. Yarrow burrowed his face into Duncan's whiskers and nibbled at the skin beneath them before going to stand behind Sasha and rake his fingers through Sasha's wet hair. Sasha groaned softly and relaxed back against Yarrow as he continued his grooming, and Duncan could no longer resist joining them. He unbuckled his plate, piled it in the corner, and stripped down to his padded trousers. When Sasha dipped the razor in the basin to rinse it, Duncan knelt in front of him and caught his wrist. "Will you let me? Please?"

When he looked up, both of his beautiful lovers smiled down at him, their eyelids drooping languidly and their cheeks coloring with lust. Sasha handed Duncan the blade and said, in a coarse whisper, "If it will please you."

"It will please me very much. Nothing pleases me more than caring for the two of you, than being allowed to do things for you." Sasha stroked Duncan's cheek with wet fingers as Duncan scraped the fine stubble from his chest, carefully avoided his hard little nipple. Yarrow took the rag and wiped away the soap, revealing a swath of silken skin. The scar the assassin at Windwake had made stretched across Sasha's chest, healed now, but still pink and puffy. Duncan ran his fingertips along the bumpy jagged line and remembered how his heart had stopped beating when he'd seen Sasha's lifeblood pouring out of it. At the best of times, life was hard, dangerous, and a struggle that could be lost at any moment. They had this moment, and Duncan swore not to let anything sour it. He soaped up Sasha's belly and scraped away the fine hair. Yarrow wiped away the residue, and both of them touched the satiny skin they'd revealed.

Duncan continued, moving the razor carefully over Sasha's pubic area, wondering if he'd trust anyone with a sharp blade so close to his manhood. Sasha never flinched as Duncan whisked away his emerging black curls, and Yarrow took extra time mopping around his cock and over his balls, kissing across Sasha's shoulders as he did much more than was necessary to remove the soap. When Yarrow lifted the cloth away, Sasha's dick pointed straight toward the ceiling, the dusky-pink tip poking out of his hood. After easing Sasha's knees apart, Duncan smeared the fragrant, bubbly froth over his inner thigh. He pulled the skin taut so he wouldn't nick it with the razor. Yarrow leaned over Sasha's chest to clean him, but before long they were kissing. Sasha twined his arms back behind himself and around Yarrow's neck, and Yarrow let the rag drop to the floor with a wet splat.

Duncan could no longer resist pressing his lips to the smooth skin on the inside of Sasha's leg. It felt like silk against his mouth and face, and Sasha trembled as Duncan tickled his freshly shorn and extra sensitive skin with his whiskers. The way he twitched and twisted on the stool enchanted Duncan, and before he knew what he was doing, he'd reached up and cupped Sasha's smooth, heavy balls, kneading them in his fist as he pecked his way toward that beautiful purple-brown cock. When he reached it, he ran the tip of his tongue up the vein on the underside and over the slit. The razor fell to the floor, forgotten, as Duncan curled his hand around Sasha's wiry waist. Yarrow swallowed Sasha's moans and cries as Duncan circled Sasha's crown with his tongue and tugged at his sheath with his lips, stretching the skin and delighting in its texture. As he closed his lips around the head of Sasha's cock, he looked up to see Yarrow pinching both of Sasha's nipples between his thumbs and fingers as the two of them slurped and nipped at each other's lips and tongues.

Sasha yanked Yarrow's tunic up and pushed their mage's belt around his chest so he could nibble along the permanent blue ink twining down the side of Yarrow's waist. Yarrow clutched Sasha hard, threw his head back, and moaned. Watching their flushed faces and swollen lips aroused Duncan more than anything ever had, and he slid slowly down Sasha's shaft, letting the head of Sasha's cock slip into his throat. Sasha rolled the waistband of Yarrow's trousers down and released his big, thick erection. He gripped it at the base and rubbed the leaking tip against his cheek, taking a deep breath of Yarrow's scent.

"You smell like winter," Sasha panted. "Cold, and… and something else. Something ethereal and… and unstoppable, like weather. Thalil, Yarrow. Duncan, I… I don't want this to end."

Yarrow pulled away and pinched Sasha's chin, making Sasha look up at him. Sapphire light spilled from his eyes, making the healthy fire in the hearth seem dim in comparison. "I told you I won't let that happen."

"Come here." Sasha pulled Yarrow back to him and closed his lips around Yarrow's cock. He soon had Yarrow muttering nonsense as thin ribbons of luminescence curlicued from between his lightly closed eyelids.

As much as Duncan loved the taste of Sasha, his skin and seed, and as much as he loved the texture of the veins and ridges of the cock he knew and adored so well, he wanted more tonight. He drew away with a slurp and got to his feet, his legs tingling after kneeling so long. He took a few moments to savor the vision of his beautiful lovers enjoying each other, Sasha swallowing Yarrow's big cock down while Yarrow made sounds almost like crying and grabbed at Sasha's hair, and then he put his arms around Sasha's shoulders and beneath his knees and lifted Sasha to his chest. Of course Sasha writhed and protested; he always pretended he didn't enjoy being taken—at first.

Duncan carried him to the bed and tossed him down. Sasha lay still and complacent, anticipation sparkling in his black eyes. "Yarrow, undress," Duncan said as he stumbled out of his own trousers.

The mage hurried to obey, and both of them crawled onto the bed. Yarrow sprawled beside Sasha, and crashed their lips together. Both of their cocks stood up, darkened and leaking white pearls onto their tanned skin.

"Yarrow, turn around," Duncan said. He wasn't usually so demanding with his younger lovers, but tonight he felt possessive, felt the need for some control. "Suck each other."

Neither of them protested as Yarrow shifted and they both rolled to their sides. Their cocks found their way between each other's puffy, glistening lips. Both moaned with satisfaction and need as they suckled and swallowed each other, fondling each other's asses, thighs, and bellies as they moved together. Duncan lay down with his chest to Sasha's back, grinding his erection against Sasha's tailbone while he reached across to wriggle his fingers between Yarrow's cheeks and over his wrinkled opening. Just the sensation of their bodies against his as they thrust into each other's mouths almost brought Duncan off. He could have just stayed still and enjoyed it, but instead he got up to retrieve the phial of oil from Sasha's pack before stretching back out behind his beautiful assassin.

Clumsy, almost drunk with his need, Duncan fumbled with the cork and spilled much of the fragrant oil across Yarrow's hip when he managed to open it. He poured a little pool of it into his palm and rubbed his hands together. Then he found Yarrow's hole with one hand, and it opened eagerly to his fingers. Duncan buried them in the mage's tight, silken heat as he rubbed himself with his other hand. Sufficiently slick, he thrust against Sasha's crevice.

"Sasha, love," he grunted, forming the words an effort, "do you need me to… open you up? Get you ready? I… I don't want to hurt you…."

Sasha pulled away from Yarrow long enough to say, "You won't. Duncan, I don't want to wait. Do it now."

"You do like to order me around, assassin. Very well, then." Duncan lined himself up with Sasha's opening and pushed past the slight resistance he encountered. Sasha stiffened for a second and shuddered at the penetration. Duncan waited, letting him acclimate to it, but he just couldn't be still for long. He began to circle his hips, and as he did, he sucked burgundy ellipses up from the skin of Sasha's shoulders, leaving a trail across the top of his back. He couldn't help it—he wanted to mark Sasha as his, so anyone who saw him would know he belonged to Duncan. He raked his nails down Sasha's ribs, leaving a quartet of deep red lines as he twisted and thrust his fingers deeper into Yarrow. They belonged to him, and he wanted his claim visible on their bodies. He didn't want anyone to doubt they were his, so he bit into the globe of Sasha's shoulder, leaving a ring of teeth marks, as he pushed into him with ever-increasing desperation. Then he dragged his teeth down Sasha's arm, leaving pink lines on his dark golden skin.

They fell into the rhythm of lovers who knew each other well but still had much to discover. From the way Sasha and Yarrow clawed at each other and bucked into each other's mouths, Duncan knew they were getting closer by the second. He pushed a third finger into Yarrow and rubbed against the bundle of nerves inside him. With a shrill cry, Yarrow pulled away from Sasha and spilled strands of white seed across Sasha's face. His anus hugged Duncan's fingers in rhythmic pulses, and it took every ounce of will Duncan possessed not to explode. Instead, he grasped Sasha's hair and turned Sasha to face him so he could lap away the delicious cords of come Yarrow had left on Sasha's lips, chin, and cheeks. He bit Sasha's bottom lip and made it swell, denting it with his canine teeth. "You're mine."

"Show me," Sasha panted. The oil was wearing thin, and he was probably getting tender.

Let him, Duncan thought. He closed his hands around Sasha's sharp hipbones and tossed him on his belly without letting their bodies separate. He pulled Sasha's ass against him as he pressed his thighs together. He wanted it to burn; he wanted Sasha to remember.

Sasha squealed in a way Duncan had never heard and dragged Yarrow to him to kiss and nibble while Duncan plunged into him.

"Sasha… Sasha… I want you to remember I love you. I want you to feel me the whole time we're apart… every time you move, I want you to feel me."

"Make me feel you, Duncan. Leave me with something…."

"I will. I won't let you forget… won't let you be alone." He pumped into Sasha with all he had until he couldn't hold his release at bay any longer, collapsed against Sasha's back, and came screaming his lovers' names. His body felt like it shook apart, and he held on to Sasha's hip and Yarrow's shoulder as he trembled so hard he felt like he'd black out. They held on to him and kept him whole as his euphoria crested, ebbed, and crested again. Duncan didn't know if he came once or half a dozen times. Every time it started to end, Sasha clenched around him again, sending him back into the ether. His legs could no longer hold him, and Duncan sprawled over Sasha, his cock softening inside Sasha as he kissed and caressed Yarrow. They lay that way for probably half an hour, until their fluids started to dry and affix them to each other.

Duncan rose and poured more water from the bucket into the cauldron over the fire. He served his lovers wine as they waited for it to heat. Then he finished shaving Sasha, washed Yarrow, and lastly, himself. When they finished, they fell back into bed and tangled together, kissing and whispering endearments, some silly and some profound, until they all fell into a deep sleep.

THE next morning, Duncan woke hard again and desperate for his lovers. He lay facing Yarrow's back, and he played in the downy white hair on Yarrow's belly until he felt the head of Yarrow's erection poke against the web of his hand. Yarrow grumbled and nestled down into the bedclothes even as he circled his hips and rubbed the crown of his cock against Duncan's palm.

"Are you awake, my beautiful boy?" Duncan whispered next to Yarrow's ear.

"Nnh-uh… maybe."

Chuckling, Duncan pushed the white cords of hair away to kiss the back of Yarrow's neck. Almost as soon as his lips touched Yarrow's skin, Yarrow began to moan and tremble. Gooseflesh erupted over his skin, and he took the hand Duncan draped across his belly and lifted it to his mouth, where he kissed up and down Duncan's fingers and then sucked on the tips.

Duncan pulled his damp fingers away to toy with Yarrow's nipples, as he knew they were sensitive. Goddesses, every inch of skin and hair on Yarrow's body was sensitive; the slightest peck or caress made him moan and roll his eyes back with bliss. The way he reacted made Duncan feel like the most talented lover in the world. He nibbled along the shell of Yarrow's ear as he rubbed his erection lightly between Yarrow's cheeks. Last night all three of them had been consumed, their desire ratcheted up so high they'd fallen into bed still covered in soap to make urgent love. Duncan wanted to take it slower this morning, take as long as he could to touch, taste, and appreciate every part of Yarrow and Sasha. He wanted to show them how much he cherished them, and commit every detail of them to memory.

Furnace-hot, slippery lips slid across Duncan's shoulder and down the back of his arm as Sasha woke up. Or, more accurately, as Sasha let them know he'd risen. Sasha had certainly grown alert at the first noise or shift in the bed.

"Good morning to you too, my love," Duncan said, turning his head and stretching his neck to kiss Sasha. He noticed the trail of bruises and bite marks meandering down Sasha's neck and over his chest before the blanket hid the rest. "How are you feeling?"

Sasha thrust against Duncan's tailbone and bit Duncan's ear, piercing the lobe with his canine. "I feel like someone mistook me for the pretty cabin boy on a ship full of very lonely sailors."

A little flush of shame stung Duncan's cheeks. "I don't know what possessed me. I felt like a wild animal marking my territory, defending it—"

"You were wonderful," Yarrow said. "I liked seeing you lose control on Sasha like that. Do you think this time you might lose control on me?" Yarrow flexed his inner muscles, and Duncan felt the ripple along the top of his shaft, the wrinkled skin gripping him and almost pulling him in.

He grabbed a handful of Yarrow's matted hair and pulled him closer. "I lost anything like reason or control in regard to you a long time ago."

"Prove it," Yarrow panted. "Prove I make you lose control." He fumbled beneath the bed, found the phial of oil, and pressed it into Duncan's hand.

Sasha snatched it away and treated them both to a smile so full of sin Duncan felt sure he'd go the Shades' Abode just for looking at it. The glimmer in Sasha's eyes told him it would be worth it, though. "I intend to return the favor you showed me last night, my love," Sasha said. "I won't be the only one remembering this room and what happened here every time he takes a step."

They stayed in that room until well past midday, making love to each other in every conceivable combination, all of them satisfying themselves half a dozen times, until no amount of desire, adoration, or love could coax their bodies to cooperate any longer.

"I don't ever want to leave this bed," Duncan whispered as Yarrow and Sasha kissed leisurely across his broad chest. He was sore and sated in every way a man could imagine and then some, and yet he wanted more. "Damn it. There are too many last times between us. I'm ready for forever."

"Can there be a forever for men like us?" Sasha asked as he carded his long, elegant fingers through the ample brown hair on Duncan's belly.

"Maybe," Yarrow mumbled, tracing Sasha's lips with his thumb. "But we still have a long, long way to go. Much more to face before we can turn our backs and walk into the sunset."

"There's no sense worrying over what we can't control," Sasha said, sitting up and stretching his arms over his head. The way his graceful muscles lengthened and popped made Duncan want to take him all over again. "Let's see to what we can control. But first, a wash. I feel like I'm coated in… our love."

After cleaning themselves and packing up, they ate a quick meal in the tavern and began walking back toward the center of Felgard. Corbin had made it clear they needed at least a few people to witness their altercation. By late afternoon, they'd reached one of the sprawling port's many outdoor markets. It went against everything Duncan had ever learned of warfare to just wait to be attacked, and he felt chilly and a bit nauseous as they perused the goods for sale. His training screamed at him to find a defensible position, dig in, and prepare to defeat the enemy. All his most deeply ingrained beliefs told him to defend what he cherished at any cost. To him, it was the most sacred duty, the very essence of knighthood. Duncan supposed it wasn't any easier for him to abandon everything he'd been taught since boyhood than it was for Sasha, but Sasha had done it, and now Duncan faced the same trial.

They inspected some surprisingly well-made weapons at a blacksmith's stall, and then Yarrow insisted on visiting a baker for a raisin muffin. As the shadows grew longer, the throng on the street thinned, and not long after the sun went down, merchants began boarding up their booths. Despite the presence of Garith's knights, Duncan got the sense Felgard wasn't a place where most people wanted to go strolling after dark. He felt a bit envious watching the butchers, fishmongers, tanners, and tailors whistling happily as they headed home to their families. They would sit down to dinner with their children and go to bed with their wives, secure that they'd do the same every evening until they died of old age in their beds with generations of their families surrounding them. Those who lived by the sword and the dagger could never expect such an end, and it pulled at Duncan's heart. He could imagine nothing more wonderful than growing old and gray with Sasha and Yarrow, teetering along on their canes, comparing their ailments, and arguing over what to have for dinner. It was a foolish fantasy, but he couldn't quite give up on it.

"There's a tavern up ahead," he said, pointing. "We might as well make our way there and have something to eat."

Sasha and Yarrow, their hoods concealing their faces, merely nodded and followed Duncan into the alleyway. After they passed a few buildings, Sasha stopped abruptly, turned to face Duncan, and pulled his serpentine dagger from the sheath at his hip. He pressed the ruby handle into Duncan's hand and curled Duncan's fingers around it. "I want you to keep it, Duncan. To return to me or to remember me by."

"Sasha—"

"Quiet. The time is up, I'm afraid. I will always love you." Sasha's lips trembled as he pressed them to Duncan's, and Duncan wanted only to shield him in his arms and dare anyone or anything to try to take him, but he had to let him go.

Sasha went to Yarrow, and as he held Yarrow's shoulders, he said, "You… Thalil, having known you, been with you, makes anything that might come a fair trade. Yarrow…."

"No one is taking you from me, Sasha," the mage said, his eyes flaring. "Never doubt it."

"I have never doubted that you would do anything for me, both of you. It's not something I ever expected to experience. I'm glad I had the chance. Now, you must both promise me you won't do anything foolish."

"Sasha?" Duncan looked around, and from what he could tell, they were alone in the narrow alleyway.

"Just, please, promise," Sasha said. "Do this for me, so I won't have to be afraid. Swear you'll keep yourselves safe no matter what. Please."

In all the time Duncan had known Sasha, he didn't think he'd ever heard him plead, let alone twice in the course of a moment. He knew with absolute certainty he'd never seen Sasha so afraid. When he reached for Sasha's hand, Sasha backed away. "Duncan, please."

"I… I swear I'll be cautious."

"And you, Yarrow."

"I'll be fine."

Sasha blew air between his clenched teeth. "I want you to promise me—"

Before he could finish, a cloaked figure materialized from a triangle of shadow thrown from a rickety three-story building. It glided toward them like a specter, reminding Duncan of a floating black cape with nothing solid beneath. Only when it stopped a few feet from them could Duncan see boots on the ground. The man threw his hood back to reveal a smooth, pale face as emotionless as a marble death mask. "So I've found you."

"You." Duncan drew his sword and pushed Sasha behind him. They had to make the battle convincing, and Duncan didn't think he'd have any trouble venting his rage on Corbin. For him, Corbin symbolized the Order of the Crimson Scythe, those vile murderers who had not only twisted Sasha's mind and walled off his heart but now thought they could take his partner away from him. He wanted to see every one of them wiped from the goddesses' light, and he would start with the one standing before him.

"Back for more, are you?" Yarrow taunted, his power forming a gemlike blue shell around him and his wide grin making him look dangerous and depraved. "Find yourself with a limb too many? I can fix that for you."

Thin cracks spread across the icy patina Corbin wore, widening and spreading until the façade fell away and his outrage was plain even to Duncan. "You… you think you're such a great and powerful mage, Yarroway L'Estrella. I know what you are now. You're an abomination, a jumble of sharp, broken things in a fragile pouch. The edges of all that debris are already tearing through, though, aren't they? Not even all your might will keep them from ripping you apart, and if you say otherwise, you are lying to yourself."

"Enough." Sasha darted between Duncan and Corbin, a dagger in each of his hands. He pointed one toward Corbin while he kept the other ready by his hip. "I won't listen to this."

"You're less than nothing to me, traitor," Corbin said with a sneer. "Everything about you makes me sick. All I heard was how remarkably talented you were, a natural. But you threw it all away for a few pieces of ass."

"Are you going to run your mouth all night, or do you think you can take me?" Sasha sank lower, stretching one leg out behind him.

"Fine." In a movement almost too fast for Duncan to follow, Corbin reached into his cloak, drew a knife, and threw it at Sasha. Sasha dodged to the side just in time to avoid it, and it pinged against the paving stones.

Sasha leapt forward, closing the distance between himself and the mage-assassin. He swiped with his blade as soon as he got within range, but Corbin raised his arm and conjured a wormy green cloud to shield himself. By the spell's jaundiced glow, Duncan could see the rust devouring the steel of Sasha's weapon where his blade had skimmed across the barrier. With the knife in his other hand, Sasha stabbed Corbin in the meat of his shoulder. Duncan knew Sasha could have plunged it deeper, drawn more than the trickle of blood dripping from Corbin's stump. The wound was just for show.

Corbin dropped down and kicked at Sasha's ankles. Though he could have avoided the blow, Sasha let himself be knocked to his back. Squares of golden light began to appear above them as people opened their shutters to investigate the commotion. They quickly blinked out as the respectable residents of Felgard decided they were better off not knowing.

Sasha moved to get up, but Corbin kicked him under the chin, and his head smacked against the hard street stones. Yarrow reached for the mage-assassin with the translucent extension of his arm as Duncan rushed at their enemy with his sword lifted over his head. Corbin pinched all his features tight, and a set of skeletal, infection-colored wings sprung from his back and closed around him, deflecting both Duncan's blade and Yarrow's spectral claw.

Yarrow stumbled back a few steps, eyes wide. "How—?"

Corbin wheezed out a laugh; the enchantment had clearly cost him. "You… gave me more than you meant to… Yarroway."

"You think you are anything compared to me? I'll tear you to ribbons!" Yarrow swung again with his ethereal talon, and Corbin's decayed wings flew apart and scattered like chunks of putrid meat, turning to blackish-green slime when they struck the ground. The force of his strike sent Corbin reeling. The enemy mage stumbled back into the nearest building and slid down the wall, clutching his ribs with his remaining hand.

"You, and then the rest of your order," Yarrow said, advancing on the other mage, too confident to hurry. "Everyone and everything in this world, if I wish. Try to stop me."

Duncan didn't know what to do. They had to let Corbin prevail, but he couldn't remind Yarrow in case the brethren of Thalil were listening, and they almost certainly were. But if he didn't do something, Yarrow would destroy Corbin and then they'd be back where they started. How would they ever secure the cooperation of another order member? Not sure what he'd do, unused to guile, he moved toward Yarrow's glowing silhouette.

Sasha threw a small knife. Though it found its mark in Corbin's thigh, it nicked the side of Yarrow's hip on the way. The minor scratch seemed to tug their mage out of his rage-fueled fugue. Yarrow's sapphire outline fizzled out, and he dropped to his knees and panted.

Corbin tugged the dagger free of his leg and threw it on the ground, ignoring the blood oozing through his leather leggings. He spread his long fingers, and a fetid cloud formed over his palm. The mist spread and grew until it surrounded all three of them. It seemed to stick to Duncan's skin as tenaciously as a cobweb, sapping his strength and resolve. The worn plate armor he barely even noticed after so many years of wearing it felt heavier and heavier, his pauldrons like boulders on his shoulders. He couldn't stay on his feet beneath the weight; his boots slipped on the dewy stones and his kneecaps smacked the ground. As he caught himself on his palm, he summoned his will and prepared to fight through the spell, fight for Sasha and everything they had together. At the last second, he remembered he had to throw this skirmish, and he stayed on his knees.

With a flutter of downy cerulean feathers and a scent like lilies and new snow, Yarrow flapped one of his luminous wings and dispelled Corbin's enchantment. Even though Duncan knew he could rise, Yarrow stayed on the ground, his face bowed toward the slimy cobblestones. Corbin got to his feet and stood straddling Sasha. Then, to Duncan's absolute horror, he lowered himself down onto Sasha's groin and brushed a swath of hair from Sasha's brow.

"What do two such formidable men see in a traitor like you?" he asked in a sensual drawl. "Mmm. Maybe I'll have the opportunity to find out."

"The rotting Shades you will!" Duncan's temper rarely wrestled down his reason, but seeing Corbin touch Sasha like that reduced him to a beast. He got to his feet, rushed at the mage-assassin, and butted him in the chest with his shoulder, knocking him off Sasha and sending him sprawling on his back and gasping for wind. Before Corbin could even sit up, Duncan had the edge of his sword pressed against Corbin's windpipe.

"I should cut off your useless head! What are you playing at?"

"You know." Corbin met Duncan's gaze, and Duncan prepared himself for what he knew would come. The mage-assassin struck Duncan in the belly with his heel, and Duncan just went limp and crumpled against the wet street. Everything inside him told him to get up and fight, and it was harder to stay on the ground than to push through the pain. Above him, the stars looked washed out and pathetic against the lights of the city. As much as Duncan didn't want to see what transpired next, he couldn't help turning his head toward Sasha.

His assassin had gotten to his feet and stood facing the other. Corbin struck Sasha in the face with the back of his hand, and Sasha didn't even try to dodge. He just took it, and the spikes at the knuckles of Corbin's glove sliced into his chin before he fell with a choked-off whimper. Yarrow rose to his knees and straightened up as Sasha curled on his side. Duncan's mage lifted his hand, but Corbin hurled a nasty, seething orb of rot at him. It struck Yarrow in the face even though his cerulean wing could have volleyed it back, and Yarrow dropped to the ground like a bag of sand. He stretched his forearm over his face as he lay on his back; Duncan suspected Yarrow didn't want Corbin to see him crying.

Corbin clutched Sasha's hair and yanked him to his feet as if he were picking a filthy wet rag from the ground. He spun Sasha and smacked his head off the corner of the stone building. Blood poured down from Sasha's hairline and coated his face. Corbin wrenched Sasha's hands behind his back and secured them with a length of thin metallic rope. Then he gagged Sasha with a strip of leather and hauled him away, down the alley and toward the congealed heart of Felgard. Just before he disappeared into the filthy gloom, Sasha met Duncan's gaze, begging Duncan to stay down. Duncan warred against his instinct to free his companion and defeat the enemy threatening him to remain on his knees. No injury he'd suffered in battle came close to the pain of watching his Sasha be dragged away and doing nothing to aid him. He felt like he was being torn in half, but he had to let Sasha be taken.

Yarrow buried his face in his arms and seized with spasms of pain. His glowing fists melted and bubbled the stone, but he didn't rise. Sasha and Corbin disappeared, swallowed up by the city's thick darkness, and soon nothing but Yarrow's truncated sobbing cut through the silence. Duncan could no longer find the strength to lift himself out of the refuse, and he prayed with every ounce of his being that he'd done the right thing.

Chapter Thirteen

ALL of his life, Sai had been perfectly content with what sweet Emir saw to carry to his feet. Like the rest of his race, he was glad to be Emiri, free from the plotting and power struggles of the land people. He and his *syrai* had been fortunate: they had a ship, a home in the warm, lovely islands of the Twenty-Nine, a little boy, and, of course, each other. Sai had the beautiful blue sea and all her bounty, the bright sun on his skin, the sky stretching on into eternity, and all the time in the world to enjoy them. He had never wished for more, and while he seized the opportunities for treasure and adventure when they came his way, he had certainly never wanted to change the ways of the world. It had always seemed like too much hassle.

Then he'd met Yarrow, and for the first time felt compelled to help someone even though he'd make no profit from it and it certainly wouldn't be fun. As he leaned against the railing at the helm of his beloved boat, watching the whitecaps churn up and splash against the hull, he remembered back to the time he'd spent with the mage, and especially to the foreign shore he'd discovered as he'd tried to liberate Yarrow from some of the pain and guilt anchoring him in the darkness.

Izu came up behind Sai and rested his hand on the center of Sai's bare back. Sai smiled and brushed the deep burgundy cords of Izu's hair back so he could kiss his cheek. His skin was warm and lightly coated with salt. The flavor lingered on Sai's lips until he flicked it away with his tongue. Sai breathed in the familiar scent of his *syrai*, and it soothed him a little, but not enough to allow him to hide his melancholy from his friend of so many years.

"Sai, what is it?" Izu asked, grazing the rungs of Sai's ribs with his fingertips. "You seem so far away."

Sai breathed out a soft laugh, remembering when he'd said those same words to Yarrow as the mage stared off. Sai could finally understand how Yarrow had felt. "I'm fine. Just lost inside my head, I suppose. Thinking back, I wish I had never sailed this way. I wish I had never set foot on that barbarian shore."

"But you did, so why worry over it now?" Izu asked, resting his chin on Sai's shoulder and winding his arms around Sai's waist. "What made you go back, anyway?"

"It called to me," Sai said. "When I dropped Tam Duncan and Tam Sasha at that port, I had a strange feeling about it, so I didn't go ashore. Then… I don't know. It just sort of stayed in my thoughts. I couldn't stop wondering what marvels waited in that savage place. What had I passed up seeing or taking? It wouldn't leave me alone until I went back. The ships there are like leaky tubs, so easy to loot and raid, and our little boy could outmaneuver them. Even the Selindrian ships were so loaded with riches they were like chasing a pregnant cow."

"But, *syrai*, it's easy enough to intercept the land people's laden boats when they pass close to the mouth of the river. There's no need for us to sail back to the shore of Johmatra if it's troubling you."

"It's strange," Sai said, relaxing back against his friend as he tried to find the words to explain his heart to Izu. A white seabird dipped toward the water's choppy surface and plucked a writhing silver fish up in its talons before flying off with a shrill call. Sai watched it until it blended with the puffy white clouds off to the ship's starboard side and disappeared. "It isn't the treasure calling me back this time. Sweet Emir, I never thought I would say anything like this, but what those bastards are doing to our people isn't right. If we don't do something about it, who will? Yarrow's cousin's fancy knights? They don't care about the people of the sea."

"It's quite a risk to take with little chance of reward," Izu said. "And it will be so much work. *And* we're as likely as not to get killed. We could just go home to the Twenty-Nine, lie on the beach, pass the *muri-ku*, and forget about it."

"You've seen them," Sai said. "They are our people; they're Emiri. Those barbarian sons of whores cut off all their hair, they chain them, beat them, burn them, and cut them. Leave them to be pecked to death by birds and suffer for days before dying. Do you think they return their bodies to Emir when they're gone? How are they supposed to find rest on dusty land? And the ones left alive! Every day they have to wake up and perform the same dull toil. Day after day, with no end in sight, no change. Can you imagine how terrible that would be? Can you really just forget about it?"

"I'm not sure what we can do," Izu said.

"I have been thinking about it a great deal," Sai told him. "If we can steal the cloth and jewels from the barbarians' ships and outrun and escape them, then why can't we steal our people away?"

"What will we do with them?" Kin had climbed down from the riggings to join their conversation. He wore a much-mended pair of heavy canvas trousers and little else besides the jewelry that sparkled against his deeply tanned skin. Ropes of dark hair swayed and brushed the sides of his waist as he walked.

Sai shrugged. He hadn't planned that far in advance. "I suppose we'll take them back to the Twenty-Nine."

Kin nodded. "This is important to you, Sai?"

"Yes."

"Then let's get ready to show these dirt-bound bastards what they get for trifling with the children of Emir," Izu said. "We should reach Johmatra by sunset if the winds stay steady."

His prediction proved correct, and Sai could see the fuzzy suggestion of the foreign shore just as the sun balanced on the surface of the water, turning the sky to a swirl of orange and rose and the sea to molten gold. The edges of the billowy clouds lit up as if on fire, bright against the darkening firmament. Sai could almost feel the heat of the day receding as the sun sank into the water, all the warmth and light bleeding out of the world and dripping off the edge. It made him even more pensive, made him want to drink away his worries and spend the time until dawn in his cabin with Izu and Kin. Instead, he went to the helm to guide his ship toward the harbor, but flashes of light and mushrooms of smoke near the shore made him stop with his hand resting on the smooth, wooden peg. He turned to Izu and Kin. "Drop the sails."

After they'd done as he asked, they came to join him at the helm. "What's going on?" Kin asked.

Sai pointed and squinted to try to make some sense of the fire and smoke. The growing gloom made it hard for him to see much more than hazy shapes, and he took a distance glass—a hardened leather tube with a lens at each end—from a loop on his belt. Looking through it, he saw a trio of ships, probably Selindrian, based on the silhouettes, facing off against four of the heavy round native ships. Sai thought he saw arrows sailing back and forth between them, just little flickers of silver. "I think they're fighting," he said to his companions without looking away. "The land people from Selindria and the barbarians. I don't think we should get in the middle of it."

An arc of flame shot from one of the Johmatran ships. When the sail of one of the Selindrian vessels caught fire, it allowed Sai to see more clearly. The barbarians shot gout after gout of fire at their enemies, and at first Sai thought it was magic; he'd seen mages conjure similar flames. Looking closer, he noticed a harpoon-like device on one of the barbarian ships. Instead of firing wooden shafts, it shot some sort of liquid. Just as the fluid left the iron tube, a spark at the end of the strange contraption set it alight. This time, the bright trail missed its intended mark and landed in the water. Sai couldn't believe what he saw next: whatever the savages had fired from the end of that weapon spread over the surface of the sea. Emir was actually burning!

"I have to have one of those," Sai said to himself. Such a weapon would make him practically unstoppable. He and his *syrai* would be able to loot anything they wished and no one would be able to stand against them. Besides, if he intended to face these Johmatran bastards, he needed weapons to equal theirs. The flames spread out over the surface of the sea and began climbing the hull of one of the Selindrian ships. The sailors hurried to the rail with pails, but they couldn't douse the white-hot blaze quickly consuming their vessel. Sai's heartbeat raced and he tingled with excitement. Fire that water couldn't extinguish! And it wasn't magery; anyone could use it!

Just when Sai thought he'd never see anything so miraculous if he lived another five hundred years, the savage sailors brought out a catapult and began loading the sling with what Sai assumed were the typical boulders and iron balls. They sailed in an arc, cutting trails through the thick smoke surrounding the ships. Something happened when they struck the deck of one of the Selindrian vessels: they blew apart somehow, and the impact shattered the mast like a brittle twig and tore huge openings in the hull. A second volley of the terrifying projectiles effectively tore the Selindrian ship in half. The helm and stern angled toward the sky, and the dark water burbled and bubbled as the ship began to sink. Sailors from the other Selindrian vessels hurried to throw ropes to their countrymen, and those who couldn't manage to make it aboard the other ships dove into the burning tide.

With their combination of liquid fire and exploding boulders, the barbarian sailors destroyed all three of the larger, sturdier, and faster Selindrian vessels in less than an hour. As the smoke began to clear, Sai could see no evidence of those doomed ships except for a few splintered boards or pieces of rope tossed about in the foam. Sai had been so enthralled with what he'd seen he'd forgotten about the distance glass pressed to his eye, and he lowered the leather tube and rubbed his face. "Emir's tits," he said to his companions. "Did you see that?"

"I saw fire shooting through the air, and ships ripped apart," Kin said softly. "I thought these foreign barbarians killed mages. What but magic could have done that, though?"

"Not magic," Sai said, gripping Kin's hand. "They had weapons that did it all: a tube that shot liquid fire. Fire that burned on the surface of the sea and couldn't be doused! And a catapult that flung boulders that blew apart when they hit the decks of the other ships. They were just devices! Anyone who possessed them could use them, and I mean to possess them."

"How?" Izu asked.

"How do you think?" Sai said, winking at his beautiful partner. "I'm— we're going to take them. Now, let's follow those barbarian ships and see where they drop anchor. Keep a good distance; we don't want them to notice us. Imagine what we'll be able to do when those weapons are ours! Ships will hand over their cargo without a fight if they think we have the liquid fire or the exploding rocks. Imagine how much gold we'll make selling them to the other *mir* around the Twenty-Nine."

"With weapons like those, we won't have to worry about the land-bound king driving us from our islands," Kin said.

"Exactly." Sai returned to the helm and guided his ship east along the coast of Johmatra, trailing the three barbarian ships until they moored a few miles down the coast, in a small harbor removed from the city. He carefully stayed clear of the shaft of light thrown from the round tower a little way inland on a bluff. He and his companions waited, and after several hours passed without any movement on or around the foreign boats, Sai carefully steered his fleet little vessel alongside one of them.

Sai and Izu slipped into their leather tunics and strapped their sword belts around their hips. Kin moved around the ship, checking the sails and riggings so everything would be ready in case they had to make a hasty exodus. When they'd finished their preparations, Sai took a large crossbow from a hatch on the deck and fired a thick bolt with a rope attached. It whizzed through the foggy air and found purchase in the mizzenmast of one of the Johmatran ships. Sai wedged the crossbow securely between the rails of their ship and gave it a tug to make sure it wouldn't move. After waiting a few moments to see if anyone noticed, Sai looked at Izu and nodded once. They had done this before, and his *syrai* knew how to move quietly and get what they were after.

Hand over hand, Sai moved along the taut rope with Izu following behind him. As soon as their feet touched the deck of the barbarian ship, Sai hurried to the mechanism that had spouted the liquid fire. It was simpler than he'd expected, little more than a metal tank, a bellows, an iron tube, and a bit of flint to light the liquid when it squirted it out. It was bolted to the boards of the other ship, and Sai knew just by looking at it that he couldn't cross the rope back to his ship while carrying it. It didn't matter; the construction was simple and he could recreate it easily enough. He could also build a catapult. They needed the burning liquid and the bursting rocks.

Sai tapped Izu on the elbow and jutted his chin toward a hatch leading below deck. He opened it, and the two of them dropped silently into the gloom, which reeked of fetid water and unwashed men. Sai would never understand what the dry-feet had against bathing in the sea while on a voyage. A few lanterns swaying from the rafters allowed Sai to see, and being Emiri, he easily acclimated to the rocking of the boat. The vessel was primitive: a hollowed-out bowl that relied as much on the oars protruding from the hull as the winds in its sails. Sai shook his head—Only these dusty pigs could turn sailing into toil. Men slumbered in hammocks between the paddles, and Sai and Izu crept quietly past them. Near the stern of the ship, they found what

Sai had hoped for: ceramic barrels full of the liquid fire and wooden crates containing the exploding rocks. When Sai knelt down to examine the boulders, he found they were actually clay orbs coated in pitch. Fuses made of oil-soaked rope extended from the heavy balls.

Sai leaned close to Izu and whispered: "Go back to our boat. Lower the dinghy. There's too much here for me to carry across the rope."

"*Syrai*, will you be all right on your own?"

Sai nodded and pressed a kiss to Izu's lips. "Go, and quickly."

The other man hurried off as Sai filled his arms with the round explosives. He snuck carefully past the sleeping sailors and up the ladder to the deck. Thank merciful Emir, Izu waited in the rowboat when he reached the foreign ship's railing. Since he couldn't just drop the clay balls without the danger of them bursting, Sai loaded them into a coarse pouch he found, probably an empty grain sack, and tossed it into his *syrai's* open arms. Quietly, taking his time, Sai made three more trips below deck and passed all of the clay orbs he could carry to Izu. Lowering the barrels of liquid fire proved more difficult. When Sai dropped the first one down, it almost knocked Izu over and practically capsized the dinghy. Afterward, he tied ropes around the ceramic canisters and lowered them slowly, though he hated risking the time it took.

The dinghy rode low in the water, piled with ten barrels of liquid fire and dozens of the exploding clay orbs. Izu waved his hand, motioning for Sai to climb down the rope and join him in the rowboat. Sai held up a finger. He had seen one more thing in the ship's hold he wanted to get his hands on: a small chest containing bags of various powdered minerals. He suspected they were the components of either the explosives or the liquid flame. Stealing the weapons was well and good, but knowing how to make them would be better. Sai stalked quietly back across the deck and lowered himself into the hatch. He passed the snoring sailors and made his way to the stern, where the chest sat next to some papers, bits of armor, and a few swords on a rack. Though he couldn't read the strange symbols scrawled across the parchment scrolls, Sai rolled them up and stuffed them inside his vest. Then he picked up the wooden box. It was small enough for him to tuck it under one arm and use the other to climb the rickety ladder back to the deck. He was just about to open the hatch when someone grabbed his ankle.

Sai swore under his breath and tried to tug his leg free from the grip of the big bald sailor. The man barked out some words in a language Sai didn't understand, and slowly the other men began to rise from their hammocks and retrieve the weapons they'd stored beneath them. Sai twisted around to face his enemy, then wrenched his leg back as hard as he could, releasing it from the burly seaman's grip. Then he drew back and kicked the man in the chin with his heel, sending him staggering and toppling on his back. Sai hurried from the hold and sprinted to the railing.

He tossed the chest down to Izu. "Get back to our ship, and hurry! Help Kin ready the sails. We're going to want to get out of here!"

"What about you, *syrai*?"

"I'm going to make it a little harder for them to follow us," Sai shouted. There was no reason to be quiet now, after they'd been discovered. Besides, the barbarians wouldn't understand Sai's language. "But before I do, I need you to put some distance between our ship and these."

Izu nodded and began rowing furiously, churning up white foam in his wake. Sai hurried back to the weapon that shot the liquid fire just as the half a dozen men who'd been sleeping below emerged onto the deck. With a great effort, Sai turned the device on its axle and pointed it toward the main mast. It was much heavier than it looked, and he grunted with exertion, his bare feet slipping on the polished deck, but he managed to aim the weapon straight at the main sheet. He pumped the bellows and pulled back the lever on top of the iron tube. With a soft swish and a few clicks of the flint, the liquid fire erupted from the chute, and the canvas sail became a wall of flame. Sai couldn't help hooting and giggling as the men who'd been closing around him hurried to open sacks and throw what looked like sand on the blaze.

The fire spread across the rigging, and in minutes all the sheets burned. One of the sailors rang a bell, probably to alert the other vessels. "Time to go," Sai said under his breath. Flames carpeted the deck now, and he didn't want to be aboard when they reached the remaining fuel and explosives stored below. He drew his thin curved sword and ran for the portside railing. Kin and Izu had already put a good distance between their ship and the burning vessel, just as Sai had hoped they would.

Three of the barbarian sailors blocked his way, two of them brandishing nasty spears with jagged edges. The other held a leather whip with rusty metal hooks attached to the three long lashes. A loud crack resounded as he flicked it at Sai's ankles, but Sai jumped and avoided it. He didn't even want to think about those barbs, longer than his fingers, embedding in his flesh. These men stood between him and the bosom of sweet Emir, and he had to get by them. He would be safe when he made it into the water; no way could these bulky dirt-walkers swim faster than an Emiri.

One of the men growled out some guttural words and swiped at Sai's belly with his spear. Sai stepped back just in time, and the serrated blade only tore through his leather vest. The other man stabbed at his right side, and Sai thrust his sword, making contact with his enemy's upper arm and drawing a spurt of blood. Turning quickly, he drove his small fist into the other man's broad nose and felt the bridge crack. Sai tried to shoulder past the two spear-bearers and dive into the waiting arms of the ocean, but the whip whizzed through the air, and one of the hooks opened a deep gash down Sai's forearm. Thank Emir, it didn't catch in his flesh, but the pain distracted him long enough for the man with the broken nose to seize his left arm. Sai pirouetted and plunged his sword into the man's chest just below the globe of his shoulder, and then he kicked him in the groin. The whip cracked again, and this time one of the barbs lodged in the muscle of Sai's waist, buried deep in the dense flesh. The man holding the handle gave it a tug, yanking Sai toward him and making Sai screech at the agony. The other man pressed the point of his spear between Sai's shoulder blade, driving him even closer to the whip wielder.

"Damn." When Sai tugged at the hook, he just seemed to bury it deeper. From the corner of his eye, he saw two other men coming toward him. He had to get off this burning heap. It was about to collapse and disappear beneath the surf, if the flames didn't reach the exploding balls and blow them all halfway to the stars first.

Sai swiped with his sword, severing the lash of the whip and freeing himself even though the barb stayed embedded in his side. He would worry about it later. He slashed again, this time opening a wide gash across the man's belly. The sailor with the spear seized a handful of Sai's hair and threw him to the deck. He lifted his weapon and thrust it down at Sai. Sai rolled just in time to avoid being skewered, and as he did, he swung at the man's leg and landed a lucky hit on the sensitive back of his ankle. He howled and doubled over, and Sai stood, stepped onto the man's back, pushed off, and dove over the railing and into the sea.

Blood-warm black water closed over him, and salt stung his wounds as Sai angled downward and swam hard. He wanted to be deep beneath the sea and as far away as possible when that ship blew. After reaching around to stow his sword in his belt, he kicked with all his might and propelled himself through the surf. Above him, the flames spread like the appendages of some strange beast over the surface of the water, casting eerie, wavering shadows and making it hard to gauge distance and direction. Sai swam until his lungs nearly burst, and then he surfaced and gulped down air. Looking over his shoulder, he saw the enemy ships blazing, sending thick, winding columns of smoke into the sky, less than half a mile behind him. Sai turned away and stroked along the surface of the ocean, toward the black silhouette of his beloved boat, backlit by a rosy half-moon probably three or more miles away.

Sai was heaving and exhausted by the time he reached his ship and caught a loose rope dangling from the starboard rail. He shimmied up it easily—he'd been swimming and climbing ropes almost as soon as he could walk—and swung his legs over the rail. A healthy wind came from the northeast, filling the sails and pushing their fleet little boat just where Sai wanted to go, toward the southern coast of Espero and then back home.

Kin left the helm and Izu dropped lightly from the rigging. They hurried to clutch Sai's hands and make sure he hadn't been injured.

"You're bleeding," Izu said, bunching up Sai's tunic and wincing when he saw the hook embedded in his waist. "Sweet Emir!"

"It's not as bad as it looks," Sai said. "Though it does hurt like a bitch. And it has backward barbs on it, just like a fishing hook. You'll have to cut it out of me."

"Come sit down, *syrai*," Kin said, leading Sai to a stack of cushions piled on the deck and then helping him recline on his side. He cut the leather around the barb to expose the injury while Izu opened a clay jug of *muri-ku* and pressed it to Sai's lips.

The sting at the back of Sai's throat, the heat in his belly, and the way his muscles went slack helped him to relax as Kin used a small dagger to excise the hook. It still hurt, though, and Sai turned to Izu to distract himself.

"We sure gave those savage sons of whores a good kick to their wrinkled sacs," he said through teeth clenched against the pain.

"That we did, *syrai*," Izu said before taking a deep pull from the jug. "Do you still want to try to rescue some of our people?"

"I think we should go home," Sai said. "If any of those men survived, they might be looking for me. I doubt they see many free Emiri, and especially not many with the stones to walk onto their clunky ships and steal their weapons from under their noses. I don't like the idea of getting boxed in by their ships and set on fire. I think we should return to the Twenty-Nine for a while, sell some of these weapons, and find a way to build the others into our boat so we'll be ready for the bastards. And then we'll come back and give them another black eye. What do you think?"

"I think that's a good idea," Izu said, smoothing the ropes of hair out of Sai's face and making the beads and shells adorning his tresses clatter softly.

"Damn it," Sai said. "I took some papers. I thought they might tell more about how these weapons are made or what goes into the liquid fire, but I guess I lost them when I had to swim for it. That's what we really need—the knowledge to make the orbs and mix the burning liquid up ourselves. When we come back, we should try to find the formula and get a hold of it."

"I think we should tell the other *mir* and their crews around the Twenty-Nine about this place—how to get here and what's going on. What they're doing to our people." Kin dabbed at Sai's wound with a clean piece of cloth, and then he wove a strand of clear filament through the eye of a fishbone needle. "As you said, the ships are slow and easy to raid."

Sai sucked in air as the needle pierced his skin, and then he released the breath with a laugh. "Easy, or so I thought until I saw what they could do tonight. At least they're still slow, and they don't look to me like they'd hold together on the high seas. It makes for an assured escape. After all, it's not like they can follow us back to the Twenty-Nine. Not if they can't sail on the open ocean."

Just then, the barbarian ship exploded, flinging chunks of burning debris high into sky. Sai held Izu's hand as he watched what looked like a shower of falling stars, and he laughed out loud. Moments later, the ship next to it blew up, and the impact reached their ship even miles away, lifting it on the swell of wave after high wave.

Kin looked up from his sewing as the ship pitched from side to side. "Yes, I think the impression we've left them of what free Emiri can do will stay with them for some time."

Sai smiled as he watched the fire on the dark water. It was beautiful. "I'm not done yet."

Chapter
Fourteen

GARITH laughed out loud when the towers of Eirion-Vayl appeared in the distance, the setting sun striking the western walls and making the fortress look like some palace carved from gold in an old story about Fane. "Goddesses be praised," he said to himself. "We'll make it home in time for dinner."

When he looked over his shoulder, he saw Sander frowning, his blue-green eyes wide and wet.

"My friend?" Garith asked softly. "What's troubling you?"

"I'm glad we were victorious, Your Majesty, but this hunt cost us dearly. I can't help thinking of those men who will never again look on these walls. I can only pray to the sisters that the beast's heart cures the queen, or it will all have been for nothing."

"I know." Garith wanted to reach over and squeeze Sander's hand, but of course he couldn't. How would he acclimate to not being able to touch him after sleeping next to him, learning the feel of his body and the wonderful sensation of Sander's hands on him? But he was being selfish, thinking of his lust when men had died and his queen lay languishing in bed because he had bothered with her so soon after bearing their daughter. "Let's ride. We're only about ten miles from home."

He kicked his horse's sides and urged it into a canter. Sander stayed beside him, his hair whipping around in the cold wind and his cheeks nipped a lovely bright pink. Before long they reached the gates, and the guards and soldiers flung them open. Garith and Sander dismounted and handed their animals off to servants. Then they waited for the other riders and the carts carrying their supplies—and the remains of their fallen comrades—to catch up. Garith went to the wagon carrying the awrythe's heart and carefully lifted the locked metal box. The sun dropped behind the western wall, and the servants began lighting the torches in their metal casings. The ancient stones turned from sparkling gold to sooty orange striated with shifting shadows.

"What will you do now?" Sander asked.

"Take this to the kitchen," Garith said. "Take an hour-long bath. Visit my wife and daughter. Then I think I'd like to speak to the armorers here. I've been thinking of a way to honor those men who fought beside me against this creature, and I had the idea to commission a sword for each of them, something sturdy and practical but with a awrythe's head on the handle, maybe. What do you think, Sander? I owe them so much. Especially the ones who didn't survive. In their cases, I'd like to present the swords to their families. Maybe one day their sons can wield them and remember their fathers were heroes."

"I think that's a fine idea," Sander said, stepping closer to Garith so he could speak softly into his ear. "And I think you are the noblest, most compassionate, and most unselfish of men. It is my sincere honor to serve you. Any other king would see those men's sacrifice as his due as their ruler. You… are extraordinary."

Tam Wyeth rode into the courtyard and looked down at them, reminding Garith of the trouble the young knight could cause for them. He stepped away from Sander, though he felt like he left his heart in Sander's gloved hand. Everything depended on whether the creature's heart healed the queen. If it did, Garith would be seen as a valiant hero, and no one would believe Wyeth's accusations. If it didn't work, people would see only the gold he'd wasted on the expedition and the men who'd died for nothing. He would stand accused of seeking help from a heathen superstition instead of turning to the goddesses. If that happened, everyone at court would clamor for more slander to heap upon him. He supposed he wouldn't know until the organ had been prepared and given to Queen Cothryn.

Garith entered the castle through a small side door normally used only by servants. Sander followed a few steps behind him as he descended a narrow staircase into the dark and smoky kitchens. At this hour of the early evening, servants filled the cavernous underground room, rushing back and forth to prepare the evening meal. In their haste, few of them even realized their king had come into the kitchens. Garith found the portly grease-smeared man who commanded the staff and handed him the metal chest. "My knights have slain the awrythe. Here is the beast's heart. Have it prepared at once and delivered to Queen Cothryn in her chambers, with the instructions that she is to eat as much of it raw as she can. Save the rest and bake it into a pie or something for her to eat at a later time. This heart is precious, and I don't want any of it wasted."

"Yes, Your Majesty," the pudgy cook said as he took the box from Garith and carried it to a butcher's block.

"Only time will tell, now," Garith said as he and Sander left the kitchen and ascended to the castle's main floor. He stopped the first group of servants he saw and instructed them to ready a bath in his suite of rooms and another in Sander's chamber. He paused at the foot of the winding stair that would lead him up to his living quarters and turned to Sander. They hadn't even left each other's presence yet, and Garith already missed him, missed the way he didn't have to put on an act when they were alone. "I'll come and find you after I spend some time with the queen, shall I? We can go to the armory and speak to the smiths together."

"I would like that, Your Majesty."

"I suppose I should also track down one of my stewards so we can plan a feast and a ceremony to present the swords. Goddesses willing, it will double as a celebration of the queen's return to health, but either way, those men—"

"By the holy sisters, here you finally are!" Tam Vartanan, one of Garith's advisors, interrupted as he rounded a corner, flanked by a quartet of high-ranking knights and generals. The old counselor's default scowl was firmly in place on his sagging face. "You have some very urgent matters to attend to after your absence, Your Majesty. This has not been the most convenient time for you to take a hunting trip, I'm afraid. I will expect you in the library in an hour's time."

"What?" Garith said, stunned. "You make it sound like I've been away on a holiday. I have not seen my wife or daughter in weeks or had a proper bath or a meal that wasn't cooked over a campfire. I'm sure whatever you need to tell me can wait until after breakfast tomorrow."

"No, my king, it certainly cannot," said one of the older knights. "To put these matters off could cost us all very dearly. To put them off could cost you your crown and cost you the alliance you have forged. Cost us our way of life. I am a simple soldier, Your Majesty. I have never been anything more. I hope you can trust me not to exaggerate."

"Yes, of course," Garith said, fear coursing like icy venom through his veins, pumping out the warm feelings of victory and returning home. "What exactly is going on?"

"Many things," Vartanan said. "They should not be discussed here in the hallway, where anyone could hear. Meet us in an hour."

"I will be there as soon as I can clean up and change my clothes." Garith tried to look regal and in control until Vartanan and the others turned and left. Then he leaned against the ancient stones of the wall and mopped the sweat from his brow with the back of his hand. "Goddesses, what now? What more? Sander?"

"Garith…. My king. I don't know. I will stand beside you through anything. It isn't much of a reassurance, but it's all I can offer."

"It's all the reassurance I need," Garith said, noting the pain behind Sander's eyes and knowing it hurt Sander to watch him suffering and to feel like he could do nothing to assuage him. "There is no reason to let our imaginations run wild until we hear what they have to say."

Sander nodded, and the two of them started up the steps. Just before they stepped onto the landing of the third floor, where both of them lived, Garith checked to make sure they were alone and quickly brushed his lips across Sander's cheek, enjoying the scratchy texture of his whiskers and the wonderful taste of his sweat. Sander stroked Garith's cheek with the back of his hand and kissed the tip of Garith's nose. The regret in his eyes mirrored Garith's own longing as they pulled away from each other.

On their way to their quarters, they passed the queen's rooms. Garith couldn't believe how many people had gathered in the hallway: maidservants, midwives, healers, and at least half a dozen priestesses of Keltha, a daughter of the Mother Goddess and the patroness of women in childbirth. The women, in their light blue robes and white scarves covering their hair, sat in a circle, holding hands around something burning in a censer. Sander buried his face in his elbow and choked at the acrid fumes. "What in the goddesses' names is that horrible stench?"

Lyorne hurried through the throng, wiping her plump red hands on her apron. "Tam Lysander, show some respect! The priestesses are burning the afterbirth of white heifers to ask for Keltha's blessing on the queen's pregnancy."

"Disgusting," Sander muttered.

"It is an obscure custom, but no more obscure than slaying an awrythe. I understand you two should be congratulated. The hunt was a success?"

Garith nodded. "Lady Lyorne, who are all these people?"

"The priestesses, Your Majesty. Healers and midwives. That young man is a follower of Ilverus, a deity of potions and elixirs. A priestess of Laud has even come out of isolation to be here." The old nurse pointed to what looked like a skeleton propped in the corner and covered in a shroud of cobwebs. Garith could hardly believe his eyes when the frail woman managed to get to her feet; she didn't look like she could possibly possess the strength.

She came to stand in front of Garith and pushed off her tattered, gossamer hood. Garith couldn't tell if her hair was gray with age or the dust of the road. Likewise, it was impossible to tell whether the deep network of lines covering her pale, papery skin came from her years or from the self-imposed deprivation she suffered in service to her goddess.

"The Thirteen Sisters are punishing you for your wickedness, Garith, son of Agarick. Laud herself has told me of your sins. Yours, and those of your harlot queen."

"How dare you!" Sander gripped the hilt of his sword. "I should run you through! This man is your king and the virtuous woman you slander is your queen!"

"For now," she said in a voice like the wind in the frozen plains grass, staring at Garith with rheumy gray eyes. "If you had any wisdom or sense, you would let that vile woman and the abomination in her belly die, and then you would throw yourself at the mercy of the goddesses and beg them to forgive your foul misdeeds. Perhaps then they will see fit to let you keep your toy crown, you ridiculous child."

"That's enough," Sander said, drawing his weapon. "I don't care who you are. I won't listen to this. Get out of here before I cut you in half, you ugly old witch."

The priestess turned and limped slowly away, cursing Garith's knight under her breath. The maids and servants stared at their king and his guard in sheer horror. No one, not even a king, spoke to a priestess of the goddesses that way. Word of what Sander had done would spread as the servants gossiped, and Garith wondered if he would be expected to reprimand his friend. Well, he wouldn't do it. He wouldn't scold Sander even mildly for defending him with so much passion. Sweet Sisters, the woman had called his wife—*the queen*—a whore!

Garith hauled in a shaky breath and tried to calm himself. "Lyorne, why are all these people in my home? Who brought them here?"

At first the old woman looked confused, then afraid; afraid to speak to Garith. She leaned in and said, "Of course you wouldn't know, my king. You have only just returned. Queen Cothryn's mother arrived a few days ago, and she brought these people with her. I'm afraid the queen's mother did not feel you were doing enough to restore her daughter's health."

"What? I love Cothryn! And my son in her belly! That is why I risked my life to hunt the awrythe. Many of my men died bringing it down."

"I am only repeating what I've heard from the Lady Ethelryn's servants, Your Majesty. The queen is her youngest and favorite child, after all, and she lost her husband not long after Cothryn's birth, so of course she's a bit overprotective. It's only natural."

"Well, let me in to see my wife," Garith said.

"That is not a good idea, Your Majesty," Lyorne said. "The queen is with her mother and a group of senior priestesses. They have been praying for hours."

"This is ridiculous," Garith said, getting angry. "I am the king of Selindria and Gaeltheon, and I don't need anyone's permission to see my wife!"

"I certainly won't stop you, Your Majesty," Lyorne said, "but you're a smart young man, and I'm sure you can see that interrupting the priestesses will not improve this situation, especially not after Tam Lysander's tirade."

"Tirade!" Though he finally sheathed his blade, Sander's cheek darkened with anger until his fair skin looked scalded.

"Peace, Sander. Very well. I'm going to bathe, and then I have to attend a brief meeting. Afterwards, I will be back to visit my wife and daughter, and I won't be turned away again, prayer or not." Garith turned on the ball of his foot and stomped off in the direction of his chamber with Sander following, his hand still on the hilt of his sword.

When they reached Garith's door, Garith grabbed Sander by the wrist and pulled him close until their chests bumped together. "Come with me. Bathe with me."

"My king… my Garith, I don't think that would be a good idea."

Garith kissed him quickly but hard, rubbing his tongue along Sander's teeth and then sucking Sander's bottom lip into his mouth. "Please. I need you. After everything's that's happened… everything that will happen…. Goddesses, I need something good to hold on to, to get me through this dreaded meeting. Before I can face Vartanan and the rest, I need half an hour to just be a man, to be with someone who doesn't expect anything from me. Sander, please."

"Goddesses, how can I say no to you? And don't think I'm doing you a favor or that I don't expect anything. I… need you just as much. I love you."

Garith smiled for the first time since he'd seen the spires of his castle rising above the frozen grassland. They would get through anything that might come. If he had Sander beside him, he could get through it.

Garith opened the door and found a tub of fragrant water steaming in front of the inglenook. He quickly dismissed the three servant girls who'd been waiting to assist him.

MANY more men filled the library than Garith had expected. He didn't even recognize all the knights in their polished armor or the aristocrats in their lush velvets and lace. He dutifully took his place at the head of the long table, and Sander stood behind him. For some reason, maybe something as simple as exhaustion, it angered Garith that his beloved friend, the man most loyal to him, had to stand while the fat nobles planted their wide asses on the padded benches. "Tam Lysander, please sit down. There's no threat to me here and therefore no reason for you to stand."

"Thank you, Your Majesty, but I will be fine."

"Sander, I insist." Garith motioned to an upholstered chair near the leaded glass window, and Sander sat in it without further argument. "Now, please tell me what is so pressing it could not wait until I have had a decent night of sleep. I would like to keep this meeting short, if at all possible. I had hoped to spend the evening with my wife and daughter, who I have not seen for weeks."

Tam Vartanan, sitting at Garith's right, cleared his throat theatrically and shuffled some papers and scrolls around, making Garith wonder if he moved slowly just to vex him. "Your Majesty, I do not even know where to begin."

"It's been less than a moon," Garith said. "What could possibly have happened?"

"Well, let us start with the good news," said a dark-haired young man. "I am Tam Firelle, tasked with overseeing the construction of the Royal Fleet. I am pleased to report that fifteen warships have been constructed so far, and we are in the process of training men to crew them. This man beside me is called Bartoum Astir, an accomplished seaman for more than a decade. I have employed him to teach our men to sail, and they've been making excellent progress."

"Captain Bartoum," Garith said, dipping his head to the big blond man. "I thank you for your service."

"It's my pleasure, Your Majesty. And if I may say so, the ships your people are building are real beauties. Real beauties indeed, m'lord."

"Your Majesty!" Tam Vartanan mock whispered to correct the ship's captain, but the other man ignored him.

"Excellent," Garith said. Maybe his advisors just wanted to catch him up on what he'd missed while he'd been away. "Fifteen ships in a moon's time seems like excellent progress indeed."

"Yes, Your Majesty," Tam Firelle said, "we are well ahead of schedule."

"And well over budget," Tam Vartanan coughed out.

"'Well over' might be a slight exaggeration," Firelle argued gently. "Granted, the wood we'd planned to harvest from along the southern banks of the river proved too difficult to obtain, so the lumber has to come from the north—"

"This venture is already more than five hundred gold sovereigns over budget, and you have plans to build another thirty ships," Vartanan interjected.

"We have to have this fleet!" Firelle said, smacking his open hand against the table. "Weren't you the one who advocated it so adamantly, Tam Vartanan? I think you will chastise the effort of any man but yourself. You are not so perfect, and you could not have done better than I have!"

"Let's just discuss this calmly," Garith said. "What is the reason why we can't cut down the lower-cost timber along the riverbank?"

"Because the filthy Emiri raid our lumber camps, and when there's nothing left for them to steal, they impede us just for sport!" Vartanan snarled.

Bartoum Astir got to his feet. "If I may, Your Majesty, I'd suggest purchasing the wood you need from the Emiri. They… er, intercept shipments coming from the barbarian lands, and that lumber is supple and strong. They'll likely sell it to you for a song, tam. I mean, *Your Majesty*."

"Buy stolen goods from the pirate scum?" Vartanan looked sick. "Disgraceful."

"It was just a suggestion, my fancy friend," Bartoum Astir said. "There's no need to insult me, and I won't tolerate it."

Garith raised his hand. "I'm pleased to hear about the progress on the fleet, and I will look into ways to cut the expenses. I will entertain any suggestions. Please write them down so I may peruse them when I have a bit more time and energy. Now, this cannot be the urgent matter keeping me from my family and my bed."

"No, it certainly isn't," Vartanan said. "I cannot imagine what we have done to invoke the wrath of the priestesses, but invoked it we have. They are speaking against you in their temples, Your Majesty, and vehemently. They claim the goddesses do not endorse your rule, that they do not recognize what we are calling the Blessed Epoch. They are preaching that your reign will destroy the kingdoms, and people are listening. They have gone so far as to call you a sinner, to say you're poisoning this nation. None of us know what could have provoked them. King Garith, I must ask. Is there anything we should know?"

"I can't imagine what you're talking about," Garith said. As he looked at the faces around the table, it all seemed surreal, as if he'd tumbled into a nightmare.

"The priestesses claim your wife's ailment is a punishment from the goddesses," Vartanan continued.

"Queen Cothryn is hardly the first woman to experience a difficult pregnancy," Garith argued.

"Be that as it may, Your Majesty, it is damning when combined with their other accusations. They claim you cannot drive back the Emiri because you do not have the blessing of the Thirteen."

"I cannot drive them back because I do not have the men or the gold I need!"

"It is much easier for the common people to blame divine wrath than comprehend vast sums of gold," Vartanan said. "Many of them are rallying to the priestess's banners, and they aren't alone."

"What do you mean?" Garith asked, sitting up straighter and gripping the edge of the wooden table.

"The priestesses, particularly those serving the Mother Goddess and Vestrafori, have put out a call for recruits. Peasants are lining up at the temples, and many of our own knights have switched allegiances."

"Do you mean to say they're building an army?" Sander said, his bench smacking the window frame in his haste to stand. "That's treason!"

"The priestesses have been quite careful, honorable knight," Vartanan explained. "They're calling the force the Defenders of the Thirteen, and while they're training and arming them, they claim they're doing so only to safeguard their temples. Even so, only a vapid idiot would miss the threat they're hanging over us. They have backed us into a corner. We can hardly fault those knights who pledge their swords to a higher calling, but at the rate they're going, the priestesses will have a force to rival our own. If not a greater one. And they're accepting commoners. They can hoard this militia until it's time to strike, and in the meantime, we can do nothing without appearing to undermine the goddesses."

Tam Firelle stood. "Your Majesty, these women are trying to pit you against the temples in the minds of the common people. It seems to me you should build a temple, or at the very least, donate some statues or fountains to the existing shrines. Let the peasants see you revere the goddesses."

"The problem being we have no money for statues and fountains," Vartanan said, "because of what we have spent on the construction of this damned fleet! There is a rift forming, Your Majesty, between those loyal to the crown and those who trust to the temple leaders. In the past, the temples needed the crown because the crown had the knights and soldiers, and the crown needed the priestesses because they swayed the hearts of the common people. We are facing a situation where the priestesses have an army of their own and no longer rely on the monarchy."

"What do you suggest I do?" Garith asked, looking at the men around the table. Almost every one of them looked down or away when he attempted to meet their gazes. "Fayelle's Fire is approaching. Will a grand and expensive gesture on my part prove my devotion to the sisters?"

"Possibly," Vartanan said. "Unfortunately you do not have the gold for an extravagant display. Not after what you've spent on your Royal Fleet."

"It doesn't have to be expensive," Sander said. "What if the king were to visit a series of shrines? It would cost very little for him to toss his twigs into a few fires each day, and the common people would see his piety. He could help out with the daily labors, just like one of them. I'll wager that will count for something, seeing the High King of Selindria and Gaeltheon splitting logs for the temple kitchens."

"Not a bad first step, I suppose," Tam Vartanan reluctantly agreed. "But it will do Garith far more good in the eyes of his subjects if his wife regains her health and delivers a healthy son. That would cancel out the priestesses' claims that the goddesses are punishing him by denying him progeny."

"The king has done all he can for his wife," Sander said. "He nearly lost his life slaying the awrythe."

"And if the creature's heart heals Her Majesty, Garith will be seen as a savior," Vartanan said. "If the cure fails, he'll look like a superstitious fool who wasted gold he does not have to spare. I must admit, a strong son would do much to allay the peoples' doubts about Garith's reign. It will provide them a sense of continuity, of security. And I reiterate that the priestesses' claims that the goddesses are denying the king an heir will ring false."

"In the meantime, I will visit as many of Fayelle's Fires as I can," Garith said. "Moreover, I will live simply, with just my guard to accompany me. I will depend upon the charity of my subjects for sustenance until the end of the virgin goddess's moon."

"Is this nonsense concluded?" An Esperon man with long dark hair and olive skin stood and came to the front of the room. The delicate beads at the end of his long sash rattled softly, and his braided leather sandals made no sound against the stone floor. "Forgive me. My name is D'Aurillian Mezzacorfii. I have traveled for weeks to be here, great and mighty king of Selindria and Gaeltheon. Espero has always been your ally, Your Majesty."

"Of course," Garith said, nervous. He hoped this young man didn't plan to say something about Tam Torkan Mellinger and the slab of stone that had started all this trouble with the priestesses. The old scholar had planned to take his discovery to Espero and show it to the mages there. "My mother is from Espero, and we still have family living there. I adored visiting the island as a boy."

"I am here because we need your help, King Garith," the delegate said. "We need it desperately."

"Go on," Garith told him.

"I don't know how much your mother has told you of our island, Your Majesty, but Espero has no military force. It has been generations since we have been attacked. The wards we place all around our islet keep most hostile forces from ever venturing near, and those few that make it through are usually little trouble to our mages. I'm sure you know Espero has many more magic-users than your lands."

Garith nodded. "And what has changed?"

"Many sailors have been traveling around our nation to the shores of Johmatra, now that the sea route has been discovered. It has been an adjustment for us, but one we have taken in stride. We are a hospitable people and have even welcomed the Emiri seafarers so long as they respect our laws. Just recently, the native people of Johmatra have constructed seaworthy vessels. At first only traders and explorers visited our shores, but the tales they told when they returned to their land has encouraged others to come— those serving the rulers of that savage place, soldiers and warriors. Furthermore, they have the knowledge to pass through our wards, and we suspect they have been somehow trained to face magic-users in battle."

"Are you saying you've been attacked?" Garith asked, horrified. The mages were a peaceful people, considered aloof and superior by some, but never aggressive.

"As far as we have been able to tell, great king, the rulers of Johmatra believe the right to wield enchantment should belong to only a select few. They think other mages are stealing power, using it up, and keeping it from those they feel deserve it. Their solution is to kill any they feel are not entitled to practice magic. Several of the smaller coastal towns, particularly those along the northeastern part of the island, have been decimated, destroyed to their last member, as they think every Esperon is a mage. Our ruling council has sent two parties of delegates to Johmatra in the hopes of negotiating, but neither of them has returned, and we are not optimistic."

"What are you hoping I can do for you?" Garith asked.

"The truth of the matter is Espero is unused to defending herself," D'Aurillian admitted. "The magic placed around our island has made it unnecessary for centuries. For the first time, we've encountered an enemy with the knowledge to dispel those wards. We need men who can fight: knights. Our mages are trying to protect our people, but we can't do it alone. Very few of us are trained in combat. I come before you to plead for men to help us put an end to these atrocities. Many of the people killed were children, Your Majesty. Babies in their cradles, even."

"Goddesses," Garith whispered. As much as he wanted to honor the alliance, to help protect the nation where half of his ancestors were buried, he barely had enough of a force to keep peace within his own borders, especially now that he had to prepare for the threat of the priestesses and the army they intended to raise. He hated to reduce it to a mere matter of figures, but the fact was there just wasn't any gold to help Espero. "I... sympathize with your situation, but my resources are spread thin here at home. I will need some time to speak with my generals and advisors to determine the best way to aid you."

"Of course. Thank you for hearing me out, Your Majesty." The young man was no fool, and he knew stalling and false reassurance when he heard it. He knew Garith had been careful to offer him absolutely nothing. His features fell with disappointment, and he dropped onto his bench as if he'd been stabbed in the belly.

"Is there any more business?" Garith felt exhausted down to his bones, his muscles so tense and tired they throbbed, and a sharp pain focused behind his eyes. When no one voiced any additional concerns, he said, "I have much to think about. Please leave me with my close advisors. I thank all of you for your loyalty and concern on my behalf, and I will meet with you in my hall tomorrow morning after breakfast."

As if Sander could read Garith's mind, he went to a cupboard, poured wine, and set the goblet down in front of him as the men filed past. Like a guard dog, Sander stood behind Garith's chair with his hand resting on the hilt of his blade, discouraging any of the knights or aristocrats from troubling Garith further. Many of them looked like they wanted to say more, and a few even opened their mouths to speak on their way toward the library door, but something about Sander's posture or countenance dissuaded all but D'Aurillian. The young mage in the brilliant, billowing blue robes clasped Garith's hand as he passed by, lifted it to his lips, and kissed one of the rings Garith wore. Garith's cheeks felt singed as he looked up and met the Esperon's dark, haunted gaze.

"I have lost my entire family: my parents, sister, young nieces and nephews, even the cousins and friends I grew up with in my small coastal village. I hope you will be able to help us, great king," D'Aurillian whispered. "Otherwise, I don't know what we'll do or what will happen to Espero."

"I will do everything I can," Garith said, and the promise sounded empty even to his own ears.

Soon most of the audience had left the library, and Sander closed the heavy double doors behind them and secured them with an iron bar.

Tam Vartanan spoke before Sander even had a chance to return to his bench. "Do I even need to mention that we have less than no gold to spend sending knights to Espero?"

"Are you suggesting we just leave those people to be slaughtered by barbarians?" one of the older knights asked. "Women and children?"

"I agree," Sander said. "How can we just stand by and let this go on?"

"Listen to me carefully, all of you," Vartanan said in an ominous tone. "For whatever reason, the priestesses of the Thirteen have chosen to make an enemy of this monarch. They have dug their heels in and taken a stance against King Garith. These women are no fools. They have been playing these games longer than any of us. Mark me on that if you hear nothing else I say. They have already used the queen's illness against the king, calling it a sign from the goddesses. They blame his ill favor for his inability to get rid of the Emiri. They are already criticizing how he spends his gold, and the sisters help us all if this last grandiose excursion to the Dairden Plains yields nothing. The fact of the matter is the people of Selindria and Gaeltheon mistrust the mages of Espero. Many see them as little better than heathens themselves. Imagine what the sharp tongues of those priestesses will twist it into if Garith sends men and money to aid them while the Emiri continue to overrun our shores and pillage *our* coastal towns."

"The Emiri are a nuisance," another knight said, "but they rarely kill except in self-defense. I have certainly never heard of an Emiri crew killing the residents of an entire village down to the children."

"They will overrun the southern coast if we do not drive them out!" Vartanan slapped the surface of the table. "Goddess-fearing people should not have to live alongside them. Their ways are worse than sinful, and they prey off people making an honest living."

"I won't argue with you," Sander said. "The Emiri must be dealt with, but I think we need to decide which is the more immediate threat. As a knight, the answer is clear to me. Innocents facing slaughter for no reason should be our primary concern."

"I will not point out that you are a simple guard, young man, and have no place voicing your opinion—"

Garith held up his hand. "Tam Lysander's opinion is welcome here if I value his counsel, which I do. In fact, I will listen to any man who thinks he can give me useful advice, and I want all of you to remember that. Noble blood does not always make a man practical, and common blood certainly doesn't make a man useless in my experience."

"Be that as it may," Tam Vartanan continued in a subdued tone, "there is no money to send knights to Espero. If you insist on aiding them, you must cut another of our endeavors: the fleet, our efforts to reclaim the land around the Kanda, the money we pledge yearly to the temples, or the guards employed to keep the roads safe and encourage trade. No matter which you choose, at least some of the priestesses will convince their flocks you have done so at their expense, to aid people they see as arrogant and impious."

"Are you saying they deserve this?" Garith asked. "Those Esperon children?"

"Of course not, Your Majesty," Vartanan answered. "I am only saying your people, molded by the words of the temple leaders, will see any money you spend as being taken out of their coffers, as food snatched from their children's mouths. At worst, the priestesses will turn this into another affront against the goddesses."

"I'll speak to the other knights," Sander said, passion coloring his cheeks in a way Garith now knew well and loved to see. "I will have messengers sent to the other castles asking for volunteers. I have to believe that I am not the only knight who believes protecting the innocent is the pinnacle of duty. I have faith at least some of those men will be willing to go to Espero without pay."

Garith was impressed. For the second time that night, Sander had proposed a simple solution to a terrible conundrum, had been able to see clearly what eluded seasoned knights and advisors.

Even Tam Vartanan argued without much enthusiasm. "Those men will still have to be fed and transported, and every soldier sent to Espero is one less to defend this kingdom should the priestesses decide to mobilize their army. It is one less against the Emiri and the warlords and mercenaries controlling the south shores."

"The cost will be greatly reduced if the men ask no salary and supply their own weapons," Sander said.

"Enough of this," Garith said. "Enough for tonight. I want to help the people of Espero if there is any possible way I can. I'll have to speak with my treasurers and assess our finances. I will have to consult records, but I simply cannot do it tonight. I have only one more question before I must retire or fall facedown on this table. Have the messengers I sent to Windust Castle returned?"

"They have, Your Majesty," one of the knights answered.

That relieved a little of Garith's tension. "Thank the goddesses. Are Bairn Duncan and my cousin Yarrow on their way here? With… with their associates? When will they arrive? I desperately need to speak with them. Will they be here within the moon?"

"I am afraid they will not, Your Majesty," Vartanan said. "The couriers returned from Windwake with the report that the bairn, your cousin, and their… the other one, rode off in the dead of night more than a month ago. Bairn Duncan even abandoned his pregnant wife. They have not been seen or heard from since, and not even the bairn's seneschal has any idea where they might have gone. Or when—indeed *if*—they plan to return."

"Damn it," Garith hissed. "Where are they when I need them? What could they be doing, and what will I do without them?"

"Garith, you're tired," Sander said, the warning plain in his tone. Garith was about to let his frustration and fear make him reveal too much. It would not do for Vartanan or any of the others to know why he wanted to summon Sasha. But what he most needed was someone who could step into the shadows, into the murky area between law and morality and cold, sharp necessity. He needed to know exactly what the priestesses planned, and goddesses forgive him for even entertaining the thought, to stop them if he had to. He needed a man whose sense of decency would not prevent him from murdering a servant of the goddesses, and he knew only one such man.

"I need to find him," Garith whispered to Sander when the others had been hurried out of the library. "I need Sasha, Duncan, and my cousin. Where could they be?"

Sander shook his head and worried his lower lip with his teeth. "I don't know that we'll find them until they want to be found. Garith, we have to assume we're on our own, at least for now, and we are surrounded by enemies. I can feel the danger against my skin, the same as when I step onto a battlefield. We need to be extremely cautious. I'm not sure if we can even trust the men who just left the room—not all of them."

Garith nodded and clasped Sander's hand, squeezing hard, desperate to feel his flesh and bone beneath his mail gloves. He wanted to tell Sander they'd prevail if they stood together, just as they had against the awrythe, but it seemed so futile. Everything felt hopeless. It was impossible to protect everyone. No matter how carefully Garith balanced everything, no matter how he moved grains of sand back and forth on his scales, he would never have enough to go around. Someone would be neglected, and someone would suffer.

"I wish I could help you carry some of this burden," Sander said.

"You do," Garith said, feeling a little better, a little less alone, when he looked up into Sander's wide sea-blue eyes. "I'd be crushed already if not for you helping me hold all this up. I have to ask you to do one more thing with me, and it won't be enjoyable."

"Of course, my king."

Garith laughed. "But I haven't even told you what it is yet."

"It doesn't matter," Sander answered.

"Well, then, I want to go to Queen Cothryn's chamber and forbid any priestess or servant of the temples to attend to her. Her mother will not like it, and I can only imagine the slander they'll hurl at us, but I don't want anyone but servants I approve bringing the queen her meals. I am loath to accuse the temples of... harming the queen, keeping her ill, as proof of the goddesses' disapproval of my reign, but I cannot take any chances. Goddesses, this is why I need Sasha! He would know if anyone... if anyone.... He would put a stop to it. Instead, I have to do it myself and face the wrath of Lady Ethelryn. I think I'd rather face the awrythe again. At least it didn't go straight for my manhood with every attack."

"We can't have your manhood threatened. It has brought me far too much happiness lately." Sander smiled and extended his hand to help Garith to his feet. "Come on, then, Garith. I'll protect you from your mother-in-law."

Chapter Fifteen

ROPES enforced with metal filament constricted around Sasha's limbs as he walked, the point of Corbin's dagger pressed to the small of his back. The other assassin had bound Sasha quite capably. If Sasha moved too quickly or fought against his restraints, they tightened around his wrists, elbows and throat, cutting off both his breath and the flow of blood. All Crimson Scythe assassins learned the art of binding, though few of them ever used it. Not often did one of the brethren have to deliver a mark alive.

Corbin brought Sasha to the safe house—one Sasha had visited before—and pushed him roughly past the threshold. When the door closed, Corbin ignored the cabbages on the countertops, the apples in the basket, and the smoked ham hanging from the rafters—all the things placed carefully to make the small cottage look like a normal home—and went to the western wall to touch the block that would open the doorway to the lower levels, to the clandestine hideout of the Crimson Scythe and the dungeons of Thalil's perverse pleasures.

Sasha let Corbin drag him down the stairs and into the light cast by crimson lanterns. He had to play along, had to act as though he couldn't pick apart his brother's knots. Sasha had played many roles in his service to the Dark and Beautiful One, and now he had to act the victim. Though his pride rebelled, Sasha kept his head bowed as he let Corbin tug him along by the fetters around his wrists.

The sanctuary was bathed in scarlet light. Fuzzy geometric swatches of red and black shifted and morphed over the padded velvet benches lining the dark paneled walls. Provocative paintings of nude young men with suggestively held swords and daggers hung between them. This sanctuary's obligatory statue of Thalil stood in the center of the room, carved from the black volcanic rock native to Espero. The Cast-Down god sat nude atop an elaborate column, one heel pulled to his groin and the point of a dagger just grazing the corner of his magnificent lips. Dozens of red candles burned on the carved skulls around the statue's base. In the low, shifting light, Sasha almost thought his master's lips curved upward when he stared at the statue's face.

Corbin pushed Sasha away, drew a dagger from his belt, and held it between his teeth as he knelt down before the idol. He lifted his wrist and nicked the inside on the edge of his blade. His blood fell in a thin stream and spattered Thalil's toes where his foot rested atop one of the skulls.

"Let me offer to him," Sasha said when Corbin stood and tucked his knife back into his belt.

The other assassin twisted his lip into a mocking, lopsided grin. "What right do you have?"

"As much as you," Sasha answered.

"Hmph." Corbin grabbed one of the ropes crossing over Sasha's chest and shoved Sasha in front of the statue. He drew his blade and slashed the back of Sasha's hand, cutting harder and deeper than necessary and severing one of the thick veins at the center of Sasha's hand.

Pain shot up Sasha's arm, though he didn't let it show on his face. A sheet of blood poured down his hand and dripped from the ends of his fingers. With his wrists tethered tightly in front of his groin, Sasha had difficulty getting close enough to the statue for his blood to touch it. Most of the blood dripped onto the candles and filled the room with a sickening smell. Sasha looked intently up into the stone face of his god, watching the flickering light skip across the solid-black orbs of his eyes. Strange shadows skittered across the polished stone of Thalil's face, deepening the darkness around his eye sockets and between his lips and playing with Sasha's mind. Steam blurred the statue's features as Sasha's blood evaporated over the flames.

I'm sorry, Sasha thought.

You'll make it up to me. The voice seemed to whisper next to Sasha's ear; he swore he felt warm breath against his skin. At the same time, the words caressed his entire body, moving over him like a silk sheet, cool, smooth, and catching against his raised pores. He shivered and fought not to reveal what he felt.

Master? I have only ever wanted to serve. Tell me what you will have me do, and I will do it.

In time.

Does that mean you have not forsaken me? I failed to offer you the prince, Garith, but I gave his father in his place….

An impressive murder, the voice said, reverberating through Sasha, making his insides tremble pleasantly. He barely even noticed himself getting erect. Sasha didn't know if it was some trick, or if Corbin had smacked his head against the wall harder than he'd thought, but it didn't diminish his absolute rapture at being complimented by his patron. He continued staring at the smooth face, hoping to commune further with Thalil, until another voice battered its way into his thoughts and dissolved the thin filament binding his mind to his master's.

"Well," said a woman in leathers much like Sasha's own. Her gray hair was pulled back from her lined, angular face. "I see you accomplished your mission, brother. None of us expected you to succeed."

"It seems you were wrong." Corbin lifted his hand and inspected his fingernails instead of looking at the master of the house.

"And his companions did not impede you?"

"They tried," Corbin answered.

"Very well," the woman said. "Someone will be here to collect the two of you within the next few days. Until then, this traitor is your responsibility. If he escapes, you will have failed in your sacred duty to Thalil."

"You need not worry," Corbin said.

"We shall see." The master of the house turned on her heel and disappeared down one of the hallways off the main chamber.

Corbin grasped the bonds over Sasha's throat and pulled him down another darkened passageway. They passed a few doors before Corbin opened one and pushed Sasha inside a small room. The other assassin had clearly been calling it home for quite some time; his alchemical equipment sat atop a chest of drawers, and some plants and fungi grew from the pots lining one wall. Corbin had arranged his knives and darts on a small round table next to a bowl of fruit and a few bottles of wine. One of the glass goblets still contained some burgundy sediment, and a half-eaten loaf of bread waited nearby.

After shoving Sasha into a corner, Corbin began picking apart the buckles of his armor. He shed his leather shirt and the hooded tunic beneath like a serpent and stood in only his snug trousers and boots as he began to unwind the wrappings from his stump. When he'd finished, he winced and massaged the remainder of his limb.

"It still pains you," Sasha observed.

Corbin spun and snarled at him, still clutching his diminished arm. "Don't be a fool. Your friend cut off my arm! Do you suppose it's a pleasant sensation?"

"But it should have healed by now," Sasha said. He'd hit a nerve, discovered a weakness in Corbin. Not only would he remember it, he'd try to push a little further and see what else he could learn.

"Yes, well, he didn't use an ordinary blade, did he? Now and then I still feel the phantom pains of his power—searing and freezing at once—and it… it is quite unpleasant. He left a few traces of his magic behind."

"I'm sure you'd like to make him pay for what he's done to you," Sasha pressed.

"He mutilated me!"

"Defending my life," Sasha said. "Did you expect him to let you kill me?"

Corbin sank down on the edge of the black iron bed draped in ebony and crimson gossamer. He rested one heel on his knee and began unbuckling his boot. "I cannot comprehend it. If he'd done it to save his own life, I would understand. Just like I can't understand a promising agent like you abandoning his mission. Is the lovemaking really so much better with them than with others? Enough to make you turn your back on your calling?"

Sasha dropped to his haunches in the corner. The ropes had started to chafe, and his muscles cramped from lack of movement, but he wouldn't give Corbin the satisfaction of seeing his discomfort. Thinking of Yarrow and Duncan proved a welcome distraction. "The lovemaking is extraordinary, but it's more than that. I don't know how else to explain it to you than to say the idea of living without them holds no appeal. If I cannot be with them, I don't care if I die."

"Ridiculous."

"I knew you would think so," Sasha said. "I would have felt the same not long ago, when I thought my heart was cold and dead. No matter what we're taught, the heart cannot just stop feeling. Yarrow and Duncan... they're everything to me."

Corbin finished undressing and stood unabashedly—and impressively—naked before Sasha. He was taller than Sasha, thin and lanky with long, willowy limbs. In the firelight, he looked like a marble statue.

"You put them before yourself?"

"Yes."

"Before Thalil?"

Sasha considered. "Yes."

"Then you truly are a traitor," Corbin said. "I should leave you bound and languishing on the floor. You're just a weak-spirited fool."

"Leave me here, then."

"No." Corbin hauled Sasha to his feet and picked apart the many knots, letting the rope coil on the floor between their feet. Sasha stretched and heard his bones popping, and then he began disrobing. His armor wouldn't save him now, so he might as well be comfortable. When he was naked, he and Corbin climbed into the bed, and Corbin pulled the cool, smooth sheets over them. He reached over and ran his fingertips down Sasha's waist, then over his belly and hipbone. "I don't suppose you'd let me fuck you."

"I don't think so," Sasha said. "Will you let me fuck you?"

"I might have at one time," Corbin answered, "but not now. I.... Am I still beautiful?"

"You know you are. It's beneath you to fish for me to say it." Sasha tried to get comfortable, but he found himself annoyingly aroused. His whole body tingled as sensation returned to the extremities Corbin's bonds had robbed of blood. Before he'd met Duncan and Yarrow, Sasha had regarded sex as either a means to manipulation or a pleasant way to pass the time. It meant more now, something deep and sacred he couldn't articulate, and he knew it would hurt his friends if he threw Corbin down on his belly and pounded him into the mattress as his body told him he should. Thalil, he wished he was alone so he could alleviate his own frustrations.

"I'm hurting," Corbin said, rubbing the pad of his thumb over Sasha's nipple. To Sasha's annoyance, his flesh budded to a hard bead. "I don't know if it's the danger we're in or our victory so far, but…. I'm willing to suck you, if you want. I'm good at it."

"No. I can't."

"Why?"

"Because it would hurt my friends to know I'd allowed that," Sasha said. "I don't want to cause them more pain than I already have. They've given up a great deal for me." He thought of the way Yarrow had resisted Sai even though they clearly wanted each other and had ample opportunity. Yarrow had declined to spare his partners anguish, and Sasha could, and would, do the same, even though his hard cock poked against his belly and his balls throbbed. Even though Corbin *was* beautiful, and their mutual dislike and competitiveness could make things quite interesting.

Rolling over, Corbin put his back to Sasha. "I'll just take care of myself, then, if you don't mind."

"Do what you need to do. I'm hardly modest."

Sasha also turned and pressed his back against the other assassin's as he took hold of himself. He felt Corbin's muscles bunching and lengthening against his own as both of them worked to relieve their tension. Corbin came with a muffled grunt, and Sasha followed him a few minutes later, thinking of Yarrow's flushed face and opened lips and Duncan's shy, vulnerable expression when he came. In his afterglow, Sasha wanted to spoon around Corbin and kiss him lazily, but he resisted. The practical part of him, the part that was Crimson Scythe, cursed himself for a fool for passing up what might be his last opportunity to lie with a man, to taste a man's skin and feel a man shuddering beneath his caresses. Death constantly looming over his shoulder had always made Sasha take pleasure where he found it, but he found he didn't want pleasure so much tonight as the security of the arms of the men he loved. By the Cast-Down, he missed them, and it hurt. It hurt in a way Sasha hadn't known he could suffer. He wouldn't pretend Corbin's warm, pale body was a substitute for what he really wanted.

The other assassin flopped on his back, sated. "Can I ask you a question, Sasha?"

"Why not."

"What did you intend to do after leaving the order?"

"Protect the men I love," Sasha said. "Destroy anything that threatens them."

"But after that." Corbin nestled a little closer to Sasha and rested his cheek against Sasha's head. "How did you intend to live? I mean, we aren't like them. We're killers. We stalk the shadows and take down our prey. We are harrow-wolves. Did you honestly intend to be a tame hound? Did you imagine the collar alone would make others forget what you are in your spirit?"

"I don't know."

"Did you think you could make yourself a part of their world, though? That you would ever be accepted?"

"No," Sasha admitted. "Not really. Not that I really want to be a part of all that foolishness. Most nobles are hypocrites, as I'm sure you know. It's nothing but ass-kissing and backstabbing."

"But not your Bairn Duncan?"

"No," Sasha said. "He is the purest, most honest, and most selfless man I've ever met. Before I knew him, nothing could have convinced me such goodness actually existed."

"Aren't the restrictions of such honor a weakness?"

"He manages."

"So it seems." Corbin rolled to his side and draped an arm over Sasha's ribs, tracing Sasha's protuberant bones with his fingertips. "And what about your mage? Do you have any idea what he holds inside? You can't. If you had any clue, you'd stay a hundred miles from him."

"No, I wouldn't. Yarrow is extraordinary, and I'm captivated by him. I have been since I first set eyes on him. What right do I have to judge him?"

"He'll destroy you," Corbin said, nuzzling his face against the side of Sasha's neck. "You have no idea...."

"It doesn't matter. I love him. Both of them. You haven't felt it, so you don't know how much you'd trade to keep it."

"You're a fool," Corbin murmured, drowsy "You've been trained against such weakness. They won't let you live, you know. The Crimson Scythe is feared because it never fails. Because no one we mark has a chance to survive. You changed those rules. They cannot let it stand. Even if you earn some sort of redemption, how will you live? You're a killer by nature. You can't be something you're not."

"I don't intend to be. The Crimson Scythe are not the only assassins in the world."

"Your lovers will be repulsed," Corbin said. "If they aren't now, they will be. You know I speak the truth."

"Maybe," Sasha said, yawning. "Or maybe you just want to make me feel alone and vulnerable. I have played these games, brother."

"Oh, I know. If only you'd play the games we both desire. Are you sure you won't let me fuck you, Sasha? I won't disappoint you."

"Go to sleep, Corbin." Sasha rolled away but didn't resist when Corbin curled around him. He tried to ignore his renewed erection, though thinking of Duncan and Yarrow only encouraged the heat coursing in his veins. Visions of their bodies writhing in pleasure above and beneath him tormented his thoughts and filled his dreams when he finally managed a fitful sleep.

PROBABLY three days later—Sasha couldn't be sure in the perpetual gloom of the sanctuary—three Whisperers arrived, accompanied by a dozen assassins. Sasha barely had time to count them as they spilled into the small room where Corbin kept him locked. The Whisperers, their faces hidden beneath heavy cowls, stood along the wall while the others hauled Sasha to his feet and bound him much more capably than Corbin had, with his hands pulled tight behind his back, and his arms wrapped all the way to his shoulders. His arms ached where the ropes nearly wrenched them out of their sockets, but Sasha stood stoic. His order detested any show of weakness and would exploit it. They moved so quickly and adeptly, Sasha saw little more than flashes of deep red leather and glints of polished steel. They tied a black scarf over his eyes and gagged him with a thick strip of leather that chafed the corners of his mouth.

Something warm, soft, and heavy, thick with the scents of musk and incense burned in the hideouts, fell over Sasha's shoulders and enfolded his chest. The dense material covered his head and brushed his cheeks and the bridge of his nose. The other assassins had likely covered him in a robe so his restraints and blindfold wouldn't attract attention. They had wrapped a rope around his neck and tethered it to one around his waist, forcing him to keep his head bowed as two of the assassins clutched his arms and pulled him through the darkness.

Sasha had to step carefully so he wouldn't tread on the hem of the robe as the assassins led him up the stairs. Soon he smelled the ham and cabbages in the kitchen, and then he felt cold, dry air on the small amount of exposed skin on his face. The hood of the cloak didn't cover everything, but the shadows it cast over his face would likely conceal most of the bonds unless someone came too close. His brothers wouldn't allow that even if some obtuse villager thought to try. It smelled like snow above the odor of the city, and somehow Sasha knew it was night even though he couldn't see. It felt like night, tasted like night, and it soothed him a bit to be embraced by his master's shadows.

I'm with you.

What? Sasha concentrated to perceive everything around him. Frost crackled beneath his boots, and the fragrance of hearth fires mingled with the distant scent of the river and the smell of the looming storm. He could even detect the aroma of the other assassins—leather and blood—though he couldn't hear their footfalls or the rustle of their clothing. Corbin, a few feet behind him, smelled distinctively of bitter herbs and a faint, sweet hint of decay. Sasha could hear the light breeze in the thatch on the roofs, the creak of the wooden structures, and the occasional slap of a shingle over a shop or the soft pads of a fleeing cat on the cobblestones, but he could find no trace of the soft voice he thought he'd heard.

They moved downhill, and before long the air grew colder and heavier. Beads of moisture collected in Sasha's hair and on the edge of his hood. The river. Sure enough, a gangplank bounced and squeaked beneath him as he walked, followed by the sturdy deck of a ship. He smelled wet rope and heard sails snapping.

"Take him," said a male voice off to Sasha's left. "He is still your responsibility."

"Understood." Corbin wrapped his long fingers around Sasha's bicep and pulled him away. "Stairs."

Sasha felt with his feet and managed to descend into the hold, though Corbin had to steady him a few times since he had neither his eyes nor his arms for balance. The other assassin helped Sasha to a damp corner reeking of mold and guided him to sit on the floor and lean against the bloated wood. "I'm afraid you'll be traveling like this." Corbin brushed his gloved hand over Sasha's cheek. "They won't take any chances. Don't worry. I'll keep my oath."

Sasha could only nod, and he barely managed that with his chin practically strapped to his chest. He tried to relax his muscles so they wouldn't cramp even worse as he felt the ship lurch forward and heard water sloshing against the hull. No matter how he positioned himself, he knew he was in for a painful journey. Worse yet, he was completely helpless. As much as he loved and trusted Duncan and Yarrow, it still went against everything he'd ever believed to depend upon others, to wait for them to save him. He had no choice, and he knew they would come. He just hoped they made it in time. Sasha didn't want to go to Thalil without seeing them one last time. Bound, blinded, and gagged or not, he didn't intend to let that happen.

Chapter Sixteen

MORE than a week had passed since Corbin had taken Sasha, but it felt like a year to Yarrow. Every glimpse he stole through Corbin's eyes of his beloved languishing in bondage threw tinder on his anger until it became an inferno, one he could barely contain. The idea of Sasha suffering made the magical fire want to gush like lava from his every pore and burn away everything in its path. With each passing moment, Yarrow's hunger for blood and vengeance grew, and it took most of his concentration to keep his wings and claws from flaring up out of the pit of his rage.

Thankfully for anyone they might have met, Yarrow and Duncan were alone, traveling south along a desolate road roughly parallel to the river. It had snowed a few days ago, and the dry powder crawled like a sparkling white serpent across the stones of the pathway and collected in the folds of Yarrow's cloak. Aside from the high-pitched cry of the wind and the rattle of the bare branches, it was quiet, almost peaceful, though Yarrow couldn't find any measure of contentment. All he'd been able to discern from Corbin's thoughts and observations was that he and Sasha were aboard a ship headed down the river, and Yarrow and Duncan were a day or two behind it. Maybe more.

"Yarrow, let's stop for a few minutes."

Yarrow whirled to face Duncan, outraged at his suggestion. "We don't have time to rest! It's already going to be almost impossible to catch up to them, and you want to loaf around? Sasha is in pain, and he's alone!"

"Goddesses, friend, I know it. I just want to sit down for a moment and have some water." Duncan, in his heavy suit of armor and carrying most of their gear, looked ready to collapse beneath his burdens. He was pale, and dark circles lined his gray-green eyes. The cold had nipped his cheekbones red and cracked his full lips. Ice crystals coated his whiskers, and the lines around his eyes looked deeper.

Yarrow turned and went to clasp Duncan's hands. "Forgive me. I'm sorry. I didn't mean to get angry with you. I'm not angry with you. I'm just… angry. Damn it, Duncan, I just want to tear something apart."

Duncan wrapped his arms around Yarrow's shoulders and pulled Yarrow against his chest. "I know. I know you get angry when you're hurt. I can only imagine how difficult it must be for you to imagine Sasha helpless and at the mercy of others, just like…."

"Just like I was," Yarrow said. "You don't have to be afraid to mention it. We both know what happened, but I don't want pity. I don't want what happened to me to be an excuse for my behavior. You have been beside me from the beginning, and you don't deserve it. Sometimes I wonder why you tolerate me."

"Oh, just close your mouth, lad," Duncan teased, toying with the tangled ropes of Yarrow's hair. "This is the worst of situations, and I know you want to punish someone for the pain you feel. I also know I'm the only one here. You want to destroy something, but you're resisting it. That shows restraint and wisdom. You're mastering whatever you hold inside, and I'm proud of you. Yarrow, I… I cannot imagine what everything you've been through has done to you. I don't know if I could handle it as well as you have, if it all."

"You say the silliest things," Yarrow said, though he smiled and some of the tension dropped from his body. "Don't treat me like a little girl."

"I'm afraid I'm the one who needs a little coddling," Duncan said, pressing a kiss to Yarrow's forehead before pulling away and lowering himself stiffly onto a rounded stone. "I'm not a young man anymore, and I feel the cold and the strain of walking sixteen hours a day." He took his canteen from his belt and drank deeply.

Yarrow stood behind Duncan, threaded his arms around him, and rested his cheek on top of Duncan's head. "You're the finest man I've ever known, and I wish I could coddle you. After this, after Sasha is safe, if you want to stop fighting, you've more than earned it. You deserve some comfort after everything you've done for others."

"If only the world would concur and be a decent place," Duncan said. "Until it does, I'm afraid I won't be able to stand to the side."

"That's why I love you so much," Yarrow said, shaking and tearing up. Damn it, he'd reached his limit as well, otherwise he wouldn't get so emotional over a simple conversation. "I'm tired too. Let's keep going until we lose the light and make camp."

"I think I can manage that," Duncan said, kissing the back of Yarrow's hand before he stood up and hoisted their packs. "Ah, Yarrow. Don't ever get old."

"I… I won't, Duncan."

"I'm sure it seems that way to you now. It felt the same at twenty, like I was too special to succumb to time as others did."

"That's not what I mean," Yarrow said. He wanted the half-truths and vague explanations cleared, and he had to start somewhere. He wanted rid of the lies and secrets between them. "I'm not going to change. Physically. Because of my creature."

"How can that be? I thought it was gone."

"No… not really. It changed me. Forever. I want you to know. I… have more I need to tell you. Much more."

"Go on, my beautiful boy."

Yarrow shook his head. "No. Not now. I am not ready."

The mail of Duncan's glove was cold against Yarrow's face when Duncan curled his fingers around Yarrow's cheek and chin. "Yarrow, nothing you can say will make me turn my back on you."

Yarrow closed his eyes and leaned into Duncan's open palm, against the metal links of his glove. "I know. I'm just not ready. After… after we see to Sasha's safety, I promise I'll tell you. I'll tell you both."

Duncan nodded and kissed Yarrow gently, his chapped lips harsh but warm and his whiskers rough against Yarrow's mouth and skin. "I suppose we should press on. Let's try to make some distance before we stop for the night."

"Agreed," Yarrow said. He took Duncan's hand and pressed his mouth to the chilly chain mail covering his knuckles, wishing he could feel warm flesh but accepting they had work to do. He let Duncan's hand fall as he returned to the snow-strewn path and forced his feet along it.

A few hours after the sun sank behind the western mountains, Yarrow stopped on the trail, his limbs feeling like porridge. "I can't take another step, Duncan."

With a forced chuckle, Duncan said, "I felt that way two miles ago. If you can manage a fire, I'll pitch our tent."

Yarrow gathered a few branches the wind had torn from the trees and stacked them into a pyramid. He bunched some dried grasses and twigs at the center and let his magic do the rest. By the time he had a decent blaze going, Duncan had erected their triangular canvas tent. Yarrow wanted so badly to crawl inside its walls and burrow into the bedrolls. He barely tasted the hard bread and dried meat they shared. Even the wine tasted like tepid water as he washed down his simple meal.

"To bed, my love?" Duncan asked.

Yarrow nodded eagerly, and when they were naked beneath the blankets, he forgot his fatigue and anxiety for a time. For an hour or so, as he lay beneath Duncan, he felt free.

WHEN Yarrow awakened on the hard ground, he didn't think he could force himself from beneath the warm blankets, from the sweet safety of Duncan's arms. His exhausted body just couldn't lift itself from beneath the furs. The light penetrating the tent's canvas walls was harsh and blinding. The wind tore across the land with a catlike wail and smacked against the walls of the tent. Yarrow buried his face in Duncan's armpit, letting Duncan's smell wind around him and shield him from the cold, hard world. Before long, Duncan's pungent, masculine scent had him pressing his erection against his knight's hard thigh.

"We have to get up, my love," Duncan said in a voice scratchy with sleep. He pushed back Yarrow's hair and traced the edge of Yarrow's ear with his finger. "We have to follow Sasha."

"I know." Yarrow scrubbed the sleep from his eyes with the heels of his hands. He sat up, letting the winter air strike his bare body and startle it awake. He retrieved his rumpled garments from the ground at the edge of their bedroll, where he'd flung them the night before, and began dressing, ignoring his hard dick until he could trap it beneath the waistband of his trousers. After he helped Duncan into his armor and they tore down their tent and packed up their things, they shared a cheerless breakfast of hard bread, jerky, and dried fruit. Then they started walking again, even though every muscle in Yarrow's body ached and every step felt like a monumental effort.

Watching through Corbin's eyes, Yarrow saw nothing much different than he had for the past week: dark wood, heavy rope, and lanterns swaying with the rocking of the ship, casting distorted shadows along the damp floor of the hold. It smelled of moldy cloth and the wormy reek of the river. It was cold, the atmosphere below the ship's deck somewhere between air and chilly water. Now and then Yarrow got to see Sasha because Corbin pulled the gag from his mouth so he could eat or drink water. Though unharmed, Sasha looked pale and thin, with discomfort pulling at his features. Yarrow couldn't imagine the pain of being bound and kept immobile for so long. A dusting of black whiskers covered Sasha's jaw, and his hair hung in greasy clumps even though Corbin brought a basin of water and a cloth now and then. Sometimes, when Corbin knelt down and reached out, Yarrow stretched his hand toward Sasha before he realized he couldn't really touch him. It made him angry, eager to make someone pay for causing the man he loved to suffer. As they walked, he envisioned more and more brutal and twisted ways of exacting his revenge. After a while, he could think of little but blood.

After another week of continuing south, Yarrow and Duncan passed a small inn and decided to spend the night there so they could enjoy a hot meal and have a proper bath. Since there were no other guests at the inn and the old man who kept the small establishment retired directly after filling the tub, Yarrow and Duncan sat together in the hot water, steam rising around them in shimmering sheets. A small fire burned off to the left, and wine, bread, and a wheel of cheese sat on a table.

"I feel guilty enjoying this while Sasha is languishing," Duncan said. "Every day I ask myself if we did the right thing by letting him be taken. It seems there's always something pulling us away from each other."

Yarrow sank a little lower, the wet hair of Duncan's chest scratching pleasantly along his back. He let the hot water close over his shoulders and rested the back of his head against Duncan's belly. "I agree. I never wanted to do it this way, but I don't know how we'd have ever found the leaders of the order otherwise. They've had thousands of years to practice staying hidden. It's really amazing, if you think about it. The Crimson Scythe have been around for thousands of years. That's longer than any line of monarchs. It's only been 879 years since Garith's ancestors, Gar the Undefeated and his people, united the tribes and destroyed the native savages to form Selindria. And Gaeltheon has been in existence only a few hundred years longer."

"I have to wonder why the goddesses allow it," Duncan said.

Yarrow gripped the wooden edge of the tub in an attempt to quell his outrage and resist railing at his friend. As calmly as he could, he said, "Think about what goes on in this world, my love. The unworthy rise to power and suck the life from the land while children die of hunger. Righteousness is not rewarded. Arbitrary things like being born with a title or land are. Those who have power get it on the backs of others and then they use it to exploit people. Do you truly believe your goddesses care what happens to us?"

"Yarrow, what a terrible thing to say."

"But it's true! How can you dispute it?"

"Your cousin Garith is a good king," Duncan argued.

"People said the same of my cursed uncle. Don't you think if these so-called goddesses cared anything about the people of this world, they would have prevented a man like that from ruling it? And let me ask you this. Have you ever seen any evidence of their intervention?"

"Of course," Duncan said in a soothing tone, stroking Yarrow's hair. "I see it every spring when the first flowers bloom, and again in the autumn when the harvest is brought in. I see it when children are born and grow, and even in common things like a soft rain over a meadow or the sun rising in the morning."

"But those things happened long before the goddesses came to power, and they'll keep happening long after they're gone."

"Yarrow, the goddesses have always been here, since before the creation of our world, and they always will be."

"But why do you believe that?" Yarrow persisted. "Just because you've been told to by others? What if it is a lie, a grand deception?"

"You should not say such things," Duncan told him sternly. "You could get yourself in a great deal of trouble."

Yarrow blew air out his nose. "Trouble from whom? Let them try. I'll tell anyone who asks me what I think of their so-called goddesses. The whole thing is ridiculous. Imagine what would happen if people found out about you and me. They would call you unnatural and take away everything you fought and bled to earn. How can you reconcile that with your insistence that the way of the Thirteen is good? They hate men like us, and it's just jealousy, and pettiness, and vengeance."

"What do you mean?"

"The only reason the goddesses forbid love between men is because Fane preferred his male lovers, and they were jealous. Hale told me so."

Duncan shifted beneath Yarrow, and Yarrow sat up so the knight could get out of the water. He watched the firelight on Duncan's wet, muscular body as he crossed the small room to fetch a towel from a hook by the fireplace, watched the trail of puddles his bare feet left on the rough wooden floor. Duncan, while he had never called Yarrow a liar, had harbored many doubts about Yarrow's time with Hale. He'd argued before that there was no proof Hale had actually known Fane, that he was anything more than a powerful and reclusive sorcerer, but Yarrow knew differently. He still hadn't been able to share the rest of Hale's revelation—that the Thirteen Goddesses were Fane's former wives and students and that they hoarded the world's magic to hold on to their power—with Duncan. He dreaded seeing the look of disbelief and pity in Duncan's muted green eyes, feared giving Duncan another reason to think him mad.

The water felt cool and oily now, so Yarrow stepped out of the bath. Duncan tossed him the towel, and he used it to squeeze the moisture from his tangled strands of hair. As he did, he stared into the dying fire, watching the small flames take the shapes of serpents with forked tongues. He meant to put an end to the deception of Fane's wives, meant to punish them for killing his beloved and usurping the world's magic. No one else could do it, he knew, and the world needed to be free. He wondered if Duncan would be able to stand beside him then, if he would one day be able to see the truth.

"We should go to bed," Duncan said as he dressed, "so we can be back on the road as early as possible. I long to put an end to this. I worry over the people depending on me back in Windwake. I need to see Sasha safe and return to my duty."

Yarrow nodded and pulled on his trousers. They walked down the hall and up the steps to their clean, if tiny, cell, one of three available at the small inn. A fire burned in the inglenook, and a pitcher of water sat on a small table. Other than that, the room contained nothing but two narrow beds and a chest at the foot of each. The rest of their things waited along the wall, where the innkeeper had left them. Duncan stretched his arms over his head, yawned, and pulled back the blankets. When he got into the bed, his broad shoulders nearly spanned the width of it and feet almost stuck out at the end.

"Join me?" he asked Yarrow.

"I'll take the other. There doesn't seem to be much room."

"All right, then. Good night, my love." Duncan punched his flat pillow a few times and rolled onto his side.

"Good night, my love," Yarrow whispered as he got into his own bed. The linens were crisp and cool, much less scratchy than those of the inns he'd slept in recently. The blanket was coarse and a faint equine smell clung to it, but Yarrow had slept far worse places, and the hardships he'd suffered made it easy for him to get by with very little. He folded his pillow double and wedged it under his neck, looking up to watch the light and shadow flickering across the rafters and the peeling plaster ceiling.

Even after a hot bath and a full belly, and even after the grueling weeks they'd spent traveling, Yarrow found sleep eluded him. He considered climbing in next to Duncan after all, creeping beneath the coverings until he could burrow his face into Duncan's thick, brown curls and wrap his mouth around Duncan's cock. His body reacted to the idea, tenting his loose trousers and making his mouth water. Yarrow licked his lips and had almost decided to join his friend when he heard the first of Duncan's soft snores. The poor man was exhausted, and Yarrow couldn't be selfish enough to disturb him.

Instead, he let his eyes lose their focus and felt for the gossamer thread that tethered the piece of his perception he'd left with Corbin to the rest of his mind. Following the sparkling silver strand, he poured a little more of his consciousness into the other mage, letting it flow drop by drop like dew down a spiderweb, and found a comfortable seat inside his head. Slowly, he let his awareness flow into Corbin's senses and down his limbs, sinking into his skin. The first thing Yarrow noticed was the absence of the ever-present rocking. Corbin had left the ship. While Yarrow could look through his eyes and feel through his flesh, he couldn't control Corbin, so he had to wait for the other mage to look around before he could get a sense of his surroundings.

The room was small, stone, with a domed ceiling and a quartet of columns along the perimeter. Fuzzy red orbs, brighter where they overlapped at the edges, shone on a bed stacked high with velvet cushions and a brocade-upholstered chair. A lewd painting of two young men, one on top of the other and holding the point of dagger near the other's mouth, hung above a small fireplace. Yarrow realized they must be in one of the order's safe houses, but he had no way of knowing where or how to reach it unless Corbin looked at or thought about something that would reveal the location. Though it frustrated Yarrow to watch and wait, the other mage had been reliable up to this point.

Finally Yarrow got a look at Sasha. Sometime between now and when Yarrow had seen him last, he must have been allowed to wash and shave. His hair fell in clean, soft-looking waves around his slender shoulders, and his face looked smooth, if still a little pallid. Yarrow watched the bones and muscles of Sasha's back moving beneath his leather, stretching it and making it catch the light, as Corbin followed him through an archway and into an even smaller room, one just large enough to hold an iron-framed bed. Sasha began pulling a glove off a finger at a time and then rolling the buttery red leather down his arm, revealing silky golden flesh Yarrow could almost feel. Corbin turned away as Sasha began unbuckling his armor, and Yarrow felt torn between wishing Corbin would stay and watch so he could drink in the beautiful sight of his partner's perfect body and being angry at Corbin for looking as long as he had. Sasha tempted the other mage; Yarrow could feel the lust like a pool of heat in Corbin's belly. He didn't know whether the almost overwhelming desire to reach out and run his hand over Sasha's exposed ribs, down his waist, and along the V of muscle disappearing beneath his snug trousers came from Corbin or himself.

Corbin turned and pulled a gauzy red curtain across Sasha's doorway before returning to his own room, frustrated with arousal. He flopped into the chair by the bed and pulled his boots off one at a time. Then, with a bit of difficulty, he managed to unbuckle his leather shirt, peel it from his arm and chest, and drape it, inside out, across the back of the chair. He unfastened his trousers and let the fly hang open as he reached to the floor beside him and took a few items from his pack.

Corbin held a small glass phial in front of his face and the viscous emerald liquid inside caught the light. It slid slowly from one end of the phial to the other as Corbin flipped it over and under his long white fingers, leaving thick trails on the inside of the glass. Then the other mage grasped the small cork between his teeth and pulled it loose. Holding the container between his thumb and pinky, he let a single drop fall on his fingertip, and then he replaced the cork and let the phial fall to his lap. Corbin sank a little lower in the chair, tilting his pelvis up and letting his knees fall open. Yarrow felt the other mage's excitement as his own, and he reached below the blankets to grope himself through his trousers. Corbin rubbed the droplet of poison into his gums above his upper teeth and then sucked on his finger, lapping with his tongue until he removed every trace of the peppery, acrid fluid. Through Corbin, Yarrow felt his tongue and lips tingle and go numb. Seconds later, a floaty euphoria spread through him, and Yarrow bit his bottom lip to keep from giggling. His body felt stretched, elongated, like it was a mile from his hand to his cock.

Corbin picked up a goblet of wine and drained most of it in a few gulps even though he couldn't taste it and could barely perceive the moisture sliding over his tongue and down his throat. The black iron posts of the bed wavered like melting wax before splitting apart into two blurry black lines. The flames in the inglenook looked smudged, as if an artist had accidentally smeared his thumb through still-wet paint and mingled all the pigments so nothing held a defined edge. Yarrow's spine felt like a warm trickle of water tickling its way down his back. No part of him felt solid. It was exquisite, rapturous, even though he felt death tugging lightly on his ankle, pulling him a few inches into the void. He was grateful he only experienced it vicariously, or panic might have spoiled his peculiar trance.

When Corbin reached into his black satin undergarment and pushed his hood back to smear his fluids over his slit and crown, Yarrow realized he was probably taking advantage of their connection, intruding on Corbin's intimate moment. Though he knew he should back away, he couldn't seem to tear his attention away, especially not when Corbin took out a beautiful, long, pale cock covered in prominent blue veins. As Corbin dragged his fist up his length, Yarrow did the same. Despite the numbing effects of the poison everywhere else, his cock felt sensitive and acute. His balls knotted tightly against him and his hole—or maybe Corbin's—clenched at the intensity of it.

Corbin paused in his ministrations and ran his tongue over his palm and up his fingers. He watched the firelight on his slick skin as he thrust into the empty air. It took a moment, but Yarrow realized Corbin was gathering magic, as if in preparation of a spell. It built slowly, like a storm, inside the hollow place between his ribs. Though Yarrow couldn't imagine what or why he intended to cast, he felt enchantment humming in his blood and moving over his skin like lightning, making the sparse white hair on his belly stand up. He had never recognized how erotic it could be, and he started to understand: Corbin loved magic—loved it in the way Yarrow loved the bodies of Sasha and Duncan. The presence of magic aroused him, and it alone commandeered his devotion.

As Corbin cast a series of weak spells, the same magics spilled from Yarrow's fingers without his conscious intent. The little speckle of frost made his balls tighten up, and the small jolts of lightning sent the most amazing sensations through his cock and along the base of his body. Finally Corbin conjured a cloud of necrotic enchantment and let the jaundiced mist hover around his head. It drew the vitality from everything around him, making the lush fabric of the chair rot and grow threadbare and the wood dehydrate until it splintered. Even the stone wall eroded, and gray powder drizzled to the floor. With a rapt moan, Corbin breathed in the fetid fog, breathed in his beloved magic as he jerked himself with short, quick strokes. The other mage lifted the stump of his ruined arm and bit into his bicep. The taste of blood filled Yarrow's mouth, towing memories not his own in its wake. Both of them came moments later, Corbin bruising the flesh of his diminished arm with his teeth and Yarrow toying with his nipple with his unoccupied hand.

Both of them panted, heads reeling, sparks flaring across their vision, and their seed drying on their bellies. Corbin looked around the room, and the motion of his head made Yarrow so dizzy his stomach lurched. Then the other mage spoke.

"Enjoy yourself, Yarroway? Hmm. I'm sure you did. But now for what you really want. We are just outside the town of Ligonier, on the Selindrian side of the Kanda. Tomorrow, we'll ride southwest." He chuckled seductively. "There. Are you… *satisfied*?"

Yarrow severed the connection between them, and with it went the effects of the poison Corbin had ingested. He was glad to be rid of the other mage's influence. He had spent too much of his life—most of it, in truth—under the influence of someone or something else. He had been so young when he'd bonded with his creature, he'd never had the opportunity to figure out what Yarrow wanted, what Yarrow valued and hoped for in life. Up until recently, he'd simply fought to survive. The time had come to choose his own path, to set goals for himself and work toward them. It was time to finally be Yarrow and to figure out exactly what that meant. In his excitement over his revelation, probably the most profound of his life, Yarrow wanted to wake Duncan and share what he'd discovered.

Now, he just had to decide what he valued and hoped to achieve. He knew he wanted to bring truth to the world, to free people from the falsehood of the so-called goddesses. The world couldn't operate under centuries of lies. Bringing down the goddesses—it was too astronomical to wrap his mind around. He'd held his own against the one who called herself the Mother Goddess back atop Starmont, but at the moment he knew no way to destroy them. Though it terrified him, he needed the spell Fane had used, the spell that could dissolve anything to a scrap of its essence. It was the only way to eliminate that which couldn't be killed. He had no idea how he'd learn the spell. As far as he knew, only Fane, the goddesses, and his creature had ever mastered it, and all of them were long gone.

It could wait; it had to. Before Yarrow could worry about anything else, he had to see Sasha safe and free from threats, and no matter how confident he tried to feel, he knew it would be the fight of their lives.

Chapter
Seventeen

ONCE again, they led Sasha blindfolded from the order hideout. The air outside was warmer and smelled of damp loam; they'd come south, probably to the fertile edge of Thulemore. From the warmth of the sun on his back when they'd hoisted him onto a horse, Sasha deduced they traveled westward. At least they hadn't bound his legs, allowing him to flex his thighs around the horse and return some circulation to his limbs. In front of him, Corbin smelled strongly of wine and mortis-root poison, with a faint hint of old sweat and semen. The Whisperers hadn't given any of them time to wash before setting out. Because his arms had been tied behind his back again, Sasha leaned his chest against the other assassin to keep his balance as the animal took off at a canter. Sasha jerked backward before his chest slammed against Corbin's back.

"Don't worry, your friends are close behind us," Corbin whispered, his voice nearly drowned by the air whipping past them.

"I'm not worried," Sasha lied. Never in his life had he felt so helpless, so much at the mercy of others, and the Crimson Scythe showed no mercy.

The procession rode hard without stopping for a midday meal, until Sasha felt the air cool with the retreat of the sun. The world felt softer and smelled fresher with the coming of night, like a fragrant velvet cloak wrapped softly around Sasha. They stopped, and after the horses had been taken care of, they entered an old mine shaft. Inside, Corbin brushed Sasha's blindfold away, allowing Sasha to see an abandoned and depleted quarry made into a sanctuary for the order. Weapons stands and armor racks stood against the roughly hewn ironstone walls of the tunnel, and Corbin hauled Sasha to a rounded alcove containing an elaborate bed that looked bizarre amongst the forgotten pickaxes and wheelbarrows. They slept together that night, and for many nights after, as the assassins continued west.

Soon the group had to cross Spearepointe Bay, between Thulemore and the valenny of West Farrendrine. That meant another three days in the dank hold of a ship, and Sasha could only be thankful he wasn't prone to seasickness. Throwing up with a leather gag in his mouth might have been more than he could stand. It was warmer when they landed on the eastern shore of the vast and wealthy valenny. The northern bairnies, Lafoer and Verneem, produced both fine wood and artisans capable of crafting it into the most beautiful furnishings. Farrendrine also boasted some of Selindria's finest hunters, and the temple to Ix, goddess of the wilds, outside the city of Syl spanned almost ten miles. Wooden carvings of the goddess and her sacred animals stood among thick but carefully tended ivy, arn trees, and burleberry bushes. Ix's sacred hares and does roamed freely without fear of predation.

Toward the middle of the valenny, flax grew and fine cloths were produced. Before the discovery of the barbarian lands to the east of the Lapir Mountains, the fabrics had been coveted by wealthy women above all others. The southern bairnies were the jewels of West Farrendrine, though. The warm climate, never frigid enough to snow but not as oppressive as the islets at the mouth of the Kanda, was perfect for cultivating grapes, olives, and koria fruit. Aside from Lockhaven, the best vintages hailed from there. To the south, on the very tip of the peninsula, stood the beautiful eyrledom of Elvara. Sasha had visited its natural hot springs, theaters, music halls, and pleasure houses many times when his work had brought him this way, though he doubted he'd have the opportunity to do so on this journey. Still, it brought him a rare smile to envision him and Yarrow enjoying the beautiful boys of the famed brothels and sipping on the delectable wine. It pleased him even more to imagine how disgusted Duncan would be with all the vice and how he'd grow possessive and protective of his younger lovers. Sasha didn't know when he'd accepted the idea of being possessed, of belonging to someone, but as he pictured Duncan shielding his eyes and trying to protect whatever innocence he imagined Sasha still contained, he couldn't help but feel warmth in his chest that had nothing to do with the southern clime.

The days crawled on in similar fashion after they'd crossed the bay. The group rode hard during the day and stopped for a few short hours each evening to rest in a safe house. For Sasha, the days robbed of his sight and the nights in darkened cells began to bleed into each other, and he grew increasingly disoriented. All the order hideouts began to look the same, and the only thing Sasha dared look forward to was Corbin removing his bonds and allowing him to wash and shave. Being tied up so much made his whole body ache, and his muscles spasmed painfully and cramped until he almost cried out at the pain.

After another week of traveling, they came to a stop near the western coast of Farrendrine. Sasha could hear the crash of the waves in the distance, and he smelled charcoal and ash. He immediately noticed the absence of birds and animals moving around them. Not even insects troubling the horses broke the eerie stillness, and Sasha knew they'd reached the Revenant Coast.

Almost a thousand years ago, the ancestors of Selindria's royal family had driven those native people who wouldn't swear fealty to them here and trapped them between slaughter and the sea, then killed them by the thousands. Some said the land itself had rebelled against the blood and pain it had witnessed; others swore those who had died had left a curse on it. Either way, the soil was powdery and bleached. It would support no life, and no one came within miles of the forsaken shore, fearing the superstitions of hungry spirits. Even the Emiri sailed miles out from the Revenant Coast and the Shores of Victory, the beach where Garith's ancestors had completed their conquest and left the bodies of their enemies piled high on the sand.

Corbin reined their mount to stop, jostling Sasha against his back and making him clutch the horse with his legs to keep from falling. He heard the shuffle of the horses' hooves and the animals' snorts of confusion. Then someone pulled him out of the saddle and grasped his shoulders to prevent him from falling. The man—judging by his rough hands and the strength of his grip—led Sasha down a steep hill strewn with rocks and loose gravel. At the bottom, Sasha heard stone grating against stone, and the next thing he knew, the musty scent of the underground engulfed him. The air felt heavy and stank of mushrooms and wet dirt. It stuck to the soles of Sasha's boots until he emerged into what he could tell was a massive chamber, and then Corbin slid his blindfold down to drape around his neck. Twelve towering columns, cut from black stone and polished to the sheen of glass, rose to meet the domed ceiling. Torches encased in red glass cast pools of crimson light across the octagonal floor tiles. A statue of Thalil pressing his blade to the throat of a victim on his knees dominated the front of the hall, at least three times the height of a man. Rubies the size of Sasha's palm comprised the idol's eyes and more large gems adorned the hilt of his dagger and the edges of his revealing garments. Hundreds of candles and sticks of incense burned at his feet, the smoke rising from them enhancing the dreamlike—or nightmare-like—aspect of the sanctuary. Thirteen seats carved from the same dark stone stood around the statue, unoccupied for the moment. More statues of beautiful, dying young men stood between the pillars. Corbin and the others hurried Sasha through the room and down a hallway lit only by sputtering torches.

Corbin shoved Sasha into a small room and waited for the door to close before removing Sasha's gag. Sasha rubbed his tongue against the roof of his mouth and pressed his lips together to revitalize sensation, his face tingling as blood rushed back. With a swipe of his dagger, Corbin severed the ropes restricting Sasha's hands, and Sasha brought them in front of himself and rubbed his palms to encourage his blood to flow. It flooded his fingers so forcefully it hurt.

"Here we are," Corbin said, sitting on the edge of another ridiculously sumptuous bed sagging beneath red velvet cushions and blankets. He let his black traveling cloak fall behind him and reached across his chest to rub his severed arm. "Did you imagine we'd make it this far?"

Sasha considered. "Why not? We aren't suspected."

"Aren't we?"

"Do you know something I don't?"

Corbin shook his head. "It just feels too good to be true. What do you think will happen when your friends get here? Do you honestly think they stand a chance of convincing the masters of the order, the Thirteen Shadows, to let you be?"

"You underestimate them," Sasha said, swiveling his waist to make his spine pop back where it belonged. His bones cracked loudly. "It's a mistake you've made before."

Corbin used his teeth to pull his glove off a finger at a time, and then he started on the buckles of his armor. "I don't dispute that, but consider: perhaps you overestimate them. You hardly see them with unclouded eyes. You abandoned not only your calling but all of your training for them. Do you honestly believe they won't just be killed? For all their skill, they're just flesh, as susceptible as any to sharp steel and numbers."

Sasha leaned his back against the wall and looked down at his puffy, throbbing hands. If he had lived his life by any sort of code, it had been the belief that every man, from the lowliest beggar to the most exalted king, bled and perished the same. Men were flesh, and flesh could be pierced, sliced, poisoned, and hacked apart. No one was immune to Thalil's touch. Sasha slid down the wall and drew his knees up against his chest as Corbin continued removing his armor. Duncan and Yarrow, while exceptional, were just men, just flesh. If injured enough, they would die, the same as anyone else. The thought of them bleeding out and going white filled Sasha with so much dread he could barely contain his trembling.

Maybe, for once in his life, he should take the noble path. He could demand to speak to one of the Whisperers, confess his treachery, and reveal Corbin's. If he divulged Corbin's connection to Yarrow, Corbin would be killed and that bond would be severed. Duncan and Yarrow would never find their way to this place. They wouldn't be able to walk into danger or possibly to their deaths. Sasha would be executed, but wouldn't it be a fair trade to keep them safe? It made sense to sacrifice one life to preserve two others.

But he didn't want to die. Not yet. Not when his life had grown so full of possibility, so rich with the satisfaction of being loved and accepted. The selfishness that had prevented Sasha from killing Prince Garith and losing the men he loved coalesced within him to an iron ball in his belly. He wouldn't give them up, and nothing would tear them out of his hands as long as he had the strength to cling to them. He wanted to keep them and he would. Let the Crimson Scythe or anyone else try to stop him. If nothing else, he'd fall fighting beside them, but he certainly wouldn't drop to his knees and stretch his neck across the executioner's block. The order had trained him to kill without compassion, forged him almost from birth into a devastating weapon, and he would give them a chance to see what they had made.

No assassin they'd sent for him had succeeded. He was better. Thalil rewarded skill, and the skill Sasha had honed, the skill that surpassed that of the others, gave him the right to endure, to keep what he valued. What he loved. He would continue to use it and to defeat anything in his path.

"I don't plan on dying here," he told Corbin. "Or letting anything happen to my friends. I am too good to fall like that."

Corbin, naked now, turned the bed down and sprawled across it, then reached his hand out for Sasha to join him. Since he had nowhere else to sleep, Sasha crawled beneath the cool satin sheets. He didn't recoil when Corbin folded his limbs across Sasha's chest and thighs; it meant nothing and he'd grown used to it by now. Even the arousal Corbin's wiry body and soft ivory skin had inspired diminished. He wasn't one of the men Sasha wanted, and he found it ever easier to resist Corbin's charms.

"Despite your confidence, my brother, we may very well die tomorrow," Corbin whispered against Sasha's cheek. "Well, you more than me. Are you sure you don't want to experience the pleasures of the world one last time, just in case? I'll let you enter me."

"That's kind of you," Sasha said, his body arguing much more vehemently now, "and I have come to tolerate you more and despise you less, but I have to decline."

"You're a fool," Corbin said, burrowing his face into his pillows. "Those men have made you soft and weak. You aren't even worthy of being inside me."

"We'll see how weak I am," Sasha said, swiping his palm over Corbin's smooth brow and soft hair. "After tomorrow, no one will doubt me. Wait and see."

EIGHT assassins and two Whisperers appeared to collect Sasha and Corbin sometime the next day. Sasha had given up trying to gauge the hour. They led them back through the winding tunnels to the central chamber. They had allowed Sasha to wash, shave, and dress in his armor, and to his surprise they hadn't bound him, instead allowing him to walk with no more restriction than one of their hands on his elbow.

Assassins in red leather armor filled the large room, probably a hundred and a half, maybe more. Many kept their faces hidden beneath their hoods or the black wrappings covering their noses and chins. Sasha felt their gazes on him like the bolts of crossbows trained on his every movement. Those few faces he could distinguish showed no sign of emotion; all order agents were trained from childhood to conceal their thoughts and motivations, to keep them from their faces and give nothing away. Sasha did the same, standing with his chin raised and his features cold and neutral, though he felt the disgust the others felt for him hanging like a noxious fog below the vaulted ceiling. It was so silent in the chamber Sasha could hear the candles sputtering behind the crimson glass.

Sasha's escorts guided him and Corbin through the throng and left them standing in front of the crescent-shaped dais. From the stairs at both ends of the platform, thirteen people, nine men and four women, all of them wearing the same scarlet armor as the rest, approached and took the carved stone chairs. The Thirteen Shadows, Thalil's perverse mockery of the holy sisters. None of them covered their faces, and Sasha judged most of them to be in their late forties or early fifties—extreme old age for those in his line of work.

One of the women, a tiny creature with dark skin and silver hair pulled tight into a knot atop her head, addressed the gathering. "My brothers and sisters, it is not often that we convene the Council of the Thirteen Shadows, the rulers of the Order of the Crimson Scythe. It is even less frequent that we bring one of our enemies—one we have marked for death—before us while he still draws breath. But as you know, it is not often one of our own turns against us, and even less often he manages to elude us. No one can live when Thalil has marked him for death, not for thousands of years. The brethren do not fail, and we have not failed today. The traitor is here before us. Do you have anything to say, traitor? Can you stand before your brothers and sisters and explain to them why you abandoned your mission and turned your back on Thalil?"

Sasha turned his back on the council and faced his brothers and sisters in the order. "I have not forsaken the Dark and Beautiful One. Thalil knows this. As for my other actions, I will not explain myself. I owe you nothing."

"You will pay for your treachery," said another of the council leaders, a stocky man with short dark hair but a face with a hint of the delicacy it had displayed in his youth.

"Do what you must," Sasha said as he turned to face them again. "There is no need to keep our god waiting."

"Well said," another man, the oldest of the thirteen, with snow-white hair but shrewd blue eyes, told Sasha. "I would not expect you to beg for your life. At least part of you is still Crimson Scythe."

"All of me is Crimson Scythe," Sasha said, his voice echoing through the chamber. "Whether you acknowledge it is irrelevant to me. Thalil sees my heart, and it is filled with shadow."

The more time Sasha could buy, the better. No matter the faith he had in his skills, he wouldn't prevail against hundreds, and he had been taught not to enter a battle he couldn't win. He'd been taught to turn it into a fight he could win, to manipulate and bide his time until the perfect moment to strike presented itself, so he did. Yarrow and Duncan were coming; he just had to keep the others at bay until they arrived.

Another woman, with a vaguely Emiri look about her features, her hair still vibrantly red despite the years carved into her face said, "Let us not forget that we have not only one traitor in our midst, but two."

Corbin's shock surpassed his training, and he flinched at what he heard. "What can you possibly mean by that? Look at what I've sacrificed to complete the task you set for me!" He pushed his cloak back theatrically and held up the stump of his arm.

"You are too much a fool to be counted among our brethren if you think we do not know of the bargain you struck," said another council member. "We have known all along of your deal with Yarroway L'Estrella. We have been watching you, and now your treachery will be answered for along with those you aided against the interests of Thalil."

"I never—" Corbin cried out.

"Enough," said the woman with the red hair. "You have forsaken Thalil, and now you must pay the price."

"How do you want to offer them to our master?" the thickly muscled man asked, as if he wondered what the others might like for dinner.

The silver-haired woman shrugged. "Let them fight." She jutted her chin toward some of the assassins to her left. "But without the advantage of the armor and weapons the order has provided."

Four assassins surrounded Sasha, and another group converged around Corbin. They drew their daggers and began cutting Sasha's red leather, grasping scraps of it and tearing it from his body until he stood practically naked. The remains of his hooded tunic hung around his neck, and a few shredded bits of his trousers draped down over his boots, but other than that, Sasha stood in nothing but his tiny satin undergarment. He needed a weapon. When the first of brethren struck at him, he dipped his head below the man's elbow, butted his shoulder against his enemy's gut, and took both the daggers he wore at his hips before he rose.

Sasha moved to stand at Corbin's back. At the moment, Corbin was his only ally, but Duncan and Yarrow were coming. He just had to survive until they made it. At least he had steel in his hands, and he used it to swipe at the dozens of men and women who closed in on him, nicking his flesh with their daggers, hurting him and making him bleed but purposefully withholding the killing blow, like marlcats with their prey.

A serrated knife skimmed the edge of his cheekbone, and the taste of blood filled his mouth. He just had to last until his friends reached him. He had to stay alive, take the minor cuts and avoid the fatal ones. He feigned and dodged, parrying blows with his pilfered daggers while necrotic smog rose from Corbin as he conjured it in an attempt to shield himself, and the council looked on without much interest.

"I REMEMBER this place, that rock with the dead tree on top," Yarrow yelled over his shoulder to Duncan as he dug his heels into his horse's side. The animal kicked up clods of dry gray dirt as it cantered past the bleached bones and scraps of dried wood, the only things breaking up the bleak monotony of the Revenant Coast. At the edge of a hill, the horse skidded to a stop and Yarrow swung his leg over its back and hit the ground running. He could see Sasha through Corbin's eyes, stripped of his gear and facing dozens of enemies who wanted to cause him as much pain as they could. They intended to cut him apart a piece at a time, and Sasha stood without anyone to defend him. Helpless and alone.

Yarrow skidded down the gravel-strewn slope and almost collided with the rounded door in the stone. Knives slashed across his Sasha's beautiful, golden skin, cutting it to ribbons while Yarrow ran his hands frantically over the surface of the door, desperate to find the way inside. It had been made all in one piece, with no indication of how to open it. Minutes later, Duncan arrived at Yarrow's back, panting for breath but holding his sword ready. Somewhere beyond these few feet of stone, Sasha fought for his life. Yarrow had to get through. Had to help him. He backed a few feet away and let his azure claw extend from his right hand. Those talons, which had torn through dozens of people and reduced them to bloody stains, ricocheted off the barrier and almost smacked Yarrow in the face when they bounced back.

"Son of a whore, they're protecting it with a spell." Yarrow smashed his ethereal hand against the barrier as he watched his partner get cut to pieces by dozens of trained killers. He had to get to Sasha, and he would not let anything stand in his way. Again and again his claws scraped along the stone, not even scratching the surface. He couldn't see Sasha anymore since Corbin wasn't watching him. Trying to stay alive while daggers swiped at him with quick, silver flickers occupied all the other mage's attention. Reaching deep into the murkiest and most clouded pools of his power—the parts it scared him to possess—Yarrow let the destruction he so craved spill out, and the stone door fell in shards. "Let's go. We must hurry."

With a nod, his sword drawn, Duncan followed Yarrow into the underground passageway. It stretched for miles, angling steadily downward.

Casting a blue orb for light, Yarrow ran harder than he ever had in his life, and Duncan grunted and panted but kept pace with him. The tunnel ceiling grew higher, and Yarrow let his wings emerge to swipe away the wards they passed through. Finally they reached a set of towering obsidian doors carved with scenes of both beauty and death—comely young men killing each other. Yarrow stretched out his hands to slow himself down, but his chest slapped hard against the cold stone. His lungs felt seared and his muscles trembled like thin porridge, but the fear and outrage the sounds of clashing steel summoned in him also drew his power. Yarrow pushed Duncan behind him and lifted his hand to the ancient door. Shards of black rock shot dozens of feet into the chamber, and Yarrow and Duncan hurtled the debris. At the far end of the huge chamber, Sasha faced dozens of enemies, and blood already covered his bare skin.

Standing shoulder to shoulder, Yarrow and Duncan fought to cut a path through the assassins, but they might as well have tried to stop the flow of the Kanda with their hands. Dozens of the brethren poured from the halls surrounding the central room, joining the hundred or so already gathered. Yarrow swiped them away with his azure claw and shot lightning from his other hand. Duncan swung his sword in wide arcs, but the assassins just kept coming.

Sasha staggered and spit up blood. Yarrow screamed for him, but then a fresh group of assassins veiled him from Yarrow's view.

DOZENS of cuts oozed across Sasha's skin, and every second he endured more as his brethren played with him, each of them eager to leave a small mark on his legendary flesh. He had defied the order and survived it. The first in centuries. They intended to make him pay with hours of pain, but he kept fighting, because he knew his friends were close. He'd managed to hold onto the two blades he'd acquired, and he used each of them to deflect a blow, stretching his arms out to both sides. Before he could lower his hands, one of the assassins slashed vertically down the side of his ribs, and Sasha felt the steel scrape along the rungs of his bones. Another poked the point of his knife into Sasha's lower belly, cutting the muscle beneath the thin layer of soft flesh. Gritting his teeth against the agony and covered in his own blood, Sasha knelt to avoid a blow to his face and spun to slash at the shins of the assassins around him. As he rose, he drove his weapon up beneath a man's chin. Blood from his first kill of this ordeal spattered Sasha's hair and face. It also angered his former brethren; their attacks came faster and their cuts deeper.

The blunt hilt of a sword struck Sasha's lower back, propelling him to his hands and knees. Buckled boots rained kicks and jabs down on him, and he felt at least a few ribs crack. He swung at the nearest pair of legs, but the assassin in front of him stepped back, and one to the side drove his knee into Sasha's cheek. Sasha landed on his side, and dozens of Crimson Scythe closed around him.

Just then, an explosion of brilliant blue light came from the hall's entrance, stealing all sound for a few seconds and washing everything to blinding white. Blinking away the afterimages burned against the backs of his eyes, Sasha took advantage of the assassins' momentary confusion and hurried to his feet. His ears rang, but he saw the council members get to their feet, point toward the edge of the chamber, and draw weapons of their own. At least half of the assassins turned and ran toward the new threat, but not all of them forgot about Sasha, and he lifted his blades to defend himself again as their daggers again slashed toward him. One of the assassins sliced deep into his thigh, while another struck him in the side, sundering the sinew of his waist. Moving as fast as he could, Sasha's daggers pinged off those aimed at him, but he just couldn't deflect them all, and one penetrated his stomach and sank deep into his guts, making him regurgitate blood along with something bitter and ominous.

Lightning flashed, making the enemies Sasha faced disappear and reappear in staccato bursts. The smell of burnt minerals filled the chamber, and even the stoic order assassins screamed as bodies went flying, tossed aside like ragdolls by Yarrow's magical appendage or cut down by Duncan's massive sword as Sasha's friends fought to cut a path to him. Yarrow screamed his name, but he sounded far away, his voice nearly drowned by the shouting of the others and the clang of steel.

Archers had emerged from the passageways abutting the main hall and released their arrows toward Yarrow and Duncan, but Sasha couldn't spare a second to see if they found their marks. A dozen assassins still surrounded him, and he was gravely injured. He kept fighting, swiping his daggers at them as fast as his arms would move and dipping and dodging to avoid as many of their attacks as he could. He had to stay on his feet, keep fighting until he could rejoin his friends. He repeated that over and over in his mind. He had to keep fighting. They were here, and he couldn't fail them. He had to fight—

The flashes of light seemed closer as Sasha leapt backward to avoid the arc of a large, barbed sword. As he did, his back collided with the chest of a larger man, and before Sasha could get away, the other assassin took hold of his hair and wrenched his head back to expose his throat.

Yarrow screamed for him until his voice broke, and everything seemed to slow down around Sasha. An intense, burning pain stretched across his neck, followed by a splash of wet warmth. Sasha couldn't believe the sheet of blood pouring down his chest had come from him. All the strength ebbed out of his limbs, and his daggers fell from his hands. The light and sound dulled, replaced by black spilling in from the periphery of his vision. Consciousness and control of his muscles drained away along with his blood. Within seconds everything went dark, and Sasha tried to draw in a breath to call to his friends, but he couldn't fill his lungs and knew he never would again. He barely felt it as he tumbled forward and struck the floor, and then there was nothing.

Chapter
Eighteen

Sai and his *syrai* had made friends on their last few visits to the barbarian coast—valuable friends. Among his people living in bondage on what the land-bound sailors called Johmatra, they had discovered a secret network of Emiri working to free their people, and Sai had found the goals of these liberators fit well with his own. He and his crew had gained their trust by carrying dozens of runaways to freedom in the Twenty-Nine and always braving the danger to return for more. With each landing, he had dropped hints to his newfound allies, hoping they might find out some secrets for him, find him the things he needed, or better yet, how to make them himself.

Tonight, Sai, Lala, Izu, and Kin piloted their ship quietly beneath a wintery silver moon edged in a blue-and-lavender halo that reflected off the waves. The night was quiet except for the gentle slap of the tide against the hull and the soft and familiar creak of the small boat's timbers. Little wind pushed the few, brightly outlined wisps of vapor along the horizon, but it was enough for Sai to steer his vessel to a neglected inlet far east of the port towns held by the land-bound barbarians.

They dropped anchor a few miles off the rocky coast and took the dinghy to shore, leaving Kin to man their ship. A group of their people, more than a dozen of them, the hair their captors had ruthlessly shorn away reaching almost to their shoulders now, stood on the lilac-colored sand. Sai hopped over the side of the rowboat and into the warm, waist-high water. He waded to meet the others with his *syrai* close behind him. White foam, bright against the purple and cobalt night, sloshed around him and dripped down his waist when he emerged from Emir to greet the leader of these people. He grasped her forearms and kissed her hard on the lips. She tasted of nervous sweat and ocean salt. Their oppressors denied his people names, but Sai had dubbed this brave woman Kori, after the brilliantly colored, beautiful, and strong stones that formed reefs around the southern pinnacle of the islands of the Twenty-Nine. While lovely to behold, the rounded barriers the *kori* formed in Emir could be deadly. They hid below the waves and could cut deep into the hull of a ship whose captain didn't know not to cross them. Besides, they matched her bright orange hair.

The two of them conversed in a stunted mélange of Emiri, the common language of Selindria, and the tongue of the barbarian overlords.

"More to come with you, *Sai-Mir*," Kori said, her golden eyes lighting up as the clouds drifted away from the moon. "And our thanks with you."

"Of course," Sai said. "Have you anything else for me? The recipe for the exploding boulders? The liquid fire?" Since she didn't seem to understand, he used his hands to mimic one of the boulders dropping and exploding, waving his fingers above his head.

"*Tama*," she responded, an Emiri word usually suffixed to others, which meant best, finest, first, or most precious. *Syrai-tama* meant beloved friend, a true mate of one's heart, valued above all others. It was not a term the Emiri used lightly, but Sai understood her intent. Kori merely meant to convey a positive response to his question, and she knew *tama* meant something good.

"You have found them?" he asked, just to be sure he understood her.

"*Tama*. Here, one will take you."

"One of you can take me to it?" Sai asked, getting excited. "To it, or to the recipe?"

Kori tapped the edges of her fingers against her forehead. Sai had learned that gesture meant the same as a shake of the head among his people: she didn't understand. He asked again, using more of the barbarian words. "*Silar jabez-khe?*"

This time Kori patted her cheek, a gesture indicative of a nod, and grinned. "*Tama*! How to make! Here, one will show you!" She motioned toward those gathered around her, and a young man stepped forth. "Here, one will take you."

Sai bit back the innuendo dying to spill from his tongue as he regarded the beautiful Emiri man, with burgundy-red hair, scarlet eyes, and an arrogant and seductive smirk stretching his full lips. If Sai could find a painter to etch a few designs on that beautiful face and body, he'd be perfect. "Hello to you, and well-met. What are you called by your mother and her *syrai*?"

The pretty young man tapped his fingers to his forehead.

Sai pressed a palm against his chest and said his name, then he pointed to the other man, but he received only the same gesture in response.

"Not called, this one," Kori explained.

"We'll have to fix that," Sai said, stepping closer to the nameless youth and running his fingers down the other's taut body, only stopping when he reached the tattered cloth concealing his best parts. The man didn't flinch or shy away; instead he arched his waist against Sai's hand and let his eyelids droop over his gorgeous crimson eyes. "Let me think. Something beautiful, something that calls a man beyond his ability to resist…. I know! You'll be called Zura. It means the line where Emir meets the sky, the horizon." Sai did his best to demonstrate with his hands, sweeping them along the vast edge of the sea behind him. "The thing that tantalizes our people most: possibility."

Sai touched his chest and said his name again, and then he touched the chest of the other man. "Zura."

"Zura," he repeated, the Emiri pronunciation, the language of the sea, sky, and winds, coming easily to him, his birthright. When he spoke in the common tongue, it sounded rough and stunted. "Here, I show you the… *boom*!" He gestured as Sai had. "I… I, Zura, make the boom!"

"Emir's tits," Sai said. "You know how to make it?" He threw his head back and laughed toward the clouds crawling past the moon, grasped Zura's wiry biceps, and kissed him hard on the mouth. Zura closed his eyes and kissed back with more enthusiasm than Sai had expected. The barbarian slavers hadn't been able to beat the Emiri out of this one, and it delighted Sai. "Emir is good to me, bringing me to you, *syrai*."

"Here, we will take boom," Zura said, pointing down the coast.

Sai followed the line of his lithe arm, his gaze skipping over the whitecaps churned up by the incoming tide. The foam glowed bright against the dark water and sky, enhanced by the moonlight, but everything else remained hidden. If he squinted, Sai thought he saw a long rectangular building a few miles or so up the coast, with half a dozen Johmatran ships anchored in front of it. Nothing he and his crew couldn't handle.

"Get those who want to come with me onboard my ship," Sai said to Kori, pointing to where his cherished little boat bobbed on the waves. "Tell them to get below deck. I don't know another way to say it, but you are Sea People, and you should understand."

Kori nodded. "Below deck, *Sai-Mir*." She placed one of her hands horizontal above the other to demonstrate her comprehension.

"*Hai*," Sai answered. The word meant good, yes, more, wonderful, beautiful, again, and many other things. Sai hoped Kori would understand, and her wide smile said she did. She pointed to the ship a mile or so offshore, and the others arced their bodies and dove into the frothy surf. Of course, they were Emiri whether they knew it or not, and they could easily swim such a short distance. It did not take them long, and Sai watched the moonlight on their wet limbs as they climbed the rope Kin lowered to them. Then he turned back to Kori. "Will you come with us this time?"

She looked longingly at the boat but then bowed her head. "Here, I can lead you more. You come back soon. More people, us people, Emiri, here waiting. More every day. Emiri will not find *Sai-Mir* if I go. Not know to look for *Sai-Mir*, will have no… no…."

"*Yu-me*," Sai supplied in a humbled whisper. The Emiri word meant "hope." The idea that these people had no word to express the concept tightened like a fist around Sai's heart, and he strengthened his resolve to help them, even if it took his time away from his most beloved pleasures of lying on the beach, drinking, pirating, and making love to his *syrai*. Though he'd never envisioned a time when something would surpass his need for those distractions, that time had thrust itself upon him, and he just couldn't forsake these people for whom he embodied *yu-me*.

He kissed Kori softly on the forehead. "I will be back, unless sweet Emir calls me to rest in her arms. Bring others. As many as you can, and wait for me here. Expect me soon."

Kori pointed toward the Johmatran ships. "Fear, *Sai-Mir*," she said. "Hate. Take care of you."

"I will, and I'll be back soon. I promise."

"Soon," she echoed, rubbing her face against his. "Thank you, *Sai-Yu-me*."

"All right, then," Sai said, his face burning at the lofty new title she'd bestowed on him. He had spent his life in the indolent pursuit of pleasure without ever desiring anything more grandiose, and he didn't know if he could live up to it. "Soon."

He and his *syrai* boarded the dinghy and rowed back to the ship. As the others had, they skittered up the rope and onto the deck. Feeling his emotions even out now that he'd returned to his truest home, Sai approached Kin, who stood at the helm. Zura stood next to him, staring with rapturous attention as Kin steered the ship about. "Want to try?" Kin asked, watching the newest member of their crew over his shoulder.

"Try?" Zura asked in a voice soft with awe.

Kin smiled his subdued grin as he stepped away from the helm to let Zura grip the wooden pegs. He moved behind Zura and rested his hands over Zura's knuckles, his chest against Zura's back, the two of them moving together with easy familiarity, already becoming *syrai*, just as Sai had expected when he'd first looked on Zura.

Izu adjusted the sails and riggings while Lala checked the curved sword strapped to her hips. She was the quickest and best fighter among them, and if it came to a skirmish, Sai definitely wanted her at his back. He tapped Kin's shoulder and pointed up the coast. "East," he said. "Toward that small cluster of barbarian ships. Right, Zura?"

Zura pointed. A gust of wind caught the sails, propelling them toward the building in the distance. Their light ship skimmed along the surface of the water, cutting through the tumultuous tide with a soft swish. In less than an hour, they'd reached another shallow bay. Sai had thought half a dozen Johmatran ships protected it, but now he saw three times that number. He also noticed men wearing the distinctive conical metal helms of the barbarian warriors patrolling the roof of the long, rectangular structure. "Drop anchor," Sai said, softly, as if the enemies might hear him. "How in the name of Emir are we supposed to get in there? It's crawling with these dry-foot bastards." He looked back over his shoulder, but nothing but the churning sea met his gaze, and he cursed again under his breath.

Zura laid a roughened palm on the bare part of Sai's arm. "Secret way. We who make boom know."

"Isn't that fascinating?" Kin said, arching one brow and smiling at Sai. "Though it surprises me that the land-bound bilge rats would trust that knowledge to one of our people."

A soft *snick* sounded as Lala pressed her sword into its scabbard. "Of course the slaves make these weapons," she said as she joined Sai and the others at the rail. "It's probably dangerous. Do you think these arrogant dry-feet are going to risk getting their own hands blown off? *Syrai-tama*, we can take them."

"What?" Sai said, surprised by his friend's passion. "In a fight? Without the other ships? The rest of the *mir* who came with us are still raiding miles up the coast."

Lala squared her shoulders and set her jaw. "They have it coming."

"Surely, but I for one would like to make it home to Toumo and our boy," Izu said. "We won't win in a direct confrontation, not on our own. There are at least a half a hundred men down there that I can see, and certainly more onboard those ships."

"I'm not afraid," Lala argued, her voice growing louder and the blood rushing to her cheeks. "Sweet Sai, we can do it. Let those below deck help us. I'm sure they'll want to fight."

Sai looked from his beloved friend to the dozens of men around the building, and then he clasped her hand. "I don't know if we can. There just aren't enough of us, even with the others. Those below deck have probably never held a weapon. Why are you so adamant about this?"

Her lips trembled, but she pressed them together to still the quaking before she spoke. "We could have been born here, sweet Sai. Our son...."

He nodded his understanding. "So let's do this in a way that lets us return to Yei. Dying here won't do our boy or anyone else any favors. Let's stay alive so we can keep fucking these fools in the ass. Agreed, *syrai-tama*?"

Lala nodded, though the anger etched in her face didn't subside. "What is this secret way, then? Let's get going."

Zura pointed to the rowboats, and he, Sai, Lala, and Izu lowered four of them to the water and then climbed the rope to get inside. Following Zura's directions, Sai sloshed the oars through the burbling foam, his three shipmates close behind him, until they reached a tiny inlet barely large enough for him to tie the dinghy to a jutting rock. He swung his legs over the side and into the warm sea, then waded onto the rocky shore while the others secured their boats. From there, Zura led them along a winding path to the back of the long, low building. He lifted a square of the thin wood covering the structure's frame, and on their hands and knees, they crept inside.

Sai couldn't believe what he looked at beneath the light of a few lanterns hanging from the rafters. Shelves stretched for half a mile or more, all of them heaped with the exploding boulders. Beyond them, hundreds of clay barrels, probably holding the volatile liquid that burned on the surface of water, stood in neat rows.

"Emir's swollen bosom," Lala said. "This is more than we can carry."

"Take what you can," Sai told her. "We have something even more valuable now—a *syrai* who knows how to make more. We'll load our ship until she scratches the floor of the sea, and then we'll set the rest alight so the barbarians can't use it against us."

Lala giggled under her breath and stroked Sai's waist. "I like that idea."

"Let's get what we can while they still don't know we're here," Izu said, filling the sack he'd brought with the boulders.

They made seven trips down the obscure little trail to the dinghies, out to the ship and back, managing to clear a great percentage of the warehouse's stores. The smudged pink line of the coming dawn lit the edges of the eastern clouds as their tiny armada made another trip. The hours of rowing had made Sai's shoulders knot up painfully, and he thought about how much he needed a few drinks and one of Izu's special massages. Despite the protests of every muscle in his body, he followed Zura up the trail and back into the storehouse, where three-quarters of the shelves stood bare and only four lonely barrels waited at the back. They'd robbed the dry-foot slavers blind right under their noses, and he supposed they might as well make their enemies' humiliation complete. Sai heard the muffled steps of boots sinking into sand, though, and he held up a hand to tell his *syrai* to wait. All of them crouched in the shadows the towering shelves cast as a group of four barbarian soldiers patrolled the warehouse, poking their nasty-looking spears into the pockets of darkness. When they saw the pilfered shelves, one of them yelled, and another ran off, probably for reinforcements.

Sai cocked his head back toward the opening, and the others understood they'd overstayed their welcome. They all crawled through the small hole and sprinted down the path toward the shore, their arms full of whatever they could pilfer without being detected. Bells began to ring, and men shouted to each other. Leaping over rocks and skidding across gravel, Sai and his friends made their way to the dinghies. Sai dropped his load of boulders, grabbed the oars, and began rowing as if his life depended upon it, because it did. All of their lives did.

They came up alongside the ship, and Kin lowered chains, which Izu attached to first his rowboat and then the other three. As those on deck turned the cranks to haul them up, Sai watched the number of torches on the shore increasing. The light within the warehouse grew brighter, and lanterns now burned on some of the ships. They had been discovered. Worst of all, the crown of the sun now peeked above the horizon. In a few minutes, their position would be clear to the enemy, if it wasn't already. "Get us out of here like our ass is on fire," Sai called to Kin as he swung his legs over the railing and ran toward the sails. Lala and Izu hurried to pull anchor.

The sheets unfurled and caught the wind with a crack. Sai thanked the sweet sea for the *eru* and their fickle affections as the boat lurched away from the shore. With Kin at the helm and their holds weighed down with the foreign weapons, they set a southwest course, planning to curve around the coast of Espero and then northwest to the Twenty-Nine, as they'd done on previous excursions. The winds favored them, and Sai didn't see a flash of the enemy sails—not until hours later, after the sun had taken her seat in the heavens.

Gray clouds moving toward them from the north promised rain, and the air felt cooler. Standing near the aft starboard rail, Sai noticed the dozen or more white squares in the distance, no larger than flecks of snow in the horrible cold climes, but gaining. "Can we pick up speed?" he called to Lala and Zura, who stood at the helm.

"I'm pushing her as hard as I can, *syrai*," Lala called over the rush of the waves against the hull. Sprays of spume pelted her face as she held tight to the wheel.

"Can we hide among the small islands along the mages' coast?" Sai shouted over the wind.

"We're nowhere near them yet, sweet Sai," Lala hollered. "We won't reach the southern shores of Espero for at least two days. Nothing but Emir surrounds us at the moment."

"We have to go quickly! They're coming!"

"Let them," Lala said, touching her sword with one hand while she steered the ship with the other.

Some of the people they'd rescued came on deck. When they saw the white sails behind them, they began voicing demands and chattering in words Sai couldn't understand. It all blended into a meaningless din, and Sai wanted to clap his hands over his ears to escape it. As he watched the dozen enemy ships, he couldn't imagine how they'd gained on them so quickly. The barbarians had been improving their vessels since coming into contact with the Selindrian ships, but no boat he knew of could outrun an Emiri vessel. Still, the white sheets grew larger every second he spared to watch. *We're too heavy*, he said to himself. *That must be it.*

If they had to dump some of their precious cargo, Sai figured they might as well hurl it at their pursuers. They couldn't let those ships get into range to use their own liquid fire or explosives. Fortunately for them, Kin was quite crafty and had spent the time since Sai had first brought the boulders back to the Twenty-Nine modifying a trio of catapults they had acquired from a Gaeltheonic boat, and they could fire much farther than those the enemies possessed.

Sai climbed onto a barrel and shouted to quiet the dozens of people. "We're not bending over for these bastards just yet! Our catapults are better than theirs, and we can hit them long before they can reach us. Get the baskets loaded, and wait for my word."

Zura, a quick study, seemed to understand most of what Sai had said, and he translated for the others. Soon, Emiri with armloads full of the clay spheres ran across the deck, filled the baskets, readied the wicks, and set more orbs at the ready. Izu and Kin swiveled the catapults on their bases, aiming them at the quickly approaching ships. Sai climbed into the rigging near the main mast to get a better view of the enemy. Through his distance glass, he saw the barbarian soldiers moving around the decks, some of them standing in front of their own catapults or the fire-shooting barrels, but not readying their weaponry yet. His pulsed raced. He didn't want to reveal their strategy to the enemy before they had a chance of hitting them, but he didn't dare risk letting them get close enough to burn his ship. Kin had been unable to improve upon the fire-barrel device.

When he could wait no longer, he yelled *"Bakei!"*—an Emiri word for "fire" or "attack."

The gray balls seemed to arc across the sky in slow motion as Sai held his breath. Most of them struck the water with magnificent splashes, before sinking, useless, to the bottom of the sea. Three or four struck the two closest ships, piercing the hull of one in two places but doing little damage to the other. Five of the six ships still gained on them. "Again!" Sai yelled. "Fire at will! Keep them coming! Lala, get us out of here!"

"We're still too heavy," she answered. Their fleet little boat wasn't used to so many passengers, let alone the cumbersome cargo.

The next barrage of boulders did little more than the first. Rain began to fall, cold and sharp against Sai's face as little bits of gravel. He stowed his distance glass to cling to the ropes as a hard wind kicked up from the north. It hit the sheets hard, stretching the canvas taut and making the bow of the ship lift from the water. It changed direction quickly, making the boat seesaw as Lala struggled at the helm. "The *eru* are kicking us in the ass," she shouted. "We need to spill wind!"

Sai leapt to the deck, unwilling to spare the time to climb down and ran to his crew. "No! No! Storm sails! We're going to run off downwind."

"You're out of your mind!" Lala yelled over the increasing rain. "You'll never keep control of her."

"I will," Sai said as he nudged her away from the helm and took his place behind it. "I sailed the Serpent's Belly, remember?"

"I don't know, *syrai*," Izu said. "Few sailors could keep her upright in a storm like the one coming." He pointed to the wall of black clouds roiling at them, bringing heavy rain and thick veins of bluish lightning in its wake. "Looks like it could be magery, *Sai-Mir*."

"Rig the jack lines," Sai said, "bow to stern." Then he trusted his crew to know their jobs and turned his attention to the increasing waves. They were going much too fast; Sai knew that. At such a speed, if he slipped up and buried their bow in the back of a swell, they'd pitchpole end over end. He knew he took a huge risk running with the storm, but it would pay off if it got them away from those enemy ships. Sai felt confident their *mir* wouldn't even attempt what he planned, not even on bare poles.

Gripping the helm tight, he steered in an S pattern between the waves, hoping the rudder would hold. The force of the water could snap it off, and then Sai would have no control. Already the boat heeled wildly, even though Lala and Kin had reefed the main sheet, but so far, Sai had managed to compensate, guiding them between the highest crests as the vessel skipped along the surface of the gray water, shooting up sheets of spume. The rain, coming almost horizontal, pelted his back. He oversteered and hit a large wave almost at the center. The stern lifted from the sea, sending people and cargo skidding down the deck toward the bow. Sai could do nothing but hope she didn't flip over or on her side, and he couldn't take his attention off the helm long enough to see if anyone had been washed overboard. He had to trust his *syrai* knew enough to get their passengers below deck.

A sheet of water hit Sai like a wall, but the back end of the boat slapped down, lifted the bow up and onto another wave. She seesawed over a few more crests before Sai got control again and resumed guiding them between the waves. The force of the rain on the surface of the ocean made it hard for him to gauge the waves, made everything into a silvery blur. But he trusted his instincts and felt out the pattern of the breakers, predicting them from the way the ship bounced and cast sideways, until he almost didn't have to try to look anymore. The seawater in his blood attuned him to the tempestuous whims of Emir. He understood her ebb and flow, her motherly compassion as well as her rage. Despite their numbers and devastating weapons, the barbarians would never be able to claim that knowledge.

Sai had no idea how much time had passed when the *eru* finally tapered off to a playful, gentle breeze and the rain reduced to a light, warm drizzle. He didn't know his hands had been trembling until he unwrapped his cramped fingers from the wooden pegs of the helm, nor how much tension he'd built up in his back and shoulders until he released it. Shafts of golden light poked through the clouds, spilling warm yellow pools between the gray shadows across the deck and making the polished wood and puddles of water glisten. It was eerie and beautiful, the way the storm clouds darkened pieces of the ship while only inches away a bit of steel shone so brightly beneath a pinpoint of radiance he had to squint.

His *syrai*, huddled together near the main mast, looked drenched and bedraggled, but unharmed. Lala pushed her sopping hair back, stepped into a column of light, and lifted her face and spread her arms, as if trying to expose as much of her body to the warm, welcoming sun as she could. She looked beautiful, haloed by the heavenly luminescence, her jewelry and the beads in her hair sparkling. She was so much to him, a capable mariner, an even better fighter, one of the loveliest creatures he'd ever seen, the mother of their son, and dear friend for most of his life. Sai suddenly decided he wanted to try for another baby or two.

As if she sensed him watching her, Lala turned and arched a brow. "What?"

Sai returned her smile and clasped her hand, pressing her palm to his still rapidly pounding heart. "I don't think I realized how much I love you until just now."

She rolled her eyes and swatted him lightly on the side of the head as Kin and Izu joined them. "I don't think I have ever found you as desirable as I do right now," Izu said. "Emir's tits, *syrai*! That was some fine sailing. I'm proud to call you mine today."

"Just today?" Sai teased, putting an arm around Izu's waist. Then he noticed a nasty bruise with a cut at the center on Kin's left cheek. "What happened?"

"A piece of driftwood hit me when we pitched forward," Kin said. "Why don't you kiss it better?"

With a grin and his blood hot and high, Sai leaned in and dragged his lips over the small wound, then down to Kin's chilled, salty lips. They parted eagerly to admit his tongue, and he drew Kin nearer with his other arm still around Izu's waist.

"We deserve a rest," Kin breathed when he broke away. "Especially you, sweet Sai. And a reward for your masterful sailing."

Sai groaned. His body agreed completely—and obviously—beneath his wet leather leggings, but he shook his head. "I don't want to heave to just yet. First, I want to make sure we've lost the others, and… and I'm not sure where we are. I think we've been blown off course, maybe even well east of Espero. I should try to figure it out and get us back on track before we… rest. Sweet Emir, I have heard the land-bound mariners can't nail down their position without the stars. I'm glad I'm not one of those poor fools."

The hatch opened slowly, and Zura poked his head out, looking around with wide eyes as if surprised at the light and calm. He said a few words to the others in the barbarian tongue, and slowly they all emerged onto the deck. Izu took the helm while Lala and Kin began to prepare a modest lunch of dried fruit, pickled fish, and any bread that hadn't been soaked to useless dough. Lala hauled out a large clay jug decorated with a starfish and some shells. "Past time they learned to drink *muri-ku*," she said, winking at Sai.

Sai laughed, genuinely happy, as he ascended up the rigging and took out his distance glass. He saw nothing in any direction but the glossy silver-green surface of the sea sparkling like a gem as they moved farther from the clouds. Below, his *syrai* and the people they'd rescued sat on the deck cross-legged, passing food and drink and talking like a family. As if his spirit couldn't soar any higher, Sai noticed a huge artificial rainbow off to his right: the one conjured by the mages above the harbor of Pala Reapaza, in Espero. The idiot land-bound's storm had pushed them closer to their destination, and Sai's gambit had shaved two or three days off their journey. He scampered lightly down the wet ropes and had something to eat with the others. Afterward, he willingly let his *syrai* pull him to his cabin for the "rest" they all desired, and as he followed them, he caught Zura's hand. After all, more *syrai* were the sweetest blessing Emir bestowed upon her children, and Sai had liked Zura from the second he'd seen him. His instincts told him the others wouldn't be disappointed.

They spent hours together behind the printed curtain, and by the time they flopped down, naked, spent, and covered in sweat, to sleep, Sai knew not a one of them was the least bit disappointed.

A FEW weeks later, Sai was sitting on the deck, mending a torn sail, when Lala approached him with a jug of *muri-ku* dangling from her small hand. He took it gratefully and wet his lips as she sat down beside him. "We'll have another little one soon," she said, smiling.

Sai dropped his needle and thread, took her face in both hands, laughed aloud, and kissed her. "Are you sure?"

She nodded. "I should have bled two weeks ago, not long after we rode with the storm. This baby will be special, *syrai-tama*, conceived on the high sea as our people were intended. I can't wait to tell Toumo."

"I'm so happy," Sai said, squeezing her wrist. "This has been a good journey."

"It has, but I'm longing for home."

After he stood and helped Lala to her feet, Sai led her to the starboard rail. "Well, look there. Has the Twenty-Nine ever seemed more beautiful?"

She giggled, and they stood watching the tiny flecks of green in the distance. Sai swore he smelled the hot sand and abundant fruit, and he couldn't wait to stretch on the beach with nothing to disturb him for at least a few days. Lala was expecting a baby, and that required a celebration—one that would last more than a few evenings. And the liberation of more of their people should be celebrated, and their victory over the barbarians… the haul they'd made….

"I'm going to stay drunk for a week," Sai yelled into the sky.

Zura joined them, resting his elbows on the rail and inhaling the warm, sweet air. He'd spent his nights in Sai's cabin with the others, and they'd made an unspoken decision to welcome him into their family, as *syrai*.

"There's your new home, my friend," Sai said, patting his shoulder. "We should see about getting you some paint first thing. Something so beautiful should be decorated, right, Lala?"

She batted her lashes at Zura. "I have found myself thinking of little else."

Almost three weeks with Sai and his crew had given Zura a better command of their language. "Here, what will I do for work?"

Sai turned and hoisted his bum up onto the rail, so he could look at his friends. "Here, you don't have to work if you don't want to. You can do whatever you like. Just live."

Zura looked a little confused, and he worried his lower lip with his teeth. "No work?"

"We are not like the dry-feet," Lala said, resting her hand on his forearm. "You don't have to justify your right to exist by making something or doing some spirit-crushing work. You're here, and that's enough. You don't need anything to show for your right to be here. Does that make any sense? We just live."

"I will try," Zura said, playing with Lala's fingers. "But I will make the boom for you?"

Sai swung his feet above the deck. "I won't tell you not to. And if you want to work with Kin to make a better barrel for the liquid fire, that would help too. But if you want to do nothing but drink, sleep on the beach, and make love, no one will mind. Among the Emiri, you don't have to buy your right to be a part of the world. Just being here is enough for us."

"I will like it here," Zura said.

Sai turned to Lala. "Have you told him the good news?"

She touched her belly and met Zura's gaze. "A baby."

"Mine?" he asked, blushing.

"And mine," Sai explained. "And Izu's and Kin's and Toumo's—you'll meet him tonight. Children among our people are just another *syrai*. You already have one. His name is Yei."

"I am happy," Zura said, his eyes misting as he watched their approach to the archipelago of the Twenty-Nine. "I will make the boom to protect my *syrai*. Emir does this?"

"Emir carries us to each other," Lala said. "She's been so good to us."

From the helm, Kin shouted for Sai, and Sai jogged across the deck. "What is it?"

"See for yourself." Kin handed him a distance glass, and Sai pressed it to his eye. Four ships waited a mile or so from the mouth of the river, and from their shape, Sai recognized them as hailing from Johmatra. Instead of attacking or even following, they were just waiting, moored a safe distance from the coast. If the enemy proceeded any farther, Sai could have a hundred ships, maybe two hundred, ready to face them in an hour. "What do you want me to do?" Kin asked.

"To the pit of a dung hole with them," Sai said. "Let them try to follow us into the Twenty-Nine if they want. If they can find us or catch us, they'll be the first." He spat over the bow and grabbed his crotch, hoping the Johmatrans saw him through a distance glass of their own.

He had a new *syrai*, a child on the way, and a hold full of valuable weapons. Sai planned to eat, drink, and fuck until he fell facedown in the sand, and these idiot barbarians could do nothing to stop him. He was home, and he'd beat them. They could rot, because he would do it again.

Chapter Nineteen

SOFT silkiness surrounded Sasha, and he slowly lifted himself from comfort and luxury beyond anything he had ever experienced. After the battle, he expected pain, but he found none—not even an itch at the side of his nose or an ache in the soles of his feet. He felt perfect, but the absence of the minor annoyances of having a physical body unnerved him. Looking around, he took in towering statues carved from black rock, polished to the sheen of glass. Red light from the hundreds of lanterns reflected off the surfaces. Sumptuous red velvet encased him, and the most beautiful man he'd ever seen reclined on his belly beside Sasha, watching Sasha with black eyes tinged with red.

A pool of thick red liquid bubbled in front of them. Sasha knew the scent well—blood. "I'm dead."

"Do you find it unpleasant?" the gorgeous dark-haired youth next to him asked. "You shouldn't. You have served me faithfully and come to your reward."

"Thalil?" Sasha asked, too disoriented to show any kind of reverence.

"My son," the other said, pinning a lock of hair behind Sasha's ear and smiling.

Sasha bolted up. Hundreds of others surrounded them, reclining on huge beds or upholstered benches behind them, all of them young, beautiful men with hunger in their eyes. They stroked their hands down themselves and each other as they looked on Sasha and…. Could it really be?

"Master?"

Thalil, a beautiful young man on the cusp of adulthood, dark waves of hair cascading over perfect tanned shoulders and brushing tiny reddish purple nipples, but with eyes as old and cold as murder itself, looked back at Sasha. Desire and defense warred within Sasha; he wanted to fall at the feet of his divine sovereign, tremble at his toes, beg to be allowed to touch his flesh, but he also mistrusted his perceptions and the intentions of his host. So he moved a few inches away, clutching his fist over his hips as he was naked and had no weapons.

"You were a good servant, Sasha," Thalil said, running his fingertips along Sasha's arm and then over his hip and thigh. "You gave me two kings, among many others. You were special, very skilled."

"But now it is over?" Sasha asked, his head still fuzzy, not sure if he dreamed it all while unconscious on the floor of the order hideout. But no— no one could have survived such injuries as he'd received back there.

"It depends." Thalil pressed against Sasha's shoulder, making Sasha lie on his back and sink farther into the luxuriant sheets and cushions. Propped on his hand, Thalil looked down at Sasha, and the Cast-Down god was the most beautiful and desirable being Sasha had ever regarded. Watching Thalil—the glint of his eyes, the perfect smoothness of his deep golden skin, the curve of his full lips—distracted Sasha to the point where he could think of nothing else. He thought he might be perfectly content to lie there looking up at that flawless face for the rest of eternity. But contentment such as he felt was nearly always a façade, and he mistrusted it.

"Say what you mean." Sasha's impertinence surprised him, but he needed whatever passed for truth in this realm.

Thalil trailed his fingers down Sasha's neck, over his nipple, and along the raised muscles of his belly. "Beautiful Sasha," Thalil said, brushing his lips against Sasha's chest, his warm breath fanning Sasha's nipples to stand up. "I have enjoyed watching you. I don't want to stop watching the havoc you can wreak in the world in my name, but I am not cruel. Not to my disciples. You have earned the rest and pleasure of my Crimson Palace, and you are more than welcome to stay. But if you want to go back—"

"Back? To Duncan and Yarrow?"

"Yes," Thalil said, drawing out the S into a seductive hiss that almost made Sasha forget his partners—but not quite. The soft sound and the breath on his skin almost whisked them from his mind, but he held on to them, to the images of their faces, clutching them as fiercely as he had his daggers in life.

"I would like to go back," he said.

Thalil flopped on his back and sank into the lush red mattress and cushions. "You don't even have to think about it? Here, there is only pleasure, and plenty of it. No pain, not even the tiniest discomfort. Not even a cramp in your toe. And I am often here, which I'm sure you'll grow to enjoy. You have earned this. Are you sure you do not wish to stay? Claim your just rewards?"

"I would like to go back to Duncan and Yarrow, if you offer me the option, master," Sasha said.

"I offer you a bargain." Thalil stared up at the high vaulted ceiling as he ghosted his fingertips along Sasha's skin. "I'm sure you realize nothing so profound can come for free."

"I'm listening," Sasha said. As Thalil's hands on his body commandeered his attention, he realized none of his injuries from that last battle had carried over to this dimension, whatever it was, but the old scars, the one his brethren had sliced across the side of his neck when he'd first defied them and the one he'd earned in his room in Windust Castle, across his chest, remained. He began to ponder it, but then Thalil spoke again, his sensual, low voice driving every other thought from Sasha's mind.

"It will take me a great deal of power to return you to the world, Sasha, to defy the very rules of life and death. To do it, I'll have to surrender a large amount of the strength I have amassed to you. I need to know I will get my money's worth, so to speak."

"What would you have me do?"

Thalil pressed a finger to Sasha's lips to quiet him, then trailed it down his chin and along the raised, satiny line bisecting the side of his throat. "Tell me. Do you know how I have managed to keep my life and youth after so many thousands of years?"

"You are a god. My god."

If the sound of Thalil speaking had been erotic and all consuming, his laughter nearly finished Sasha. "I suppose I am, now, at least in the same way those thirteen bitches are goddesses. Did your mage not explain this to you?"

"No."

"Well, none of us were born divine, you see. We were born as flesh, the same as you. The thirteen the others of the world revere were the wives of the emperor Fane, and I am his son. While they have used his teachings and magic to become what they are, I have used life. It is a spell I put in place long ago, ten thousand of your years or more. When one of my disciples, one bearing the mark of my crimson moon, offers me a life, I receive two things. First, I get whatever years are left, the years between the person falling to one of my children until their lifespan would have ended by whatever way fate originally decided. I also get souls." He stood and offered Sasha his hand. Though Thalil was naked, a golden chain rode low on his hips, and dozens of others dangled down the sides of his legs, decorated with red stones and black pearls. The train in the back dragged several feet behind them as they walked toward an arched window, the delicate links tinkling in a musical and enticing way against the bone-colored tiles.

When they reached the opening cut in the dark rock, Thalil leaned one hip against the broad sill and pointed. Beyond his palace stretched a starless red sky smudged with feathery black clouds. Beneath it stood a dark, undulating plain devoid of any vegetation. Nothing broke the monotony but an errant formation of sharp rocks. Across it, comet-like wisps darted and fluttered, millions of them or more, just white flickers with long gossamer tails. They continued for as far as Sasha could see. "What are they?"

"The souls of every victim of my children," Thalil said, watching them with a hungry smile. "They are the source of my power. They are why I'm greater than the rest of them put together. Fane's wives would put an end to me if they could, you know. But because of them, because of the devotion of my children, they do not dare try."

Thalil clasped Sasha's elbow and led him back to the sumptuous round bench encircling the pool of blood. They sat on the edge, their backs to the gurgling font, and Thalil draped his hand over Sasha's thigh. "You have served the Crimson Scythe and served well. I would have you serve me directly, as my emissary in the mortal realm. If you do, I will give you enough of the years I've collected to live as long as you want, and to stay vital and beautiful. All I ask in return is obedience. If I ask something of you, you must do it."

Sasha considered. The bargain seemed more than fair, a little too easy, and that roused his suspicion. He could think of very few things he would refuse his master—in truth, he could think of only one. "I will do anything you ask of me, master, with one exception. I will not hurt Yarrow or Duncan. Not for you, not for anyone."

"Ah, my little killer with a chink in his armor. No matter. I was already aware of this slight imperfection in you, and I'll agree to your terms. I will never ask you to lift a hand against either of those men, or—before you say it—cause them suffering indirectly. You will take over command of the Crimson Scythe and dissolve that ridiculous council. You will take your orders from me directly and see they are carried out as you will. You'll see that the order continues to flourish and the supply of years and souls reaching me remains steady. I… will have need of power very soon, I suspect. Do you agree?"

"I…. Will the others, the rest of the order accept this?"

"I will see that they do," Thalil told him.

"Then I agree," Sasha said. He could see no reason to refuse. It would be a good thing to be part of the order again, to have an identity and a place he belonged. "I have to ask, master. Why me?"

"I'll tell you in time. Now, do you wish to spend a few more moments recuperating here? The pain will be—quite exquisite when you return, especially after this short time in its complete absence."

Sasha shook his head. "I am eager to have cold iron in my hands, as it should be. Will I see you again?"

"Not in this form," Thalil said. "Not until you return here for the final time, but you will hear from me. Are you ready? To say that this is going to be unpleasant would be to say the man who cut your throat gave you a playful scratch."

"Best to get it over with, then," Sasha said, scarcely able to imagine enduring more pain than he had during the battle. But the idea of spending eternity here, without Yarrow and Duncan, hurt more.

Thalil kissed Sasha softly. He placed his hand on Sasha's right side, at the bottom of his ribs. A burning blast shot from his palm. Sasha smelled scorched flesh, and then pain obliterated everything else, filling his entire universe, his every perception, with agony, until he could no longer find the place where the pain ended and he began. Before long, he even forgot he was screaming.

On HIS knees in the pool of thickening blood, Yarrow held Sasha's lifeless body on his lap. With his face toward the vaulted ceiling and tears pouring down his cheeks, he screamed and screamed, inarticulate cries of raw pain. The brilliant blue energy kept the rest of the assassins at bay, clutching their weapons in the shadows beyond Yarrow's flaring power. Duncan stood at his back, clutching his sword, though he didn't know if he'd be able to use it. When he'd seen Sasha fall, he'd tried to hold on to hope as he fought his way to Sasha's side, but when he'd seen the quantity of blood, Sasha's throat cut almost to the bone—Duncan had seen too many battles to delude himself into thinking his friend could survive. His first instinct had been to drop his weapon and fall to the floor, screaming his rage to the heavens like Yarrow, but he still had Yarrow to protect and Sasha to take from this hideous place, because he would be damned if he'd leave Sasha's body here. So he pushed his grief back to deal with later, though tears flowed hot down his cheeks and sobs he couldn't quite choke back shook his chest.

How were they going to live? Duncan couldn't imagine spending the rest of his time in the world without Sasha beside him. He didn't want to. How would he survive without seeing Sasha look up at him through his eyelashes or glimpsing one of his rare smiles? Without Sasha walking beside him on the road, or sitting next to him quietly in front of a fire? It couldn't be. It just couldn't be possible Sasha couldn't get up and walk—

"No," Duncan choked before he realized he'd intended to speak. The tears he'd tried so hard to hold spilled hot into his mouth, and it took all his strength to keep his sword in his hands as sobs wracked his chest. What did it matter if he cried or screamed? Duncan had failed Sasha; he was gone forever. If not for Yarrow, who would need him desperately in the aftermath of all this, he might have given up.

Yarrow's voice finally faltered, and his screams tapered to dry moans before stopping altogether. Hauling in shaking breaths, the mage stared down at his blood-soaked hands and then at Sasha's contorted corpse. Sasha's skin had already started to gray and his lips were blue, and his black eyes stared into the void of eternity with no light behind them. With a quivering hand, Yarrow touched Sasha's cold cheek and gurgled out another whimper. Then, after several moments of silence, his power flared so brightly Duncan shielded his eyes. When it faded enough for Duncan to focus his vision again, Yarrow looked out on the gathered assassins with a hideous snarl, cerulean light pouring from the corners of his eyes.

"You're all going to pay for this," the mage said in a low voice, sounding almost calm. When he next spoke, he sounded completely, violently insane, shrieking so hard spittle flew from his mouth. "You're going to pay! All of you! I'll kill every last one of you! I will rip every shred of evidence this order ever existed from the face of the world!" He laid Sasha down gently and touched his forehead. When he spoke again, he addressed Sasha's corpse with a sad smile. "You avenged me, my dear love, and now I'll avenge you." His wings shot from his back, spanning almost the width of the chamber and liquefying the stone of the walls where his feathers brushed them.

Duncan tensed. He should have expected this. Yarrow possessed a singular predictable trait: he responded to pain with anger. Though Yarrow had had more than his share of pain heaped on him in his short life, he had probably never hurt like this. Duncan knew he never had himself—not even when he'd lost his first love, Aubrey. The hurt and loss built in his belly until it spilled out in another trio of dry sobs. Duncan had seen Yarrow level an entire army, and he knew he'd obliterate everything around him and maybe even himself. Sensing the threat, the assassins backed away from him. One of them fired an arrow from somewhere off to the left, but the bolt turned to powder the second it touched the glowing light around the mage. Yarrow shot a blast of energy in the direction from which the arrow had come, and it tore through the three people it struck, cutting them almost in half and making blood bloom around them in a red mist. Afterward, Yarrow laughed, a cruel and frightening sound Duncan knew well but had hoped to never hear again.

He dared a few steps toward the mage, the enchantment surrounding Yarrow making Duncan's teeth wiggle and his hair stand on end. What would he say to his friend? "Yarrow, my love, you must keep control of yourself. You know what can happen if you do not. Try to calm down."

"Calm down? They took him, Duncan! They took my Sasha! My beautiful Sasha! He was… everything. My beloved. They killed my beloved! *Our* Sasha!" Yarrow's aura faded and his wings drooped as he looked at their partner's pale face, and he started sobbing again. Sensing his momentary weakness, the assassins crept forward. Duncan heard the stretch of bowstrings, and he turned to face them, willing his numb, spent arms to hoist his blade. Though he knew nothing at the moment but anguish, Duncan's body knew how to fight, and he let his instincts guide his movements. To his surprise, Corbin limped over to stand next to him, the dead order brother he'd resurrected with his magic lurching behind him, ready to fight under the control of Corbin's enchantment. Duncan had neither the time nor the energy to be disgusted by the forbidden magic. All of them might be joining Sasha soon.

They faced off, the three of them, four if Duncan counted the corpse Corbin controlled, and if they could even include Yarrow, against the hundred or so assassins. Before either side could deliver the first blow, a loud grating, rock against rock, like the stone floor cleaving in two and sliding apart, drew their attention. All of them turned to the towering statue of the Cast-Down god, though Duncan kept one eye on the armed people surrounding them. He'd been around Sasha long enough to know they would exploit any opportunity—

The floor shook, almost knocking Duncan off his feet. A round lip of rock broke through the tiles, shattering the thick black marble as if it were nothing more than a thin sheet of ice. It encircled the idol, rising to the middle of its shins. The stone victim began to bleed from his eyes and an unseen wound across his neck, crimson rivulets flowing heavy and fast, like the melted snow down the mountainside in the spring. Duncan could only stare with his mouth hanging open and his heartbeat floundering. Somehow, he knew neither Yarrow nor Corbin, nor any of the other mages of the order performed this macabre miracle. Even the assassins shuffled and whispered to one another. The blood burbled, and in no time it had filled the newly formed pool, an area the size of a small pond.

Then the statue spoke through unmoving lips, the playful, sensual voice emanating from deep within the stone, making the whole cavern quiver. "Brethren of the Crimson Scythe, my children, hear your master. I give to you my chosen, my ambassador. This one alone will control my order. Obey him as you would obey me, and I shall be pleased with you. Disregard his wishes and risk my wrath."

As quickly as it had begun, the blood ceased flowing and the statue went still. The cavern seemed smaller and much less impressive after the departure of whatever had possessed it. Duncan couldn't quite bear to acknowledge that he'd stood in the presence of the foulest of the Cast-Down, one whose name the righteous refused to speak....

All of them looked around, waiting for this chosen one to appear, wondering if he or she might already be among them. Duncan imagined most of the assassins would love nothing more than to be selected.

"Who is doing that?" Yarrow shouted. "Stop it!"

Duncan turned around, ready to defend his friend—the only one he had left—but what he saw almost made him drop his sword. Sasha's limp form floated a few feet above the floor, bent backward, arms stiff at his sides and his poor head almost touching his back, the horrible wound stretched open.

Duncan whirled back toward the assassins. "There is no need for this disrespect. You slaughtered him outnumbered a hundred to one! At least have the dignity to—"

A tug on his elbow cut Duncan off, and Corbin, his face whiter than usual, pointed back toward Sasha. Sasha's body flew to the side, as if someone had hit him below his right rib, and a glowing handprint appeared on his skin for just a second. Crimson light poured from his mouth and eyes until it engulfed him in a scarlet cocoon. Inside it, the black silhouette writhed and let out earsplitting screams of the purest agony, ten times worse than Yarrow's. Only moments after it appeared, the light faded, and Sasha fell to his hands and knees, his head bowed and curtained by his long, dark hair. When he lifted his head slowly and looked up at them through the cleft in his tresses, his eyes glowed red.

With a sound between a sob and a giggle, Yarrow scrubbed at his cheeks with the heels of his hands as he ran toward their friend. "Sasha," he whispered, then yelled. "Sasha!" He gripped Sasha beneath the armpits and helped him to stand, tears streaming down his face as he looked into his friend's eyes, touched Sasha's cheek, his chin, and lips. Then Yarrow threw his arms around Sasha and dropped his face to Sasha's shoulder, his whole body convulsing as he wept unabashedly against Sasha's skin. Sasha laid his cheek against the top of Yarrow's head and returned his embrace. For a few minutes, they just held each other.

Duncan approached slowly, still reeling with the shock of it all. Nothing felt real or solid, not even his feet against the gory ground. He felt like he moved through a realm of ether, of shadows and phantoms where nothing, not even his own senses, could be trusted. Sasha had been cold and dead, as lifeless as the black stone and now…. How? Had his god done it, and if so, what would it cost? Goddesses forgive him, Duncan didn't care.

Yarrow and Sasha broke away from each other as Duncan joined them. He looked at Sasha warily, as if he expected the whole illusion to collapse, leaving him to once again regard a mutilated corpse. He let his sword drop and clatter against the floor, then reached for Sasha with a shaky hand, almost afraid to touch him. Sasha met his gaze, his black eyes with their slight slant and decadent, dark lashes just as Duncan remembered. Thank the goddess the red light had faded; Duncan wasn't sure he could stand to look at it. Sasha blinked a few times, waiting, gauging Duncan's reaction. Duncan laid his palms on Sasha's shoulders, and they felt solid, rising and falling slowly with Sasha's breath. Duncan tugged off his chain-mail gloves and tossed them aside, then ran his bare palms down Sasha's arms, over his belly, the rungs of his ribs, his chest and neck. The ghost of a handprint, black against his skin but smooth and raised, like a long-healed burn, remained above his right hip. Though still covered in clotting blood, he was whole, unwounded. Warm and alive, and Duncan didn't care how or why. He folded Sasha in his arms, pressed their foreheads together, and wept as Yarrow had as he held him, never wanting to let Sasha out of the safety of his arms.

Finally he pulled away, unclasped his filthy cloak, and draped it over Sasha's shoulders. Then he picked up his sword and replaced it on his back as Sasha turned and walked toward the dais at the front of the room. The assassins parted to allow him to pass, some of them touching the hem of Duncan's bloodstained cloak with quiet reverence. He ascended the stairs and stood looking over the sea of his former brethren. Were they his brethren again, now?

"I have been judged by Thalil," he said. "He has named me the head of this order. Do any of you dispute my claim?"

A murmur moved across the sea of red, and Sasha waited impassively for it to die down. No one challenged him, and how could they, after what they'd seen?

"Good. I absolve this man of any wrongdoing. His status within this order is restored." He indicated Corbin with a nod.

"Thank you, chosen one," Corbin said.

Sasha shook his head. "I have no desire for fancy titles. What I would like is a room, with a large bed and a healthy fire. I would like a bath, a meal, some wine, and something to wear until I can have another set of armor made. I would like to do that tomorrow, and I would also like the weapons I have lost replaced." Without another word, he left the platform and motioned for Duncan and Yarrow to follow him.

"Right this way," said a young man said, leading them down a hallway.

Duncan noticed an odd occurrence as they passed between the pools of crimson light the lanterns cast and the shadows between them. When Sasha stepped into the darkness, he melted into it, disappearing and losing all semblance of solidity until he moved into the hazy light again. It frightened Duncan, especially since Sasha didn't seem to do it intentionally or even notice.

When they reached an elaborate chamber with a huge round bed with a heavy red velvet canopy, fires burning in twin hearths, and a rich feast spread across an iron table, Duncan didn't know if he wanted to sleep for a week or never close his eyes again.

Sasha wandered to the platters of food and picked up a slice of apple. He sniffed it, popped it into his mouth, chewed, and swallowed. "It's delicious," he said. "Tart and sweet and crisp. Moist and juicy. It tastes just as it should. Better. I didn't know whether it would or not."

"None of this has turned out as I expected," Duncan said as he leaned his weapon in a corner. "Not at all."

"I expected all of us to perish," Sasha said, "but only one of us did." When he moved to rest his hand on Duncan's shoulder, Duncan flinched, and Sasha frowned. "I am not a phantom. Are you afraid of me, Duncan? Disgusted by me as I am now?"

Duncan reached for Sasha and folded him into his arms. "No. I'm just very confused. I love you, Sasha. That has not changed. Do you... remember anything from when you were... gone?"

"Yes," Sasha said. "I'll tell you all of it, if you'd like."

"I would," Duncan said, "but not tonight. I don't need anything else giving me nightmares."

Yarrow came up behind Sasha and laid his head between Sasha's shoulder blades, against Duncan's old cloak. "I suppose we have been victorious. We're all alive, even Corbin, and I have a feeling the order won't be bothering Sasha anymore."

"But what does this all mean for us?" Duncan asked.

"It means I must lead the Crimson Scythe," Sasha said.

"I suppose that's quite an honor," Duncan forced out. He'd hoped this doomed mission would sever all Sasha's ties with the order, but it had only strengthened them.

"It is a gilded cage," Sasha said, shaking his head.

"Will they expect you to live here?" Yarrow asked.

"I don't care if they do," Sasha said. "I have no desire to live here, and I won't. I will have to come here, of course."

To send murderers for hire off to fulfill their contracts, Duncan thought. He kept quiet, though, because the last thing Sasha needed right now was his judgment. He didn't want to consider the implications, not tonight. Tonight, he just wanted Yarrow and Sasha sleeping across his chest, sheltered in his arms, where he could protect them. He never wanted them in danger like this again, but he didn't know if he could force the world to acquiesce to his wishes.

"This blood on me," Yarrow said in a timid whisper, "most of it's yours, Sasha. I wish I could burn these clothes. I never want to look at them again. I don't want to think of this—"

"Burn them, then," Sasha said. "I can have armor made for you here. It will be of excellent quality. You too, Duncan. If you want."

Duncan was hardly a materialistic man, but he'd grown quite attached to his battered old suit of plate and his greatsword. "I'll keep them, but they'll need a polishing. And some repairs when we get home to Windwake."

"I can have them repaired for you here," Sasha offered.

"No," Duncan said, a little too quickly.

"I'm going to do it," Yarrow said, stripping off garments almost completely soaked through with blood. "Thinking about what happened.... It still makes me want to go out there and slaughter them." After he'd disrobed and thrown everything he'd worn into the hall, he glanced down at his brown skin, almost as fouled with gore as his clothing. He looked like he'd be sick.

"Come, my friend," Sasha said, taking Yarrow's hand. "There is a bath just through this doorway. You'll feel better after you're clean. Will you join us, Duncan? The tub is big enough, and I'd like your company." There was a plea in Sasha's eyes Duncan had never seen before, but he understood it. Sasha needed Duncan to accept him, to touch him and prove he didn't consider him some sort of abomination.

"I'll be there as soon as I get out of my armor." As he began working the leather buckles loose, Duncan let his gaze wander over the room's decadent furnishings. It lit on a painting of Thalil, and Duncan stared at the beautiful youth, unable to trust his own heart. Everything about the Cast-Down god and his cult horrified Duncan, yet this creature had given him Sasha back. Sasha would never be free of Thalil now, and Duncan wasn't yet sure exactly what that meant. He just knew they were together, and he wouldn't have to face life without the man he loved. Perhaps it was just selfishness. After he finished undressing, he went to the painting and touched the canvas. A numbing chill shot through the bones of his finger, but he didn't pull away.

"Goddesses forgive me," he said, feeling a little faint, "but…. Thank you."

Chapter Twenty

THE last night of Fayelle's Moon belonged to Thalil. On that night, the hours of darkness outnumbered the hours of light, and most of the mortals cowered in their homes, burning white candles and stoking their fires in a vain attempt to keep the shadows at bay. Small golden squares from their windows painted the stones of the street, but they were little more than feeble flickers against the vast, silken, glorious expanse of the longest night.

Thalil twirled his daggers in his hands and whistled to himself as he made his way to the grandest of Fayelle's temples, an ivory palace in the city of Sarfylle, between Meadow's Edge and the coastal lands held by the Emiri. It had been carved from the white rock of the Revenant Coast, hundreds of miles away, and transported here at the cost of a great many mortal lives. The thirteen spires, each topped with a gilded rosebud, made any king's palace look like a hovel. A candle flickered behind each of the frosted-glass windows, and fires burned in the braziers lining the parapets.

Thalil rolled his eyes at the ridiculous spectacle. The whole thing looked like a spoiled princess's birthday cake.

All of the priestesses and servants slept inside, deluded by the false security the white walls offered. Even a novice of Thalil's order could creep into their hallowed halls and slit all their throats while they slumbered on their ivory sheets. He considered ordering his new emissary to see to that, just to heap more gruesome glory onto his name, but then he saw the one he sought.

Fayelle sat about halfway up the grandiose stair leading to the temple doors, covered in layer upon layer of coarse white cloth, a white veil and silver circlet hiding most of her pale blonde hair. Thalil, in nothing but a gauzy red skirt with beaded fringe, red leather boots with long, sharp spikes on the toes, and a single ebony pauldron accentuated with delicate chains draping his chest and hanging below his opposite arm, skipped up the steps. A crown with a crimson crescent carved from a ruby sat atop his dark hair, the curtain of gems and dark pearls attached to the sides brushing his cheeks.

When he reached the plain-featured woman with the frozen gray eyes, he bowed theatrically and kissed her knuckles.

"What are you doing here, you hideous creature?" she asked, snatching her cold, dry hand out of his grasp.

Thalil planted a boot on the step between Fayelle's legs and bent in half to rest his elbows on his knee. The spike on his toe stuck up between her thighs in an obscene way that made him smile. "I am many things, Aunt, but hideous is certainly not one of them, and we both know it."

"You are, and have always been, too confident in that beauty of yours, you sin-soaked abomination," Fayelle said. "If you think you will find a repeat of what happened between us all those centuries ago, you are very much mistaken."

He laughed and tossed his head, rattling the decorations dangling from his crown. "You flatter yourself, hag. Do you suppose I enjoyed the night we spent together? I could barely force my body to perform. Unlike you. You screamed your pleasure to the stars. I remember it well, how you let me do anything I wanted and begged for more—"

"Enough. What is it you want, monster? You are planning something, and all of us know it. Why did you use so much of your power to return that assassin of yours from death to life?"

"Ah, you know about that."

She pursed her bloodless lips. "That act defied the most scared and irrefutable laws of nature. Of course we felt it. And we know what it cost you. So… why? You have many others. What is so special about this one?"

"I have a good feeling about him. He's lovely, and very skilled. A killer born."

"Indeed?" Fayelle asked. "Is it really this Sasha you want to secure? Or his companion? For know this, Cast-Down, we thirteen will obliterate Yarroway L'Estrella."

"Will you? What's keeping you?"

"We do not need to justify our decisions or actions to one such as you," Fayelle said, turning her small nose up.

Thalil grasped her face and tilted it toward him, leaning in until the tips of their noses touched. "Deceit, like making love, is a skill, my lady. You must practice to be even passable at either. You haven't, and you're not. At either. You thirteen cunts can't touch that boy, or you would have."

"Get your hands off me."

"You love my hands on you, Fayelle. You're a worthless liar, as worthless as you are a bedmate. But very well. I prefer men, anyway. Just like my father did. Go on and deny that as well."

"What are you doing here, Thalil? Did you come just to torment me?"

"Only partly. I wanted to give you and the others the chance to step aside, to fade gracefully into the realms of history and myth. I'm tired of sharing the world with you, and I don't like any of you, least of all my bloated sow of a mother. Leave the world to mortals. It's theirs; let us see what they make of it."

"Will you relinquish your power?"

"No, but I won't use it, either. Resurrecting Sasha took more from me than I thought it would. I'd be happy to rest for a few hundred years, see what the mortals do with their world. Just a few hundred years. Five, maybe six. What's a few hundred years? Agree to sit and watch, and I will do the same. Refuse, and, well… I *will* aid those who stand against you."

"The others will never agree to this," Fayelle said. "Nor will I. This is our world. We are the Thirteen."

Thalil brushed the back of his hand down her face, watching as color trailed his touch. Could any other being but him make that pallid flesh bloom red? Probably not. "I hoped you'd say that. Well, then, may the best of us win, and we all know that's me. This will be quite a diversion. I'll be going, unless you'd like me to stay?"

"I… sweet Thalil…."

"But I jest! Good night, you dried up old buzzard!" He resumed the tune he'd been whistling as he skipped back down the steps.

AFTER a month on the road, visiting temples and offering his vices into Fayelle's Fires, Garith returned to Eirion-Vayl a few pounds lighter and much dirtier than when he'd left. The courtyard seemed unnaturally empty when he entered it with Sander, though a single servant appeared to take their packs. It was early, just after dawn, cold but still, and frost had etched delicate patterns across the face of the ancient stones.

"It's Sarmine's Moon," Sander said, leaning in toward Garith's ear. "Do you suppose all the lads are out courting the country girls?"

Garith shook his head, the contentment of coming home evaporating as anxiety took its place. "All of them?"

They proceeded into the castle and found it equally abandoned. No servants tended the fires or refreshed the flowers on the tables in front of the statues of the goddesses. The fortress felt cold and decrepit as Garith and Sander ascended the stairs. Many of the torches in the alcoves had gone out, and no one had relit them.

"Let us just hope the queen is recovering," Garith said.

"Should we stop in and see her?" Sander asked.

"Absolutely." One advantage of the empty castle was that Garith could reach over and squeeze Sander's wrist. He'd grown so accustomed to spending his days with no one else it would take an effort to remind himself he couldn't just touch Sander whenever he wanted, which was practically every minute. If Garith could see Sander, he wanted to put his hands on him, especially after the nights they'd spent traveling, when he'd finally gotten the chance to push inside Sander and to feel Sander within him. He had never imagined anything could be so wonderful, but now they had to pretend they didn't love each other, didn't draw comfort from each other's touch.... Garith had begun to question why others considered the love and loyalty they shared so wicked, but the idea of seeing his wife, hopefully ruddy with health, convinced him to leave the questions for later.

Not the queen, but Garith's mother, met them on the landing. Denna Corinna clutched a fox-fur cape around her shoulders. She took Garith's hand and led him into an alcove where a statue of the goddess Myint held sword and shield ready. In the war goddess's shadow, Garith's mother stared into his eyes. Sander waited a respectful few feet away, but Garith motioned to him.

"Your Majesty?"

"Sander, please don't. You are the other half of me, and I don't care if my mother—or, frankly, anyone else—knows it. I would have you beside me. You have supported me, defended me, lov—Please, my friend."

"You will have need of loyal friends, my son," Garith's mother said. The lines around her dark eyes looked deeper than Garith had ever seen them, and the mouth that had curved up at the corners now hung in a frown.

"How is the queen?" Garith asked.

"Better, but not fully restored. She will live to deliver her... your son, but she is weak."

"And what of the knights?" Sander asked. "Where are they?"

Garith's mother shook her head. "A great many of our men have joined the army the priestesses are forming. The priestesses speak against you in the temples. They say the goddesses do not bless your rule. Many of your nobles defend you, as you have been a good king, but I'm afraid the rift is only growing, and it's beginning to divide this kingdom."

Garith flopped down on a wooden bench and rested his elbows on his knees. "I have spent the past month visiting temples, sweeping their floors and peeling turnips for the priestesses. Has it all been for nothing? What are they trying to do? Do they honestly want to depose me?"

"No, I don't think so," his mother said. "I don't think they'd risk outright treason. They want to turn you into a puppet by constantly holding the power they're amassing over your head. They might not want to rule directly, but I have little doubt they want your every decision made with the threat of their growing army, centuries of wealth, and influence over the people first in your mind."

"That's even worse!" Sander said.

"They aren't going to get it," Garith said, balling his fist and watching the thin layer of dirt on the back of his hand crack. "I will act in the best interests of this kingdom. But if it is becoming a divided kingdom, how do I heal it? What more can I do?"

"You have read history," his mother offered gently. "What is the one thing that will unite a people faster than any other?"

"An outside threat," Sander said. "A threat to everyone, something they must stand together to face. Something dangerous and terrible enough to make them put their differences aside."

"But what? Goddesses, are you actually advising me to start a war?"

"The invaders are already on our shores," his mother said. "Two weeks ago, a fleet of ships from the lands of Johmatra reached the mouth of the Kanda. The same barbarians who have been sacking cities along the coasts of Espero and killing my countrymen are now attacking the Emiri. They are bloodthirsty and merciless. This is your common enemy, my son, the one that will unite your people under your banner once again—both your supporters and those knights who have joined the priestesses."

"But that's insanity!" Sander said. "No one is going to fight to save the Emiri! Everyone hates them. If Garith sends knights to defend them, he'll just be giving the priestesses more fuel to turn people against him!"

"He's right." Garith's head started to pound as the muscles across his shoulders and up the back of his neck tensed. "I can just hear Tam Vartanan now. He'll say the barbarians are doing us a favor, that we should just let them wipe the Emiri out and move in when they've finished. None of my nobles are going to send their knights to defend the Emiri. Even asking them is likely to push more of them toward the loyalty of my detractors. Goddesses, what am I going to do?"

"I can tell you what your father would have done," his mother said. "He was a very shrewd man when he had to be. He would have found a way to unite his people against this common enemy. He would have done whatever was necessary to keep this kingdom whole and undivided. Not far from the Emiri lands, on the coast near Meadow's Edge, is the great temple to Fayelle. Can you imagine the outrage if the barbarians were to attack, even destroy it? Not a single person—noble, knight, or priestess—would dare to argue against making them pay and driving them from our shores. They would stand together, behind their king."

Garith wiped his roughened palm over his face, his cheeks hot and his head light and swimming. "So I'm left to hope these enemies will attack and kill a temple full of innocent women. Has it really come to this?"

"Not hope," his mother said.

Bile splashed the back of Garith's throat, and he barely managed to choke it back. He clutched the edges of the bench as everything grew fuzzy and started to spin around him. She couldn't mean—Not his mother. His mother was kind and fair, and he'd always valued her counsel above all others because of her sensitivity, her empathy, her unique ability to see a situation from every point of view—She couldn't mean it. But she did. Garith reached over and clutched Sander's hand, finding it trembled almost as hard as his own.

"You are honestly suggesting I... I somehow see that temple destroyed and place the blame on the Johmatran barbarians?"

"You are a king, the king of Selindria and Gaeltheon, of the Blessed Epoch. You must do what needs doing to hold all that together."

Garith kept expecting to wake up from some horrific nightmare. "All those innocent lives. Their blood on my hands...."

"The war cry against the enemy would be deafening and unanimous," his mother continued, her voice seeped in sorrow and defeat. "This rift between you and the priestesses would be forgotten in an instant, and afterward, you would be a champion of the goddesses for avenging the defamation of one of their shrines. I have thought about this a great deal, and I can see few other options."

"I can't," Garith said softly. "No. I should protect my people, not slaughter them for my personal benefit.... Goddesses."

"Will your people be protected if they come under the rule of the priestesses? Do you have so much faith in their benevolence? My son, this is your kingdom, and one day it will be your son's. You must do what it takes to keep it whole."

"No. No good can come of doing something so... so reprehensible. I will be a righteous king, and I have to continue to believe being good, doing good, will result in good."

"You are young and an idealist," his mother said. "I wish we had the luxury of allowing you to remain so. Where has doing good gotten you? Did not this whole ordeal result from one righteous act?"

That cursed tablet! All this over an old, dusty slab of stone! "If I'd had any idea, I would have just let them have the damned thing."

"You are not a clairvoyant," his mother said, "and neither am I. Nor can we change the past. I have not arrived at this solution lightly, but I know this kingdom can become a paradise under your son's rule. You must prepare it for him."

"Even if I could reconcile this... this thing, I would not even know how to do it," Garith said, aching all the way to his bones, stomach churning. He just wanted to go to his bed and curl in a ball beneath his blankets, as he'd done when he'd been upset as a child. Back then, his mother had been the one promising him everything would be all right, driving the night terrors away, and now—

"You know very well who to ask," his mother said in the firm tone she'd used when he'd misbehaved as a boy, "and, I might add, it will not be the first time."

Garith stood, released Sander's hand to grab at his hair, and kicked the bench. "It isn't the same thing! I sent him against traitors, people who wanted to overthrow me and murder *me* in my bed! Cloistered sisters! Has it occurred to you that even *he* might refuse that?"

"Don't be a child," she scolded. "Do you know how many knights you've lost since you've been gone? How many do you think, Garith? Out of the thousand men here at Eirion-Vayl?"

"I... I don't know." Garith nudged the bench back into place and practically fell back onto it.

"More than three hundred. And among the lowborn soldiers and infantry, the numbers are even worse. Assuming the figures are the same throughout the kingdom, you've lost a third of your army to the priestesses. Are you going to wait until they decide some indiscretion or other is great enough for them to march against you? Is that the kingdom you want to leave for your children? It is not the one I want for you, my son. You must remind them they need you as a leader, prove to them you can defend this land, and to do that, you need a common enemy, an enemy no one can stand up for. To drive these barbarians from our shore, after what they've done, you'll be justified in demanding all your men return to your banner, and the priestesses will not be able to refuse. What will you do?"

"I cannot do this," Garith said. Sander nodded once, decisively, and it bolstered Garith's convictions. He reached for Sander's hand again, needing something to hold on to. "I will not do it, and I will not accept that the world has fallen so low that resorting to something like this is the only way to keep hold of my kingdom. I believe it's still possible to be a decent man and succeed. I have to believe that. I will not blacken my heart or my spirit by doing something like this."

His mother looked from Garith's face to Sander's, her lips forming a tight, pale line. "The temples have more to use against you than you know, my son. Do you remember a young knight named Wyeth Ashlinn? I see you do, both of you. Then I do not need to tell you what he has reported to the priestesses and what they are now sharing with their congregations. Soon, they'll have enough men to punish you for what they're telling everyone you've done."

"That young man is mistaken," Garith argued feebly. "He does not know what he saw."

"It hardly matters to me if you did it or not, Garith," his mother said. "It does not even matter if the priestesses believe it is true. What matters is that the common people, and many of those who fight for you, are starting to believe it. They are starting to believe you are unnatural and therefore unfit to rule. They're beginning to fear the wrath of the Thirteen. You must direct their fear and anger at something else, and soon."

"No," Garith said firmly. "My ability to rule this kingdom with wisdom and justice is hardly contingent upon who I lie beside at night. I will not do it. I have made my decision."

She stood, brushed a lock of hair from Garith's brow, bent, and kissed him on the forehead. "I will not ask again. Let your heart and your spirit remain bright and pure. Perhaps that's as it should be. Now, your wife will want to see you. She is feeling well enough to sew and read in the afternoons, whether from the awrythe's heart or the absence of the food brought to her by the priestesses, I cannot say. I'll leave you to it. The swords you commissioned for the men who joined you on the hunt are ready, and we should see about a feast so they can be presented. And to celebrate the queen's health. Her appearance at dinner should boost everyone's bleak moods. I have much to do, it seems."

Her skirts swished as she hurried off down the hall, and Garith let out a sigh. He didn't get up from his bench; he wasn't sure his legs would hold him yet. Sander's hand felt cool and damp between his fingers. Garith brought it to his face and rubbed his cheek against Sander's knuckles. "I'm thankful for you."

After looking up and down the corridor, Sander bent and pressed a kiss to the top of Garith's head. "I'm here. Anything you need, just ask it."

"Some days, it's hard for me to imagine anyone envying a king," Garith mused. "Thinking about bakers or tailors wishing they could be me…. It all seems so absurd. Who would want this over a life of just kneading bread or mending trousers? Honest work, a well-earned meal, a chair by the fire, sleep undisturbed by worry…. Is a home with a hundred rooms and fifty sets of clothes in my closet really a fair trade?"

"You feel that way because you are a good man," Sander said. "Others would covet the power, the chance to tell everyone else what to do, to be in charge of everything, but not you. That's exactly why you must remain king. You… you're a treasure, and these people are lucky to have you. So am I, and don't think I don't know it. You put everyone before yourself, down to the lowliest beggar, when anyone else would put himself first. I'd follow you into the Shades' Abode, even if I didn't love you, because that's what a king should be."

Warmth replaced the cold, spoiled feeling in Garith's gut, and slowly, he began to feel better, more solid, more rooted in reality. Blood seemed to flow back into his limbs and chase away the numbness. Even with everything he faced, Sander gave him such hope. "Part of the reason I couldn't agree to what my mother suggested was because I knew you wouldn't be all right with it. I knew you would think less of me if I said yes. You're the treasure. You make me a good man."

"It doesn't matter why you refused," Sander said. "You did, and that's enough. I'm just a guard and you're the king. I would never question your decisions. But you *are* a good man. The best of men."

"Let's hope it will be enough. What's better, Sander? To hold to your beliefs and be destroyed, to lose everything? Or to adapt, abandon your convictions, and survive?"

"I don't know."

Garith leaned back and rested his head against Sander's belly with no intention of moving until he absolutely had to. What if they had been common born, Sander a farmer and Garith a leather worker or something else, maybe a miller or a grocer? They could have had a little house together, a stone hearth to cook their meals and a small bed covered in coarse blankets and furs. No one would have cared that they wanted to share their lives; no one paid much heed to the people who made their food and clothing. Garith wanted that, and he decided once this fiasco with the barbarian invaders had been resolved, his conflict with the priestesses smoothed over, he would buy a little stone house, maybe in Everdale, where the meadow flowers bloomed so beautifully in the spring, and he'd take Sander there for a few weeks of the year. They would till their soil and chop the wood for their fireplace, cook together, eat together, sleep together, mend the tears in their clothing, gather eggs, barter for meat and an occasional bottle of wine, and just be men for a short time—men with nothing weighing on them, nothing to worry over but each other. So long as Sander agreed to pretend, it would be a pleasant daydream, Garith's one indulgence: to be ordinary for a bit.

Now, though, he had to be a king, had to be the one who decided how to keep his hundreds of thousands of subjects safe, had to decide what was best for them. He just hoped he wouldn't fail when he faced danger and doubt in every direction. So many lives depended on the words he chose to say, and he couldn't fail. Garith felt like he'd been holding his kingdom by a gossamer strand since they'd set the crown on his head, and now, with it slipping through his fingers, he just didn't know if he could hold on.

Chapter
Twenty-One

AN ASSEMBLY of about two dozen children, all of them between probably five and seven years old, stood facing their master in a room far below the great hall of the order hideout. From the shadows of the corridor, Sasha watched as their tutor led them through the motions of drawing their daggers, blocking an enemy blow, and attacking with their opposite hands. The children went through five or six choreographed routines designed to teach them the basic moves of combat, and then they paired off to practice their thrusting and parrying while the man who instructed them offered advice and corrected small mistakes, such as an elbow drooping too low or a lax wrist.

Next the teacher brought out a trio of lifelike dummies made of canvas stuffed with straw. Red paint indicated the organs and major blood vessels. The children eagerly took out their short, tapered throwing knives and lined up to show their instructor what they could do. Nearly all of them managed to embed at least one blade in a vulnerable area: the side of the neck, the throat, the eye socket, the inner thigh, or the meeting of the shoulder to the chest. The children clearly enjoyed the exercise, and Sasha remembered enjoying it too. He knew what would come next. Another assassin brought out lengths of black-dyed linen and blindfolded the young order members. They would now be expected to remember the location of their targets without the benefit of their sight. The lesson was meant to impart to them the importance of observation, at all times, even when they thought they would not need it, and, of course, memory.

Predictably, few of the children managed to hit the dummies with their throwing daggers, having not known to plan for the loss of sight. Sasha recalled himself at six or so—he'd never known his exact age—drawing in a steadying breath and imagining the position of the mannequins. When he'd pushed his blindfold into his hair, he hadn't been surprised to see one of his knives sticking in the figure's forehead, another in its neck, and the third in the model's lower belly. He had been able to envision where his iron would fly from his memory of the dummies' positions. It had been a challenge, but hardly impossible. His peers had marveled at his ability, as most of them had failed to even hit one of the mannequins, much like the newest order recruits. One boy managed, out of sheer luck, to strike a figure's leg, and the others missed entirely, except for one.

A fair-haired child—Sasha thought it was a girl, and probably a northerner, maybe of Lockhaven or Windwake—drew in a deep breath and waited as he had. With calculated movements, she threw her daggers. One pierced the dummy's eye socket, another struck its cheek, and the third landed between its neck and collarbone. Sasha blew air out between his teeth. She had surpassed even his example by grouping her daggers closer together.

The girl pushed the wrappings off her eyes to regard her accomplishment and merely nodded once at what she saw—already cold, devoid of all emotion, even the pride of a young child seeking accolades from an elder. Sasha saw she had large, sky blue eyes and full pink cheeks. Her innocent beauty would serve her nearly as well as her lethal skill, and he decided to learn more about her.

As the children put away their throwing knives to practice with staves, Sasha turned and left them to their lessons. He had loved combat training as a boy; he'd been better at it than any of the others, but his teachers had warned him against overconfidence, and it had stuck. One could always improve, become faster, better, deadlier—

As Sasha had watched the young assassins spar, he'd realized that, as the leader of the Crimson Scythe, he held their lives in his hand. He would choose which of them would be sent on important missions, and he'd have to gauge their skill and predict which of them might succeed—survive. Many of these children would perish before they reached Sasha's current age, and he would be the one sending them to Thalil.

But he had seen the respite Thalil offered after good service, and it had tempted even him to stay. Sasha turned back to watch a few more moments. The blonde girl used her staff to knock her opponent—a much larger boy—off his feet. He landed on his back, but before he could rise, she pressed the blunted end of her stick to his throat, and he held up his hands in supplication. Their teacher patted the victor's shoulder, and Sasha resolved to learn and remember the name of that girl. She was, as he had been, a killer born.

They were all his responsibility now. His decisions would mean life or death for them. Sasha felt the weight of it on his shoulders, and he started to understand what Duncan had always said about duty. He now ruled the Crimson Scythe, but it wasn't so much a privilege as a burden; he had to decide what was best for all these people, the thousands now under his command. He had to keep them safe, hidden from the forces in the world bent on destroying the order, and keep them alive as best he could.

Sasha turned away from the children, desiring some training himself. His body felt a little different after returning from his master's realm, and he thought he might be faster, more agile, and he itched to put it to the test. Luckily, on his way down the winding staircase to the vacant practice rooms, he met the only two men who might prove worthy adversaries: Duncan and Yarrow.

"I thought I could use a bit of training," Sasha said. "Care to see what we can do against each other?"

Yarrow grinned wide. "Sure! I have learned a lot from the order mages, and I'd like to practice some of those spells."

"Duncan?" Sasha asked. His heroic knight looked uncomfortable. He had for the past few weeks, ever since Sasha had assumed leadership of the order. Though he tried to conceal it, Duncan hadn't been trained to school his every facial expression to the desired result as Sasha had, and it was easy for Sasha to see he misliked staying among the Crimson Scythe. "My friend?"

"Practice is never a bad idea," Duncan said. "Let's go."

Soon they reached an expansive space several floors below the hall. Though mostly empty, a few weapons stands holding blades, bows, and arrows lined the chamber, and some round targets—painted cloth over round bales of straw—leaned against the black stone walls.

Yarrow picked up a small bow—one meant to train children—and stood a few dozen feet from one of the targets. "I used to enjoy archery as boy," he said, "before I manifested the gift." The mage drew back and loosed an arrow, barely hitting the outermost rim of the target. "I guess it's been a long time."

"I didn't know you'd trained for combat," Duncan said, aiming his much larger bow and pulling the string back. When he released it, his thick arrow stuck only an inch or two from the center of the bull's-eye.

"If it had been up to my parents, I wouldn't have." Yarrow shot again, and this time his arrow landed closer to the target's center. "They had Rayne and Rowan—one son to inherit the valenny and another as a backup in case he died." Yarrow pulled back and loosed another arrow. It struck the target only inches from the center. "I was useless. I don't think my mother and father cared if I even survived childhood. And as soon as they realized I was a mage, that I'd never be able to rule Lockhaven—I'm surprised they let me learn to read." His next arrow struck the target almost at the middle, right next to Duncan's. He fired again, planting an arrow only an inch from the last. "I don't care what they think of me. What does their opinion matter?" His next shot embedded in the dead center of the red circle.

Sasha grinned. His mage continued to surprise him; he'd been full of unexpected delights from the first night they'd shared. It hardly shocked Sasha that Yarrow proved a crack shot with a bow. And his mage looked fantastic in the gear Sasha had made for him by the order armorers: black leather trousers that hugged his spindly legs, matching boots with a trio of buckles up the sides, a snug gray shirt with a long triangular hood that reached the tops of Yarrow's thighs, a black leather vest, hardened leather pauldrons held in place by straps crisscrossing his chest, bracers, and gloves. Now Sasha had an idea for another gift for his mage. "Yarrow, you should carry a bow. You're adept with one. It would be good, in case you got too tired for your magic."

"Too tired for my magic?" Yarrow asked in a shrill, amused tone. "You want me to use arrows when I can do this?" He wiggled his fingers at the target. Four comet-like bursts of blue light shot from his fingers and made a fizzling sound as they hit the straw circle. It flared with azure flames for a few seconds, then a pile of gray ash drifted to the floor.

"Even so," Sasha said, "it can't hurt to have an extra weapon. I can have the fletchers here make something for you, and it will be a finer bow than you could get anywhere in the world. It would please me."

Looking over his shoulder at Sasha, a faint blush staining his cheeks, Yarrow grinned and said, "All right, then. I like pleasing you."

A warm tingle spread up Sasha's back. "Duncan, are you sure you won't at least let me have your sword and armor repaired?"

The big knight frowned slightly and looked down at his dinged and dented breastplate. "I would rather have the blacksmith at Windust see to them."

"Afraid they'll be tainted with the order's evil if one of ours touches them?" Sasha asked, watching Duncan's face closely.

"Nonsense," Duncan muttered.

"What, then?" Sasha pushed.

"I… do not know, Sasha. This place unnerves me. I am ill at ease here, and I won't tell you otherwise."

Sasha stood in front of Duncan and took his hand. "This order is mine now."

"And that seems to please you very much," the knight said.

"Of course," Sasha answered. "Why should it not? I have power now, power enough to bring down any kingdom I choose. I am the deadliest man in the world. My power can benefit you—both of you. You two are the only things in this world I have ever valued, and now I have the strength to keep you safe. But I must lead this order, and I intend to keep it strong, aid in its growth if I can. This is my purpose, my duty, my place in the world. At least that much you should be able to understand."

Duncan squeezed Sasha's hand and finally met his gaze, a look of wistful regret in his gray-green eyes. "You could have had another place. A place at my side at Windust Castle. You still can. You need not do this."

"Ah, my love," Sasha answered. "Do you not see? I *want* to. I never belonged at Windust Castle. I did not fit, and I never would have, no matter how many years I tried. You feel ill at ease here? Try to imagine making this place your home, finding a sense of belonging here. You could not. I would not ask you to; it isn't who you are meant to be. It *is* who I am. Who I'll always be. You can either accept that or you can't."

"I'll try," Duncan said, eyes shimmering. "I'll try every day."

Sasha smiled. "Good. Then I will lead the Crimson Scythe, you will rule Windwake, and Yarrow can… do whatever it is he feels destined to do."

"Ride the great wyrm asleep in Estrella Lake," the mage said, looking up at the ceiling, eyes far away. "Raise a great white fortress atop Starmont and look down over all the world. Make a war against… against those who would keep mankind on its knees. Liberate the world from tyranny and champion truth."

"Not much, then," Duncan said. "Accomplished before lunchtime." His rich, deep laughter broke through the web of tension lying over them, and soon Sasha and Yarrow joined in it. "Though, in reality," Duncan said when he caught his breath, "I must think about returning to my bairny, making sure all is well there. We are into Sarmine's Moon. I suppose my wife will be expecting a gift of some sort. Do you think we could make for home tomorrow morning?"

Sasha thought. He had seen little need to change the way the order functioned; it had been operating efficiently for thousands of years. In truth, it really didn't need a leader, so Sasha had little to see to before he could depart. "I think I'll leave Corbin in charge in my stead. I have a few things to see to, but we can depart in the morning. We should ride overland. It will take a month and a half, so I'm afraid you won't be able to celebrate the goddess of love beside your dear wife, Duncan. I suppose we'll have to do. How does that sound, Yarrow? Back on the road, sleeping in a single tent with the snow swirling outside, just the way you love most."

"Actually, I think I'll stay a little longer," Yarrow said. "I'm learning a great deal here. There's a… there are a few spells I want to figure out, and I think Corbin can assist me. Besides, I promised to teach him what I can in exchange for his aid. And he did aid us, in the end."

"Will you be safe?" Duncan asked in a voice soft with concern.

Yarrow laughed. "What, surrounded by about a thousand of the best killers to ever live? I think I'll manage."

"We'll miss you during those cold nights on the road," Sasha said, a little disappointed.

"I'll miss that too," Yarrow answered. "But I… I still need to figure some things out."

"What aren't you telling us?" Sasha asked. He saw it plainly in every movement of Yarrow's brows, every nudge of his teeth against his lower lip.

Yarrow shrugged, toyed with the feathers at the end of an arrow, and worried his lip some more. "Very well. I don't want to lie to you anymore. That is not the man I want to be. I-I wish to figure out the spell Fane used to dissolve my creature's physical form and bind it to that pool of water. I want to be able to cast that spell."

"What enemy would you possibly need to use something so dreadful against?" Duncan asked in a shaky whisper.

"One that cannot be killed the conventional way," Yarrow answered. "I should know the spell—my creature knew it and he taught it to Fane—but I can't seem to find it in my head. When I think of it, it's like hearing a language you barely know, being able to almost understand a word here and there but making no sense of the whole."

"But I don't understand," Duncan said. "Why do you need to understand it?"

"I *want* to," Yarrow answered. "It's the same as you wanting to become a better swordsman."

His words reminded Sasha of something he'd wanted to ask. "Yarrow, Thalil told me he had once been mortal. He told me you could explain. Will you explain it to me now?"

Yarrow's eyes went wide and he looked nervously at Duncan. "You will not like it, especially you, Duncan. Perhaps we should sit down."

They sat in a line on the floor and leaned back against the stone wall. Yarrow drew in a deep, faltering breath that made Sasha dread the words he would say, and then he began to speak. "I have told you Hale was Fane's lover and apprentice, more than ten thousand years ago. When I mentioned the Thirteen Goddesses to him, he had no idea what I was talking about. Then I told him their names. They—the Thirteen—had all been powerful mages, Fane's wives. He taught them everything they knew, taught them immortality, taught them the very spell I want to learn so they could rid the world of creatures like the one that possessed me—the very one Fane had learned his magic from. They became very strong under his tutelage, and they became jealous of the love his people showed him. They betrayed him in the end, and used the spell to dissolve his physical form and trap him in that puddle—right where we found him."

Duncan, pale, a line of beaded sweat across his brow, looked back and forth as if he expected a horde of priestesses and temple guards to rush in and arrest them. "That is blasphemy, Yarrow! You should not say such things. Ask the goddesses' forgiveness!"

"I will ask no one's forgiveness for speaking the truth! They are the ones who are the liars, liars who have been deceiving the world for thousands of years! They are not divine, and they didn't create us or anything else! They only have the power they hold because they learned it from my be—from

Fane before they turned against him and because they're keeping the world's magic from mortal spellcasters. Why do you think fewer mages are born with every generation? All the world is operating under a falsehood."

"No," Duncan said firmly. "I will not believe that. This Hale you spoke to is a heretic and likely mad as well."

Yarrow stood and began pacing the perimeter of the room, waving his arms wildly as he grew more and more frustrated. "Damn it, Duncan! Have you ever seen any evidence of the so-called benevolence of the goddesses? Any proof of their divinity?"

"Of course," Duncan said in the careful tone one used to soothe a hysterical child. "I have told you I see it all around me, in things growing, the beauty all around us, in the love between us."

"Love your goddesses condemn as a sin," Sasha reminded him in a deliberately neutral tone.

"I am not talking about common things," Yarrow railed. "All those things happened long before the goddesses stole their power, and they'll happen long after they're gone. I mean miracles. Truly divine things. I can say I have only ever seen one such miracle, and that was when Sasha came back from the beyond. And who did that? Who gave us back the man we love? Your goddesses? No. Because they don't care about the people of this world! It was Thalil! Thalil, Fane's son to the Mother Goddess, just another mortal who learned to amass power. If you feel so desperate to be led, told what to think and believe, maybe you should worship him! At least he's done something for you!"

On his way out the door, Yarrow kicked one of the weapons stands, sending bows and arrows clattering across the floor. Duncan moved to go after him, but Sasha rested his hand on Duncan's forearm and shook his head. "Let him go, burn off his anger. If you chase after him, he'll only end up saying something he doesn't mean and feel guilty over it later."

Duncan drew up his knees and dropped his head between them. "You're right. He is still filled with so much rage. I just wish he wouldn't aim it at the goddesses."

"What if it's true?" Sasha said.

"No—"

"Duncan, what if it is? Thalil told me something very similar. Will you deny the truth just because you'd rather not believe it? That's not the kind of man you've ever been."

"No. But I also won't believe it based on the words of this Hale, who could be anyone, or your Cast-Down god. I will believe in the goodness of the goddesses until I have good reason not to."

It hardly mattered to Sasha either way; his life would be no different whether no goddesses reigned or they increased to a thousand. He served

Thalil and would continue to serve, especially with the debt he now owed. In fact, he should see everything was in order for his departure, seek out Corbin and let him know of his new tasks. He rubbed the back of Duncan's neck and swept his hair away to kiss the edge of his ear. "Pack your things, my love. I have a few matters to attend to, and then we can get on the road."

"I do long for the open air," Duncan said. He lifted his head to give Sasha's lips a gentle peck. "Go on, then. After I see to my belongings, I'll go and find Yarrow. He should have calmed by then, and if we are to be parted again, I want to make sure we give him some incentive to hurry home."

Sasha smiled and kissed Duncan again. "Absolutely."

CORBIN had claimed for himself a sprawling suite of rooms on the lowest level of the hideout, four floors below the great hall. The round central chamber held his bed, a few chests of drawers, some upholstered red benches, a table, and a rack for wine bottles. Thick rugs covered the black stone floor, a fire burned between the elaborate pillars of the hearth, and a massive painting of Thalil—as poisoner, pouring the contents of a phial into the parted lips of the nude young man across his lap—hung on the wall. Dozens of candles burned beneath it.

Three small alcoves abutted the main chamber. One held a variety of poisonous plants and fungi growing beneath greenish, magical orbs. Another contained tables covered in bones, cats, erkits, twirl-horns, various fish and birds, and even a harrow-wolf mounted on metal spikes in a semblance of life. Sasha found the mage-assassin in the third room, where Corbin had set up his alchemical equipment. Concoctions of every color bubbled over small flames, light reflecting off the glass decanters and dozens of feet of looping copper tubes. Noxious fumes hung in the air and clung to the back of Sasha's throat and the roof of his mouth. The mage sat on a stool, his black hair curtaining his face as he leaned over to grind something with a mortar and pestle.

"To what do I owe this great honor, chosen of Thalil?" Corbin asked without looking up from his work.

"I'll not have you, or anyone else, calling me that," Sasha said flatly. "I won't be made into some silly cliché. I am leaving with Duncan tomorrow morning. I would like you to take my place as leader while I'm gone."

Corbin tilted his head and locked his dark gaze with Sasha's. Though no emotion showed on his features, his voice dripped with offense when he said, "Do not make a joke of me."

"You have made a joke of yourself, brother, through your failures. I'm giving you a chance to reverse that. I'd like you to lead the order in my absence. If you'd rather decline, I'll choose someone else."

"Why would you choose me in the first place?" Corbin asked, the black marble grinder clutched in his hand.

"I have come to trust you to a degree," Sasha said. "You did what you vowed to do without trying to deceive me for your own benefit. I can't say I'd have done the same in your place. Do you want to stand in for me, or shall I ask someone else?"

"No, Sasha. I'll be honored, and I'll do my best."

"Good. You should not have to do much beyond choosing which agents to send on the most important missions, but that is a weighty task. Choose well. I want missions carried out efficiently and my brothers and sisters making it home unharmed. If they don't, I won't be happy."

"Of course. When are the three of you leaving?"

"Yarrow would like to stay," Sasha told him. "He enjoys working with you for some reason, and he feels he owes you a debt. I don't have to tell you how I'll react if anything happens to him."

"No, though I can't imagine how I could harm him. Have you not yet realized how dangerous he is?"

"I have other matters to attend to," Sasha said, and he turned and left without another word.

As he walked up the stairs leading back to the room he shared with his friends, the fine hairs on the back of Sasha's neck began to stand on end. He paused and listened, but heard no footsteps, no breathing, anywhere near. The silence was so profound and complete it almost had a physical presence, a weight, and Sasha's pulse and the sound of his breathing seemed a cacophony. Still, his instincts told him he wasn't alone.

He scanned the shadows between the sputtering patches of light the torches spilled across the walls and floor. He'd been able to see far better in the dark since returning from Thalil, but he couldn't locate anyone or anything, and so he turned and started walking again. After ascending a staircase and emerging into another darkened passageway, he heard the softest scrape: a boot against stone. On instinct, he slid one of the daggers hidden in his sleeve past the hem and into his hand, keeping it concealed as his attention focused on the soft footfalls he now detected. Sasha gave no indication he knew he was followed, and let his pursuer come closer and closer. At the last second he spun, reached out, caught the person by the collar, and pressed his dagger to the other's throat. Then he let his hand fall.

He recognized the blonde child from the training session he'd observed and lowered her to her feet. "What are doing following me?"

She shrugged, showing no fear, not even the tiniest twitch, on her round little face. "Wanted to see if I could."

"You need more practice," Sasha told her.

"You're him, aren't you?" the girl asked, her blue eyes widening just a bit. Anyone else would have missed it, especially in the gloom of the corridor. "You're the one who died and came back."

"Yes."

"Did it hurt?"

"Dying?" Sasha asked. "Yes."

"I suppose I'll have to avoid it, then."

"Yes," Sasha said. "That would be wise. I saw you practicing earlier. What did you learn from your lesson with the blindfold?"

"To always be aware of the position of everyone around you? To burn it into your mind? I knew that already."

Sasha wondered how. "Where are you from? What's your name?"

She rolled her eyes at him, crossed her arms over her narrow, leather-wrapped chest, and rested her back and the sole of one foot against the wall. Practiced nonchalance. She wanted to convince him she hadn't been unsettled by his questions, and it almost worked. "You know I don't have a name. I won't get a name until I get my first mission, but you do. It's Sasha, isn't it?"

"Yes."

"But isn't a name just something else to get attached to?" she asked. "Doesn't getting attached to anything make you weak?"

Sasha didn't know how to answer. He had thought so—once. He still wondered, still worried that the value he placed on Duncan and Yarrow made him weak. They were everything to him, his world and sun and stars, morning, night, everything. Losing either of them would destroy him, and if that wasn't a vulnerability, he didn't know what was. Still, should this child be deprived of the chance to feel the happiness, the sense of completion he felt when he was with them?

She spoke again after a few minutes of awkward silence. "So the others say you're our leader now."

"Yes. And that means if I say it's all right for you to remember your name and tell it to me, then no one else can overrule it. What was your name? You remember it; I can see it in your eyes. Tell me."

"It was Asphodel."

Sasha smiled. "You are named after a flower. One of my best friends is named after a flower. It's a beautiful name."

"Sasha, I followed you because I wanted to tell you I am ready. I'm ready to spill blood for Thalil." She clenched her tiny fist. By the Dark One, she was so small. Sasha could have crushed her little head in just one of his hands.

"Our master would admire your enthusiasm," Sasha said, kneeling down to meet her gaze. She was a beautiful child: golden ringlets of hair, eyes the color of a summer sky, ivory skin, red cheeks, and lips like a rosebud ready to open to the sun. "I'm sorry to say you're not quite ready. Don't make that face! You must never let your anger or disappointment show. How about this? We'll go get something to eat, and then I'll show you some tricks."

Little Asphodel beamed, and Sasha couldn't bring himself to reprimand her for letting her happiness show so plainly. He even leaned in and touched her pink chin before standing and taking her hand. Together they climbed the stairs and finally entered the great hall. The kitchens waited on the other side, and Sasha knew the girl would be hungry. He'd always been hungry at her age.

Something compelled Sasha to stop beside the colossal statue of Thalil as he passed it. He let go of Asphodel's hand and wandered over to look into the pool of blood. It was so still and shiny, like a sheet of scarlet glass, that Sasha could see his face reflected back at him in perfect detail. He let his gaze travel up the glossy, black stone until it met the face of his patron. Then a whispery voice ghosted across his consciousness like a faint brush of chilled fingertips along his spine. Everything around Sasha blurred and faded away, until it was only him and Thalil.

Sasha.

Yes? I am here.

Good. I have two tasks for you. Two messages you must deliver. The first is to Corbin. Tell him he will receive an important mission, an assignment from the priestesses of my mother and aunts. He must complete this task himself. He must not fail me.

It will be done, master. What is the second message?

The second message is for your mage. Tell him only this: Not yet.

Chapter
Twenty-Two

NOT yet.

What had Thalil, through Sasha, meant by that? Yarrow wondered. He'd been turning it over and over in his mind for weeks, ever since Sasha and Duncan had left the order hideout for Windwake, and he still had no idea what the Cast-Down god wanted to impart to him.

Corbin was making poison, mixing various elixirs together and adding pinches of different powders. He had offered to teach Yarrow the art, but Yarrow had found it complex, a lot of work, and, frankly, boring. He had grown bored. Bored, and... frustrated. He missed his lovers, missed Duncan's skillful mouth, the catch of his whiskers on Yarrow's skin, Sasha's slender fingers and the marvelous way they pressed into Yarrow's flesh, always finding just the right place inside.... It grew harder by the day to resist Corbin's thinly veiled suggestions, but Yarrow had resisted Sai, and he would not give in to the mage-assassin's invitations, no matter how tempting they became.

Boredom, the lack of something to occupy his mind, threatened Yarrow, because it invited thinking about the past, and that led to anger and the lust to lash out at something. His lack of control over his own emotions led him to disgust, and the hurt drove him back toward anger, around and around in an endless circle. He hated feeling like such a slave to his fears and the rage they inspired, but he knew of no way to break the chains, so he endeavored to keep himself distracted with his research. He'd slowly begun to understand himself a little, but knowing all the ways something could be broken didn't help him understand how to make it whole.

Wine helped sometimes, but other times it only distilled his despair, focused it, and besides, Yarrow knew he drank too much already. Better to work.

Yarrow and Corbin had worked together for weeks, yet they were no closer to discovering the spell Yarrow needed. Corbin had taught Yarrow to hasten death—he could reduce an apple to a slimy black puddle or a bird to a skeleton draped in desiccated sinew—but he had no insight on the enchantment Yarrow needed. Yarrow thought he should probably leave. He had nothing else to gain by staying, and he had taught Corbin more than enough magic to repay his debt.

Someone knocked at the door, and Corbin stood from the cauldron he'd been folded over. In nothing but his snug leather trousers, he strode to the threshold, the vapors from his latest concoction condensing to beads that sparkled over his pale skin. One of the Whisperers waited in the hall; Yarrow knew him by the sumptuous black cloak he wore. He and Corbin exchanged a few breathy words, and then Corbin closed the door. Corbin went immediately to his toxins and started stoppering phials to prepare them for travel.

"What is it?" Yarrow asked.

"I have an important mission," Corbin said as he continued to prepare his potions and weapons. "One Thalil himself has dictated must be mine alone. One I must not fail."

"Well, can I come with you?" Yarrow asked, desperate for any diversion.

Corbin paused in his preparations and studied Yarrow's face. "The kills will be mine."

"Of course. I am not an assassin. I just want to watch."

"All right, then," Corbin said. "Why not? Make yourself ready. We'll depart within an hour."

YARROW and Corbin traveled northeast on horseback, around Spearepointe Bay, through Thulemore, and across Meadow's Edge toward the river. Then, when they reached the disputed territory, they commissioned a ship and crossed into Gaeltheon. Corbin rented another pair of horses, and they rode until they reached the foothills of the Lapir Mountains. From there, they progressed on foot, with Corbin reading the markings he found in the snow. Though no tracker, even Yarrow could see many people had ground the pristine white crystals into the mud beneath and left a slimy, dirty trail headed into the foothills. Cart wheels and the hooves of horses, along with frozen piles of their dung, marked the path up to the base of the great mountains. Whoever they followed had made no effort to cover their passing.

After following the trail for three days, Yarrow awoke on the fourth morning, alone in the tiny tent they had been sharing. He reached for his heavy cloak—the only thing he'd removed before going to sleep—draped it over his shoulders, and left the tent in search of the other mage. The world looked frozen and sharp beneath the morning sun, brittle, the edges of the mountains as delicate as jagged glass. The air tasted pure and metallic, and it stung Yarrow's lungs if he breathed it too deeply.

Corbin stood on the edge of a precipice, his breath misting around him as he held his cape tight to his chest and gazed at the valley below. Hearing Yarrow's boots compacting the snow, he turned and smiled. "Can you feel that, Yarroway? Taste it on the wind? That's destiny, ripe and ready to split open."

Yarrow did sense something, a storm-like tingle moving up his arms and making the fine hairs rise. He stepped to the edge of the cliff and looked down on a small circle of simple tents. A few people, their gender impossible to determine beneath their heavy furs, cooked over the small fires and heated water for washing. Four knights—Royal Guards in plate polished to mirror sheen and wearing bright blue capes, stood at the outskirts of the camp.

"Which one?" Yarrow asked.

Corbin looked over his shoulder and dragged the tip of his tongue along the edge of his upper teeth. "All of them."

Yarrow watched a few more minutes. The people in the bulky furs loaded provisions and tools onto simple sleds and began dragging them slowly up the mountainside. The knights followed a few hundred yards behind them. After half a mile or so, they unloaded their equipment to chip away at a piece of blue-gray rock with hammers, chisels, and hand-operated drills.

"What is their crime?" Yarrow asked.

Corbin shrugged. "That is not my concern."

"Well, how will you do it?" Yarrow pressed. "Four Royal Guards are more than a small obstacle. And there are at least six others. Ten people, and one of you. Unless you'd like my help."

"I am more than capable of accomplishing it without you. Watch and learn, Yarroway. We'll follow them and stay hidden until after dark. I trust you can keep yourself from being seen or heard?"

"You know I can."

"Good. Let's go."

They spent the day lying on their bellies between some jagged, snow-capped rocks, looking down through a cleft as the people chipped at the stone, dug, shared a simple lunch, and finally packed up their gear to return to camp. Yarrow wondered what they could be doing even as he reminded himself none of them would see morning. Had they done something to deserve death? What if they hadn't? Who was he to judge? He had asked to accompany Corbin knowing full well what he would likely witness, and if he didn't want to see it he should turn away now. Corbin, like Sasha, was an assassin, and this was what he did—he murdered people without questioning the righteousness of the act. Yarrow had never questioned the moral implications when Sasha described his past deeds, and he had no reason—no right—to start now.

Not after everything he had done, the blood he'd spilled over the centuries, often just to entertain himself. Though the hands now shivering in the folds of Yarrow's cloak hadn't been the ones soaked in blood back then, since he'd chosen to bond with the creature who had committed the slaughter, they might as well have been.

And on the other hand, he wasn't that creature anymore…. And yet he was. Better, Yarrow decided, to stay silent and observe.

The sun dropped off the western edge of the world, and not long after, a full moon rose and hung low in the sky, the white disk seeming to balance atop the mountain peaks. Beneath its light, the snow glowed until it was almost as bright as midday. As the people in the camp cleaned up after their supper and retired to their tents one by one, Corbin opened his small pack and began sifting through his items. He took out a long reedlike tube, a device used for firing poisoned darts, considered it, and then laid it aside. He located a rolled-up leather strap, unfurled it, buckled it across his chest and pulled the end tight with his teeth, then slipped a half a dozen small throwing knives into its sheaths. Next he dribbled some thick black elixir on five other daggers before stowing one beside each hip, one in his left boot, one at his side below his ruined arm, keeping the last in his hand. He pushed his hood up over his hair and started down the hillside, just a shadow flitting across the snow as if a cloud had moved in front of the moon. He melded so completely with the few shadows, Yarrow had to concentrate to keep track of him.

Two of the Royal Guards stood just beyond the small ring of tents. Their comrades had retired, probably in preparation to take the second watch. As Corbin knelt behind a small knoll, Yarrow wondered why he had neglected his darts. From where he crouched, he could have easily eliminated both knights with no danger to himself. Instead, he crept slowly up behind them. Did he seek to impress Yarrow? What did he suppose he would gain by doing so?

I'm thinking like Sasha, Yarrow realized with a small smile before he returned his attention to Corbin. The assassin had moved to within a few feet of one of the guards, and in one smooth, quick motion, he rose to his feet, reached around the man, and cut his throat. His companion must have noticed the sound his body made as it fell facedown in the snow, because he managed a few strides toward Corbin, trying to yell something that sounded like "assassin" before Corbin flipped the blade in his hand and drove it into the base of his neck. Blood fanned out and fell in a wide arc, black against the snow. Unlike the first knight, he gurgled and flailed on the ground for a few moments before falling still.

A light came on inside one of the tents, making it look like a hand cupping a small candle. A man emerged from the flap. "What is this racket?"

he asked, rubbing his thin bare arms against the chill. "Some of us are trying to sleep, you know."

Corbin crouched in the shadow at the edge of the splinter of light coming from the small tent and drew his arm back. He threw, but Yarrow couldn't see his blade flying through the darkness, even though the moonlight shone down. His dagger struck the man in the chest so hard it knocked him off his feet. The canvas walls crumpled and fell as his body struck them, the spikes holding it in place torn from the frozen ground and the ropes whipping around.

Corbin turned on the ball of his foot and sprinted deeper into the darkness, leaping atop a pile of rubble a few dozen feet away. When he knelt down, bowed his head, and let his cloak cover his knees, he looked like nothing more than a smooth black boulder. Yarrow didn't even sense him using magic to conceal himself.

Predictably, the noise from the man's collapsing tent drew the others, the two remaining Royal Guards leaving their shelters first, swords drawn. The rest of the people huddled together and whispered and muttered fearfully as the knights began searching the small camp for the assassin. They poked about on the ground with the points of their blades while Corbin perched above them, completely undetected. One of the people lit a torch, and then another. The laborers in their coarse clothes and matted furs held lights, swiping at the darkness as if they could drive it back. One of them—a woman—began wailing, high and long, when she uncovered the body beneath the heap of wrinkled canvas.

Yarrow almost wished he could see through Corbin's eyes as he once had, feel his emotions along with him. Yarrow bet the peoples' panic amused the other mage, and he hid a crooked smile beneath the shadows of his hood. But, at Corbin's vehement insistence, Yarrow had completely severed their connection. Not even he would sink so low as to invade Corbin's thoughts without his consent, and so he watched from the bluffs above them all, thinking about the beautiful bow made of ebony Shade-Willow and the quiver of arrows strapped to his back, and how easily he could have assisted Corbin.

A greenish-yellow fog outlined Corbin, though Yarrow didn't think the others—those without the gift—would see it. A few tendrils of the jaundiced mist twined through the still night air before settling over the two fallen guards like a shroud. After a few minutes, the corpses began to spasm and twitch, and then they lurched to their feet. With stiff movements, the knights lifted their swords and advanced on the small group of people, who screamed and ran away. One of the living soldiers hurried to stand in front of the others, facing his former companion. The deceased man's head lay on his shoulder, flopping around horribly as he staggered forward. Their swords clashed, the dead man moving with more speed and precision than Yarrow would have expected.

As the two knights sparred, the others tried to keep the dead soldier under Corbin's control at bay, and it worked for a few minutes. Then, with one swipe of his greatsword, the dead man knocked both torches from their hands, slicing one of them across the middle at the same time. The others ran and tried to cower behind tents and wagons. The shaggy ponies screamed, and one of them managed to break its rope and escape into the hills. As the dead soldier went from person to person, blood began to spread out, melting the snow.

The living guard was tiring, losing ground to his deceased adversary. Where was the other soldier? Yarrow cast around but couldn't find him at first. Then he saw him, the moonlight glinting off his armor, as he crept around the pile of rock where Corbin sat. Yarrow remembered Corbin admitting how much of his concentration it took for him to animate dead things. While this spell was a little different—the dead soldiers fought of their own volition, attacking anything in their path rather than being controlled by Corbin's will directly—it still seemed to command most of his attention. Otherwise, he would have seen the man trying to creep up and flank him, heard his heavy boots on the snow. Sasha would have. If Corbin had been Sasha, the man would already be dead.

Yarrow kept waiting for Corbin to turn and throw a knife or a dart. Even from his vantage point, Yarrow could hear the man's loud footsteps. If he crossed a few more feet, ascended just a little farther up the hillock, he'd be in range to drive his large sword right into Corbin's back. Corbin had told Yarrow not to move in on his kills, but—

Yarrow couldn't wait. Abandoning stealth, he got to his feet, spread his wings, and glided down to Corbin, making it just in time to raise his claw and deflect the knight's blow. The sword struck his enchanted limb so hard Yarrow staggered back into Corbin, almost sending both of them toppling off the mound. It seemed to knock Corbin out of his trance, and he took one of the throwing knives from the strip across his chest. It soared past, missing Yarrow's cheek by an inch or less, and pierced the soldier's face just below his right eye. Two more blades followed, one sinking into the man's left eye and the other finding a mark in his throat. He fell backward off the rubble pile and landed with a thud in the snow.

Yarrow let his magic sink back into its recesses, stood, and looked at the camp, his senses still acute and his skin prickling with vestiges of enchantment. Aside from the ponies nickering and pawing the ground, it was quiet. Surreally quiet. The bodies of the simple laborers littered the ground, and the knights Corbin had revived had finally been allowed their rest. Blood soaked the snow between the tents, the metallic smell strong and making

Yarrow glad of the cold. At the same time, it stirred something in him, made him want to taste raw flesh and feel his talons slicing through muscle, skin, and bone. No. He would not be a slave to desires not his own. He turned his attention to Corbin, trying to ignore the way the other mage's veins looked plump and blue beneath his ivory skin.

The other mage glowered at Yarrow before picking his way down the rocky slope to crouch and pull his knives from his victim and wipe them clean on the dead man's gambeson. He replaced the three blades with soft clicks and looked over his shoulder at Yarrow. "I told you to stay out of my way."

"I saved your life," Yarrow said. "I thought you might forgive me now, for—"

Corbin cut him off, his teeth bright white when he curled back his pale lips. He pointed his dagger at Yarrow's chest like an accusatory finger. "You think I forgive you?"

"Why not? We have been working together for months. I just saved you when it would have been no detriment to me to let you die. I don't need you any longer, but I saved you anyway. What do you want from me?"

"I want my goddess-damned arm back! What do you think I want?"

"Not even I can do that," Yarrow said. "At least, not yet. It's much harder to create than tear down. Still, I have given you no reason not to trust me."

"You want me to trust you?" Corbin whispered. "Tell me what in Thalil's name you are."

"I-I'm Yarroway L'Estrella. Born twenty years ago in Lockhaven, third son to Lady Asaria and Valen Rayne L'Estrella the First."

"Don't pretend like I haven't seen inside you," Corbin pressed. "More, I think, than you intended. There is something else. A power—and a violence and rage—like nothing I have ever experienced. Where does it come from? It is not human. What committed deeds that would make even a son of Thalil sweat icicles in his bed at the mere memory of them?"

"I don't know what you mean," Yarrow said, looking away. Then he thought about what Sasha would advise, and he met Corbin's gaze and tried to show no doubt or deception on his face.

"A fair attempt," Corbin said, arching a brow. "But you're lying. You're barely holding it at bay, aren't you? That lust for complete destruction. You worry it will claim those you love most. I bet it would not be the first time."

"Shut up!" Yarrow ran at Corbin and shoved him hard in the chest, cerulean light trailing like a cape behind him. "You don't know anything about me!"

Corbin stumbled a few steps before he caught his balance. "You've just proved me right. You'd like to rip me to shreds; I see it in your eyes. I might not be able to figure out the rest, but I know murder when it's looking right at me."

Goddesses, he's right! I can hear the blood singing in his veins, and I just want to spill it! I am not a monster. I am not a slave to this thing. Not anymore. Not anymore! He hauled in a breath of the chilly, gore-scented air and held it, tasting death at the back of his throat. What did he want? What did he want behind the anger and fear? The answer was simple: "I wish to return to my friends. Your work is done here, is it not? Can we be going?"

Corbin cocked his head and regarded Yarrow, his black eyes glittering. Yarrow knew he had surprised the other mage by regaining control so quickly. That seemed to worry Corbin more than Yarrow's rage. *He wants me broken, coming apart, but I'm not. Well. At least I'm trying to mend. I'll never be free until I'm rid of the burdens of the past. I have to let them go, before—*

Not yet, Thalil had said. *Not yet.*

I cannot do it out of rage or the lust for destruction. If I do this thing, I cannot do it to entertain savage appetites.

"Actually, there is another facet to this assignment," Corbin said, stowing his final blade as he turned toward the ruined camp. "I am to gather everything these people might have found in the mountains and deliver those items to my employer."

"Who is your employer?"

"I suppose it can do no harm to tell you, since you'll see soon enough if you continue to travel with me. I must deliver these artifacts to the grand temple of the Mother Goddess in the city of Belphora, in Gaeltheon."

"The… the priestesses hired you? Hired the Cast-Down?"

"It is not the first time. Hardly. Surprised, Yarroway?"

"I shouldn't be. Bitches. Who but deceitful bitches to serve deceitful bitches?"

Corbin chuckled. "Well said. Now, if you're still interested in assisting me, you can help me take a look at the contents of these wagons. We'll need to search the tents as well. It might not be pretty work, what with all the blood."

"What about the place where they were digging?"

"Good idea," Corbin admitted, "though we may need the daylight to do it."

"What for?" Yarrow asked. "I can conjure a light for us. I've been doing it since I was a boy of six, when I wanted to stay up past my bedtime reading. Can't you?"

"Of course I can. Don't insult me."

"I wasn't," Yarrow answered honestly.

Corbin flipped his hair off his shoulder and met Yarrow's gaze, a vulnerability in his eyes that Yarrow couldn't tell if he meant or used as manipulation. "The truth is, I don't wish to venture into that pit without the light of day shining in."

"But I thought you—the Crimson Scythe—preferred the night. Sasha's always saying things about 'my master's shadows.'"

"I do not have to explain myself to you, Yarroway. Either help me or stand over by the carts and be quiet."

They spent the rest of the evening hours rifling through the contents of the wagons: mostly worthless junk, broken bits of carved stone columns, shattered pottery, and a few bits of jewelry tarnished by the centuries. In the collapsed tent of the first worker Corbin had killed, a thin, elderly man, Yarrow found a gold pendant with a blue stone the size of a coin at its center, not even cracked. A faint hum of enchantment, one Yarrow almost thought he recognized, emanated from the jewel, and Yarrow slipped it into his pocket before Corbin saw. He smiled; Sasha would have been proud of his speed and stealth. As the sun's watery pink spines stretched across the sky, rosy blades that pierced the retreating darkness, he and Corbin consolidated what they'd discovered into a single cart. Yarrow found he didn't want to look at the freezing corpses, their limbs jutting at odd angles, mouths agape and eyes clouded, scattered across the camp. He didn't know why—he had seen and caused more than his share of death—but he wanted distance from them.

"Let's make our way up the mountain and take a look at what they were excavating," Yarrow suggested. "Do you know what the priestesses are looking for? Precious metal, or gemstones?"

"I have no idea," Corbin said. He drank wine from a skin canteen and passed it to Yarrow. It was the heavy, earthy, plummy-tart vintage from the order hideout, and Yarrow's eyes almost rolled back when it hit his tongue. Ferrous and mineral, almost like blood, it warmed him all the way to his toes, leaving a faint hint of burleberry and charred oak on his tongue after he swallowed. Corbin wiped his lips with the back of his hand before continuing. "I was told only to deliver anything I found here to the temple. Seeing all this, I can't imagine what they'd want with it, but that isn't my concern."

They made their way up the well-worn trail and discovered a cavern about the size of a small room. More crumbling columns held it up, but other than that, it seemed filled with only dust and distant memories. Though he had to bend nearly in half, Yarrow went inside. As much as he hated confined spaces, especially those underground, something drew him on: a pulse of enchantment near the back of the chamber. It felt alive, seemed to synchronize with his heartbeat as he got nearer, a cautious step at a time. "I-I know this magic."

"Come out," Corbin ordered sharply. "There's nothing left here, and it doesn't look safe."

Yarrow ignored him. He pulled off his gloves to press his bare palms against the mirror-smooth stone at the end of the hollow. Power, ancient and familiar, moved in waves up his arms and into his chest. If he squinted and looked from the corner of his eye, he could almost see a faint shimmering line around the slab of rock. He pushed. Nothing happened, so he let a faint echo of magic flow from his hands.

The sound of grating stone filled the chamber, and rocks the size of apples, as well as clouds of choking dust, rained down on Yarrow. He shielded his head with his forearms and coughed.

"Come out, by Thalil," Corbin urged. "The whole place is about to fall down around you, and don't think I'll dig you out if it does."

"Either help me or shut up and leave me be," Yarrow choked out. "There's something here. You're a mage. Do you feel nothing?"

"Just… great age. It's incomprehensible," Corbin answered. "It's almost like magic, but so different. I have never experienced anything like this."

"I have." Yarrow remembered the enchantment veiling Hale's island, the illusions he had encountered in Fane's cave. He remembered how to pull apart the delicate, tightly woven threads, and he started to tug on the ends. This spell, old and worn thin, unraveled easily, quicker than the others without a living caster to maintain it. After only a quarter of an hour or so, the panel dissolved and he looked into a dark narrow tunnel sloping sharply down. "I'm going in."

"You're out of your mind."

Yarrow chuckled. "I have heard that before and will again, I'm certain. Your concern warms my heart, though, Corbin." Though his whole body trembled with the recollection of past horrors, he reached his foot into the blackness and found something like a step, worn to a mere bump by time. He reached out to put his hands on the walls, so close around him, and slowly felt his way down, his heart in his throat and his stomach close behind it.

When the ground evened out, Yarrow conjured an orb for light. Eerie drawings on the walls sprung into being: barely clad women fighting horned and winged creatures twice their size, the same women shooting lightning into a fair young man, the young man dying… then rising from a pool of water.

"Goddesses." Yarrow's whisper echoed through the tiny chamber. He flinched at the sound of his own voice. He knew he was witnessing Fane's wives' war against the creatures, those ancient beings who had first dominated the world, and their betrayal and decimation of their husband and teacher. Then… his resurrection. Had Fane known he would come back? How? Yarrow almost felt he had been meant to come to this place, but why? How? The odds he would discover it were astronomical. Anyone with even a trace of the gift in their blood would have been able to find the door, yet only he had. There was nothing here, just a round empty space with some archaic paintings on the walls. If Fane had meant to impart something through this place, in his name, what could it be?

Yarrow walked to the painting of Fane emerging from the pool. He studied the crude lines depicting the simplistic, nude male form. A dim light emanated from its chest, and Yarrow pressed his hand to the barely perceptible glow. Nothing happened until he offered it a little of his own heart, his own magic, in exchange. Then the rock opened, bisecting the image of Fane down the center and swinging out toward Yarrow with the groan of something very, very old. Inside, resting on a plinth, sat a box with no seams, the size of a loaf of bread. Yarrow ran his hands over glossy blue stone shot with branching white veins. It reminded Yarrow of the sky during a lightning storm, but he had never seen nor heard of such a stone. Made all in one piece, the box offered no clue as to how it opened, if it was meant to open at all, so Yarrow held it to his chest and jogged back toward the stairs as a low, ominous rumble shook his feet. The ceiling cracked and fell in pieces as he ran, taking the crude steps two at a time. He made it to the room where the laborers had been digging. No sooner had he cleared the steps than the walls fell in and obliterated the worn staircase. He only just made it past the chamber and out into the snow before the entire mountain seemed to collapse, destroying any evidence of the little room or the hidden crypt beneath it.

Crypt? Not exactly. It held no remains. More like a vault—a place for treasure. The prospect excited Yarrow.

Yarrow, having dived free of the falling stone, had landed hard on his belly. Corbin grasped his hand and helped him up as he fought to fill his lungs. The other mage dragged him clear of the collapsing mountainside, and Yarrow dropped to his knees in the snow.

"You found something down there," Corbin said.

Fighting dizziness, whether from lack of air or euphoria at his discovery, Yarrow didn't know, he managed, "No."

"Liar."

"Whatever I found is mine, Corbin. Do you really think you can take it from me?"

"I should try, on Thalil's orders. For the sake of my mission. I was told to deliver *everything* to the priestess."

Yarrow rolled his shoulders back to make the knobs of his spine stretch and pop. "We can fight, if you want. I'll beat you and we both know it. Or you can let me keep what I have found, study it. Who will reprimand you—Sasha? My lover? No one need know what we discovered here. It's come from Fane. Who knows, with his knowledge, maybe we can restore your arm."

"Do you really think so?"

Yarrow shrugged. "I can't promise anything, but he was the greatest mage to ever live. He was capable of making flesh immortal, so maybe he also knew how to recreate it. If we have any chance, it's with his wisdom. Let me take this, see what I can make of it. If I learn anything, I'll share it with you."

"You'd help me?"

"Why not?" Yarrow said. "I have very few friends, and I'll soon need as many as I can get."

"Why?"

"Because I'm going to change the world. Right down to its foundations."

Chapter
Twenty-Three

THEIR leather armor hidden beneath ragged cloaks coated in road dirt, Yarrow and Corbin guided the wagon carrying their spoils along the western road toward the city of Belphora, a little southwest of their current position. For the first few days, they encountered no one. After they left the foothills of the Lapir Mountains, they passed rangeland and a few farms, but both men and animals remained indoors, waiting out what was left of the winter.

As they got closer to the many villages of Gaeltheon's fertile southwestern plain, they began to pass companies of knights on the road, all of them heading west, toward the river, into hostile territory still ruled by warlords, mercenaries, criminals, and the Emiri. The groups ranged from a few dozen men to regiments of several hundred. Yarrow tried to ask a few of the soldiers they encountered what was going on, but they either ignored him or offered him some feeble explanation that told him nothing.

"By saying nothing they tell us a great deal," Corbin said, flicking the reins against the flanks of the two shaggy ponies pulling their cart. "What is not said can mean more than what is."

"So what are they saying by not saying anything?" Yarrow asked, watching the dust cloud surrounding the latest batch of several dozen knights and twice as many soldiers on foot recede as they descended the crest of a hill.

"It can only mean one thing," Corbin said, his gaze on the road before him and his hand tight on the reins. "This many men on the march only ever means one thing: war."

ABOUT a week later, Yarrow and Corbin reached the pretty city of Belphora, a picturesque town built of grayish-white stone nestled into a shallow valley about a day's ride from the fabled Bay of Blossoms. At the center of the city, the temple to the Mother Goddess dwarfed every building around it, including the stronghold of the noble family ruling the area. Twelve white spires, each of them five or six stories tall, surrounded a massive dome, atop of which a thirteenth pillar stood, dozens of feet higher than the rest. At its pinnacle, a golden statue of a voluptuous woman stood, arms raised to the sun. Though it was hard to tell from the hillock where they waited, Yarrow estimated the idol must have been four or five times larger than any living woman, and he curled his lip. Hypocrites. If they cared as much about the plight of the poor and the peasants as they claimed, the priestesses would melt that monstrosity down and use it to feed and clothe the beleaguered they claimed to love. It would keep every beggar in Gaeltheon plump and happy for decades.

Corbin guided the rickety wagon carefully down the winding trail until they reached the edge of the city. The market stalls were just closing down and the vendors packing up for the evening as they made their way through the center of the lovely hamlet.

"Ever been to Espero?" Yarrow asked.

"Of course," Corbin said a little testily. "Why do you ask?"

"I just wish to talk to pass the time," Yarrow said, appropriately defensive. "Why do you assume everything I say to you is some sort of veiled insult? Are you so quick to defend yourself because you have failed in the past?"

"I suppose that wasn't meant to be an insult either."

"No," Yarrow said. "I have failed too, made terrible decisions, so many terrible decisions. You might say my entire life is a string of them." He laughed, and Corbin flinched at the bitter, broken sound. "Anyway, I was just thinking this city looks a little like Pala Reapaza, in Espero, only the stone here is white, and in Espero it's black. But it's clean and neat, not like Meritage or Felgard."

Corbin kept watching the road from beneath his hood, said nothing, and didn't even glance in Yarrow's direction, so Yarrow kept talking to keep himself company. He still hadn't quite acclimated to the loss of his creature, to always having someone to speak with, even if the other had done little but hurl hurtful abuse. "It's strange. This is one of the oldest temples in the world. The one back home in Lockhaven, on the shore of the lake, is a little older, 2400 years, I think I remember my tutors telling me. If Fane fell ten thousand years ago, what took them so long? The goddesses, I mean."

"How should I know?" Corbin answered. "Who cares?"

"I do. Why does it please them to waste so many resources on a building where no one even lives? What do they get out of it? Is it just vanity?"

"Probably. Why does this mean so much to you?"

Yarrow considered. "I just don't understand why they did what they did. If they were already immortal, why destroy my—why destroy Fane? Why keep us all under their heels?"

"The only god who concerns me is Thalil," Corbin said.

"But what about that? If Thalil is a god, why does he need the Crimson Scythe? If he wants someone dead, why doesn't he just shoot a bolt of lightning at them or something? Why haven't the sisters destroyed me? Why don't they just make the ground open and swallow me up?"

"Because you could avoid being swallowed?" Corbin turned to look at Yarrow then, eyes narrowed and one brow arched.

"Damn. I could, couldn't I? I… I wish I could trust you. Trust you to really share what I have learned of truth and the nature of magic. There are things I'd like to discuss that only another mage would understand."

"You hold many secrets," Corbin observed. "You have not even shared them with those you claim to love, so why would I expect you to share them with me?"

Yarrow fell silent, thinking about Corbin's words. How had the other mage seen it when he had not? He didn't want to lie anymore, not to them, not to the only men who had ever trusted him. Sasha had suspected Yarrow kept things to himself—before, he'd had to. Now, he wanted to be Yarrow, a man who could confide in his partners. But could he? He still held much that could hurt them.

Sometime after dark, Yarrow and Corbin entered the temple grounds through a small gate near the back of the complex. Corbin steered the ponies into a small shed used to store hay and sacks of grain, and there they waited until well into the night. When the hundreds of bells around the grounds announced the midnight hour, a short, plump woman draped in a purple velvet cloak and carrying a lantern entered the little barn. Corbin leapt from the driver's seat and strode to meet her, while Yarrow waited with the wagon, careful to keep his distinctive hair and paint hidden beneath his hood.

"Cast-Down," the priestess said by way of acknowledgement.

"Lady," Corbin responded. "I suppose you think you insult me by calling me thus. You are mistaken."

"No matter. Were you successful?"

"Do you need to ask? The children of Thalil do not fail. Ever."

Even in the gloom, Yarrow saw the big woman shudder and pull her cloak tightly over her heart. "Do not speak that name in this scared place. Show me what you have recovered. The sooner this holy place is free of your corruption, the better."

"I couldn't agree more," Corbin said, catching her elbow like a suitor might and leading her around the wagon. He whisked away the sheet of oiled canvas covering what they'd found at the dig site. The pudgy priestess rifled through the bits of stone and broken pottery. The longer she shifted the debris, the more agitated she became, huffing and hurling chunks of rock. Yarrow held the strange box he had found, now hidden in a leather satchel, close to his heart beneath the folds of his cloak.

"Am I to believe you found nothing else?" She'd worked up a sheen of sweat Yarrow could smell from where he sat.

"I removed every artifact I found in the camp, as instructed," Corbin said. "Now, I assume you have my payment? Thalil"—he emphasized his master's name—"was promised five hundred gold pieces per person."

The fat priestess huffed. "You expect me to pay you when this is all you have brought me? A cartful of junk!"

"Yes," Corbin said with a shrug.

"Well, I won't. The temple will not pay for a load of refuse!"

"You should reconsider." Corbin sounded so much like Sasha a tingle of arousal spread down Yarrow's body, and he crossed his legs to hide his reaction. "Though I should not, I will offer you one last chance to pay what is owed."

"You are out of your mind! Pay for this… this rubbish?"

"Very well. The choice is yours." Before Yarrow could stop him, Corbin drew one of the small knives from the strap across his chest and slashed it across the priestess's throat. She collapsed into the sawdust, a pool of blood spreading out from her body.

"Now why in the Shades' Abode would you do that?" Yarrow asked.

Corbin cleaned his blade on the woman's cloak before replacing it. "It is standard practice when an employer refuses payment. No one denies Thalil. You can bet that when I ask her successor for the agreed-upon gold, it will be produced. What's the problem?"

"Nothing. I just wanted to ask her about the war. I want to know why the knights are marching, and against whom."

"The order will know."

"But I don't want to wait that long!" Yarrow shouted. A hound bayed somewhere nearby, and he lowered his voice. "Duncan is a knight, a bairn. If he'll be fighting, I want to know where and why. I should be beside him."

"Think he'll fall without you and your awesome magic?"

"To the Shades' with you, Corbin. You know nothing, understand nothing. I'm sick to death of your stupid games, and I'm leaving."

"Oh? And where will you go?"

Yarrow thought. "All of the soldiers we have encountered have been marching south and west. I'll go that way for now. I'll find my way to my friends."

"Go on, then. What do I care?"

"Fine." Yarrow turned on his heel and left the shed. He walked slowly at first, giving Corbin the opportunity to call him back. When he didn't, Yarrow made his way out of the temple compound and onto the city streets, trying to convince himself he wasn't disappointed, that he could care less if

Corbin considered him valuable or interesting. At the edge of town, Yarrow bought a small, swift, gray mare and urged her west, toward the river. He needed to be beside Duncan and Sasha. He knew he never should have left them. If there was fighting to be done, he'd do it at their sides.

SAI worried as he looked out across the mouth of the river. The Emiri had come together and proved a formidable force as they defended the only homeland they'd ever known, but the barbarians seemed never-ending, as many as the drops of water in the sea. They just kept coming, dozens of ships a day to face the Emiri forces. So far, the Emiri, with the weapons Zura had crafted for them, had managed to keep the invaders from entering the mouth of the Kanda. But with their numbers, Sai didn't know how long they could keep the enemy at bay. They'd already lost too many ships and even a few of the southernmost islands. He worried what would happen to his *syrai*—and his son—if the Johmatrans advanced much farther.

Out on the water, a pair of Johmatran ships fired on an Emiri vessel, the exploding boulders tearing the ship in half. Emiri dove for the safety of the sea as their boat burned on the water. A trio of Emiri vessels returned fire, but on the horizon, another dozen or so barbarian ships appeared.

"We can't keep this up," Sai said to Izu, who stood next to him at the helm. "There are more of them than there are of us."

"They seem intent on wiping us out," Izu said, holding Sai's waist. "What will we do?"

"What can we do? People with babies and children are hiding farther up the river. We have to make sure the barbarians don't make it that far."

"But how?"

Sai shook his head. "I don't know. But we have to hold the line. We can't let them get any farther. This is the most important thing we will ever do, so we'd better do it as well as we can. Full sails. Let's get over there and help our people."

"All right, then," Izu said, going to the chute Kin had installed on the ship to spray liquid fire while Lala and Kin adjusted the riggings. "Let's send as many of them to the pits of Emir as we can while we still draw air!" A gust of air stretched their sheets tight and propelled them toward yet another battle.

YARROW rode west, skirting the edge of the Bay of Blossoms. Legend told that one of the first priestesses of the Mother Goddess, a princess who gave up her wealth in favor of service and piety, had planted a tree for every blessing from the sisters she recognized in the world. According to the myth, that had been two thousand years ago, and today hundreds and hundreds of flowering trees surrounded the bay. It would be a few more weeks before they reached their pinnacle, but already pale pink, lavender, and powder blue clumps of blossoms covered their boughs, weighing down the thinner branches and scattering their petals like snow across the trail beneath Yarrow's mount. The delicate flowers swirled in the air around him and tumbled off the cliff, covering the surface of the sea near the rocks and scenting the air. Pilgrims sat praying or meditating beneath the lacy ceiling of blooms.

Yarrow rode beneath the trees until he neared territory still outside the control of Garith and his knights or even the priestesses. Luckily the area beyond the bay contained mostly Emiri, as it wasn't far north of the Twenty-Nine, and Meritage lay just across the river. Yarrow would blend in among the Sea People, since he wore their paint, spoke their language, and knew their customs. Dozens of ships with brightly colored striped sails bobbed in the water near the river's edge, but as Yarrow got closer to them, he noticed this settlement felt different somehow. It pulsed with a sense of urgency he had never experienced among the Emiri: every man and woman worked loading ships, mending sails, adjusting ropes or tinkering with some strange, cannon-like weapons affixed to the decks. No one sat fishing from the piers, passing the *muri-ku* jug, or napping in the rapidly warming springtime sun.

Yarrow dismounted and found a pole near the end of a wooden walkway to secure his horse. He found an old bucket and filled it with water from a pump for the animal. Emiri rushed past him carrying cargo as he wandered down toward the quayside. They called out to each other in their language, mostly ignoring Yarrow. Finally he caught the arm of a young man with red hair that leaned a little more toward brown than Sai's brilliant vermillion. The Emiri spun around to face Yarrow, confusion in his yellow eyes.

Yarrow greeted him in Emiri, and the other man relaxed a little. "You wear Emiri paint, yet you are not Emiri," he said to Yarrow. "Are you here to help us?"

"Help you with what?" Yarrow asked. "What's going on here?"

"What? You mean you don't know? Have you been hiding in a cave the last few moons?"

"Er… sort of."

"Well, a few moons back we started sort of… helping ourselves to the fancy cloth and spices coming from the barbarian lands east of Gaeltheon. The barbarians didn't have seaworthy vessels when we started, but they learned to build them, and then they managed to follow us here somehow. They're after one of our *mir*, who has been freeing the slaves in the Johmatran lands, as well as making the dry-foot pigs look like fools. They've been attacking us, and we're holding the mouth of the river, but some of the outer islands of the Twenty-Nine have fallen. We've moved everyone who can't fight—old people and children—to the inner isles.

"We thought it might get a little easier to defend our homes when the dry-foot king declared a war against the barbarians, but there are just so many of them. All of us are on our way down to the Twenty-Nine to see if we can help. You're welcome to come with us."

"You have a ship?" Yarrow asked.

"Of course. Want to join my crew? Can you do anything useful?"

Yarrow grinned, opened his hand, and produced a small blue flame across his palm.

The Emiri man nodded and patted Yarrow's shoulder. "One who knows magery is most welcome, as long as you're willing to fight alongside and for the Emiri."

"I'll fight for the Twenty-Nine," Yarrow said. "It's my valenny, after all."

The Emiri man laughed and patted Yarrow on the shoulder. "Of course it is, *syrai*. And I'm next in line to rule the council in Espero."

Instead of explaining his long and complicated path to his claim on the lands, Yarrow just swore his magic would be with the Emiri, and he'd fight until they drove their enemies from the Twenty-Nine. "I have a few more questions, though, if you don't mind."

They began to walk along the shore, Yarrow following the other young man. "Go ahead and ask," the young Emiri said.

"How did it happen that Garith… er, the land king, started a war with the foreigners? I'm sorry, but I know he wouldn't go to battle for the sake of the Sea People."

"He certainly wouldn't, syrai. We were on our own against the barbarians until a few weeks ago."

"What changed?"

The Emiri shrugged. Like most of his kinsmen, this one was lithe, graceful, and beautiful, with an intrinsic sexuality behind his every gesture. The Emiri, Yarrow had always thought, must be made up of more water than his kind, because their movements were so much more fluid. "I don't understand land-bound religion very well, but from what I've heard, the barbarians attacked some temple to their gods or goddesses. Sacked it and forced themselves on the women. Took all the treasure, and from what I hear, it was a good bit. Now, not only the land king's soldiers but those working for the temple women are on a path to destroy the invaders. That doesn't mean they're helping us, though. But you will?"

"Oh, I will," Yarrow assured him. "If we'll be fighting together, I should know your name, *syrai*. I'm called Yarrow L'Estrella, of Lockhaven."

"Born to the mountains and the frost, then. I was born on the sweet western seas to the south of the Revenant Coast. My mother and her *syrai* called me Ibo."

Yarrow put his hands on Ibo's waist and kissed him on the lips, greeting him in the traditional way of the Emiri. "The sea has carried us to each other. Let's make the best of Emir's gift. I'll help you drive these dirty whoresons from your shores, and along the way, maybe you can help me get back to my friends."

"I'll help you if I can," Ibo said. "Come along, now. My ship is just this way, and I want to make it to the Twenty-Nine as soon as we can. When we get there, I'm afraid we'll be up to our ankles in blood. But we can't let these bastards take our beaches and islands and drag our people away in chains to languish in some dusty land."

"No, we certainly won't let that happen," Yarrow said as he followed his new *syrai* over the gangplank. Just before stepping onboard the ship, Yarrow looked over his shoulder toward where he'd left his horse. Not surprisingly, after leaving his mount unattended in an Emiri port, she had already been stolen.

Chapter Twenty-Four

"WHERE is Yarrow?" Duncan asked, raising a hand to shield his eyes against the soft spring rain. The moisture over the past week or so had intensified the rich, fecund scent of the soil and the promising hint of green things starting to push forth from it. It also made their gear bloated and heavy and the hundreds of men following them miserable.

"I've done all I can for the moment," Sasha said quietly. "Three of my people are looking for him, with messages to deliver when they find him. They will find him, Duncan."

"What's taking so long, then?" Duncan looked worried; he didn't bother trying to hide his concern, and he looked to Sasha for comfort. Sasha was still learning how to provide it, but he would do his best.

"Most likely Yarrow is among the Emiri," Sasha said, looking over at Duncan where he sat mounted on a huge bay charger, rain running down his face and dripping from the tips of his whiskers. He completely exposed every vulnerability, his very spirit, in his eyes, leaving himself open to Sasha. What Sasha had once seen as naiveté, he now understood as courage. "We know from my information that he left Corbin's company many weeks ago, near the end of Sarmine's Moon, and Corbin said he planned to ride west. He was seen near the Bay of Blossoms at the full moon of your Mother Goddess, on the holiday your people call the Afternoons of Content. He would have encountered Emiri as soon as he reached the river, and he may very well have traveled with them. He's always had a fondness for them, and them for him. If he's with the Emiri, it will take my people a bit longer to locate him. We do not often hunt among them. The Emiri have a way of swallowing people up, much like the sea. They hide people without ever meaning to."

"I know it," Duncan said, looking out over the muddy, rutted road that would, within a few more days, take them to Meritage. "I can't help but worry. I know Yarrow can take care of himself—I mean, he can defend himself, but I worry. He isn't you. He doesn't think before he speaks or acts, never weighs the consequences of his decisions. For all his power, he's—"

Sasha grinned at Duncan and arched a brow. "Mad?"

Duncan pursed his lips into a tight smile. "I was going to say fragile."

"He would be very cross at that assessment," Sasha said.

"Oh, undoubtedly. But am I wrong?"

"No." A little trickle of cold moved across Sasha's chest and down to settle in his belly. As he wondered at the novel sensation, he remembered all Yarrow had suffered and wished yet again he'd met his beautiful mage sooner, spared him some of it, made those who had wronged Yarrow pay for it in blood and pain. He couldn't, of course, but he could make sure no one hurt Yarrow again. "I'll also be glad when we find him. Not only can we protect him, he can protect us, and will want to."

"Goddesses," Duncan muttered, shaking his head. "War. It's always war. Will men never learn?"

"If you're tired, my friend, you have every right to stop fighting. Your gods know you've earned your rest. If you want to go home, I'll go with you."

Duncan reached over his shoulder and touched the hilt of his sword, both a nervous and sentimental gesture Sasha had noted on many occasions, often accompanied by the same faraway look his knight's eyes held right now. "I would stop fighting, my… my friend. If the world would only be a decent place and a place where innocents aren't exploited and the defenseless don't suffer and die for nothing. On that day, I'll lay my sword down and find myself a chair by the fire. Maybe raise some cows. Or dogs. Dogs are fine creatures, loyal and strong. But while horrible things keep happening, a temple burned and priestesses raped and murdered by heathens, I'll never be able to stand by, not while I have strength to resist such atrocities. If I can still lift my weapon against such senseless horror, I must do it. Tell me. Do you think the world will ever agree to my terms? Will there ever be a world where men such as you and I aren't needed?"

"No," Sasha answered honestly.

"I guess a death in battle, then. It could be worse. I hope you'll be beside me at the end. You and Yarrow."

As he remembered what Thalil had said, what he'd granted, Sasha realized he would outlive Duncan and Yarrow; he'd have to watch them die, somehow deal with losing them, somehow continue going through the motions of life after they were gone. The icy weight of fear, something Sasha had never experienced before meeting and loving Duncan and Yarrow, settled so heavy on his chest he could scarcely breathe. How would he live without anything to live for? Killing for Thalil had been enough… once, but Sasha didn't know if it could be again. Succumbing to the weak feelings, to fear, would do nothing for any of them, though, so Sasha forced it away, forced himself to concentrate on what he could control. Still, he had to wonder if the

Dark and Beautiful One intended to punish him after all. Many things could be twisted to one's advantage, though.

Sasha looked over and saw Duncan watching him with a bemused expression. He wondered if he'd given some of his turmoil away through his features (though he doubted it) or if Duncan simply wondered why Sasha hadn't answered his question. He let the apology he felt show through, even though doing so still felt wrong. "I'll be beside you as long as I can, Duncan. The Cast-Down help anyone who tries to stand between us. *Anyone.*"

YARROW had to get the wounded farther up the river, to the safety of the northernmost islands and the coasts around them, that tiny bit of land the Emiri still held. He'd been confident he could help people who had always treated him with more kindness and respect than most when he'd set off with Ibo, imagined using his magic to destroy their enemies, render them all to ash and dust. He'd had no concept of their numbers, though. Hundreds of ships, more than he could count, surrounded the archipelago of the Twenty-Nine, with reinforcements arriving almost daily. And they had mages, some of the most powerful casters Yarrow had ever encountered.

He'd joined the Emiri near the midmoon of the Mother Goddess, expecting a fight lasting a week, at most. Now, at almost the end of Myint's Moon, they had succeeded only in losing most of the Twenty-Nine. Today, after yet another devastating attack, they'd salvaged the ten boats that could still float, loaded the survivors onboard, and ran. They ran against the current, upriver, toward the scant eight islands they'd managed to defend. At least a dozen enemy ships pursued them.

Yarrow stood at the stern of Ibo's ship, trying to protect the flank of their small fleet. He estimated four or more of the twelve ships close on their heels had casters onboard, and they hurled all manner of spells: lightning, gouts of flame, and spears of ice formed from the river water. One of them used a spell similar to those Yarrow had learned from Corbin; when the greenish mist touched the hull of a ship, the wood began to rot until it lost all integrity and water flooded the hold. Another devious enchantment thickened the water, trapping the fleeing ships like bits of garbage stuck in a slimy puddle of city mire or a gutter on a hot day. That, combined with the liquid fire and the exploding boulders the enemy hurled at them, could destroy a fleet three times their size; Yarrow had seen it happen, too many times. He'd seen too many die and been helpless to save them.

So he stood balancing on the aft rail, arms stretched out in front of him, long tangles of hair streaming out behind and all his muscles trembling with the effort of maintaining the shield he'd conjured. The sparkling blue filament stretched in a dome over the retreating ships, extending several feet down into the water and high into the sky. The spell itself was simple enough—Yarrow had figured it out at about twelve—but casting it on such a massive scale and sustaining it against an almost constant fusillade of enemy attacks took all his concentration, all his energy, and he knew he couldn't keep it up for much longer. They had to reach the large island where most of their people gathered. Hundreds of Emiri vessels surrounded that final stronghold, and these dozen enemy ships would not get past them. They had to make it, but they still had miles to go—Yarrow didn't know how many, only that they hadn't yet spotted the Big Island's southwestern tip.

The four ships closest behind them each shot a ribbon of fire so bright against the twilight sky the afterimages burned into Yarrow's eyes. Gritting his teeth, he pushed back against the skin-melting heat and the force accompanying it. He managed to keep the flames from touching the ship, but it lurched forward, banging against the one in front of it. The Emiri cursed loudly as they, along with everything not tied securely in place, went skidding across the deck and, in some cases, overboard. One of the women grabbed her crewmate's arm just before he tumbled into the river. Yarrow tasted blood as a thin rivulet poured from his nostril into his mouth. No matter—his body could withstand almost anything. It would mend. He was more worried about his magic running out. He couldn't help wondering if he'd have access to more power if the greedy, glutted, so-called goddesses weren't hoarding so much.

Too late, Yarrow saw a trio of burning arrows sail over his head and over his shield. Though one missed its mark, the others hit the main mast of Ibo's ship and one of the topsails. The canvas caught fire instantly, and Yarrow knew if the barbarians had coated their arrows in the liquid fire, water wouldn't douse the blaze. He hopped from the rail and turned sideways, one hand, fingers spread wide, still preserving his barrier. With the other, he reached toward the burning sheets and drew the heat from the fire, pulling away the air it required to burn. The flames dwindled and died as glittering black began to pour over Yarrow's vision. He willed it away, willed his eyes to bring the blurring, watered-down world back into focus as he turned toward his shield once more. Archers had already lined up on the decks of the enemy boats; Yarrow could see dozens and dozens of tiny bright orange balls of flame. From their current location, they could fire over the arcane wall he'd constructed. He had to build it higher, stretch the magical fabric just a little thinner without letting it rip—

He took a step toward the rail and darkness poured into his perception like a sudden summer storm on the high sea, one of those unexpected rains that smeared the ocean and sky together and reduced everything to variegated sheets of gray. Strong, slender arms caught Yarrow around the waist and kept him on his feet, and after a few seconds, the spell passed. Those few seconds had cost dearly, though, and a storm of burning arrows sailed toward the now defenseless ships. Yarrow stumbled out of Ibo's grasp and held on to the rail with one hand. He stretched out the blue claw, extending it from his shoulder like a wing, and swatted at the arrows, sending some of them back at the enemy. From crow's nests and riggings, Emiri returned fire, but small blazes had already sprung up on many of the vessels.

After conjuring a shield, a much smaller version that protected only the very back of Ibo's boat, Yarrow turned to the Emiri captain. "We have to move faster, *syrai*. If we can't reach the Big Island soon, we're all dead."

Ibo shook his head. "We can't go any faster. The *eru* just aren't cooperating. By Emir, I feel like I've wandered into the Dredges. It isn't natural. Can't you help?"

"I… I don't know." By the cursed goddesses, he was tired, so tired he almost couldn't keep caring. But then he thought of the Emiri dead the invaders had left floating in the bloody water, some of them not even old enough to produce children yet. He thought of those the marauders had captured and hauled away in chains. He thought of Duncan and Sasha, fighting somewhere without him, maybe hurt… maybe dying. He had experienced losing one of them, a pain like nothing he had ever imagined, and he would not do it again. Who did these bastards think they were, coming to *his* valenny, attacking *his* people? Rage began to churn in his stomach, and this time Yarrow didn't push it away. Angry was better. Angry was better than frightened or hurt.

"To the Shades' with them," he spat between clenched teeth. "Ibo, tell your crew to hold on!"

The Emiri ran, shouting to the others in their language, as Yarrow raised his hands to the heavens. He would show these damned barbarians who they dared to trifle with. First, he drew in a breath, drawing the air toward the Emiri ships as hard as he could, roping the wind with tendrils of magic and pulling it against their sails. It smacked against the canvas with a resounding crack, driving the fleet little boats forward so fast they almost lifted out of the water. They knocked together, scraped alongside each other, but they'd soon put some distance between themselves and their enemies. What he was doing was dangerous and rash, and it put the Emiri ships in almost as much danger as it did their enemies. At this point, Yarrow had no choice but to resort to it. The unpredictable magical winds tossed their fleet around, giving the sailors at the helms a challenge, but they pushed them farther from their pursuers. Yarrow turned his attention away; he didn't need to maintain the airflow. By sucking the air toward them, he had essentially created a hole, and more air rushed in to fill it without his direction. He turned to the water, drew it up in a wall, and drove it against the pursuing ships. He had to be careful not to pull them backward in its wake, but he judged well.

Two of the enemy vessels capsized, driven below the surface of the river before bobbing back up, their masts shattered and their sails drenched. Two other ships crashed into them, and one pitched on her side, tossing men and weapons into the gray-green water. The others steered around them and continued to chase Yarrow and the rest of the Emiri. That horrible, diseased fog began to spill from one of them, roiling over the surface of the river like a hideous rash spreading over skin, and the wind Yarrow had summoned to aid them only hastened its approach.

"You're not going to beat me!" Yarrow yelled, and a clap of thunder echoed his words. With his magic, fueled by his ire and frustration, he lifted one of the capsized vessels high into the air and slammed it down into the ship spewing the putrid vapor. The impact shattered both boats to splinters, while lifting a third high on the crest of a swell and sending it into another nearby, damaging both. *Seven more,* Yarrow thought as he dropped to his knees and rested his elbows on the rail. *Seven....* He dragged in great quaffs of air and tried to fight the dizziness. While they were now out of the range of the enemy archers and their devastating weapons, it also meant the Emiri couldn't attack. It was all up to Yarrow.

Six of the barbarian ships pursued them, while one remained, probably to aid their survivors. One of the enemy mages imitated Yarrow's tactic, drawing wind into their sails. It closed much of the distance between the two fleets of ships, but it also wreaked all sorts of havoc with the ether above them, and soon crosswinds pitched the ships back and forth and lightning flashed as air collided against air.

With the enemy ships drawing closer, Yarrow couldn't use the water to drive them back, not without pulling his own ships along with it. He tried to lift another up and toss it against the rest, but this time he couldn't manage it, and vertigo hit him like a blow to the face. His tailbone struck the smooth wood of the deck, making him bite his tongue. Spitting out the blood, he climbed back to his feet, but his knees buckled and he doubled over, hitting the rail with his chest.

In minutes, the enemy ships would be close enough to use the liquid fire and exploding rocks. The Emiri fired at them, but fell short. Yarrow didn't know what else to do. For the first time, he understood why Duncan felt so protective of the people of Windwake. These Emiri were his, each of their lives precious, each of them depending on Yarrow to save them, and if he failed, they would all die. Yarrow didn't know exactly when it had happened, or how, but he had come to care about people other than himself. He couldn't say it was a good feeling, either. It had been much simpler when he only had to protect himself, and to the Shades' with the rest of the world.

Once I ripped the sky open and made it rain fire. I burned an entire army to ash—Why can't I do it again? Why? What's missing? Well, now's no time to think on it. Do what I can. Save these people. My *people....*

He forced his legs to straighten, forced them to hold his weight. He took a few steps back and lifted hands that trembled so badly they made his whole body jerk. *Fire. Need fire. Fire to alight that cursed liquid they keep below decks, those damned boulders—Damn it! I'll blow them halfway to heaven!*

A little crack of reddish light appeared between the blackish clouds the sorcery had drawn, but not even a spark issued from the fissure. Yarrow couldn't do it; he had no more to give. Even when he tried to replace the shield, he managed only a pale wash of bluish light that faded into nothing seconds after it appeared.

"I don't know what to do!" he screamed against the sky.

"Yarrow?" Ibo yelled from the helm. "What do we do?"

"Fight," Yarrow answered. "We have no choice but to fight." Though he could barely keep his grip on it with his trembling hands, Yarrow lifted his light, ornate black bow and notched an arrow. How weak and frail the supple piece of wood felt compared to his magic, and he felt so helpless... helpless, alone, and afraid... like... like a child....

"Fight?" one of the other Emiri shouted. "We've got wounded! Our ships are damaged, and they have Emir knows how many mages! They'll destroy us."

Another member of the crew, who stood on the rigging and looked through a distance glass, cried, "More ships coming from the east! Twenty, no, twenty-five... maybe thirty ships."

"No," Yarrow whispered. "No!" He managed a gout of flame, but it landed in the water and fizzled out dozens of feet away from the enemy boats. Biting his bottom lip, he tried again. None of the Emiri would survive— Yarrow knew that—and all he could do was take as many of these bastards with them as he could. *Thirty more ships....*

Yarrow reached into the ether, into the space beyond reality, into the place inside that held nothing but power—no reason, no desire, no words or thoughts or emotions—and he found the flames. The crack in the sky gaped a little wider, and a small storm of sparks began to spiral down.

"Yarrow, wait!" yelled the Emiri sailor with the glass. "Don't do it! Those ships, the thirty ships, they're ours! They're ours! Yarrow, not yet. Not yet!"

The words penetrated Yarrow's haze, and he slowly remembered he had flesh, muscle, and bone, weight, and... and it hurt. It took all his strength to stow his bow and replace his black-tipped arrow in the quiver. "What do you mean?"

"Those are Emiri ships," the sailor called down.

Yarrow stumbled to the mast, feeling like his feet weighed a hundred pounds each, and grasped a length of rope to remain standing. "Let me see."

The Emiri dropped the glass. Yarrow caught it and pressed the narrow end to his eye. Yes, he could see the brightly colored stripes on the sails. Thirty ships, firing catapults loaded with exploding rocks, and with what seemed a much greater range than the enemy, fanned out around the remaining barbarian vessels in a crescent. Before the Johmatrans knew what had hit them, the fresh Emiri force decimated them. In less than half an hour, nothing remained but burning debris, flotsam floating on the darkening water, and the dead. The Emiri on Ibo's ship shouted their victory, hugged, kissed, and brought out the *muri-ku* jug. Yarrow just sank down and leaned his back against the mast, too tired to manage more than a small smile. He let his eyes close—just for a few moments. The next thing he knew, someone was shaking his shoulder, and the stars twinkled in a clear sky above him.

Ibo handed Yarrow the jug, and Yarrow took it gratefully, wincing against the burn of the strong liquor. "Yarrow, the *mir* responsible for saving our asses has come onboard. If it wasn't for him, and you, we would all be under water now. Would you like to meet him?"

Still numb, wanting nothing more than a week of sleep, Yarrow nodded and let Ibo help him up. The crowd of Emiri gathered on the deck parted, and a man with red hair turned and opened his arms. Sheer joy gave Yarrow a fresh surge of energy, and he ran and hugged his old friend, kissing him again and again until the kisses began to grow into something beyond gestures of victory and gratitude, and Yarrow pulled away. He still held tight to Sai's hands, though.

"Sweet *syrai*," Yarrow said, a quiver in his voice. "I'm racking up more debt to you than a man can hope to repay in a single lifetime. I am glad to see you, my wonderful, beautiful Sai."

"Emir is good to me, bringing you back to me," Sai said, and Yarrow sensed a trace of the sadness Sai had expressed when he had wanted Yarrow as more than a friend. "When I heard of someone using magery to aid the Twenty-Nine against these Johmatran bilge-suckers, I hoped, maybe…. Well, I couldn't let you pass so close without seeing your face again." He rubbed his warm, smooth cheek against Yarrow's, and Yarrow couldn't help himself. He kissed Sai again, hard, with fire. It just felt so good to know he wasn't alone. The other Emiri clapped and hooted at their display, and Yarrow pulled back, his face hot and a ripple of guilt in his belly. It wasn't fair to give Sai false hope just to comfort himself.

"We must make it to the Big Island," Sai said, mostly to Ibo. "The barbarian bastards were about half a day behind us, and we have news of more coming up from Espero. Fifty to a hundred ships."

Ibo swore. "We're losing ground every day. It's only a matter of time until they take the rest of the islands. We'll all either be dead or slaves."

Sai laughed and kissed the other man's cheek. "They have a name for me in Johmatra. They—the Emiri in bondage there, those struggling for freedom—call me *Sai-Yu-me*. If those people, those who have never been surrounded by the open sea, those who have never laid naked beneath the sun with their *syrai*, those forced to cut their hair and perform the same drudgery day after day, if they can hold on to hope, then so can we. I have rescued hundreds of our people from that awful place, maybe thousands, and I have hidden them. They are safely tucked away, learning to sail and learning to fight. One way or another, we're going to drive these bastards from our islands and make them sorry they ever saw an Emiri. My *syrai* Zura, here, and my *syrai* Kin can make us weapons. We'll make them, put them on every ship, and fire them straight up these Johmatrans' fat pimpled asses. But for now, we have another problem."

"What more?" Yarrow groaned.

"The *mir* who have come down from the north to aid us bring word of a huge land-bound force gathering just south of the land city of Meritage," Sai said, looking in that direction. "Three hundred knights, triple that number on foot. More than a thousand in all."

"Wait," Yarrow said, trying to quiet the buzzing in his skull and the whispers of doubt hiding just behind them. He was tired, almost too tired to shut the voices out. "The king is fighting the Johmatrans. Would he really split his force to come after us?"

"The dry-foot king has been intent on getting rid of us since he took his throne," Ibo said.

"But at the risk of losing to the invaders? Garith wouldn't be that stupid. Sai, do you know what livery… er, did your people notice what color capes these men wore? Maybe they're coming from Merryvale or Meadow's Edge to join the king against the enemy."

"I don't know what they were wearing," Sai said, "only that there were a lot of them, and they're heading our way. We should be ready for them."

"Can one of you take me to them?" Yarrow asked. "It shouldn't take more than a day or two."

"Why?" Ibo asked.

"I'm a valen's son and the king's cousin."

All the Emiri looked at him without comprehension, as they had no leaders and no one had more value than anyone else, so Yarrow clarified. "I'm important enough to the dry-foot king that those men might listen to what I have to say. Then again, they might not. But if you take me to them, I can at least try to find out what they plan to do, maybe save us from fighting two enemies at once."

Sai caught Yarrow's hand and kissed the back. "I'll take you. You know I will. I've never told you no, have I? Do you want to go right away?"

"If you can sail while I sleep, sweet *syrai*," Yarrow said. "I'm afraid I just can't stay on my feet another moment. I need to be in bed."

Sai grinned wide, opened his mouth as if to speak, then closed it and looked away from Yarrow's gaze. "You'll be safe with me, don't worry. You'll be able to rest. We'll look out for each other as we always have, my… my friend." He hugged Yarrow close and whispered into his hair. "I love you as I always have."

"I love you too, my friend," Yarrow whispered back. "You are one of the best men I've ever known."

Sai pulled away. "Then—"

Yarrow shook his head. "You'll have to be content with my friendship."

Though he looked like he shattered just a little more, the existing cracks widening and spilling out a little more sadness, Sai nodded. "I'll take what I can get of you."

"I can only try to give you something worthwhile. God—No. I won't call out to them again, whether I mean anything by it or not. We'll do this on our own. I want to do something good for once. I'm curious how it might feel to see something end and not experience regret. But this isn't for me. This is for the Emiri, for the Twenty-Nine…. I-I won't fail you…."

Sai shushed Yarrow and took his elbow to pull him away. "You're rambling, *syrai*, and your poor eyes look like two piss holes in the sand. Come back to our ship, and I'll get you into bed. By the time you wake up, I'll have ferried you to your dry-foot friends. Hopefully it will do some good."

Chapter
Twenty-Five

AFTER half a day of blissful unconsciousness, Yarrow woke in Sai's cabin, unable to return to sleep despite the ache in his limbs and the throbbing in his skull. He lay on the comfortable pile of colorful cushions and blankets, breathing the scent of Sai and the others: salt water, leather, *muri-ku*, wet rope, and the grease they put in their hair. Lanterns, made in the Emiri way by cobbling together broken bits of glass into prismatic orbs, swayed back and forth from the rafters above. Yarrow watched their gentle motion through heavy-lidded eyes, trying to let the rocking of the ship lull him back to ease and rest. He would need his strength. Who knew what waited for him at Meritage? He hated nothing more than dealing with the nobility and their petty games, and he wanted to be ready to match their manipulative and duplicitous banter. Questions tossed about and collided in his mind, like the ships on the river had, and he could do little more to still them.

What had Corbin said back in Felgard? That Yarrow was just a mess of broken bits barely held together? Right now, his words rang true. Yarrow felt pulled apart, fragmented. What had happened during the battle? Why had his magic abandoned him? Was it because after being with Sasha and Duncan, after being accepted, cherished, protected... maybe he just wasn't as angry anymore? Anger had always brought out his greatest power, and if it had diminished, had his magic gone along with it? Yarrow closed his eyes and reached out with his consciousness, into the sky, the ether, the place beyond the stars, and at the same time inward, to the infinite space within, the miniature universe he held inside. In there, funnel clouds of power and endless maelstroms of magic extended to the limits of his understanding and beyond. The enchantment was there, he just couldn't access it without the rage, and he was sick to his core of being a slave to rage, to fear. Damn it, this was his! Yarrow's!

Yet, who was Yarrow? Was there anything to him beyond the boy who ran from pain, seeking power, willing to barter anything for the ability to protect himself? And then came the boy full of violence, ready to make the world pay, along with his creature. The lonely boy, so desperate for someone to love him, who pushed everyone away. But then came two men who would not be pushed….

And now? Was there anything behind the fear and pain and anger? Again, Corbin's words echoed in Yarrow's thoughts: *Tell me what you are.*

But I don't know! If he could have heard its voice, his creature would have called him a mewling baby. Its voice. Its thoughts. Now those impulses were his own, inseparable from whatever he had been before. Was there any Yarrow left, or had Yarrow died long ago? Died when the creature took control of him, or maybe even before, when the king and his knights held him down and—

A shard of light fell across Yarrow's bare chest, disrupting his maudlin introspection. He sat up and rubbed his face, glad for the distraction. He needed to sort things out, but a bit at a time, or he would break apart just as Corbin had predicted.

Sai sat cross-legged by the bed and offered Yarrow a platter of grilled seafoods. Though he felt hungry, the fishy smell turned Yarrow's stomach. It smelled of death and decay, and he pushed it away. Sai sat the plate behind him and looked at Yarrow, his brilliant orange eyes wide with concern. Without thinking Yarrow pressed his palm to Sai's cheek, still warm from the sun. Sai draped his hand over Yarrow's and leaned into Yarrow's touch. "What is it, *syrai*?"

"Sai… sweet Sai. What am I?"

Sai swiveled his head and kissed the inside of Yarrow's wrist. "Whatever you want to be."

"Whatever I want," Yarrow repeated, considering.

"Of course. What else?"

"Yes…. Yes! You're wonderful!"

Sai chuckled as he ran his fingertips down Yarrow's bare arm. "I am. Ask anyone. Or better yet, let me show you."

"Sai…."

"I know, Yarrow. I remember what you told me, and I don't want you to hurt your *syrai*, but… after all this time, I still want you so much. Don't hold it against me for trying."

"No. I adore you." Yarrow adjusted the blankets before Sai could see just how much. "You have really helped me, *syrai*. Anything I want to be…."

"And why not?"

"Why not?" Yarrow echoed. "All that's left is to decide what that is."

"Well, we've arrived at Meritage," Sai announced.

Yarrow shook his head in a vain attempt to clear it of phantoms and distant voices still seeking influence over him. "What? I've only been asleep a few hours. I'm still exhausted."

Sai's laughter brightened the dim cabin, and he stroked Yarrow's cheek with the back of his other hand. "*Syrai*, you've been dead to the world for more than two days."

"What? No, I-I don't even feel refreshed."

"Well, I can drop anchor and let you rest a while longer," Sai said. "After all, no one's expecting us."

"No. We should get this over with."

Sai nodded. "Are you sure you won't have something to eat?"

Yarrow looked at the oily bits of flesh on the platter and remembered how annoyed he would have been a few years back at someone urging him to take sustenance. Now he saw it for what it was: concern and love. "Ah, Sai. Is there anything besides fish?"

Sai laughed again with an ease Yarrow envied. "Yarrow, we're Emiri. It's fish or nothing. Unless you want *muri-ku*."

"No. No, but thank you. You're good to me, better than I deserve. I should wash and dress, though. Appearances, frivolous things, hold weight with the land-bound."

Almost as if summoned, Izu entered the cabin with a pail of steaming water, a cloth, and a cake of yellow soap. Yarrow used them and dressed in the fine garments he'd received from the order. Never, not even as a child, had he decked himself in laces to impress the aristocrats, and he wasn't about to start now. He followed Sai out of the cozy room and into the bright spring sunlight. The gangplank extended from the ship to the pier, and a mile or so away, hundreds of tents stood, twice as many fires burning between them. Banners snapped in the warm breeze, but Yarrow couldn't discern their allegiances from such a distance.

"I suppose you should go on without me," Sai said, resting a hand supportively on Yarrow's shoulder. "Your people have no respect for mine."

Yarrow tensed at his words. "No. I would ask you, as a friend, to come with me. I don't want to face them alone; I can admit that now. Besides, you're worth more than all of them put together. I dare anyone to say otherwise."

Sai nodded once, sheathed his small curved sword by his hip, and said, "Let's go, then. Together."

Shoulder to shoulder, they made their way to the shore and then up the rocky trail to the encampment. First, they encountered plum-colored tents with gold trim and knights in bronze plate with matching cloaks. The knights eyed the pair warily but didn't impede them. Yarrow didn't recognize their colors or the strange pattern of stars on their tabards, and he had been educated to know the heraldry of all the noble houses. The nascent bones of his wings curled at his back as they ascended the hill.

Their feet sank in the sand, and nothing but an errant cluster of sea oats grew from the barren expanse as Yarrow and Sai crested a rounded hill. Tents stretched to the horizon on the other side: yellow tents emblazoned with heraldic eagles. Yarrow turned to Sai and grasped his hands. "Windwake! I can't believe it! Duncan!" He turned and ran into the circle of gold-and-black pavilions with Sai close behind him. Not long after they had breached the perimeter, men with swords, spears, and halberds surrounded them, demanding they state their business.

"I'll tell my business to the bairn of Windwake and no one else," Yarrow responded, to Sai's muffled laughter.

"The bairn cannot be troubled with such nonsense," one young knight declared.

"I'll bet he can," Yarrow countered. "Go and ask him, won't you?"

"I certainly will not, Emiri filth," the overzealous soldier shouted.

"What is all this commotion?" Duncan, looking tired and frustrated in nothing but his gambeson, leggings, and boots, asked as he emerged from his tent.

"Windwake!" Yarrow shouted, jogging across the open space to his Duncan and throwing himself into Duncan's strong arms.

Duncan chuckled as he lifted Yarrow off his feet in a hug. "Lockhaven."

"Hardly," Yarrow chastised. "South Coast. Twenty-Nine, maybe. I haven't decided."

Duncan set Yarrow down and held him at arm's length to look him over. "You look tired. Where have you been? What have you been doing? We've been looking for you."

"I've been defending my valenny, or trying to," Yarrow answered. "The Twenty-Nine is overrun with invaders from Johmatra. They're killing everyone or hauling them off as slaves. But now you're here. You and your army can help us."

"Yarrow," Duncan said cautiously, "I've been summoned by your cousin to aid him in his war against the very same barbarians. I am on my way to meet him in Gaeltheon, across the river."

Sasha leaned against the side of a small shed and crossed his arms over his chest. Yarrow hadn't seen or heard him approach, and he hardly recognized him. Instead of his order leathers, Sasha wore a silver chain-mail tunic and some light pauldrons and greaves with the Windwake tabard over top. He'd tied his black hair up in a tight bun at the back of his head. Yarrow laughed as he hurried over to wind his arms around Sasha's waist and kiss his cheek. "You almost look like a respectable soldier," he teased.

Sasha kissed him back and pinned a clump of hair behind Yarrow's ear. "Appearance is just a tool, my friend, one I see you still haven't learned to use. I'm glad you're back."

Yarrow broke away and faced his companions. "I need your help."

Duncan rubbed his hand over face. "The king is expecting these reinforcements. I don't know that I can lead these men down the river when I've been ordered to take them across it and join the Royal Guard."

"You did swear an oath to help Sai, should he ever need it," Sasha reminded Duncan with a barely perceptible smile.

Duncan sighed loudly and curled his shoulders in defeat. "The decision isn't mine alone."

"But you have been put in command of these men," Sasha said.

"Besides, what does it matter where we fight the enemy?" Yarrow asked. "Kill them along the shores of Gaeltheon or kill them in the Twenty-Nine. What's the difference?"

"A fair enough point," Duncan conceded. "But I will have to meet the commander of the Defenders of Thirteen, and—"

"Defenders of the Thirteen?" Yarrow asked, curling his lip.

"Much has happened while we attended to our own business," Sasha said. "It seems while we were... away, the various orders of the goddesses formed an army. They were at odds with the king, at least until the sack of Fayelle's temple. Now they've joined with us to fight the common enemy, but their loyalties are with the priestesses, not your cousin. Make no mistake about that."

"As I was saying," Duncan continued, "I will have to meet with their commander, as well as your brother."

Yarrow groaned. "Which one?"

"Rowan," Duncan said. "He is here with a company of two hundred of his knights from Greyrclif and almost six hundred soldiers. The valen of Lockhaven, your brother Rayne, marched across the Starlight Bridge a few weeks ago with almost five thousand men, toward the southwestern coast of Gaeltheon, where the fighting is worst. The skillful fighters of the new bairny of Rosecairn joined him and are headed in the same direction. That's where we are also supposed to go. Meadow's Edge and Thulemore are holding the Spearepointe Bay, and the invaders haven't made it as far as the Revenant Coast. Goddesses help them if they do. King Garith hopes that if we can defeat them at the peninsula nearest Espero, we can drive them back where they came from before they ever make it that far. Of course, we have had to leave men to defend the western coast in case they do."

"So, how many do we have here?" Sai said, joining the conversation.

"Sixteen hundred men from Windwake, eight hundred from Greyrclif, and almost two thousand Defenders of the Thirteen." Duncan cast his gaze at

Sasha without turning his head to face him. "We could always use more… skilled people. If any were available and could be convinced to aid us, it would be most beneficial."

His face neutral, Sasha said, "No. We have talked about this, and if you wish everything repeated, we should go inside the tent, at the very least."

Duncan turned on his heel and slapped the tent flap open. Sasha entered after him, and Yarrow shared a confused glance with Sai before they hurried to follow. They waited just inside the entrance while Duncan and Sasha stood facing each other, Sasha with his hands on his hips and Duncan drumming his fingers on the map-strewn table.

"How many people in the order?" Duncan said, his tone as tense and tight as his features.

Sasha shrugged. "Thousands. I have told you this already."

"Thousands of people under your command," Duncan said. "Practically an army—a very deadly army. You could order them to help us, and yet you refuse."

"I am their leader, and I must do what is right for the order," Sasha said. "We have never forged political allegiances, and they are not necessary to us. The order will remain unchanged no matter who holds power. I won't turn a system that has operated for thousands of years upside down. My people are, of course, always available for hire. They are not available as an army. That isn't what they're for."

Duncan shook his head. "I beg you to change your mind."

"I can't," Sasha said. "Those people are my responsibility now. They're not, have never been, a force for the battlefield. Find me a single, powerful target, and then maybe I can use my position to help. Duncan, you should be able to understand this."

"I-I do," Duncan said. "I'm just desperate. The situation is desperate. We need more men. The enemy seems never-ending, and so many of our best knights volunteered months ago to go to Espero. We'd have been outnumbered even if they'd stayed. We need—someone."

"Then help us," Sai said. "Come to the Twenty-Nine, where you can make a difference. We'll fight alongside you."

"I will need some time to convince the others," Duncan said.

"Should we come with you?" Yarrow asked.

"No," Duncan said. "I don't think that would be a good idea."

FOUR days later, the force under Duncan's command marched south. Sasha rode near the front of the company, next to Duncan, Yarrow, and Sai. It surprised Sasha little how easily Sai acclimated to riding a horse when he had never been on one before. The Emiri were a graceful people, with good balance and strong, slender muscles. Sai had opted to let his crew sail their ship back downstream so he could guide the soldiers along the safest route, and after a few hours in the saddle, he rode better than many of Duncan's knights.

With so many men on foot, it took them more than a week to reach the riverbank the Emiri occupied. The area looked nothing like the Twenty-Nine had the last time Sasha had visited, on their way back to Windwake after retrieving Yarrow. Instead of brightly painted little houses, quaint bridges, and rows of lanterns hanging between the eaves, the Emiri had constructed pitiful shelters from scraps of rowboats, errant pieces of wood, and tattered, stained strips of canvas that had probably once been sails. Some groups occupied little more than lean-tos with a few dirty blankets beneath. No one sang, played music, fished, or frolicked in the water. They all held weapons— even the children had filet knives or at least pointed sticks, and they eyed the knights and soldiers warily as they dismounted and began unloading carts. The soldiers looked at the Emiri with unmasked hatred and disgust.

Some of Duncan's men came to take their horses. Another group began setting up a yellow-and-black tent that would seem like a palace compared to the hovels barely sheltering the Emiri. In the meantime, the common soldiers began erecting their own small tents and scavenging for driftwood to build fires. Then something unexpected happened. One by one, the Emiri stood and walked over to the infantrymen. At first, the men moved their hands to their weapons, but as the Emiri offered them firewood, fresh water, and food, they relaxed. Soon the Emiri were helping them pitch their tents. Working together, they had the camp set up in only a few hours.

Sasha wandered to the edge of the water and looked south at the hundreds and hundreds of Emiri vessels moored about a half a mile away. Beyond them, more ships surrounded the islands of the Twenty-Nine, and past that, at the very limits of Sasha's vision, black smoke rose in puffs and columns.

Footsteps, muffled by the sand, approached, but he recognized the rhythm of the gaits and didn't turn around. Yarrow and Sai stood on either side of him, and Yarrow caught his hand and twisted their fingers together. The setting sun warmed their backs, and soon the smell of food cooking rose from the camp. The three of them just stood watching as the light painted the water with rose and gold, then, slowly, retreated altogether. Not long after, Duncan called them over for the evening meal, and all of them sat on the ground around the fires—knights, soldiers, servants, and the Emiri alike.

Afterward, Yarrow's brother Rowan came to call them to a meeting, and they all followed him to a huge octagonal tent near the center of camp. Inside, three men sat at a long wooden table: the Defenders of the Thirteen.

The one at the head of the table, a man almost as tall as Duncan, with red-brown hair and a thick curly beard, stood and furrowed his brow. "Bairn Duncan," he said, bowing slightly. "Welcome. Eyrle Rowan, we have not met. I am Tam Bertrand Slige, commander of this branch of the Defenders of the Thirteen, by the grace of the sisters. These are my knights, Tam Wyeth and Tam Kendall, both brave and capable men. Now, please dismiss your servants so we can discuss our strategy."

Sasha wanted to smile, but that would ruin what he knew was coming, so he just waited, and he wasn't disappointed when Yarrow came to the front of their group and stood chest to chest with the much larger man. "Who are you calling a servant? This happens to be my land you're standing on, tam."

Tam Bertrand looked pleadingly at Duncan, who only smirked in response. Then he turned his confused gaze to Rowan. "Who is this… *person*?"

"My brother, Yarroway, one day to be valen of the South Coast." Sasha detected Rowan's shame in his miniscule grimace and the edge to his voice, and he tamped down the flare of anger it ignited.

The big knight's eyes widened, and he took a few steps back. "The-the Hero of the Starlight Bridge? I apologize, Valen Yarroway, but your appearance—"

"Is no one's business but my own," Yarrow said. "Now, can we sit down and attend to this?"

"Absolutely, a fine idea," Tam Bertrand said. "Tell this soldier and the Emiri they can go."

"I will not," Yarrow said. "They are my friends, and I value their advice. I would ask you to treat them with respect."

"But… an Emiri?" one of the knights at the table, this Tam Wyeth, said before Yarrow silenced him with his glowing glare. No one else spoke, and all of them took their places around the table, which was already covered with maps and documents.

Duncan pulled the largest of the charts in front of him and studied it. Yarrow edged closer to him on the bench and pointed. "All of these islands are already lost. The enemy is using them to repair their ships and accommodate their people. There's plenty of shelter and ripe fruit. Between here and here"—he held his fingers a few inches apart, indicating different points along the river—"are probably four hundred Johmatran ships."

"And we have no ships at all," Tam Bertrand said.

"We do," Sai said, stretching across the table to point at the largest of the northern islands. "Here. Five hundred, at least. Our boats are smaller, but they're also faster, more maneuverable. We also know how to make the liquid fire and the exploding boulders. And we know the territory like we know the bodies of our *syrai*."

"Are you suggesting we come aboard with you?" Tam Kendall asked. "Fight with the Emiri?"

"How else are you planning to reach the enemy?" Duncan asked. "Swim?"

"Will my men be safe?" Tam Bertrand asked.

"Our goals are the same," Sasha said. "What sort of fools would the Emiri be to harm men who could fight for them?"

Tam Bertrand glared at Sasha. "I don't recall your name, soldier."

"I didn't offer it."

"And have you completed many successful campaigns?" Bertrand said, clearly trying to anger Sasha, the blind fool.

"You might say I have completed hundreds," Sasha said, offering the other man the sweetest smile he could muster.

"This is getting us nowhere," Duncan said. "*Sai-Mir,* even with your many ships, you have been unable to drive these barbarians from your islands. How will more men onboard make a difference? Tell me about your attack strategy so far."

"Well, we always travel in groups of at least five ships, and when we think we can, we pick off an enemy boat or two. Lately we've been doing more running than attacking, though."

Duncan rubbed his chin as he continued to scrutinize the map. To Sasha, anything his friend devised would be more effective than what the Emiri had been doing: fighting leaderless with no real plan, no strategy. They had vast resources, but they didn't know how to put them to the proper use. Unfortunately, at least from Sasha's perspective, they'd let themselves be backed into a corner.

Duncan echoed Sasha's concerns, tapping the northern cluster of islands with his finger. "The biggest problem I see is that all our ships are bottled up here. Trapped. We'll have to fight through all those enemies, trying to reclaim islands along the way. With the number of ships the Johmatrans have, and their weapons and magic, it would a difficult endeavor at best. But with more ships coming from the east...."

"What we need, if we're to have any chance of success, is to eliminate the ships already here. At least that way, when more arrive, they won't be doubling the number we have to face."

"I don't see how we can do that," Duncan said.

"We have to flank them," Sasha said. "Surround them from the north and south. If we can manage that, we'll be able to destroy them."

"How?" Duncan asked.

For a long time, none of them spoke. Only the crackle of the fires in the braziers around the tent broke the awkward silence. Finally, Yarrow spoke, and his words surprised them all, even Sasha, who had expected his mage to offer to wipe the barbarians out in a storm of fire. But instead—

"Sai, you told Ibo you'd sailed to Johmatra and rescued hundreds, maybe thousands of people, and that you had them tucked away, learning to sail and to fight. Are they building ships?"

"Of course," Sai said. "Ships are how we set our spirits free."

"And where are they?" Yarrow asked. "Where do you have them hidden?"

Sai looked from the three Defenders to Yarrow's brother, gauging whether he could trust them with his secret. Sasha couldn't blame him; people in power had been trying to eliminate the Emiri since they'd set foot on the shores of Selindria and Gaeltheon. Sai said a few clipped words to Yarrow in his language, and Yarrow answered him. Sasha had yet to learn the nuances of the language of the sea. To him, it always sounded like they just repeated the same few dozen words, so he had no idea what Yarrow had said, but it seemed to reassure Sai, and he leaned in toward the map, pointing.

"Here." Sai indicated a small, deep but narrow inlet, running east to west on the Gaeltheon side of the Kanda. "We call this the Blink of an Eye, because that's all it takes to miss it if you don't know to watch for it. There's a reef of *kori* at the mouth of this cove. If you don't know just where it is, it will rip up the belly of a boat. Also, here, near the entrance, are some caverns large enough to hide many ships. My people are there, building boats and making weapons."

"Perfect," Duncan said. "From there, they could do just what Sasha suggested. If we can lure the enemies farther up the river, the others can sail south from the cove, then into the mouth of the river, and close them in from behind. We'll still be in for a fight, but…. It could work. This could be the chance we need."

"There's only one problem," Rowan said. "Everything south of here is swarming with enemies. No Emiri ship can reach this Blink of an Eye. No one will be able to sneak past that many barbarians."

"I can," Sasha said.

"This young warrior is full of surprises," Tam Bertrand said.

Sasha didn't let his face reflect the smile he felt. *If he only knew.* "I can make it past the enemies, I assure you. The bairn of Windwake and the valen of South Coast know I speak the truth." Then, just to rankle the man a little further, he added, "So does this venerable sea captain, *Sai-Mir*."

"So do I," Rowan added, looking a little pale. Sasha wondered if Yarrow's brother remembered when he'd handed him Taran Edercrest's rotting head, and he suppressed another grin.

"Getting those ships here will be critical," Tam Bertrand said, still not convinced. "If you fail, we'll be decimated."

"I won't fail. I never fail."

"Confidence is beneficial, to a point, but you are very young and still just a foot soldier," Bertrand argued.

"If you have a better candidate, name him," Sasha said.

"Oh, very well," the man finally conceded. "But we'll have to plan this down to the smallest detail if we are to have any chance of surviving it."

They spent the next several hours going over their plan. Sasha was glad to leave the smoky tent and step out into the cool damp night. Hundreds of small fires dotted the land, burning holes in the mist rolling off the river. Sasha took a deep breath of the wormy air as he followed Duncan back toward the tent they'd been sharing. When they reached it, they stood facing each other, Sasha standing next to Duncan and Yarrow beside Sai.

"If you need a place to sleep, Sai, we have plenty of room," Duncan offered.

Sai smiled and laughed, but Sasha could tell he was forcing it. "I appreciate that, *syrai*, but my ship will be here by now. I'll make my way there." He kissed each of them, Yarrow a little longer than the others, before turning and disappearing into the gloom.

Sasha appreciated Sai's intuition—the three of them needed some time alone, and, of course, Sai could tell—and he planned to make the best of it. He caught Duncan's hand and reached for Yarrow, pulled them inside the tent and drew them both close, burying his face between their necks and breathing the perfume of their skin and hair before tasting it, dragging his lips over Yarrow's smooth neck and Duncan's rough whiskers. Duncan rumbled deep in his throat, and Yarrow wriggled his hands beneath Sasha's mail and spread his fingers over Sasha's belly. They searched for and found each other's lips in the dark, nipping, licking, sucking and slurping hungrily, desperately, and tore at metal, leather, and cloth.

"We should push these cots together," Duncan panted. "Now."

"It'll take too long." Yarrow dropped to his knees and clawed at the leather lacings of Duncan's trousers. When he managed to open them, he swallowed Duncan down in a single smooth motion. At the same time, he groped at Sasha's ass, making the cumbersome links of his tunic rattle to rival the obscene noises his mouth made on Duncan's flesh. Duncan held Yarrow's hair and grabbed the fabric of Sasha's tabard, pulling Sasha into a brutal kiss. Before long, they were naked on the bearskin rug covering the sandy ground, and they remained there for many hours.

Chapter
Twenty-Six

SASHA relished the feeling of the soft leather hugging his limbs, this new set of armor so deep red it was nearly black, and his hair loose beneath his hood. After two weeks of traveling only at night, staying well away from even a goat trail, he'd finally reached the inlet Sai had described. Though the sun tinted the eastern sky, Sasha's desire to get back to Duncan and Yarrow compelled him to continue. He only hoped they'd managed to keep the invaders at bay. They'd agreed to wait a month before springing their trap, and Sasha had to make sure he did his part. After securing the small amount of gear he carried, he dove into the blood-warm water.

The swim took longer than he'd estimated, and as the sky brightened, Sasha took in the beauty of the crystal blue water, full of fish in colors he'd never imagined and strange, underwater rock formations of prismatic orange and purplish red. He wished Duncan and Yarrow had been with him to see it. He wished they would see each other again, and contrary to everything he'd been taught, his forbidden attachment—his overwhelming love—brought focus and urgency to his mission, and he pushed his body past exhaustion.

By midmorning, he'd dragged himself out of the water, gasping for breath, muscles quivering, and made his way toward the entrance of the largest cave. His vision adjusted instantly to the darkness—much faster than it had before—lit only by a few sputtering torches. Around twenty ships stood moored farther in. Though it was quiet save for the lap of the waves against the sandy shore, Sasha sensed hundreds of people watching him. He stretched his arms wide, palms to the ceiling, so they would see he held no weapons.

A single Emiri man appeared a few dozen feet away, his simple arrow trained on Sasha. He must have noticed Sasha's attire, because he cried out "*Shagiri!*" The word echoed through the cavern. It was one of the few Emiri words Sasha knew; it meant death in their language, and it also meant a member of the Crimson Scythe. The Emiri, wiser than their land-bound counterparts, used the word interchangeably.

Bowstrings stretched and steel clattered around Sasha. He resisted the instinct to reach for a hidden weapon of his own and spoke in a commanding but neutral voice. "I am not here to harm any of you. If I was, I would not let you see me. You know this. I am here to deliver a message from *Sai-Mir*. He needs your aid defending the islands of the Twenty-Nine against those who once enslaved you. Is there one of you who understands my words, who can speak with me?"

He waited a few moments before an Emiri woman with beautiful golden cords of hair to rival the necklaces worn by queens leapt lightly from one of the boats and walked to meet him, a sword in her hand. "I can speak your language," she announced. "You speak the name of my *syrai*, the one who rescued me from the Johmatrans. What are you called by your mother?"

Sasha released the tension in his shoulders and let his hands fall beside his hips. "I have no idea. I am known now as Sasha, a friend to *Sai-Mir*. He needs your help. What is your name, *syrai*?"

"You have not earned the right to call me that," the woman said, her grip sure on the hilt of her blade. "I am called Yomu, and I'll need more than Sai's name to prove you are a friend."

"Tell me what you need to know," Sasha said. "Time is of the essence."

"Why would *shagiri* visit us here?" Yomu asked. "*Shagiri* is never a gift from Emir."

"It is this time," Sasha said. "*Shagiri* has come to those who would keep your people in bondage and take the Twenty-Nine from them. *Sai-Mir* and his *syrai* have devised a plan to destroy them, but they cannot do it without your help. Is the mage Yarrow known to you? He is my… *syrai-tama*. He has been fighting for you, but he can't prevail alone. Are these people ready to fight? Death is on your side."

"We are ready to fight," Yomu said, sheathing her blade. "Come, sit with me, death. Tell us what we must do."

SEA spray struck Sasha's face as winds from the east pushed their ship toward the mouth of the river. The crew claimed the *eru*—another word Sasha had added to his Emiri vocabulary—favored them. Sooner than he'd expected, they reached the Twenty-Nine. The absence of enemy ships told him his friends had succeeded in luring them farther up river, just as they had planned. For several days, they sailed through empty water and past abandoned islands. Then, at the center of the archipelago, Sasha saw the fighting. Johmatran vessels faced Emiri ships, and fire and smoke filled the air. The debris in the water and the bodies, told Sasha they'd been struggling for at least a few days, maybe a week. Wrecked ships and more corpses littered the shores of the Kanda. Duncan, Yarrow, Sai, and the others had been fighting to hold their adversaries until Sasha and his reinforcements arrived, and the battle continued, both fleets firing the exploding boulders along with more conventional weapons like arrows and ordinary rocks. Blue light flashed as Yarrow struggled against the enemy spell casters.

Sasha ran to Yomu at the helm of her ship. "Fire on them! Quickly, before we lose the element of surprise!"

The sea captain shouted to her crew, and they loaded catapults with the exploding rocks and raised torches to their wicks. The boulders soared through the air, struck the barbarian vessels, and tore many of them asunder. As the secret Emiri fleet drew closer, the sailors readied their cannons to shoot the liquid fire, and the enemy armada, caught off guard, burned.

As the boats at the north of the river fought their way down, Sasha and his people boxed the Johmatran forces in, pushing their ships toward the superior numbers of their allies at the Big Island, where the Emiri force beat them down, or toward the shores of the river, where Duncan and Rowan's knights waited to slaughter them as soon as they came ashore. With the fresh boats barricading the Kanda's mouth, the enemy had nowhere to go. They had trapped them, just as they'd intended, and now they simply killed them off, like the proverbial fish in a barrel. For his part, Sasha boarded any ships that got near enough, and with the fine new daggers he'd commissioned, as well as his trusted old serpentine blade, he killed the enemies onboard with ruthless efficiency. Afterward, one of the Emiri or someone from Duncan's force took control of the ships and added them to their armada. It took a day and a half, but the barbarians were slaughtered within the snare. The Kanda ran red, and Johmatran ships burned on the crimson water. Some of the Emiri even went ashore to make sure they finished the enemy to the last man.

For the next few days, the Emiri went from island to island, slaughtering every foreigner they found. Better to be sure, to leave no enemies to appear unexpectedly. Sasha watched from the deck of Yomu's ship as the Emiri cut the throats of those who would oppress them.

"Can you give us any counsel, death?" Yomu asked as they arrived on one spit of land where a small cluster of Johmatran tents stood.

"Yes," Sasha responded. "Alive, those who oppose you can try again. Dead, they cannot. The decision is a simple one."

She licked her lips and drew her sword. "Thank you, *shagiri… syrai.*" Sasha waited while she and the rest of her crew went ashore. They didn't require his aid, and they would relish the kills far more than he would. Less than an hour later, they returned, covered in blood, the enemy encampment blazing behind them. A few knights of Greyrclif, who had been captured, joined them, and together they sailed for the Big Island.

Hundreds of ships surrounded the land mass, but Sasha cared only about finding Duncan and Yarrow and making sure they'd survived the battle, since so many hadn't. He went below deck and changed from his order leathers to a simple pair of faded tan trousers, old boots, and a scratchy ochre shirt a bit too large for him. Then he made his way toward shore. With so many ships packed together so tightly, Sasha was able to leap from one to the other until he could swim the last few hundred yards to the beach. Though it looked like the combined force of Duncan's men and the Emiri had prevented the enemy from coming ashore here, Sasha still passed piles of bodies wrapped in white shrouds. In the heat, the stench was strong, and the seabirds circled overhead. Beyond them stood the tents, and Sasha made his way toward the yellow-and-black ones bearing the crag eagle banners.

He found Duncan and Yarrow sitting on the ground around an overturned barrel serving as their table, the food untouched upon it. Despite their victory, both of them looked miserable. Yarrow got to his feet, walked slowly up to Sasha, and practically collapsed against Sasha, clinging to Sasha's shoulders. "*Syrai*," he whispered into Sasha's hair. "I'm glad to see you unhurt."

Duncan stood and rested a hand on the center of Yarrow's back. He looked more tired than Sasha had ever seen him, and… something else. There was something weighing on him, dragging him down, something beyond the battle they'd just won and those they had yet to fight. Duncan's gaze drifted to Yarrow for just a second, and Sasha understood. Whatever troubled Duncan had something to do with their mage. He would have to wait until they were alone to ask him about it. For now, he was just grateful to see them both alive. Anything else could be fixed.

They broke apart and sat down again, close, letting their knees touch when they folded their legs. Yarrow picked up a piece of bread, examined it as if he was considering eating it, then let it fall to the ground and reached for the wine.

"My love," Duncan said softly, "haven't you had enough?"

Yarrow shook his head and drank, his attention fixed somewhere over Sasha's shoulder, perhaps on the birds. After he set the bottle down, he said, "We did it, didn't we? We took the Twenty-Nine back from the enemy."

"Yes," Sasha said. "Everything went just as we had hoped. What has you so upset?"

"We lost so many," Yarrow said.

"We are at war," Duncan said gently, resting a hand on Yarrow's shoulder. "Men die during war. Killing is part of it."

Yarrow looked at Sasha. Red ringed his pale eyes. "Do you remember Lala?" He waited for Sasha to nod. "We lost her. She's dead. She… she was expecting a baby. Sai…. There's nothing I can say to him. Nothing I can do. Sasha, what do we do now?"

"We can do nothing for the dead but avenge them," Sasha said.

"I'm afraid to," Yarrow whispered.

"Because we might lose more friends?" Duncan asked.

Yarrow, still watching the sky, reached for the wine again with a trembling hand. "No. I'm afraid of how much I like doing it. Fighting. Killing. I've been trying to control it, the anger, but if I don't give myself over to it, I'm just not as strong. And now I need the strength. I have to be that other, the one who burned the army at the Starlight Bridge. What if I let it overtake me and I don't come back?"

A chill moved over Sasha's skin despite the heat. "What overtakes you, though? I'd understood the thing that controlled you was gone."

"It's me now," Yarrow said. "The part of me I'm trying to get rid of… the scared, angry part… the part that wants to make the world pay. It's not who I want to be anymore, but now I need it."

"You don't," Duncan said firmly. "We have plenty of men to fight. You don't need to go to that place. Your magic aids us well enough without you becoming… that."

"But I might have to use that power," Yarrow said. "If I have to choose between using it and losing one of you, it's no choice."

"But you mustn't lose yourself, either," Duncan said. "You're just beginning to find out who you are and what you hope to get from life. Don't lose that for me."

"Or me," Sasha said. "You must not worry about me."

"I saw you die!" Yarrow hissed. "I held your body! I have never hurt like that. I didn't think I would survive it."

"I'm different now," Sasha said. "Thalil's power protects me. I won't be killed as easily."

"Are you saying you're immortal?" Duncan asked.

"He told me I could live as long as I chose."

"Goddesses," Duncan whispered.

"He told me 'not yet,'" Yarrow said, tracing small swirling patterns in the sand with his fingernail. "At first I thought he meant not until I could control my rage, but now I wonder if he meant for me to take care of these enemies before I attend my own pursuits."

"I don't know," Sasha said.

"He wants something from me," Yarrow said.

"I think so, yes," Sasha admitted.

"I knew this would come with a price," Duncan said, "and as much as that frightens me, I won't hesitate to pay it."

"You are a much different man than the one who didn't even want me to accompany you because of what I am," Sasha observed. "Back then, you preferred risking your life to tolerating my presence."

Duncan rubbed his eyes with his thumb and finger. "Back then, I still thought it was possible to protect what I love with my honor intact. I have learned to adapt since then. I… am no longer sure it's possible to have it both ways. Now, if I must choose between the two of you and upholding what I once believed? Well, some things just don't feel as important as they once did."

Sasha reached over and squeezed Duncan's hand. For some reason he couldn't even begin to fathom, the idea of Duncan compromising his honor and abandoning his beliefs hurt Sasha. Though he had once found it ridiculous, an inconvenient weakness, he found he missed Duncan as he had been, with his spirit bright and unblemished. But all things changed, and Sasha didn't think his opinions would lift his friend's mood, so he stayed quiet.

They picked at their food but mostly sat in silence. After a while, Sai approached them, dragging his feet through the sand as if the effort of walking took all his strength and then some. "*Syrai*. I would ask you to come with me."

Yarrow hurried to stand, but by the time he reached Sai, Sai had already turned and begun walking in the direction of the water. After giving Duncan a questioning glance and getting a shrug in response, Sasha followed them back through the camp and to the rowboat Sai had waiting. Sai rowed in silence as the setting sun turned the river water to molten gold, and then the four of them boarded his ship. He went to the helm without a word and began sailing south, followed by around a dozen other Emiri vessels.

Sasha looked back at the ships following theirs. Now that evening had fallen, hundreds of the mosaic lanterns the Emiri made burned against the dark blue sky. The stars shone so bright and numerous it looked as though someone had strewn silver sand across the heavens. Not far from where Sasha stood, Kin played an atonal melody on a flute made from a conch shell, while Izu held their child and Toumo sang. The rhythmic swish of the water against the hull accompanied their melody, and while Sasha didn't understand the words, he felt everything they conveyed: pain, loss, possibilities cut short, the sense of being small and helpless, just a speck of foam adrift on the great expanse of the sea, beneath the endless breadth of the firmaments. Though he knew he was not helpless, the song moved through Sasha's chest, evoking a strange and novel emotion he couldn't name, something akin to hollowness. It made him want to reach for Duncan and Yarrow and hold them close. Since none of the other knights or soldiers had been invited onboard and seeing three men holding each other would hardly surprise the Emiri, Sasha opened his arms and pulled Duncan and Yarrow to him.

From the time he had been a boy, younger even than little Asphodel, Sasha had known life was brief and cruel, that it rewarded neither righteousness, selflessness, charity, or purity, and sometimes not even skill kept death at bay. Nothing kept death at bay; cleverness and talent only managed to slow it down a bit. From the time he'd made that realization, Sasha had accepted death as inevitable. Now, for the first time, it felt unfair.

"Where are we going?" Duncan asked Yarrow softly.

"To the open sea," Yarrow answered. "The Emiri are returning their dead to the ocean, to sleep in the arms of their mother. I... I'm going to help with the winds. It's the least I can do." He closed his eyes, rested his chest against Duncan's chest, and fluttered his fingers. A warm, strong, but even breeze filled their sails. By heading southeast from the Big Island, they reached the open water in a few hours. With only a sliver of a moon hovering near the horizon, the night was especially dark, making it hard to tell where the water ended and the sky began. Only the glimmer of the stars marked the boundary between sea and air.

The ships slowed as the winds died. Sai continued to stand at the helm, looking out over the water. "I did that to him," Yarrow said. "I ruined him."

"Ruined him?" Sasha asked. "You fought for these people when no one else would have. It's not your fault his friend died. They might have all been lost if you hadn't been here."

Yarrow shook his head. "It was long before any of this. He changed back when we first sailed together. He said I left a little of myself in his head when I freed him from Hale's enchantment. That was when he just... stopped being as happy, as carefree."

"Yarrow, this is not your fault," Duncan agreed.

"Enough about me," Yarrow said. "This ceremony is not for me. It's for the lost and the *syrai* they've left behind. Come. We should pay our respects to them."

Sasha and Duncan followed him to the bow, where about a dozen Emiri lay on the deck, adorned with jewels, pouches and pockets stuffed with coins and their stiff arms wrapped around smooth stones, fruit, flowers, and jugs of *muri-ku*. Yarrow knelt down beside Lala and touched her waxy white forehead. A small bump protruded from her slim belly, barely covered by the tight leather of her worn and patched vest.

"*Hai mira*, Lala," Yarrow whispered before standing up.

"What does it mean?" Sasha asked.

"It means 'good sailing to you,'" Yarrow said, swiping at a tear with the back of his hand. "It is both hello and"—he choked and drew in a shaking breath—"and good-bye to the Emiri."

Sasha crouched down next to Lala. Truth be told, he remembered little about her. "*Hai mira*."

"*Hai mira*," Duncan said. "What a waste. A sad waste."

Yarrow clasped their hands and led them a respectful distance away while the other Emiri bid farewell to their companions, some of them offering a coin or a piece of jewelry. When Sai's turn came, he dropped to his knees beside his fallen friend and curled over her, pressing their foreheads together. His body shook with repressed sobs, though he made no sound. Everyone waited quietly for many moments, until he exhausted his grief. Then Sai stood, scrubbed at his face, and nodded to his crew.

One by one, the sailors lifted their dead over the railing and dropped them into the tides to more cries of "*Hai mira*," along with plenty of tears. When they were finished, Sai turned and looked at them.

"Thank you, *syrai*."

"It was our honor, *syrai*," Duncan told him in a rough voice.

"Sai…." Yarrow took a step toward him, but Sai shook his head, turned away, and walked slowly toward the helm.

"What happens now?" Sasha asked Yarrow as Sai and the other *mir* turned their ships about to return to the Twenty-Nine.

Yarrow gave a mirthless laugh. "Now? Now we drink."

LATE the following afternoon, Sasha woke facedown in the sand, certain someone had driven a dagger into his skull. At some point he'd shed his shirt and boots, though he didn't remember doing it. Nearby, Yarrow lay on his side in a similar state of undress, his cloak twisted around his legs. Duncan sat on a piece of driftwood, looking a little reproachful as he offered Sasha a large ceramic bowl filled with steaming, fragrant liquid.

"What's this?" Sasha asked as he reached for it. His mouth tasted like the inside of an old boot.

"The Emiri claim it will make you feel better," Duncan said with a shrug.

"Sea oats." Yarrow stretched his arms over his head and then brushed the sand from the side of his face and bare chest. "I know from experience it works. Drink it, *syrai*, but save me some."

After a few sips of the vaguely citrus liquid, Sasha's head started to clear and his nausea subsided. As he passed the dish to Yarrow, he expected a mild lecture from their upstanding knight, but it never came. Instead, Duncan gathered the clothes strewn along the beach and handed them their garments, then petted their hair and kissed their cheeks before he suggested they find some breakfast.

"And a wash," Duncan clearly couldn't resist adding with a grin. "Both of you reek of that swill."

Bread and some leftover stew made Sasha feel even better, and by the time they'd washed and dressed, he felt basically restored, if a little ashamed. Turning to Duncan, he said, "Not so long ago, I wouldn't have dreamed of leaving myself in such a compromised position. I left myself completely helpless."

"Well, I suppose you felt safe enough surrounded by a few thousand knights."

Sasha smiled and ran the back of his hand over Duncan's cheek and whiskers. "Not a few thousand. Just one."

Duncan returned his smile. "Yes, well, you're welcome. But don't make a habit of it. I may need a drink myself after we meet with the others."

"Must we?" Yarrow groaned. "I'm in no mood for this. My head hurts enough already."

"I'm afraid we must," Duncan said. "After all, we were supposed to join forces with your cousin a month ago."

"We've made a difference here!" Yarrow protested passionately, moving his hands. "We might not have defeated the enemy, but we certainly gave them a black eye."

Duncan curled a hand around Yarrow's shoulder, and it seemed to calm him. "Save it for the council. I've asked Sai to meet us there, and I don't think we should leave him to face the others alone."

"You're up to something," Sasha said.

"No," Duncan said as he held their tent flap open. "I just think Sai and the Emiri should have a say in what happens next."

"So do I," Yarrow said. "Thank you, Duncan."

Sasha still wasn't convinced as they walked to the large pavilion at the center of the encampment, but he trusted Duncan as he'd never trusted another person, so he waited to see what his friend had planned. Inside the tent, Tam Bertrand sat with his Defenders, along with Rowan and some of his knights. Sai perched on the edge of a large chest in a corner, still looking wan and weary, but with his chin raised defiantly.

Bertrand stood. "So the bairn of Windwake and his companions have finally recovered enough from their night of revelry with the pirates to join us."

Sasha didn't expect Yarrow to let such a comment go unchallenged, but it surprised him when Yarrow grabbed the big knight by his tabard and attempted to lift him off his feet as he yelled into his face. "Shut up, you swine! We were celebrating the memory of our fallen companions. Don't you dare make it sound petty! Don't you dare! Don't you plan to honor the men you've lost?"

Tam Bertrand pushed Yarrow off, and Duncan hurried to get between them. "I'll honor the men who died according to the customs of the goddesses and not in some obscene heathen ritual! As if drunken unnatural acts honor anyone."

"You have no right to judge us or our ways!" Yarrow shouted back, the blue glow growing behind his eyes.

"You're as mad as everyone says, Yarroway L'Estrella! You are not Emiri, whether you have defaced yourself with their markings or not. These are not your ways!"

"This is my land, and these are my ways! They are the ways of my valenny!"

"Enough of this!" Duncan said, his strong voice cowing everyone. "Tam Bertrand, there is no need to disrespect these people. You have fought beside them, bled beside them, in the name of the sisters! More than that, I won't have you speak that way to my friend."

"Nor me," Sasha added.

"We should sit down," Rowan said. "All of us are exhausted, and that can lead to quick tempers and words that can't be taken back."

"I take back nothing," Yarrow snapped, and his brother rolled his eyes.

"Yarrow, please," Rowan said, a little crease forming between his brows. "Now is not the time. Now, sit down, and stop proving all the things others say about you are true."

Sasha shot Yarrow's brother a glare, and it pleased him when Rowan flinched and moved a little farther down the bench. He considered sitting next to Rowan, just to make him uncomfortable, but decided if they were in for another few hours of poring over fading maps, he'd rather be between Yarrow and Duncan.

"Have we received any reports from the east?" Duncan asked.

Tam Bertrand nodded. "High King Garith is facing the bulk of the enemy here, near the southern end of the Bay of Blossoms, though there is fighting all along the coast. His Majesty's forces have managed to keep the invaders from claiming any land or even making it ashore, but without reinforcements, they will be overpowered eventually."

"Then we must make our way to them," Rowan said. "What is there to discuss?"

"What we need are ships," Duncan said slowly, in a cautious tone. "Without them, we might be able to hold the enemy off, but we'll never be able to defeat them or drive them back where they came from."

"His Majesty has a small fleet," Rowan said. "Most of the ships and crews should be ready by now. We won't know until we speak with the king, but I'm sure those vessels must be en route by now."

"How many ships?" Duncan asked.

"Maybe fifty," Rowan said.

"Fifty. And how many in the barbarian fleet?" Duncan continued.

"Our scouts say around two hundred in the bay, with smaller groups attacking up and down the coast," Tam Bertrand said.

"So you see our dilemma," Duncan said.

"And what do you propose as a solution?" Sasha had known Duncan had been planning something; he'd seen the secrecy in the flit of Duncan's eyes and the tightness of his lips.

"Isn't it obvious?" Duncan looked at the men seated around the table, meeting each of their gazes in turn. When none of them responded, he continued. "We have, assembled right here, perhaps the finest seafaring force anywhere in the world. *Sai-Mir—*"

Sai leapt to his feet. "What are you saying? Are you honestly suggesting I ask my people to sail to the aid of your dry-foot king, the same man who has been trying to drive us from our homes since he took the throne? That we risk losing more of our *syrai*? No! Why should we?"

"We fought for you!" Bertrand said, getting to his feet, followed by Yarrow.

"I made no agreement with you," Sai said.

"Ungrateful little—"

"Stop," Duncan commanded. "Sai, listen to me. You and your people owe us nothing, but what do you think the Johmatrans will do if they defeat the king? Where do you think they'll go next?"

"Why would we want to do this?" Sai asked again. "We should stay here and protect our islands. Why should we care what happens to the land-bound king?"

"You shouldn't," Sasha said. "But don't you want to kill the people who took your *syrai* away from you? I have no stake in this, so I have no reason to try to persuade you either way, but I will say this: every one of them you kill is one less who can attack you another day."

"We can use the same tactic," Duncan said, pointing to the map. "Garith has thousands of men along the coast. If groups of Emiri ships can flank the enemy, we can drive them onto the land, trapping them between us just like we did before. It could mean a decisive victory against them."

"And what will that get me?" Sai asked. "My *syrai* back? My baby? No. I will not help you. I won't ask my people to help you. What would I even say to them?"

"Tell them what we have said," Duncan practically pleaded. "If Garith falls, the Twenty-Nine will be next. The Johmatrans could conquer Selindria and Gaeltheon if we don't stop them now. What will happen to the Emiri then? You have seen it, seen how the barbarians treat your people."

"I can't," Sai said. "I won't ask more of my people to die." He turned and ran out of the tent.

"Yarrow, perhaps you can speak to him," Rowan suggested. "You've always had an understanding of these people and their ways."

"No," Yarrow said, staring into his lap. "I've taken too much from Sai already. I won't ask anything more from him."

"Then we have little choice," Duncan said as he stood up. "We should make ready to march in the morning. Without the Emiri, I don't think we have much chance of victory, but we'll have to fight anyway. It's either that or just hand our kingdom over, and that won't happen while I'm alive."

Chapter Twenty-Seven

From the cliffs overlooking the Bay of Blossoms, Garith's archers fired on the enemies rowing toward the strip of white sand beneath them. Duncan gave a shout, and a dozen soldiers fired catapults, raining boulders the size of ale barrels down on the invaders, tearing their dinghies asunder and sinking some of the boats when they connected—but not enough. Duncan shouted for his men to refill the baskets, and the soldiers grunted and strained, stumbling under the weight of stones it took two or three of them to lift.

"Fire!" Duncan shouted. The rocks arced through the hot southern air. While the catapults were devastating, they were difficult to aim, and only five out of the dozen hit the enemy. The rest of the boulders hit only seawater with fantastic but useless sprays, and hundreds of Johmatrans continued to advance. By now, the enemy soldiers had made it close enough to shore that many leapt into the ocean and waded through the waist-high tide.

Sasha stood among the archers. While he continued to refuse to involve the order in a political dispute, Duncan had convinced him to share his poisons with the other bowmen. A year or so ago, Duncan would have considered the use of such toxins dishonorable on the battlefield, but today, he saw only a death from what otherwise would have been a mere flesh wound— one less enemy. As hopelessly outnumbered as they were, every man they brought down, no matter how, mattered. Every dead Johmatran might mean one of his men could live.

As he instructed his men to ready the catapults again, Duncan looked east. Yarrow stood on a thin outcrop of rock, and the dark clouds gathered above him. Looking at that boy—for in so many ways Yarrow was still little more than a youth—Duncan just wanted to drag him away from the blood and violence, away from everyone and everything that expected him to kill. He wanted to shelter Yarrow, finally let him see what it meant to be cared for and protected. But they were at war, and the king needed Yarrow's abilities. Duncan wondered if Garith had any idea of the price his cousin paid. Duncan did, and he'd made Yarrow swear not to push too hard. Now he could only hope Yarrow would listen and remember.

Lightning crackled above Duncan's mage as he waved his arm toward the horizon. A few dozen feet from the shore, the bright blue water rose up into a wall capped with white foam, drawing back from the shore until it reached dozens of feet above the enemy rowboats. When Yarrow dropped his arm, it engulfed them, pulling them under, the riptide dragging them away from the coast. Those that managed to claw their way to land found arrows trained on them, and they didn't get far. Still, for every man they shot down, four others made it ashore.

Duncan could wait no longer. He turned to the men behind him: men of Windwake, of Greyrclif, of Meadow's Edge, Thulemore, and Merryvale, Royal Guards and Defenders of the Thirteen. "Men of Selindria and Gaeltheon, you in service of your king, and you in service of the goddesses, the time has come. The enemy is at our door, and there is no one but us to hold it shut. We don't know what these invaders want, except to take our lands and kill our loved ones. It is time to tell them no. No more will we tolerate their blasphemous presence on our coasts; no more will we watch Selindrian and Gaeltheonic blood flow. This land is ours! Our fathers and grandfathers fought and bled to secure it, and now it is our turn. If you love this kingdom, if you love the people who call it home, follow me. If you would lift your sword out of love instead of greed or conquest, follow me now! If you believe there is no force stronger than love, men defending a land and people they love, follow me!"

A resounding cry answered Duncan, and thousands of men followed him as he drew his sword and ran down the steep trail toward the beach. Steel met steel as the two forces clashed, and men fell on both sides. Within moments, blood soaked the shore and stained the water. Duncan swung his trusted old blade as he cut down foe after foe, ignoring the minor injuries they inflicted. From above, the archers took the shots they found. From his vantage, Yarrow fired strategic bolts of magical lightning, deftly breaking up clusters of enemies before they could overwhelm any single fighter. It pleased Duncan to see his mage holding back, not reaching into the inky darkness he held for power, but he couldn't spare much time to contemplate it.

Duncan and his men, with Yarrow's help, held the shore. They held it for an hour before another dozen Johmatran ships joined the fray, sending hundreds more men toward the exhausted fighters. Gradually, the enemy began to push them back. The fresh Johmatran fighters soon had Duncan's men's backs against the cliffs, waiting to be slaughtered. Duncan fought until fatigue drove him to his knees. Though he could barely lift his sword, he hoisted it in front of him to block the enemy blows. Four, maybe five enemies bore down on him, and he attempted to parry their strikes as the strength abandoned his body. His muscles felt like pudding, but he would die on his feet. He backed against the support of the white stone of the cliffs as he swung his sword and an enemy's head fell and bounced along the beach. Duncan shouted his victory as the warm blood spattered his face. He drove his blade below the chest plate of the next adversary, and the man gurgled up blood before falling. A third man swung a mace at him, but Duncan dodged, severing his enemy's leg above the knee as he rose and finishing him with a blow to the back of the head when he fell. He fought past his body's capacity for pain and exhaustion—not for his country or his king, but because he wanted one more chance to hold Sasha and Yarrow close to him, to breathe their scents and taste their skin. He fought for a world where they'd be free to love and enjoy each other, though he soon found no ideals rivaled the weariness of the flesh. He dropped to his knees in the sand and crushed flowers and blood and crossed his armored wrists over his head to protect it. Goddesses, all he wanted was a few more days with them….

Please, merciful sisters, give me another day…. One day! Don't let it end here….

Not the goddesses, but his men answered his plea. A fresh group of soldiers, Yarrow's brother's men, rushed down the trail and spilled onto the beach, getting between Duncan and the other exhausted fighters and the enemy. After taking a few moments to catch his breath and summon his willpower, Duncan got to his feet and lifted his sword. At the periphery of his vision, Sasha fought with a set of long daggers, spinning like a dark whirlwind and cutting down everyone in his path until he'd made his way to Duncan's side so they could fight together. As always, they made an effective team, with Duncan drawing the adversary's attention and Sasha moving in with quick, precise strikes to any vulnerable spot the enemy exposed as they battled. Men fell around them, but for every one they defeated, three or four more came ashore.

A blinding blue flash washed everything away for a second, and when Duncan blinked and brought the world back into focus, Yarrow stood a few hundred yards away on their right, aiming comet-like balls of energy into the fray. Yarrow's wings stretched behind him, bright against the overcast sky, but he attacked with restrain and intent, still in control. If he hadn't been, everyone along the shore would have likely been reduced to ash—Duncan, Sasha, and Rowan included.

After Yarrow had thinned the throng coming from the rowboats, giving Duncan and the others a chance at holding them back, Yarrow drifted closer and stood just at the edge of the battle. He lifted a hand and swept it in an arc in the direction of the sea, and the water began to burble and churn around the dinghies and the men disembarking from them. Hands made of grayish-blue water shot from the surface, grabbing men and boats and dragging them under or swatting them and sending them flying far from the shore. At first, the enemy panicked, but they were men used to dealing with and fighting against mages, probably more so than Duncan's people. They knew how defeat a magic user, and within moments their surprise passed, and a group of them began to converge around Yarrow. They knew to divide Yarrow's attention, strain his concentration, and attack him while he focused elsewhere.

"Sasha!" Duncan yelled, pointing with his sword.

Without looking at Duncan, Sasha nodded, swiped at the man he faced and cut his throat before turning and throwing his dagger. It struck the archer closest to Yarrow in the back of the neck. His next thrown blade hit another enemy in the lower back, sending him to his hands and knees. Sasha sprinted toward their mage, hurdling the dead and slashing at the enemies he passed, leaving a trail of death in his wake. Most of the men surrounding Yarrow were dead, stabbed in the back or their throats cut, before they had time to turn toward Sasha. Duncan tried to follow him, but a group of soldiers got in his way.

"Protect our mage!" Duncan shouted to his warriors as he faced the enemies in front of him. "We can't afford to lose Yarrow!"

The enemies' tactic had accomplished one thing: they'd distracted Yarrow enough to prevent him conjuring the liquid hands. Once again, their boats approached the coast and men made their way ashore, tipping the numbers back in their favor. Just as Duncan defeated the last of the fighters standing between him and his friends, Yarrow grabbed Sasha's arm, pulled Sasha tight against him, pushed Sasha's head against his chest, and protected it with one arm while he reached the other out in front of him. His wings stretched dozens of feet into the darkening sky, long, curved horns protruded from his forehead, and a savage smile twisted his lips.

"Get down!" Duncan shouted to his men. He dropped, pressed his forehead against his knees, and covered the back of his head with his hands.

A wave of light passed over him, smelling of lilies and burnt minerals, searing hot and numbingly cold at the same time. For a few seconds, it stole all sensation from the world: sight, sound, the pressure of Duncan's armor against his skin, the solidity of the ground beneath him. Until it passed over him, Duncan felt like he existed in a universe containing nothing but that light and energy, with some scrap of his fleshless perception hovering at the center. It didn't cause him pain, though. Quite the contrary. He felt giddy and light, hopeful and happy, just as he had when Yarrow healed his hands back in Fane's cavern. Magic, he thought, was much like a beautiful wine and just as harmful to grow too fond of or indulge in too frequently.

Blinking, remembering the weight of his limbs and that he could direct them, Duncan stumbled to his feet. Slowly, shapes began to form against the blinding wash of bluish white, and he looked around with dread, expecting to see friends and enemies alike burned to nothing. Instead, his soldiers helped each other to stand, rubbing their eyes and looking about in confusion. Only Johmatran fighters lay in the sand, their skin and eyes as white as Yarrow's hair, their faces frozen into masks of pain and terror. Somehow Yarrow had managed to sort them apart, which meant Yarrow hadn't given in to the destruction he craved. He hadn't lost himself to it. To Duncan's left, Garith, Lysander, and a small group of Royal Guards made short work of the few enemies who'd escaped Yarrow's spell. Out on the water, only a few bodies and some errant bits of splintered wood indicated the invading fleet had been there at all. Down the beach to the right, Sasha crouched, holding Yarrow's flaccid form in his arms. A prickle of alarm spread through Duncan's chest until Sasha met his gaze and nodded, telling him their mage was unharmed, just exhausted.

Trying to ignore the ringing in his ears, Duncan addressed his men. "We've held them off. Retreat back to the camp. Station a fresh group of archers on the cliffs and send scouts in both directions. I want to know if the enemy is moving, if they're getting reinforcements."

A few of the men acknowledged his words, but most just hoisted wounded comrades off the ground and helped them up the trail. Others collected the dead. Duncan knew Sasha considered it a waste of time and energy, but he understood the soldiers' need to look after their fallen friends. Dead or alive, these men would be going home, to rest beside their families and predecessors in the good soil of Selindria. He knew it gave the men courage when they entered a battle to know, one way or the other, they would be going home.

Sasha swung Yarrow's knees over his arm, stood, and fell into step beside Duncan. Duncan reached over and touched Sasha's sweaty hair, then Yarrow's still, cool cheek. To the Shades' with what anyone thought. They were alive, and they might not be tomorrow, and he would touch them whenever he got the chance.

THIS cousin of Yarrow's, Garith, was a strange king. Sasha was glad he'd let him live, in retrospect. Instead of holding council in a tent and hearing the advice of his generals, Garith held an open meeting around a large fire at the center of their encampment, and he invited everyone, down to the boys who scooped up the horses' dung, to attend and speak their minds.

Hundreds surrounded the fire and the table where Garith, his guard Lysander, Duncan, Rowan, and Tam Bertrand sat. Yarrow had been invited to take his place among them, but had declined, and now stood beside Sasha at the edge of the gathering, close enough to watch the others and hear what they discussed, but still sheltered by the shadows beyond the firelight.

"Today was a good day," Rowan said timidly, clearly attempting to start the discourse on a positive note.

"Because your mad brother decided not to destroy us all… this time," someone shouted.

Sasha stiffened, but Yarrow clasped his hand. "I do not care what they say about me, any more than you care what they think of you."

Though Sasha agreed, he didn't like standing by while others slandered his mage. From the time they'd met, Yarrow had defended him to others. His training had taught him to pick his battles, though, and this conflict wasn't worth it.

The guard, Lysander, stood. Sasha could tell from his facial expressions and the way he looked at the king that the two of them had been intimate, that they loved each other. He wondered where a king who loved another man might lead the world as Sander spoke. "We don't have time for insults tonight. The goddesses have granted us a rare victory and an even rarer few moments of peace to plan what we'll do next. Let's try not to squander it."

Duncan spoke next. The men's silence proved their respect for him. "We were lucky today, but the fact is we cannot win with circumstances as they are. We barely held the coast today, and the enemy ships are still out there, a few miles from shore, waiting to try again. More may well be on their way. Without ships of our own, we have no way to defeat them."

"I have a fleet on the way," Garith said. "The scouts say it should reach our location within a few days."

"I mean no disrespect, Your Majesty," Duncan said, "but fifty ships against three hundred?"

"It's hopeless," yelled a man from the crowd.

"We're all going to die," said another.

Duncan slapped the table, the resounding crack drawing all attention to him. "And what will you do? Run home, like a dog with his tail between his legs? Wait for the enemy to take our shores and make their way inland? Because rest assured, that's what they'll do. They will take our land, our women, and our children."

"But why?" someone shouted.

"What does it matter?" Duncan answered. "Do you want to be remembered as one of the men who stood his ground, who told the enemy 'no farther,' or as one who cowered and waited to kneel? If any of you are the second type of man, you might as well go and start painting your faces now. I'll stand against the Johmatrans, the filthy scum who burned a temple and raped its priestesses, until I can no longer stand."

Cheers and hollering met Duncan's words, but as Sasha watched Garith, he saw the king look away with shame. Interesting. Had Garith had something to do with the sack of Fayelle's shrine? Had he wanted this war? If so, why? Sasha decided he would find out. Such knowledge could prove valuable currency in the days to come.

"Are you asking us to fight with no chance of victory?" one of the men asked.

"Yes!" Duncan said. "Yes. Because we either fight, or we stand aside and allow injustice. I know what I'll do. The chance to prevail is irrelevant. What matters is not standing idle and letting it happen."

"Hear, hear!" someone yelled, and dozens of voices joined in assent.

"All men must die," Duncan continued. "For my part, I'll go to the goddesses regretting nothing, and I'll take as many of these bastards with me as the sisters will permit!"

The men cheered, hollered, and punched the air. Rowan stood and said, "Enjoy tonight, brave men of Selindria and Gaeltheon. Enjoy our fine wines and ale, the beautiful women who have accompanied us"—he looked toward the scantily clad wenches grouped to his left, those opportunistic women who followed armies—"or just the camaraderie of your fellow warriors." Sasha wondered if he meant that statement as it sounded. "Tomorrow, or sometime not long after, we'll face the enemy again, and most of us will not walk away. But we will die, not on our knees before the barbarian oppressors, but on our feet, with our weapons in our hands."

The soldiers shouted their assent as they started to disperse, and soon only the people at the table, along with Sasha and Yarrow, remained.

King Garith looked over at Duncan. "It's lost, isn't it?"

Duncan sat with his neck and shoulders curled down. "We can't prevail. Not against the seafaring force the enemy commands. It… it is lost. We cannot beat them."

"But we'll fight," Sander said in a whisper.

"It's that or run," Duncan said. "The men are ready to fight, to die. Goddesses forgive me."

"We'll do what we can," Garith said, standing and resting a hand on Duncan's shoulder. "At least history will remember that we did not give up." With that, the king departed with his guard.

"Duncan, get up," Sasha said. "Get your things. We're leaving."

"What? Sasha. What are you saying? Where do you expect me to go when the king is facing certain defeat?"

"Back to my order's hideout. We'll be safe there, safe until this conflict is decided."

Duncan rubbed his temples with the heels of his hands. "You honestly expect me to run, to leave the others here to die while I save myself?"

"Yes," Sasha said. "Get your things or leave them behind. We're going."

"Sasha, I-I cannot leave. I have to fight beside these men," Duncan said. "I'm their leader."

"No. Out of the question. You can come with me willingly, Duncan, or I *will* poison you and drag you to safety."

Duncan scrunched his eyes shut and shook his head. "What makes me better than these men? Why should I live while they're slaughtered?"

"You're mine, and they aren't," Sasha said with a shrug. "Do you want to get your things?"

"No," Duncan said. "I'm not leaving. Sasha, if you care about me, you will not take me from here against my will. I want to fight. I won't forgive you if you take me from here, though I'm sure you can if you wish to, especially as you are now. I want to face the enemy."

"To die?" Yarrow cried, fisting Duncan's tabard and drawing him close.

"If… if there is no other choice."

"No!" Yarrow shrieked, his face tipped to the heavens and his eyelids peeled back, exposing the entire orbs of his strange eyes. "I'll burn them, burn them all, everyone and everything, first! To the Shades' with all of it! I'll save you no matter what it costs."

"I don't want that," Duncan said calmly, stroking Yarrow's flushed cheek. "I don't want Yarrow burned away."

"Yarrow can't bear the world without his Duncan and Sasha," the mage whispered. "There's nothing else holding the broken pieces inside him together. I can't even bear to think of what I'll become without you. I-I think we should go. Back to the order safe house."

"I can't," Duncan said.

Sasha understood; he knew Duncan so well now. Duncan felt responsible for each and every one of these men, and he would ask them to risk nothing he wasn't willing to risk himself. Sasha found it both admirable and infuriating. If Duncan wouldn't leave, Sasha would have to conceive of another way to save him. "Let's at least go back to our tent."

Duncan turned and cupped Sasha's face in his big hand. "I can agree to that."

SECLUDED within the six black-and-yellow canvas walls, Sasha, Yarrow, and Duncan removed their armor in silence, without meeting each other's eyes. Sasha didn't need to see the blue light spilling from the corners of Yarrow's eyes to perceive his mage's turmoil. Firelight glinted off the hard planes of Yarrow's back as he stood facing a corner in nothing but his snug trousers, the rest of his clothing held tightly balled in front of his chest.

Naked, Sasha dipped a cloth in a bowl of water and twisted out the excess before wiping down his face, underarms, and groin. He dragged his wet fingers through wavy black hair that had grown past his shoulders since winter, since they'd left Windwake to seek the Crimson Scythe. Yarrow's white ropes of hair hung past his waist, and Duncan's ponytail trailed down his back between his shoulder blades. Sasha picked up a simple iron comb and began dragging it through the tangled ends of his tresses. Duncan stood and came up behind him, the smell of his damp skin strong and the hair of his chest tickling Sasha's back. Gently he took the comb from Sasha's hand and took over combing Sasha's hair. After kissing the top of Sasha's head, he leaned forward, the touch of his skin against Sasha's familiar, comforting, and exciting all at once. Sasha relaxed back and let his head rest against Duncan's shoulder.

"How am I going to comb your hair now?" Duncan asked, running his fingers down Sasha's arms.

"It will be fine," Sasha said.

"It's beautiful long," Duncan said, resting a hand just above Sasha's left hip. "Like black silk."

Sasha shook his head and smiled. "The things you say. I thought you told me you'd changed, adapted to survive, and yet here you are, as silly and sentimental as ever. And just as stubborn."

Duncan forced a chuckle and wound his arm around Sasha's waist, drawing them tighter together and planting a few light kisses on Sasha's shoulder. "Maybe I have not changed as much as I'd thought. Perhaps I'm just too old and set in my ways."

"I'm glad," Sasha whispered.

Yarrow finally turned to face them. From the look on his face, Sasha expected to see a knife stuck in his belly. "Duncan, I can't do it," Yarrow said in a high, frail voice. "I can't let you die. Don't ask me to do it. I can't. You… you and Sasha are the only people who have ever meant anything to me or given a damn what happens to me, except for maybe Sai. But I lost him. I destroyed him. I can't lose you."

"Come here," Duncan said, reaching for Yarrow. Yarrow wrapped his arms around both of them, and Duncan rested his arm protectively across Yarrow's shoulder.

"Tell me you're not going to die," Yarrow practically pleaded.

"I can't," Duncan said. "But I can tell you that if I do, it will be with no regrets. My life has been full and wonderful, especially since you two came into it. I think I've been the luckiest man in the world the past couple of years. I cannot ask for anything more."

"Damn it, Duncan, I can! I just turned twenty-one, but I feel like my life is just starting. I'm finally figuring out the man I want to be, and that man is largely based on you. I've never had anyone to model my life after. I need you. There it is. I'm selfish and greedy, and I place what I want above all the rest of those men. I admit it. To me, you're more important than all of them put together."

"Hush." Duncan pinched Yarrow's chin between his thumb and finger, making Yarrow look up at him. "My beautiful boy. I hate seeing that pain on your face. Won't you let me see you smile?"

"How can you ask me to be happy?" Yarrow stiffened against them and lashed out with a measure of his old anger, but Duncan, used to it by now, just laughed softly and stroked Yarrow's hair.

"Why shouldn't you be happy? It's a lovely summer night, and we have it all to ourselves. We're here together. We even have a bit of wine. So smile for me, for everything we're blessed with at this moment." Duncan stepped back, turned Sasha toward him, and looked at them both with an expression not even Sasha could decipher. He smiled and shook his head. "My beautiful boys. Look at the men you've become. You're strong. You'll change the world. I want you to remember one thing if…. Remember to do what's right and not what's most effective… at least now and then."

"I wish you'd do what's effective instead of what's right, some of the time," Sasha said, surprised at the strained sound of his own voice. That cold weight—fear, he now knew—had never felt heavier against his heart. Duncan didn't plan on surviving the coming battle, and Sasha could conceive of no way to save him.

"I'll do what I must," Yarrow said. "I will not let you die. So if you don't want to see how far I'll go, you should get yourself out of danger."

"Yarrow, you know it's not fair to ask me to make that choice," Duncan said.

"Life's not fair," Yarrow snapped, a sheen of blue light crackling over his skin.

"My love, you told me you wanted to learn about yourself and your dreams and desires without the chains of fear holding you down. Let go of that fear. You can't be so afraid of losing me that it stops you from discovering what you can become."

"Duncan, I have no dreams or desires that don't include you," Yarrow said, stroking Duncan's whiskers with the back of his trembling hand. "I love you both so much. I don't want to be alone. I can admit that now. I'm worse than useless on my own."

"We're here now," Sasha said, burrowing one hand in the hair of Duncan's chest while running the other up the prominent knobs of Yarrow's spine. All of them stepped in, pressing their bodies tight and finding each other's lips. They opened their mouths and the tips of their tongues met in the center, bumping and twisting together as they explored each other's warm skin with their hands. Sasha reached down to cup a cheek of each of their asses. They were so different, Yarrow with barely a thin layer of tissue between his glass-smooth skin and his bones, and Duncan with a soft dusting of hair over the meaty, muscular crescent of his ass. They even smelled different: Duncan of sweat and steel, honest, concrete things, and Yarrow of wind and ice and burning minerals, things difficult to hold or even comprehend. Iron and ether. Sasha never thought he'd have been able to admit it, but he loved them, valued them even over his own existence, and he needed them both.

He dropped to his knees on the bearskin rug, pulled Duncan and Yarrow down beside him, and then he stretched out on his back, letting his legs fall open. Yarrow lifted Sasha's foot into his lap and began kissing the inside of his ankle, then moved his lips up Sasha's calf, raising gooseflesh as he went. Duncan, sitting beside Sasha on his heels, spread his fingers and placed his hand right over the print Thalil had burned into Sasha's ribs. Yarrow lifted his head, stretched out his hand, and draped it overtop of Duncan's before leaning across Sasha to kiss Duncan. Sasha's body reacted as he watched their cheeks and throats working as their kisses grew sloppy and rough. Together, they moved their hands down Sasha's belly to his root. Yarrow cradled Sasha's balls and Duncan gripped the base of his shaft. With his other hand, Yarrow raked his nails up the outside of Sasha's thigh, and Sasha bucked his hips up off the ground. He reached around Duncan and pressed against the small of his back, urging Duncan closer so he could get his mouth around his wonderful cock and breathe in the musk of the brown curls framing it.

Sasha propped himself up on his elbow and moved his head into Duncan's lap. As Sasha took Duncan into his throat, swallowing around his cock and earning a deep groan from Duncan, he spread his legs wider and tilted his pelvis up, communicating to Yarrow where he wanted to be touched. They knew each other well, and Yarrow understood. He knelt down, spread Sasha's cheeks, and lapped at his opening. Sasha gasped. He liked this, which Yarrow knew, but Duncan was usually the one to pleasure him that way. This was the first time Sasha had felt Yarrow wriggle his tongue inside him, and the sounds of enjoyment Yarrow made drove him wild. He had to grasp Duncan's wrist and push his hand away from his cock before he shot his seed all over himself. He twisted his fingers around a handful of Yarrow's hair and pulled his face away, then twined his body onto his knees and elbows without ever moving his mouth from Duncan's cock. As soon as he could, Yarrow burrowed his face back into Sasha's flesh and resumed his work. The small sounds of delight and discovery he made reverberated up through Sasha's body, making his inner muscles clench around Yarrow's tongue. Yarrow soon had Sasha so wet and open Sasha doubted he'd need any oil, but Yarrow reached beneath the cot and found the phial anyway. It felt as warm as blood as Yarrow drizzled it between Sasha's cheeks.

When Yarrow pushed into him, Sasha tensed at the penetration, a shiver moving up his back and through his belly. Yarrow paused and waited for Sasha to adjust to his size, and Duncan looked down at him, his eyes dilated with lust as he swiped away the tears Sasha hadn't realized he'd shed. He buried his other hand in Sasha's hair and rocked his hips, thrusting into Sasha's throat and leaving Sasha free to enjoy the sensations.

Yarrow began moving, dragging his teeth up Sasha's sweaty back as he pushed into him, his fat cockhead hitting Sasha's sweet spot with every stroke. Soon Sasha heard Duncan and Yarrow kissing above him, Duncan growling with pleasure as he sucked Sasha's flavor from Yarrow's lips.

"Goddesses, that's delightful," Duncan grunted. "The taste of you both...." He began thrusting faster and deeper, and Yarrow matched his tempo, both of them smacking against Sasha as he braced himself against the wonderful onslaught.

When he broke away from Duncan's mouth, Yarrow began practically wailing, a high, clear note of pleasure escaping him each time he pushed into Sasha. Sasha loved the sounds of utter abandon and bliss his Yarrow made, and for once, not even Duncan scolded him to be quiet. The whole camp would be able to hear what they were up to, but none of them cared—not even Duncan. His more subdued groans echoed Yarrow's as he reached out to kiss their mage again. Yarrow let out a ragged scream into Duncan's mouth as his wet heat filled Sasha. Quivering and muttering nonsense, Yarrow dropped his forehead between Sasha's shoulder blades and caressed Sasha's waist before slipping out of him.

Sasha sat up and looked at Duncan's flushed face and swollen lips. He kissed Duncan hard as he climbed into his lap and straddled him. With his body open and Yarrow's seed easing the way, Duncan slipped easily inside him. There was no pain, just a magnificent feeling of fullness. As Sasha circled his hips, Yarrow moved behind him and pressed his chest against Sasha's back. His cock, softening now, left little wet trails above Sasha's tailbone as Yarrow kissed and nipped across his shoulders. Sasha turned his head and found Yarrow's lips as Yarrow found his cock, letting Sasha thrust up into his fist as he rode Duncan. Thalil, they were going to destroy him. Sasha shook all over, barely realizing he was moaning like a cheap whore into first Yarrow's mouth, then Duncan's. He clutched Duncan's shoulders and sank his nails into the dense muscle, trying to hold on to something solid as the intense pleasure pulled him in every direction. Yarrow bit the side of his neck and twisted his hand around the crown of Sasha's cock. Sasha came so hard everything went dark for a second, and he wondered if they'd actually killed him.

Duncan followed him a moment later, trembling and panting hard against Sasha's collarbone as Yarrow smeared Sasha's come over his chest. Then Duncan fell onto his back, his face glistening with sweat and his body still joined with Sasha's. Tingling everywhere, Sasha rolled off him and lay beside him, his chest heaving. Waves of pleasure still moved through him as both his men's seed mingled within him. Yarrow laid his cheek against Sasha's belly, oblivious to the mess. Duncan lifted Yarrow's hand to his mouth and licked Sasha's come from Yarrow's fingers. For a while, they just basked in their afterglow and tried to catch their breath.

"I wish it was safe to go into the ocean," Yarrow said wistfully. "I miss swimming in the sea."

"Put your pants on," Sasha said. "A swim sounds wonderful. We're filthy. What's the worst that can happen? I'll keep us safe." He expected Duncan to argue, but his knight simply found his trousers and pulled them on.

They left the tent, ignoring the stares and accusing expressions some of the men sent their way, and went down the trail to the strip of white sand. It felt good between Sasha's toes, as did the light breeze against his heated skin. Stripping off his trousers and diving into the churning surf, letting it wash the coating of sweat and semen from his skin, felt amazing beyond description. As the three of them played in the water, chasing, splashing, and dunking each other, as carefree as boys, Sasha could almost pretend he didn't notice the sails of the enemy ships a few miles away, white as bleached bones against the night sky.

Chapter
Twenty-Eight

THE days that passed with no movement from the enemy felt maddening to Yarrow. He wanted to fight; he was ready. But the Johmatran ships just waited, a hundred of them or more, anchored a few miles from the coastline. He sensed mages aboard those ships, and he longed to face them, show them what happened when they threatened what he loved. He spent his nights, when he wasn't wound up in a sweaty knot with Sasha and Duncan, contemplating Fane's box. He had never had such a need of power, but he couldn't figure out how to make it reveal its secrets, and it remained nothing more than a lump of cold stone from a forgotten world.

Today, Yarrow practiced with his bow while Sasha and Duncan sparred. He did it because it made them happy, not because he thought arrows would ever compete with his magic. Even so, he'd gradually become better at using the weapon and could hit targets from farther and farther away. If nothing else, it distracted him, at least until he noticed his brother walking toward where they trained. Feeling Rowan's scrutiny on him, Yarrow loosed an arrow and it whizzed to the center of his target.

"You're a capable archer," Rowan said. "I never knew that about you."

"You don't know anything about me," Yarrow said tersely, securing the bow on his back. "I wasn't useful to your aspirations, so you could never be bothered to find out."

"Brother, I—" The approach of Duncan and Sasha cut short anything Rowan had intended to say. "His Majesty has asked to see the three of you in his tent."

Duncan mopped his sweaty face on the sleeve of his gambeson and sheathed his greatsword. Sasha slid his daggers into their places by his hips, and the three of them followed Rowan to the king's pavilion. Garith and his guard, Lysander, waited inside. All of them helped themselves to water and then sat down around the long wooden table.

Garith looked weary, pale beneath his dark Esperon complexion. "There has been some news, mostly good. Messengers arrived earlier this morning.

Windwake, Bairn Duncan, I'm happy to inform you that your wife has given birth to a healthy baby. A little girl. Congratulations, my friend."

"A girl," Duncan said softly. "I thank the goddesses. A daughter. I'll never have to worry about her losing her life on the battlefield. That is a blessing."

"And my wife has borne a son," Garith said, unable to suppress his smile. "The Blessed Epoch has an heir. His name is Thaneyael Garron da Verrichi. A good, Selindrian-Gaeltheonic name, with a little Esperon tacked on at the end, yes? I'm sure someone will find a problem with my decision, but my son, and his mother, are doing well. It makes me feel better about dying here. At least what we've tried to build won't end with me. He's a big boy, and already alert, I'm told. Already able to clutch a rattle."

"Do you know the name of my daughter?" Duncan asked.

Sander consulted the scrolls. "Marlythe Helwyn Purefroy, after your wife's grandmother and Helwyn, the goddess of solitude. She's dark of hair, with green eyes."

"Green eyes," Duncan said, smiling. "I have a little girl."

Yarrow wanted to know more about Garith's child, because he knew the boy was his, conceived on the night of Duncan's wedding, with the aid of a potion. Garith's mother and his wife had wanted to produce a mage, and they'd asked for Yarrow's assistance. In his disgust over Duncan being forced to marry, Yarrow had agreed to spite his cousin. Now he had a son, one he could never acknowledge. Unlike Duncan, Yarrow couldn't reveal his joy, though he felt sure Sasha sensed something as he watched Yarrow worrying his lip. "What does your boy look like, Garith?"

"Esperon," Garith answered. "He's dark but has bright blue eyes. I'm told they almost seem to glow."

"Really," Sasha said, turning his eyes, but not his head, in Yarrow's direction. "Interesting."

"But-but certainly not what we were called here to learn," Yarrow hurried to say. "What other news?"

"Your brother, Valen Rayne of Lockhaven, has secured the port city of Oreeta, to the south. He and his forces are marching to join us here."

"Good news," Duncan said.

"The last of it, I'm afraid," Sander said. He stood and left the tent, with Garith behind him. Yarrow and the others followed Sander to the edge of the cliffs, where the sails of the enemy ships almost obscured the horizon. "There are at least two hundred of them. They'll come ashore, and we won't be able to hold them back." Imminent death trumped his modesty, and he grabbed Garith's hand and squeezed it. "We're all going to die on this beach."

"At least I have a small fleet. My ships will be able to offer some resistance," Garith said. He took a distance glass from his belt and surveyed the horizon. All the men turned to look in the direction Garith faced.

A surge of excitement raced through Yarrow, and he tore the glass from his cousin's hand and pressed it to his eye. Scanning over the enemy boats and the king's small number of ships, he fixed upon the hundreds of brightly colored striped sails he saw to the west. Yarrow jumped and punched the air. "You call that a fleet, cousin? Look. *That* is a fleet. *My* fleet, from the Twenty-Nine, my valenny."

Duncan shielded his gaze from the sun with his arm and squinted to see what waited on the horizon. "Sweet goddesses, the Emiri?"

Yarrow bounced on the balls of his feet. He turned and hugged Duncan, then Sasha, then Garith, and even his brother. "Oh, my wonderful Sai! He changed his mind. He came after all. Tell me, Duncan. Are our chances still so hopeless?"

A wide grin split Duncan's face. He looked happy enough to cry. "Not so hopeless at all."

IT TOOK four days for the Emiri ships to fight their way through the enemy armada. By flanking the Johmatrans, they'd been able to take them by surprise and eliminate many of their ships before the invaders could even turn their vessels to face them. Then half of the Emiri fleet cut a swathe through the invaders, separating them into two smaller, weaker groups, before the rest of the Emiri boats appeared from the west, decimating the first batch of enemy ships. When the fleet came back together, they had little trouble driving the remaining Johmatrans southeast toward Espero. Sasha respected how quickly the seafarers had learned to organize their force and form battle tactics. On the sea, united, they were force to be reckoned with.

When the victorious Emiri came ashore, Duncan and Garith's men ran to meet them at the beach, rushing out into the water to lift the smaller sailors off their feet, hugging them and twirling them around, even kissing them in many cases. Yarrow located Sai and threw himself into Sai's arms so hard both of them ended up on the sand, the water breaking over their backs as they held each other, laughing and crying. Sasha and Duncan greeted the rest of Sai's family—what was left of them. Toumo had remained in the Twenty-Nine to care for their young son, and the quiet, dark-haired boy, Kin, had been badly injured and remained behind as well. Izu and their newest syrai, Zura, didn't know if he would recover.

Yarrow clasped Sai's hand as they made their way up the hill. "Not that any of us are complaining, *syrai*, but what made you change your mind? I thought you wanted nothing to do with this war."

Sai looked far away, his gaze fixed on some point in the distance. "I suppose I just realized I'm part of the world, not separate from it. We all are. What happens beyond our islands and ships and beaches affects us." He looked over at Yarrow. "You're the one who started to make me see there are things beyond drinking, pirating, and making love. These dry-feet took my *syrai* and my baby from me. They keep my people as slaves. If I can stop them, even slow them down, I have to do it, or I can't live with myself. I can't just lie in the sun and pretend it isn't happening."

Yarrow squeezed his hand. "We'll send them to the Shades', *syrai*."

Sai stopped at the top of the cliffs and faced Yarrow. "We will, but I must ask you something first. Yarrow, if I don't make it home, will you promise to take care of my *syrai*? Will you protect the Twenty-Nine, make sure the Emiri aren't driven from there?"

"You know I will," Yarrow said. "But it won't be necessary. I'm not letting anyone else die. You can count on it."

"We can't waste any time," Duncan said. "The Johmatrans have retreated, for the moment, but they're likely to regroup, maybe refresh their ranks, and come back. We have to plan for that. Sai, would you accompany me to the king's tent?"

"Me?"

"Who else?" Yarrow said. "You're the leader of our fleet."

Sai looked both proud and a little nervous. "I suppose I am. You'll come with me, won't you, *syrai*?"

"Of course," Yarrow said. "Sasha?"

Sasha paused. "Actually, I think I'll sit this one out. I have little to contribute to discussions of sea warfare and tactics, and to be blunt, I make the others uncomfortable."

"They'll deal with it," Duncan said.

"It doesn't offend me, my friend," Sasha said. "Go on. I'll find some way to make myself useful, and you can tell me your plans later tonight."

Duncan nodded, and the others continued toward the center of the encampment. Sasha waited a few moments in the lengthening shadows, until the sun disappeared completely behind the western hills, leaving the sky rose pink and the land bathed in cool blue shade. Sasha slid his hood over his hair as he made his way north, toward the outskirts of the military camp, and then a few miles inland, beyond the famed flowering trees and into a stunted little wood thick with bracken and briar bushes. By the time Sasha reached the tiny, abandoned cemetery near the center, full night had fallen, and a bright three-quarter moon shone above, though little of the silvery light penetrated the thick, twisted vegetation.

Sasha touched the crescent dripping blood carved into the stone of a dilapidated mausoleum. Woodbine, ivy, and moss nearly obscured the structure, but those who knew what to seek here would find it. One by one, six figures in black cloaks emerged from beneath the trees, stepping silently toward Sasha, not so much as a twig snapping beneath their boots. The one who reached Sasha first threw his hood back to reveal a face as pale and smooth as the moonlight. Corbin tipped his head in slight deference to Sasha and said, "Brother."

Sasha offered Corbin an even smaller nod. "Brother. I'm glad you received my message and were able to make your way here so quickly."

"What will you have us do?"

Sasha leaned his shoulders and one foot against the old crypt. "I want you to protect the bairn of Windwake, my friend Duncan. See that no harm comes to him. Do not be seen, and do not let him become aware of what you're doing. The order can't be seen as choosing a side in a political conflict."

Corbin arched a brow. "Using the order for personal gain?"

Sasha shrugged. "It's my order. Or will you ignore the commands of our master?"

Corbin bowed theatrically, sweeping his cloak out behind him with a flourish. "It will be done." He and the others melted back into the night, and Sasha headed back toward camp. He had one more matter to attend to before he joined his friends.

Half a dozen Royal Guards stood watch around Garith's tent, but none of them noticed Sasha, standing only six feet away, beyond the light of the torches. Since he'd returned from Thalil, he'd been able to blend almost effortlessly into the darkness, as if his body repelled any light. He waited until one of the guards wandered a few steps away to speak with another, and then he darted below the hem of the tent.

Once inside, Sasha crouched behind the table. Garith was alone, stripped to his trousers, washing at a basin, his back to Sasha. The recent conflict had added a fair amount of muscle to the young king's frame, as well as a few scars. Clearly, he wasn't a leader to send his men into danger while he cowered behind them. He didn't consider himself above lifting a sword or suffering a wound. For a king, he wasn't a bad sort, and though Sasha didn't dislike him, he wanted Garith to maintain a healthy respect for him, even a measure of fear. He slipped quietly into the chair and rested his elbows on the table. A little squeal escaped Garith when he turned and saw Sasha.

"Sweet sisters, Sasha! If you wanted to speak with me, you could have used the front entrance. Wh-what can I do for you?"

"I want to know who you hired to sack Fayelle's temple and blame it on the barbarians."

"I don't know what you're talking about." Garith's face screamed otherwise. Every hint of color drained from his skin, and muscles bulged along his jawline as he clenched his teeth.

"Please. You didn't come to us, so who?"

"And why should I tell you?"

Sasha leaned forward a few inches, and Garith flinched. "Little king, do I even need to list the debts you owe me? I'm not a fool. The Johmatrans were fighting the Emiri. They were retaliating against Sai for freeing their slaves and stealing their weapons. They had no reason to go to that temple, let alone the knowledge of its location. But since the attack, your kingdom has never been more unified. You started this war, solidified your rule at the cost of thousands of lives."

"How dare you presume to judge me?" Garith asked. "I should call my guards."

"Go ahead."

"Just what do you plan to do with this knowledge, Sasha? How can it possibly benefit you?"

"I don't know yet," Sasha said. He didn't tell Garith, but he would store away what he learned, as it would inevitably be of use at some point. "I misjudged you, and that doesn't sit well with me. I didn't take you for a man who could devise something so ruthless, let alone carry it out. Being able to understand a man's character, especially a man with as much power as you have, is an essential part of my work. I have to say, you played the innocent idealist with absolute aplomb. I don't think one of us could have done as convincing a job." Sasha indicated the wine with a tilt of his head, and when Garith nodded, he poured a glass for each of them and then lifted his in salute. "Well done. You are dangerous, Garith, and you managed to make me think you weren't. Sit and have a drink with me, one killer to another."

Garith sat and reached for his goblet with a trembling hand. "You're wrong about me. I'm no liar; I doubt I could deceive a child. I didn't want this war, but the kingdom was splitting apart. The priestesses were turning my people against me…. We needed a common enemy. I still wouldn't have done it, though. I feel sick every time I think of it, and I haven't slept through the night since it happened."

Sasha didn't let his surprise show. "Who?"

"My mother," Garith said softly.

"I see." Sasha understood. Denna Corinna had probably been ruling the Blessed Epoch from the beginning. He wondered just how much she'd set in motion. She'd been less than horrified when she'd discovered Sasha murdering her husband. Had she planned that too? To get her son on the throne and herself in a position to rule from behind the scenes? Had she known Yarrow would tell Sasha what the king had done to him? Thalil, if so, she had managed to manipulate him, and masterfully. He would have to keep a closer eye on her. She could make a powerful ally—or enemy.

"I don't think she had any idea how strong the enemy was, though, or how many. It's too late now, isn't it?"

"Yes."

"Sasha, are you going to tell my cousin? Duncan?"

"I don't know. No, not at the moment. It will only scrape away another layer of Duncan's waning faith in justice, and I honestly don't think Yarrow will care."

"Yarrow idolizes my mother," Garith said. "He'd do anything for her. If it hadn't been for her, do you think he would have ever set foot at my father's castle, after what happened to him there? I don't know what hearing about what she's done will do to Yarrow. Is… is he any better, Sasha? Is he still in so much pain?"

"It will take time," Sasha said, and Garith nodded. They sat quietly for a few minutes, sipping their wine.

"Can I ask you something?" Garith finally said.

"You can ask."

The young king took a deep breath. "You were hired to kill me once. If your… the one you serve, asked you to kill me again, would you do it?"

Sasha smiled as he looked up at Garith's pale face through his eyelashes. "You can sleep soundly. Thalil cannot ask that of me. He has promised to ask nothing of me that would hurt Yarrow or Duncan, and both of them love you and would mourn you."

"And you, Sasha? Do you consider me a friend, at least?"

"I find you interesting, you and your handsome guard. You and your fireside councils with the stable boys included. I'm curious to see how the world will react."

"We're at a cusp, aren't we?" Garith mused, looking into his swirling wine. "A threshold. Once we go over this cliff, we'll never be able to go back, unless we can sprout wings like Yarrow does. But the world is about to change, isn't it?"

"Yes, I think so," Sasha said as he stood up. "I should go. Let you rest. We both know this fight isn't over."

Before Sasha returned to Duncan's tent, he went to find Corbin. "I have another task for you."

"I live to serve."

"You are head of the order in my stead. Get a message to them. I want four of my people sent to Windust Castle and another four sent to Eirion-Vayl. They are to pose as servants, insinuate themselves into the households, make everyone trust them. They are to watch, listen, and await my orders. In the meantime, they are to see no harm comes to Duncan's daughter or Garith's son."

"The children are in danger?" Corbin asked.

"I don't know yet," Sasha said. "For now, just tell them to watch and wait."

Chapter
Twenty-Nine

THREE weeks after the arrival of the Emiri, they, along with the newly established Royal Fleet, under the command of Fleet Commander Bartoum Astir, had driven the invaders from the Bay of Blossoms and chased them southeast, almost to the coast of Espero. Out of necessity, they'd put their differences aside and learned to fight together. Knights and Royal Guards fought alongside the Emiri on the decks of their fast ships, and they'd quickly learned that following the orders the *mir* gave kept them alive.

Duncan, their best strategist, along with Sai, their finest sailor, had informally assumed command of the force, and they proved a magnificent team. The fleet had faced the Johmatrans three times and won three victories, each time reducing the enemy's numbers. So far, Yarrow had been able to counter most of what the barbarian spell casters aimed their way. Morale soared among the men; they felt invincible—until the two fleets faced off on the westernmost edge of the Esperon islands.

With nowhere to go but into the Serpent's Belly, the Johmatrans had circled their remaining ships, clearly keeping those carrying their mages protected at the center, and conjured a storm unlike anything Duncan had ever witnessed. Winds strong enough to lift a boat from the water assailed them for days, along with rain that felt like a hail of arrows, able to draw blood if one stood in it too long. It forced their ships back toward the coast of Gaeltheon while keeping the enemy protected beyond an impassable barrier.

Yarrow stood on the aft rail of Garith's flagship, the Queen Cothryn, his arms spread wide, blue light pouring from him in sheets. For the past three days, he'd been trying to dispel the arcane storm without success. From the deck, Duncan watched the cerulean energy Yarrow conjured slamming against the black vapor of the storm, the two forces pushing back and forth, each gaining and losing ground in turn. It was eerie and unsettling watching the light and darkness advance and recede over the surface of the tumultuous water.

Once again, Yarrow lost the battle. He crumpled and fell to the deck of the ship, the blue light blinking out, and the storm rushed in to take its place, battering the boats and tearing their sails as their crews hurried to furl them. The rain felt like sharp rocks against Duncan's face as he made his way toward his friend. He tried to shield his head with his arms, but the water stung his eyes as if tainted with poison. He ran to escape it.

Sasha reached Yarrow first and dragged him into the captain's cabin. As Duncan slid the final few feet across the deck, Sai swung from a rope and landed lightly beside him. Together, they hurried to see to their friend. Inside the cabin, Yarrow lay in Sasha's lap, blood dripping from his nose and the inner corners of his eyes. Garith, Sander, and Rowan stood over him, looking worried and defeated.

Duncan and Sai sat down on the edge of the bed, and Sai curled his fingers around Yarrow's hand. "He's cold. His heartbeat is weak and uneven. You can't let him keep doing this to himself. He's one mage against who knows how many dozen the enemy has onboard their ships." Sai met Duncan's gaze, and Duncan nodded.

"I agree."

"What do you suggest, then?" Rowan asked. "If we can't breach that storm, we have no choice but to let the enemy retreat. If they escape us, we know what they'll do: fall back to the territory they've taken on the Esperon coast, regain their strength, and attack again. No. They can't be allowed to escape."

Duncan, not a man to let his temper get the better of him, wanted to throttle Rowan. "He's your brother, for the love of the goddesses!"

"And if he wasn't… whatever he is to you, Bairn Duncan, you would agree with me. You're letting your unnatural feelings for Yarroway cloud your judgment. We must do what's best for the kingdom."

"No," Sasha said. "Yarrow can't continue. I won't allow it."

"You have less than no say in what we decide, tam!" Rowan said.

"We'll see about that," Sasha responded.

"So… we have to let them go," Sander said, resigned.

"No," Sai said softly, drawing everyone's attention. "I have another idea."

Before he could continue, Yarrow's eyelids fluttered. He tried to sit up, but collapsed back against Sasha's lap. "I can destroy them," he said in a hoarse whisper. "Let me. Let me open up the sky—"

"No," Duncan said, smoothing the hair out of his face. Yarrow's skin felt as cold and damp as a fish's belly. "That is not an option."

"And why not?" Rowan protested. "If he can do it, then what are we waiting for?"

"You don't know what it costs!" Duncan shouted. "He is your brother! He is my… my friend."

"Don't be a fool," Rowan continued. "If we can keep our men alive, so what if my brother needs a few days of sleep? If we can be rid of the enemy—"

"I can do it," Yarrow croaked. "I've done it before. I'll be all right. I told you my body is changed. Ordinary flesh couldn't handle what's inside—"

"No," Sasha said, and in minutes, all of them were shouting, arguing, and struggling to be heard over the cacophony.

Sai's clear, sure voice rose above the din. "Shut up, all of you! Listen to me. I have eighteen barrels of liquid fire, and four dozen exploding boulders, the last of what we brought from the Twenty-Nine. It's enough to take out the last of the enemy ships, especially the way they're clustered together."

"But how will we get it there?" Garith asked.

"Easy," Sai said. "I'll sail to the edge of their fleet. They won't have time to run. Then I'll light the barrels. The blast will destroy them all."

"And you, too," Sasha said.

Sai shook his head. "I'll dive overboard and swim. I can make it."

"No one can guide a ship through those winds and waves," Rowan said.

"I can," Sai said, without boasting. "I sailed the Serpent's Belly, and I ran with a storm like this once before. Ask my *syrai*, Sasha and Duncan. They know I can make it."

"No," Yarrow said, tightening his grip on Sai's hand. "You could die. I should go, I… my body is different."

Sai laughed. "No one but me can sail through that mess. You can't sail at all, *syrai*. It's a job for me, and you know it. Besides, I'll need your magery to shield me from their spells. I can manage the *eru* and the tide, if you can do that."

"It's too dangerous," Yarrow said. "You'll have to put a lot of distance between you and your ship before those boulders explode. If you don't—"

"But I will." Sai bent down and kissed Yarrow's forehead, a lingering last kiss. "I'm Emiri. You doubt my ability to swim?"

Yarrow wrapped his arms around Sai and held Sai against his chest, speaking into the hair near Sai's ear. "I don't want you to. Please don't."

"*Syrai-tama*, my dearest Yarrow. I have to. Don't you see? If I do this, my *syrai*, my people back at the Twenty-Nine, my son, will be safe a little longer. It isn't just me. I want to do this for them. I'm one person, and I could save thousands. You have to let me go."

"You-you're sure you'll make it back?" Yarrow asked.

"Absolutely," Sai said.

Tears stung Duncan's eyes, because he recognized the resigned tone in Sai's voice. Sai knew he wouldn't make it back; he was ready to die for his people. Duncan had been in his place only a few weeks ago. He'd made it, and maybe Sai would too. Sai's people called him *yu-me*—hope—so maybe he would come through.

"We have a priestess who can bless you, if you want," Sander offered.

"No, thank you," Sai said. "Emir will take care of me. Yarrow, let me know when you're ready."

To everyone's surprise, Yarrow rose from the bed. "I'm ready. The sooner we get this over with and I know you're safe, the better."

Sai went to his ship and dismissed the rest of his crew. Alone, he went to the helm, looked over his shoulder, and waved at the others, looking as happy and free from worry as he had when Duncan had first met him, so long ago. Yarrow blew him a kiss as he sent a soft wind to start him on his way. Scrunching his eyes closed, Yarrow surrounded Sai's little boat in a blue bubble. Everyone on every other ship came aboard, braving the rain to watch his progress. The azure orb moved closer to the storm, Sai guiding his vessel between the huge, swelling waves, until he passed between the barbarian ships guarding the perimeter. Their spells, fire, lightning, ice, and necrotic mist bounced harmlessly off the boundary Yarrow maintained, and Sai was able to guide his boat near the center of the group. Yarrow dissolved his protective dome, and the resulting explosion lit the firmaments and shook the ship where Duncan stood, miles away. A wall of water shot into the sky, leaving a crater in the sea for a few moments until the frothy water, littered with flotsam, blood, and bodies, rushed in to fill it. The resulting waves hit Garith's fleet hard, dousing the men watching from the decks and washing gear overboard. Flames spread into the heavens and crawled across the water, obliterating everything. Ship after ship sprung alight, and the spells the enemy mages attempted to contain the blaze failed. A series of smaller explosions followed the first as the liquid fire and weapons aboard the barbarian vessels caught. Splinters of wood flew in every direction. The Johmatran ships were ash in moments.

The quiet that followed the attack was eerie as the storm, without the casters to maintain its fury, blew itself out and a few shafts of watery sunlight punched through the clouds. Bits of debris still burned for miles across the roiling sea, sending black smoke into the clearing sky. Yarrow grabbed a distance glass from one of the Selindrian sailors and practically pitched himself overboard as he leaned across the rail. Duncan rested a hand on the center of his lower back, but Yarrow didn't seem to notice. Sasha looked over at him and shook his head.

They waited hours for Sai, and when he didn't appear, they sent ships out in search of him. They combed miles of water for a day and a half before giving up. Yarrow stood, day and night, at the southernmost tip of Gaeltheon, maintaining his vigil for two days without food or sleep, using his enchantment to seek for some trace of his friend. It took both Duncan and Sasha to drag him away.

Chapter Thirty

ON THEIR way home, Yarrow, Sasha, and Duncan stopped at Eirion-Vayl to welcome the newborn king of the Blessed Epoch. Queen Cothryn sat holding her son in the throne room, and Yarrow flushed and turned away when she met his gaze. She had known him, though he didn't remember, and the boy on her lap was his. Thaneyael Garron, the mage-emperor of the Blessed Epoch, Yarrow's son. Yarrow ascended the steps to the dais and let the baby wrap his chubby fingers round Yarrow's hand. Though the infant babbled and drooled, something intelligent and powerful resided behind his bright blue eyes— something Yarrow recognized.

Yarrow opened the clasp of the pendant he'd found at the site of Corbin's assassinations, in the tent of the old scholar Corbin had been sent to kill. It had been Fane's, he knew. When he wrapped it around the child-king's throat and closed the clasp, the stone shone a bright blue for a second, so bright the afterimage stayed with Yarrow as he tried to blink it away. The others gave no indication of having noticed, not even the queen.

After a short visit, Yarrow's brothers, Rowan and Rayne, along with Duncan, Garith, Sander, Tam Bertrand, Fleet Commander Bartoum Astir, and dozens of other high-ranking knights and sailors left to discuss improvements to the fleet and land forces, in the event the Johmatrans returned. They planned to sail for Espero, along with those Emiri willing to accompany them, and purge the mages' island of the stragglers and make their victory absolute. Despite the blow they'd delivered, they had no assurance the enemy wouldn't return. Garith wanted to send delegates to Johmatra, to at least make an attempt at diplomacy. Sander expressed his plans to recruit spell casters from Espero and build an allied force of fighters from both lands.

Yarrow decided not to join them; he couldn't find it in his heart to think about war even a minute longer. He stood in the throne room, the light shining through the tall, narrow windows warm on his shoulders, but his insides cold. He couldn't stop thinking about Sai and how, for all his power, he'd failed his friend. He shouldn't have let Sai go; he should have stopped him… somehow….

"I'm going down to the kitchens," Sasha said, his soft voice dragging Yarrow's attention back to the present.

"Why?"

"For something to eat and to talk with some of the servants," Sasha said. "Do want anything? Wine? A sweet roll?"

"I'm not hungry."

"All right," Sasha said, stroking down the outside of Yarrow's arm, "I won't pester you, but if you don't manage at least a little at dinner, Duncan will make you eat something if he has to force it down your throat."

Yarrow just nodded and rested his hand on the stone ledge of the window. Beyond the leaded glass, the grounds were a brilliant green, dotted with flowers of every color. Fruit ripened on the trees, and the gardens thrived. Life went on, and all Yarrow wanted was to destroy it, burn it to dust, make it as desiccated and gray as he felt.

With nothing better to occupy him, Yarrow wandered back to the platform, climbed the stairs, and sat down in Garith's chair beside the queen. He suspected it wasn't proper for him to sit there, but he didn't really care. Who was going to make him get up?

"He likes your gift," Cothryn said as the baby gummed the blue gem, larger than his hand. "Where did you come by it? It's beautiful."

"I found it along the road," Yarrow said, watching the striations of energy within the gem trail the infant's touch.

"Well, it's a generous present, Tam Yarroway. Although I suppose I must address you as valen now, the valen of the South Coast."

"Of the Twenty-Nine," Yarrow corrected.

Soon Yarrow's aunt, Denna Corinna, joined them, holding the hand of a little girl in a soft blue dress edged in white lace. Her dark brown hair hung in ringlets that bounced as she walked, and she had Garith's dark eyes. Three ladies-in-waiting followed them.

"Look, my darling," Aunt Den said, crouching down to speak to the child. "This is your uncle, Yarroway L'Estrella. Can you say hello to him?"

The girl's eyes went wide. Yarrow's appearance, his white hair, washed-out eyes, and permanent ink probably frightened her. She recovered quickly, though, held out the edges of her skirts, and curtseyed. "Pleased to meet you, my lord."

"And what is your name?" Yarrow asked.

"Denna Borea, my lord."

Yarrow gestured with his left hand and offered Princess Denna Borea the single, perfect blue lily he'd conjured. She giggled with delight as she took it.

"And what do you say to your Uncle Yarrow?" Aunt Den coached.

"Thank you, my lord. Can you make me a pony?"

"Denna Borea," the queen scolded mildly.

Looking excited, the little girl pointed to the head of a monstrous beast mounted above them, an awrythe, if Yarrow wasn't mistaken. "My father killed that horrible creature," she said, smiling and tugging on the hem of Yarrow's tunic. "He stuck his sword in its belly and its insides fell out on the ground." She leaned in and whispered conspiratorially to him. "I'm not supposed to know that part, but Sander told me."

"That is not something appropriate for a young lady to discuss," Cothryn told her daughter. "Go with your ladies, now. I wish to speak to your gran. One of you, come and take the prince."

"I can take him," Yarrow offered. "I'll take him for a quick walk around the garden while you two talk."

The two women looked at each other, unused to noblemen offering to tend babies, but Aunt Den nodded, and Cothryn handed Yarrow her son—their son. At first the boy seemed asleep, as he made no noise as Yarrow took him and settled him into his arms, but when Yarrow looked down, Thaneyael stared up at him with eyes holding too much understanding to occupy such a young face.

They strolled across the grounds, past women in plain dresses and white aprons and bonnets picking peas in the garden, past young men in dirty trousers hoeing the flower beds, and past ducks swimming in the pond. Yarrow found a secluded spot beneath an apple tree and sat down in the dappled grass. He shifted his son to rest against his left arm and opened the leather satchel he had kept by his side since he'd found the box. Seeing Fane's amulet react to his son had given Yarrow an idea, but he didn't want anyone to see what he was about to do, especially not the Thirteen Goddesses. They didn't know Yarrow had bonded with his creature, and they didn't know he had found and freed Fane from the prison where they'd left him. Yarrow wanted to keep it that way.

He just needed a simple, believable illusion, and it only had to cover the small area they occupied. Hale had used a similar spell to conceal an entire island, so Yarrow figured he could manage this. He projected the image of himself and the young prince lounging on the lawn, reading from a book of poetry. The spell, while modest, was woven strong and solid. Anyone who looked at them would see just what Yarrow wanted them to see. Confident the illusion would hide them, Yarrow slid the box onto his leg and placed Thaneyael's chubby pink hand on the surface.

Almost immediately, a gossamer thread of light bisected what had been a solid piece of smooth rock. Yarrow's pulse sped as a lid appeared and then opened. Inside the box, he found papers, charts, a small book bound in black leather, and an elaborate round sigil that looked carved from a single sapphire. A language Yarrow didn't recognize shimmered around the edge, and bumps and whorls protruded from the surface, the largest, almost a miniature tower, rising from the center. Yarrow quickly replaced the contents of the box, glad to see it didn't return to its previous state and the lid remained. He'd have to guard it even more carefully now. He had no idea what to make of the things it held, and he couldn't read the words Fane had written, but at least he'd managed to get to them. He could study them now, get ready. Thalil had said not yet, and Yarrow didn't know when it would feel right to proceed, but he intended to be prepared when that time came. His mage son wouldn't be begging scraps of power from the castoffs of those thirteen charlatans.

AFTER spending a few leisurely weeks at Garith's court in Gaeltheon, Duncan, Yarrow, and Sasha left to return to Windwake. Summer was ending by the time they reached Windust Castle; there was a chill nip to the air, the wheat stood high and golden in the fields, and the farmers they passed filled cart after cart with the fruit of their labors. It looked as though the harvest had been good, and the sweet goddess Berris quite generous.

Duncan's daughter, Marlythe, had an unruly tuft of red-brown hair, huge green eyes, and fat rosy cheeks. She smiled when Duncan lifted her and tossed her into the air. He'd been looking forward to seeing her, but hadn't expected to fall so instantly in love. The dog he'd given his wife, grown now and reaching almost to Duncan's hips, growled low when Duncan handed his daughter to Yarrow.

"And here is your Uncle Yarrow and your Uncle Sasha," he announced. Sasha moved his fingers in front of Marlythe's face, and when her gaze followed his motions, he pronounced her reflexes quite impressive.

"Is there any magic in your line?" Yarrow asked.

"No, tam," Lady Aurauna said, clutching her skirts and pressing her back against the wall as if she could sink between the blocks and disappear.

"Sasha, Yarrow, would you excuse me?" Duncan said. "I'm sure you want to go to your rooms, unpack, and clean up for dinner."

They took the hint and left Duncan alone with his wife. "What's troubling you, my lady?"

"Those men are not related to you by blood," she said cautiously, darting her gaze around as if Yarrow and Sasha might reappear out of nowhere, and Duncan supposed that wasn't an unreasonable worry.

"No," he said, unsure where the conversation headed and afraid to upset her further. "They're my friends."

"Why did you call them 'Uncle Yarrow and Uncle Sasha' as if they were your brothers? Is that how you'll teach our daughter to think of them?"

"Why not?" Duncan asked. Little Marlythe tugged on his whiskers. He smiled even though it stung. She had a grip like iron. "You should be happy. Yarrow and Sasha are strong and skilled. They'll help us protect our daughter."

"I worry about the influence those men will have on her."

"What do you mean by that?"

Aurauna sighed. She narrowed her eyes and pressed her lips together, her expression turning cold and a bit nasty. "If you want me to say it in no uncertain terms, very well. Just remember you asked for this. Yarroway L'Estrella is dangerous and deranged. Everyone knows it. Everyone knows what he did to the former king and why he was sent away. He is mad, he's unnatural, and likely a criminal."

"He has saved my life more times than I can count, he is a valen now, and King Garith values his counsel. You shouldn't slander him. In fact, I won't have it."

"What about your Sasha, then?" Aurauna continued, her cheeks coloring. "What exactly does he do?"

"He fights alongside me," Duncan said.

Aurauna shook her head. "Do you take me for a fool? To be quite plain, I know exactly what he is, and he isn't something I want my daughter exposed to. No mother would."

"You will have to find a way to reconcile that, my lady. They are my family, and they aren't going anywhere."

"Your family! I know what you do with them. Must you say it aloud? Do you know how my ladies, and even the servants, talk behind my back? I'm an object of pity." Marlythe began to cry as Aurauna raised her voice, and Duncan patted her back.

"I have tried to make you happy," he said in an even tone. "I have given you everything you wanted, and I'll continue to do right by you. I will ask you never to speak that way about my friends, however. Goddesses, this is hardly the homecoming I looked forward to."

"I-I am sorry, husband." Aurauna took the baby to nurse. "I thought the birth of our daughter might change things between us. A foolish hope, it seems. I suppose we'll just have to make the best of this life we share and try to tolerate one another if nothing else. We still need a son to inherit your title."

"I cannot think about that right now," Duncan said, eager to leave the too-warm sitting room and escape the disappointment on his wife's face. "Forgive me, but I need to be alone."

As he left the castle to walk across a fallow field toward the bay, Duncan decided he would send a message to the king. If the Johmatrans returned to their shores, he would offer to lead men against them. Here, it seemed, he could do nothing but make people unhappy.

"WHAT'S this, then?" Sander asked as Garith reined his mount to a halt in front of a little stone cottage with a wide chimney and a thatched roof. A vegetable patch stood out back, with a pricklefruit tree to the left, and a small stable, a fenced-in paddock, and a few chicken coops to the right. All around the quaint little house, the leaves of the old trees burned red, burgundy, golden brown, and yellow.

Garith dismounted and reached for Sander's hand as Sander leapt down from his horse. They led the animals to the small paddock, let them inside, and locked the gate behind them. Together, they walked along a garden path edged with berry fronds and stopped a few dozen feet from the simple wooden door. "It's just something I've been dreaming about," Garith said. "I want to stay here now and then, chop wood, grow turnips, cook stews, bake bread, and wash dishes. I want just a week or two out of the year to forget I'm a king, just be a man, and just live—with you. If you'll agree to it, Sander."

"It's a lovely idea," Sander said, pink staining his cheeks and the bridge of his nose, "but it won't be real, just illusion."

"I think illusion can have its place sometimes," Garith said. "Don't you? Here, no one will know who we are or care what we do, how we sleep, or—"

Sander stepped in front of Garith and leaned in to kiss him. His lips tickled the corner of Garith's mouth when he spoke. "Do you want me to do it properly and carry you over the threshold, then?"

Garith laughed. "No. I think we should just walk in together, hand in hand."

They did, then closed the sturdy door and left the rest of the world and its troubles locked out, at least for a time.

A MONTH and a half later, after checking up on his people at the order hideout and attending to some business there, Sasha arrived in the valenny of the Twenty-Nine. Though they neared the end of Jelsyn's Moon, here it was still warm enough to make Sasha sweat beneath his leathers.

Yarrow and Duncan met him at the river's edge, and together they boarded a new Emiri ship with bright blue sails. Above the main sheet, emblazoned in soft silver against a blue background, Yarrow's new livery, a man with a fish's tail, holding three stars in his outstretched hand, drawn in a swirling, stylized way reminiscent of Emiri paint, flapped in the warm wind. As Izu steered them through the archipelago, the Twenty-Nine looked much the same as it had the last time Sasha had been here, before the war. The Emiri built ships, sewed sails, mended nets, fished, played music, or just lounged on the warm golden sand with their characteristic disregard for any semblance of modesty. Sasha smiled because Yarrow looked much happier than he had when they'd parted ways at Windust Castle. Even Duncan looked out over the water, his posture relaxed and his features soft and content.

"I can't wait for you two to see the home I've been working on for us," Yarrow said, the ornaments in his long hair rattling softly as the wind whipped the white ropes around.

After a few hours, they arrived at a midsized island not far from where Sai and his family had lived. They rowed ashore, and Yarrow took their hands and practically dragged them up a gravel path lined with large shells and interesting pieces of driftwood. Mosaic Emiri lanterns hung from iron crooks. The house sat atop a gentle knoll, surrounded by a sand-colored wall adorned with all manner of starfish, shells, and bits of colored glass and metal. No gate, just an arched opening, led them to the palace of the valen of the Twenty-Nine.

Five houses, each of them two or three stories tall, had been joined together by covered walkways, forming a star-shaped enclosure around a courtyard, where a group of naked Emiri children splashed in the large pool at the center. More lanterns had been strung between the structures and along the many porches and balconies. Instead of windows and doors, brightly colored curtains and strings of small shells covered the entrances, and, along with the chimes hanging from the eaves, filled the air with soft music. In the Emiri way, the outer walls of the structures had been painted in ornate loops and swirls, with shells and other treasures from the sea pressed into the plaster. Triangular banners bearing Yarrow's heraldry waved from the roofs of a few of the houses.

Tugging Sasha and Duncan along, Yarrow showed them the many rooms. Many still stood empty, while some held stores of food and, of course, jugs of *muri-ku*. Others contained piles of cushions and mats for guests to sleep upon. Some rooms simply stored heaps of loot and bolts of cloth, and one, on the ground floor, held a huge round tub in front of a latticed wall covered with flowering vines. Yarrow had made one room into a sort of study—it held a desk, a few benches, and several shelves covered in books and scrolls. Some locked chests lined the walls. Sasha and Duncan crossed the room and followed Yarrow through the strings of colored shells covering another doorway.

It opened to a large room, long and rectangular, with a balcony and a spectacular view of the sea along one side. Lanterns and plants in hanging baskets hung from the eaves. Yarrow pulled a cord, and a veil of sheer blue cloth, darker toward the bottom, closed in front of the veranda, though the sun penetrated easily, giving the room a softened, ethereal quality.

"In case we want some privacy," Yarrow said, grinning and canting his head toward the dozens of pillows piled in the corner. "What do you think of our new home?"

"A second home," Duncan said wistfully, drawing Sasha and Yarrow against his chest. "We have this and Windust Castle now. A valenny and a bairny. If we could acknowledge each other as family, we might rival High King Garith for land and property."

"We certainly would," Sasha said, nuzzling his face against Duncan's whiskered cheek and stroking Yarrow's smooth bare arm. "Don't forget that you are both welcome in the headquarters of my order as well. I think we have done well for ourselves. Home for me is anywhere we're together, even if it's a tent along the road."

"I wish it hadn't all come at such a cost," Yarrow said. "I wish Sai could have seen this." He pulled the cord to draw back the curtains and expose the sea and the dozens of Emiri ships bobbing along the surface. "I don't think anyone will dare try to drive the Emiri from this place now, and if they do, they'll have not only me but the finest fleet the world has ever seen to deal with. That's all because of him. That reminds me. I have something else I'd like you so see."

They followed him out of the house, beyond the wall, along a wind-strewn trail edged in high, pale grass, and over a bridge to a sandy spit of land only a little larger than Yarrow's new estate. A statue carved from the golden brown rock common to the islands stood at the center. The figure was idealized and a little simplistic, but Sasha still recognized the sensuous curve of the waist and the cocky, seductive grin. "Sai. Did you do this, Yarrow?"

"No. An Emiri artisan made it, and I put it here. The others have been visiting, leaving coins and jewelry, little baubles." He indicated the piles of shiny items near the statue's feet. "Sai was especially important to those Emiri he rescued from slavery in Johmatra."

"Important enough to be made into a god," Duncan said.

"No," Yarrow said, tracing his fingertips over the single word carved in the swirling, Emiri script below Sai's feet. Sasha knew without asking that it said *yu-me*—hope. "Gods and masters are not welcome in the Twenty-Nine. We have no need for them. He's a memory, a memory of what one person can do. Sai won this battle for my cousin, not the goddesses. I don't seem to recall them assisting us at all."

"You should not say such things," Duncan told Yarrow without much real conviction in his tone.

"This is my valenny," Yarrow said. "I'll say and do what I like."

"I don't wish to have this argument," Duncan said. Sasha agreed. All of them sat down in the pulpy afternoon sun and soon stretched out on the sand, holding hands and watching the white clouds drift past above them.

Some had died while others lived, and the world continued on, oblivious to it all. The sky spun overhead, the waves lapped at the shore, and the sun shone down on Sasha's skin. He knew it likely would not last—peace rarely did—but he had it now, and he let his guard down, shrugged off his mind's armor of constant observation and planning. He could replace it if he needed it, but he was safe here. He was happy.

HOW his creature would have laughed at Yarrow as he led his lovers through his house like a proud new wife. At first, he'd felt a little foolish showing them his cookpots, chairs, and rugs, but as soon as he'd chosen to stop doubting himself, he'd been able to see that Duncan and Sasha liked what he had built, that they didn't find him puerile or laugh at him.

The sun felt good against Yarrow's body as the three of them lay on the beach by Sai's statue, quite literally at the feet of hope. Hope was not something Yarrow had ever expected to experience. There was still much to do: deal with the barbarians, protect his lands, free the rest of the Emiri, decipher the mysteries in the small stone box, and one day, when he gathered enough strength and knowledge, put an end to the lies and tyranny of Fane's wives. But today, on the warm, blessed shore of the Twenty-Nine, with the wind skimming their skin just enough to dry their sweat, he lay with his friends—his lovers— his *syrai*—his family. The temptation to pretend nothing existed beyond them and the edge of the islet proved too strong, and Yarrow gave into it, understanding the bliss and contentment he felt for the illusion it was.

But illusion had its place sometimes.

A time would come, and soon, when all of them would have to get up from where they rested, don their armor and weapons again, and fight for their lives and a place in the world. The warmth of the island sun would fade, replaced by cold uncertainty. The future always promised bloodshed, conflict, loss, and pain. But as Yarrow braided his fingers into Sasha's and Duncan's and lifted their hands to kiss the back of each, he thought: not yet.

Not yet.

Check out this excerpt from

Cairn and Covenant

Blessed Epoch: Book Four

By August Li

An assassin's unexpected mercy granted Octavian Rose his life and freed him from his father's control, but it left him with little more than the clothes on his back and the determination not to waste his chance at a life of his choosing.

As Octavian sets out to make a name for himself, he refuses to compromise his ideals for money or status—a decision tested as he works his way up the ranks as a mercenary fighter and novice mage. Along the way he forges friendships, takes lovers, and makes bitter enemies, all while striving for the power he feels he deserves and can wield fairly.

With the advent of the Blessed Epoch and the discovery of new cultures, the world is changing. Octavian's decisions will affect not only those closest to him but will have profound worldwide consequences that he cannot begin to imagine. For twenty years, Octavian does what he must, and his choices bring him brilliant victories alongside crushing losses. Time and again, he must choose between what is right for all and what is beneficial to him, while hoping for the wisdom to tell the difference.

Coming Soon to

http://www.dsppublications.com

Chapter One

AS ALWAYS, the road stretched out before Octavian Rose looked long, barren, and lonely. The last of the autumn foliage had shriveled to a few curled brown leaves that skittered across the dirt path, and the tall grass alongside it had withered to hollow, washed-out stalks. Octavian hoisted the pack containing all his worldly possessions onto shoulders that didn't feel strong enough to bear it. He checked the dagger he kept on his belt to protect himself and the pouch on his opposite hip that held a handful of copper coins. After a last look back at the quaint farmhouse and barn, he turned toward the muted gray sky and landscape and started out. The lower the sun sank beneath the mountains to the northwest, the less the contrast between the ground and the heavens. Slowly, all the color bled out of the world, leaving it chilled, numb, and as void of life and energy as Octavian felt as he forced his feet to carry him along the path.

He was dead, at least in the eyes of his father and anyone else who mattered. That spring, he'd left his torn and bloody cloak in the lair of the bandits who had kidnapped him. The memory of the unlikely accomplice he'd found for his ruse coaxed a rare smile to his chapped lips. Whenever he felt like he could no longer be strong, Octavian summoned the memory of the assassin—probably not much older than his eighteen years—who'd killed a dozen men and aided Octavian in feigning his demise. That assassin, who'd refused to tell Octavian his name even after they'd been quite intimate, had been strong, more than capable of taking care of himself against anything the world hurled in his direction, and Octavian aspired to the same.

With renewed determination, Octavian headed north, hoping to encounter a village, a tavern, or a small camp before full darkness fell. He'd slept along the road before, but it was dangerous, not to mention cold this time of year in northern Selindria. He'd spent the summer helping a family mow their hay and harvest their wheat, and in exchange, they'd given him a share of their meager food stores and a cot in the barn. With winter pounding insistently at their door, the farmers could no longer afford to offer Octavian hospitality, and he didn't expect their generosity or pity, not when he'd never received either from his blood relatives.

The assassin who could have just as easily killed him had granted Octavian a chance to make his own way in the world, to choose his path and live without another's yoke around his neck. Octavian shivered. His belly hurt from too many months of too little food, his muscles ached from too many hours of work for too little coin, and he wanted to collapse in the dry grass by the roadside, but he couldn't. He'd partially earned and partially been given his freedom, and he couldn't squander it, so he forced himself a few hundred yards farther along the rocky path.

Goddesses, he didn't know what he wanted to do with his independence, but he knew it wasn't this: working odd jobs from dawn until dusk for barely enough food to sustain himself. The assassin who had let Octavian go after killing his captors had warned him against displaying weakness, and so Octavian had never asked for charity. He'd earned his keep, but he wanted more. He wanted much more: power, respect, and influence, though not in the way of his Cast-Down savior. He didn't want to live relegated to the shadows, cutting life down from the periphery, unable to walk into the light and claim his just rewards. No, if he played the game, he wanted to win, and more than that, he wanted to hoist his spoils into the air to the cheers of the masses. He wanted greatness, and he wanted recognition. As he trudged along the road, he tried to formulate a plan to achieve his goals. He knew he needed to make a name for himself, a name others would one day speak with reverence.

By the time the sickle moon had risen, frost sparkled on the desiccated grass and rounded stones lining the road. Octavian's breath wreathed his head in a frozen halo, and he rubbed his tingling hands together. Up ahead, a few fires burned a little way from the road, a semicircle of high, jagged rocks partially sheltering whoever warmed themselves beside them. Octavian paused and touched the hilt of his dagger. Campfires could mean many things: traveling merchants, farmers, people visiting friends, or bandits and worse. The small blazes punching holes in the cold and darkness could indicate a group of men who'd slit his throat for the few copper pieces in his pouch, who'd possibly do things that made him wish for death first, so Octavian moved off the road to escape their notice. He may have been raised the son of a wealthy merchant, but life on the road had been a harsh tutor, and he wasn't a fool. Slowly, trying to squelch the crunch of the grass beneath his holey boots, he hid himself behind a copse of stunted, leafless trees to listen to the men seated around those fires.

A quick count revealed six men, and horses snuffled and pawed the ground somewhere beyond the circle of light. Octavian didn't see any wagons or carriages, which meant these men rode. Few people beyond knights and sell-swords rode rather than traveling in coaches or drays. Octavian crouched down and crept a little closer. Being a thief would never bring him the glory he coveted, but hunger had forced his hands to close around the possessions of others before. Growing up, he'd never imagined feeling such desperation, and he'd remember it—being stuck between starvation and dirtying his hands—before he ever judged another man.

Even now, the distant heat of the campfires lured Octavian closer. He trembled, hands losing feeling and nose running, as he observed the men sitting on the ground. They wore mismatched—probably scavenged—bits of plate, chain mail, leather, and furs. An argument seemed to rage between the man in the nicest armor, probably the leader, and a big fellow in a dented breastplate partially obscured by a heavy fur-lined cloak. Plumes of fog, orange in the firelight, sprayed from their mouths as they shouted at each other.

"And I'm telling you, Lyman, reputation is everything in this business! See how many more jobs we can get when word gets around we not only failed in what we were hired to do, but let our patron, the patron paying us to provide safe passage, be captured!"

Lyman, a stout man with an ample belly and a dark beard, pointed a gloved hand at the other man. "We were paid in advance for our work, you goddess-damned fool. We still have the coin, whether the ones who provided it were captured or not."

"You have no honor, you serpent!"

Lyman spat on the ground and wiped his mouth on the back of his arm. "I'm a fucking mercenary, and so are you, Myrddin! You'd do well to remember it."

"It doesn't mean I'm a filthy coward!" the man called Myrddin said. "We need to make this right. It's the only decent thing to do."

Lyman's supporters outnumbered Myrddin's two to one, and the one man sitting behind Myrddin looked even younger and smaller than Octavian. Part of Octavian thought he should cut a quiet path back to the road and put as much distance between himself and an altercation that looked ready to escalate to bloodshed as possible, but more of him sensed a glimmer of an opportunity. If this group of mercenaries split, both sides might be looking to bolster their ranks. Perhaps Octavian could convince whichever side seemed more promising to take him on. Mercenary work paid better than farmwork, and with the tenacious fingers of winter wriggling into the land deeper every day, farmwork would be drying up, and sleeping along the road would no longer be an option. Traveling alone would become more dangerous as men grew hungrier and more desperate.

"What are you suggesting we do?" Lyman got to his feet faster and with more grace than Octavian would've expected from a man his size, and the three men behind him followed suit.

Myrddin neither flinched, stood, nor looked terribly impressed with his leader glowering down at him. When he spoke, he didn't even raise his voice, his tone calm and practical, but defeated. "What I think we should do is track the people who took our patrons and their goods. We should liberate both, and then we should see them safely to their destination, just as they paid us quite well to do."

"Fucking fool. We're in Cracked Tooth territory here. Likely as not, the Teeth are the ones what took 'em. You honestly want to go up against them with a group as small as ours? When we already have the coin for the job?"

"And you honestly want to abandon a family to goddesses know what terrible fate?"

"What do I care, Tam Myrddin?" Lyman drawled the other man's name into a mocking snarl. "You'd do well to remember you're not a knight any longer, just a sell-sword like the rest of us. You'd be smart to take the gold we earned and buy yourself a pint of ale, a bed, and a whore to warm it. That's our lot, my fine friend, not your misguided nobility."

Myrddin shook his head. "I'm paid to fight. Paid for my sword. That doesn't mean I'm a swindler, a thief, or a callow-hearted bastard who turns his back on the people he swore to protect. I have my honor, whether or not I have my title."

"Oh, and what are you going to do?"

"What do you think, Lyman? I'm going to do everything in my power to save those people. I want to be able to stand the sight of myself the next time I see it reflected back at me from my wash basin."

"You're on your own, then!" Lyman shouted, spittle flying from his mouth.

Myrddin stood. "I am hardly surprised." He lifted a large sword, slid it into the scabbard on his back, turned in the direction of the horses, and disappeared into the darkness, with the gangly youth scampering behind him. A few moments later, the trotting of a pair of horses sounded on the road and quickly faded into the distance.

Still squatting in the shadows, arms wrapped around his knees, Octavian considered his options. Offering himself to Lyman would be more practical; Lyman had a camp only a few dozen feet away, with fires, bedrolls, and something savory smelling crackling over the flames. Lyman had more men following him, and he planned to move on to another lucrative job while his former comrade, Myrddin, planned to undertake a mission with no chance of recompense and even less hope of success. But some of what Myrddin had said resonated within Octavian. The big mercenary had a point when it came to reputation. Who in the world would ever hire Lyman after word of his cowardly indifference spread? He'd practically swindled those who'd employed him. What would it mean for Octavian to have his name associated with men who couldn't finish a job? Besides, Octavian had no desire to be like his assassin, taking any job for coin. He'd been desperate before, but he was not yet desperate enough to let life force him to that, so he snuck back to the road and started to jog along it. With nowhere else to go, the two mercenaries would be found along this path before long.

After an hour or so of running through the frigid night, his muscles twitching, his chest tight, sweat freezing to his face, Octavian spotted a candle-sized flicker of light about a mile to the east, in another narrow cleft sheltered by ironstone. Taking a deep breath, he readjusted the straps of his pack and raked his sweaty hair back from his forehead. He had to make these men see him as capable, someone they wanted by their sides. He could not let them see the pampered son of a wealthy merchant, a boy who'd been handed everything and waited on in exchange for obedience, approaching their camp. As he walked from the darkness into the light of their fire, he held his hands open and out to his sides.

Both men heard Octavian before they saw him, and before he'd taken three steps into their light, the point of a sword and a knocked arrow pointed at him. He refused to cower and forced himself to keep walking until Myrddin said, "Stop there, lad. Who in the Shades' are you?"

"My name is Octavian Rose." If he wanted it known, he had to say it, and say it as if it meant something. "I am looking for work."

"Move along then, son," Myrddin said, lowering his blade a few inches. "Neither of us is looking for a pretty lad to warm our bedrolls tonight."

"You think—What? No! I am not a whore." Later, he would have to isolate the part of him that gave that impression and cut it out. Perhaps his desperation shone through some part of him worn too thin to hold it in. When he had the luxury, he'd find the tear and patch it. "I understand you are about to undertake a dangerous mission, and I thought you could use another blade by your side."

The two men looked at each other. The younger one rolled his eyes, stowed his arrow in the quiver on his back, and went to rub his hands together over the fire, having obviously dismissed Octavian entirely. Myrddin sheathed his sword, and Octavian resented them not seeing him as a threat worthy of holding weapons against, but he didn't let it show.

"Can you use a man to help you rescue your patrons that were taken?" Octavian persisted.

Shoulders slumping and expression softening, Myrddin offered Octavian an indulgent smile. "Aye, a man we might be able to use, but I'm afraid I have less than no time to play nursemaid to a boy with dreams of grandeur. You should get home to your family before you worry your poor mother, lad."

That feeling of desperation, the one he despised controlling him, wrapped around Octavian as he stepped closer to the much larger man. "Look at me. Look at my clothes. My boots. The bones beneath the skin of my face. Look at them, and tell me if I am a man being fed by a loving mother."

Myrddin pursed his lips, then said, "We can offer you something to eat and a seat by the fire." He gestured toward the little blaze with his big hand, and his companion made an exasperated sound and shook his head.

"I can help you," Octavian persisted, struggling to keep the anxiety from tainting his tone. "I am not looking for charity."

"Sit," Myrddin insisted, and Octavian obeyed. He took the canteen the man offered and gulped at the bitter wine within, letting it warm him from his throat all the way to the pit of his empty stomach. He couldn't suppress his sigh of satisfaction any more than he could turn away the strips of dried meat and chunk of hard bread the man offered him, though he resisted his instinct to shove them into his mouth whole and swallow them barely chewed.

After he'd eaten, disgusted at the way his basest needs interfered with his ambitions, Octavian said, "I want to help you on your mission."

The young archer snorted, but Myrddin patted his shoulder to silence him. "Lad, I've no idea how you know what we're planning, but it isn't something we want a novice involved in. Do you know how to use a weapon? Do you even carry one?"

"Aye." In a smooth, swift motion, Octavian reached beneath his thin, tattered cloak, drew his dagger, and presented it, hilt first, to Myrddin.

From a few feet away, Octavian saw the mercenary was probably ten years older than he, maybe more, with long, knotted, blond hair and neatly trimmed whiskers a few shades darker. He had strong, dark brows and pale eyes, though Octavian couldn't discern their color in the flickering light of the dwindling fire. Still, something in his gaze made Octavian want to trust him. Myrddin's eyes were not cold and dead, as his assassin's had been. Again, he thrust his blade toward the other man's waiting hand.

Myrddin reached for the dagger, but at the last moment, he recoiled as if it were on fire. "Sweet goddesses, boy! I—Where in the world did you get that? You—you're not—"

"No, I'm not," Octavian reassured him with a smile. His assassin had done him more than one favor. The dagger the Cast-Down had offered him was distinctive if one knew what to look for, and apparently Myrddin did. Many people doubted the existence of the Order of the Crimson Scythe, the world's most dreaded cult of assassins, but belief or no, everyone feared them.

"Then how?" Myrddin asked. "Goddesses, how do you hold that and still walk in the light of the world?"

"It was a gift," Octavian explained. "The one who offered it to me… I like to think he saw something in me he didn't want destroyed by a petty thief or someone who would accost me on the road. Why, I cannot say."

The young archer grunted and made a few quick gestures with his hands.

Myrddin laughed. "Dirk thinks perhaps it was your… uh, beauty the assassin did not want lost." Clearly, "beauty" wasn't the word the archer had expressed, but Octavian didn't ask for the truth. He probably didn't want to hear it.

"He could have killed me," Octavian protested. "I certainly could not have stopped him."

"No, my lad." Myrddin stirred the coals in the fire with a stick. "No one can stop one of them. Still, it does not mean you can handle yourself in a fight, or that you wouldn't be worse than an annoyance to Dirk and me. We have our hands full as it is. You are not trained to use that blade. If you were, we'd both be dead without having ever heard your breath on the wind. Is there anything else you can offer us?"

Octavian sighed. "Are you wounded anywhere?"

"What?"

"Are you hurt? A bruise? A scratch?"

"Why?"

"Just…." Octavian slipped his dagger back into the scabbard by his hip, frustrated. If he could just convince someone to give him a chance, he'd show what an asset he could be. He knew there was more to him than a small man who'd led an easy life until the past spring. The assassin who had let him live had seen it. But Myrddin still looked at him like he'd sprouted two heads.

Dirk came to his rescue, rolling up his sleeve to reveal an infected cut a few inches above his wrist. Octavian wrinkled his nose at the rotten smell emanating from the wound, but he closed his eyes and rested his fingertips at the edge of the old cut. He felt the life and vitality syphoning from him to the other man, and he grew dizzy. He was vaguely aware of his body curling backward and prepared himself for the impact of the frozen ground against his back and head, but thick arms caught and steadied him. Myrddin's breath warmed his cheek when he spoke.

"Bleeding Shades, you're a mage!"

Hard steel plate pressed against Octavian's cheek, and he leaned against it despite the cold of the metal. "So far, I'm best at healing."

At the edges of Octavian's vision, Dirk the archer gestured wildly.

"Aye," Myrddin said. "I can see it would be useful. So, you want—"

The archer grunted.

"If you say so," Myrddin grumbled. "I hope we're not sorry for taking him on. Personally, I had hoped to avoid the need for a healer's skills. Give me a few big lads who know how to swing a blade over a mage any day."

Octavian wriggled out of Myrddin's grasp and forced himself to sit up straight even though the world still wiggled and spun around him. He didn't want pity; he'd show them he could stand on his own. Though he knew he shouldn't use his magic again so soon, that it would strain him, this was his chance to get himself in with what seemed an honorable and capable couple of men, a chance to do something others might talk about. "I can do more than heal."

Over the summer, alone in the barn where he'd slept, he had been practicing, struggling to understand his gift and make it do his bidding. He'd only been partially successful, but he hoped it would be enough to impress the two mercenaries. Mages, after all, grew rarer with each generation. Noticing a pile of small stones stacked about a dozen feet away, Octavian took aim. No sound or flash of light came from his fingers, but the air rippled with the familiar scent of burnt minerals before the rocks flew apart and scattered in every direction. Octavian willed away the gray glitter pouring in at the edges of his vision. He kept his voice even and strong. "I can knock down at least a few men with that spell."

It was a lie; he'd never tried it against a living thing, but the mercenaries looked impressed. Octavian had to press his advantage. Laying his palm flat against the frigid ground, he closed his eyes to concentrate. A moment later, a tremor ran through the frozen soil, making the gravel strewn over it quiver and bounce. Myrddin swore under his breath, and Octavian opened his eyes in time to see Dirk poke out his lower lip and nod. Octavian pulled his knees to his chest and held them tight, letting his cloak fall around his arms and legs so the others wouldn't see his hands trembling. "So do you think you have a use for me?"

Dirk moved his hands so fast they made Octavian's head spin. In response, Myrddin shook his head.

"What's he saying?" Octavian asked, hoping Myrddin answered before he passed out. Goddesses, he just had to endure until he could pretend to fall asleep of his own free will.

"He doesn't like you," Myrddin said. "He thinks you're soft, inexperienced, and think too much of your magic."

In the world of wealthy merchants and their noble patrons where Octavian had been reared, things weren't said so plainly. The rich and so-called civilized men and women traded snide, subtle insults and backhanded compliments, but no one spoke his mind. In a way, Octavian appreciated not having to decipher the hidden meaning, but the assessment stung—probably because he knew it was true. When he looked over at Dirk, the archer raised his chin and met Octavian's gaze defiantly. Instead of relying on Myrddin to translate, Octavian spoke to Dirk directly. "I thought, earlier, that you said my skills might be useful."

The archer slashed and stabbed at the air, scowling as he moved his fingers at various angles.

"Dirk says you'd be worth having if the fight goes poorly and we need patching up, but he doesn't think you'd last long enough in battle to draw that cursed knife. Why do you carry that thing, anyway, he wants to know. He says it is bad luck and you should throw it into Estrella Lake or bury it in holy ground."

Octavian skimmed his fingers along the dagger's hilt. "I am fond of it, and it has served me well." He didn't tell them it represented the first stroke of good luck he could remember having, and that it held a deeper, more personal meaning than he'd ever share with another living soul.

"Well, Dirk says he doesn't want to take you on just to watch you die, that you'd do better to look for work on a farm, or a shop, or a—Oh, Dirk! There's no need for that! Lad can't help being nice-looking. Doesn't mean he should resort to selling—"

"I suppose I should be on my way." They might not want him, might not see any value to him, but Octavian would be damned if he'd sit idly and let them make him the butt of their crude jokes. One day, when he showed the world what he could do, they would be sorry for turning him away. One day, as soon as someone gave him the chance to prove it. It would not be tonight, though. He'd depleted his energy and left himself vulnerable for nothing.

As Octavian stood, his eyes stinging and his cheeks hot, eager to escape before the mercenaries noticed his childish reaction to their rejection, Myrddin caught his wrist, pulled him back to the ground, and met his gaze. "I have told you what Dirk thinks. I have not said I agree with him. Likely as not I'm an old fool, but the way I see it, a lad who can walk into a mercenary camp as you did has stones, at least. Stones can count for more than skill sometimes."

The big man indicated a bedroll near the fire. "Get some rest. You'll need it. Have some wine, too. It may be your last chance. I'm still not sure you won't get yourself killed tomorrow."

"Thank you," Octavian said.

Without meeting his gaze, Myrddin waved his hand at the pile of blankets and furs. "Save it. You can thank me if you survive."

AUGUST (GUS) LI is a creator of fantasy worlds. When not writing, he enjoys drawing, illustration, costuming, and cosplay, and making things in general. He lives near Philadelphia with two cats and too many ball-jointed dolls. He loves to travel and is trying to see as much of the world as possible. Other hobbies include reading (of course), tattoos, and playing video games.

For more info, visit Books by Eon and Gus:
http://www.booksbyeonandgus.com

Don't miss how the story started!

http://www.dsppublications.com

Don't miss how the story started!

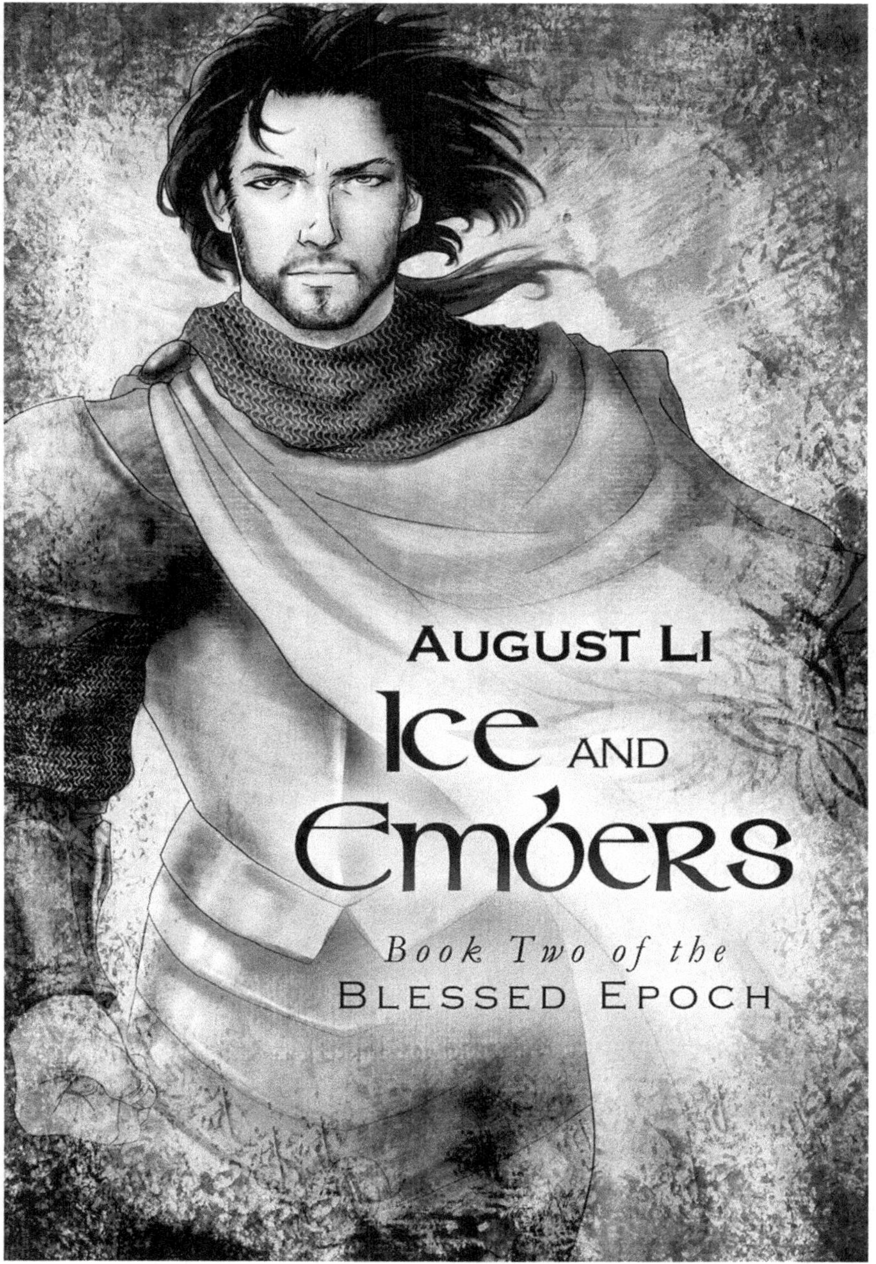

http://www.dsppublications.com

The
Bastard's
Pearl
CONNIE BAILEY

9 781632 169518